THE BOOK OF FLORA

ALSO BY MEG ELISON

THE ROAD TO NOWHERE SERIES
The Book of the Unnamed Midwife
The Book of Etta

THE BOOK OF FLORA

THE BOOK OF FLORA

MEG ELISON

Text copyright © 2019 by Meg Elison
All rights reserved.

No part of this book may be reproduced, or stored in a retrieval system, or transmitted in any form or by any means, electronic, mechanical, photocopying, recording, or otherwise, without express written permission of the publisher.

Published by 47North, Seattle

www.apub.com

Amazon, the Amazon logo, and 47North are trademarks of Amazon.com, Inc., or its affiliates.

ISBN-13: 9781542042093 (paperback)
ISBN-10: 1542042097 (paperback)

Cover design by The Frontispiece, Inc.

Printed in the United States of America

*Dedicated to all the radical queers
in my life.
Rage on.*

CHAPTER 1

The Bambritch Book
Fog moon, summer
Year 144, Nowhere Codex

Last night I dreamt I was back in Nowhere again.

I don't know why. I haven't seen Nowhere in so many years that I can't number them, and I only ever stayed there for a few days, maybe a week.

But it was where I met Alice. Alice, the drugmaker with the impossible curls and the cruel, clever mouth. Alice, the keeper of som for sleep and hands for waking. Where Eddy brought me when I decided not to go home to Jeff City. Eddy, living child of Ina, killer of the Lion and liberator of the Lion's harem. Eddy, my lover and my hero, whom I lost in the end. Eddy, raider of the road and hero of Nowhere. Eddy, forever in my heart. Alice and Eddy gave me my first taste there of something I hardly knew was possible, and it was where I learned something I would never forget. Nowhere. Nowhere. Nowhere.

Nowhere was beautiful in my dream. The old women with their wooden baby bellies were coming and going across the open square, with Hives of men trailing after them, carrying baskets and buckets and babies. I saw Ina clearly, though she was younger than I ever knew her. I saw her wide smile, and I looked down to see that her belly wasn't wood but flesh. She was pregnant with Eddy, close to giving birth. She was carefree, having no idea that this child would almost cost her her own life.

I saw Connie, my living child. Connie who was neither boy nor girl, neither breeder nor horsewoman, not he or she but always *they*. Connie was never in Nowhere. Or maybe they were; I have no way of knowing what they've seen on their long walk in the world. Seeing them in a dream always crushes my heart like a tomato in the hand. I wake up crying. I end up calling out. I could only see them from the back; even in dreams, Connie is lost to me. As Nowhere is lost. As so much is lost.

I wasn't there when the Paws of the Lion took Nowhere. I was locked up in his harem, far away. Alice held out as long as she could; she was strong. But she had everything there to make som, and he always needed more. The men who kept harems in those days almost always had a drugmaker. Once the Lion had Alice, he was never going to let her go. He sent his Paws after her lab and told them to take the town.

In my dream, I was there when they took it. They burned houses and fields. They caught women and children and tied them up like cattle; they cut men down where they stood. They took apart the careful work of more than a hundred years in so little time.

Destruction is easy. Creation is so much harder.

Nowhere wasn't much, but it was the first place I felt free. It was imperfect, but it was as if there was a piece of me waiting there, ready to join the whole, that I hadn't even known about. I suppose that is why I dream it still.

That, and the Midwife.

I understand her better now. For years I thought I never would, since she knew the old world and had lost a peace I couldn't imagine. But I've done that now. I've seen peace. I've seen cities that have lights at night and free people and I've been loved as I was meant to be loved. I have grasped all possibility, felt its enormity, and lost it all. Like she did. I can follow her now. Not literally, like we tried to. But in my heart.

The Midwife didn't build Nowhere; it waited for her as the dark earth waits for a seed. But all that we have now of Nowhere is its story, and that was hers first. She was the one who survived the Dying, all the way out on the coast, and came across endless miles to find a safe place. She saw the old world destroyed by plague, countless numbers dead and no Mothers left alive. She was the one who walked in the world as a man when being a woman wasn't safe. She was the one who waited through the years for a child to be born, never letting her tools go rusty. She knew the world would need Midwives once again, and she helped build Nowhere on that hope. Her work goes on; Motherhood lives forever on the doorstep of death. She understood that. She brought this new world out of fever and into being. I have tried to do the same.

I have kept her books all these years, through all the times I have moved and fled across this broad continent. She is always with me, though I will never know if my copy of her story is complete. Eddy used to say that no two copies were perfectly alike, since the boy scribes of Nowhere made mistakes, and some volumes were not as popular as others. Mine might be the last copy, but I doubt it. She meant just as much to so many others.

When Nowhere was burned, the people who were there barely got out with their lives. The people who returned to rebuild were able to recover a few things—tools and seeds and the odd scraps of remembrance.

But books are so fragile. Paper and leather and wood cannot stand up to fire or water or time.

And there is one thing I know is true in this world: only what is remembered survives. Only what is written has a chance in the future. People forget. Rivers rise. Stories and songs are snuffed out every time some town takes a fever or loses to a man with a little power.

Destruction is common. Creation is rare.

Because I know this truth, I must do two things. First, I must collect and keep as many pieces of record and evidence as I can, to ensure that they do not pass out of this world. Second, I must write my own record so that it survives. I must write the people in my life into the record as well, just as the Midwife did, so that they survive, too. I sometimes do as she did, putting the book into their hands. I write it for them. I did it more when I was younger. I trusted too much then.

I know why I dreamt of Nowhere, but I'm afraid that by writing it down I will make it real. I know why I taste ashes on the wind, why I cannot sleep, why I keep thinking of friends and lovers I have lost not to age or sickness but to the hands of wanton destruction.

I do not want to face what is coming. I cannot imagine my life's work wiped out. I will not.

I will instead finally set myself to the task of telling what has not been told.

I began to write the stories of my days when I was already a grown woman, thirty summers gone and sure of who I was and my place in the world. I did not begin until I had read the Midwife's story, until I had seen the blank pages of Eddy's book. Eddy left home with that leather book from his mother and never found a way to put himself or his story in it. The Midwife told it all and Eddy held it all inside. I guess everyone who shares their story gets to choose. I wanted to land between them somehow. I started late, but I went to the task with determination and detail. The volumes of my life are already too numerous to move them with me if I have to flee this place when the army advances on us. If they have all the power of thoughtless destruction people say that they have. And there are other books I would choose first, if I had to carry them out of here in a hurry.

They are coming. Every raider and scout and smallholding farmer and fisher tells the same story. They are coming in numbers we can't imagine, in old-world war machines that cannot be stopped. Tanks. Long guns mounted on trucks. Missiles that can destroy a whole village. Plague-weapons, like the ones that caused the death of the old world. I don't know what to believe. One of the raiders, Speel, draws pictures of everywhere the army has gone. Flowers and deer and lizards and crumbling cities. They brought one back of a mass grave, where the army had made the people dig a pit and stand before it, so that they could shoot them and let them fall in. The bodies weren't covered. Speel drew them as they were, with bugs crawling in their open eyes.

Yesterday, someone told me the army has a plane, maybe more than one. I cannot believe that. If they did, they would be here already.

They are taking cities and towns. They are headed straight for us, intent on the old city of Settle. The people in Settle cannot fight them. Neither can we.

I am undertaking this work in the hope—no. In the firm belief that there will be eyes to read this story, and people to keep the pages safe from fire and water and time. This is my act of faith. I am not going to live my death until it comes for me, not even in my imagination. I will not turn what has not yet occurred into a memory. I will spend these next uncertain days turning memory into record. One will last. The other will not.

Many of the books I have read and kept here begin with wonderful sentences, like doors opening into a vast, untouched building from the old world. I would love to begin like one of them, but I cannot think how. I would begin my life with the beginning of my life. I would tell you that I was born with a gift or a sense, or under the shining of an auspicious star. I would tell you to call me by my name or acknowledge a universal truth. I would like to say that I was born twice, but I was not. I would promise you that this is my best, my saddest, my only, my very true story. Even here, at the top of this entry I have nearly stolen another. I have been told many times that the tale begins with "In the beginning" or "Once upon a time," but neither of those is right.

I cannot begin at the beginning; I wasn't there. I cannot even begin at one particular moment in time; I do not remember how this got started. Neither does anybody else. We only know the story we are given, unless someone writes the truth of it down. And even then, it isn't the whole truth. Only theirs. As this is mine.

I can only tell you what was told to me, and most of that was probably lies. The person who told me who I was and showed me my place in the world very seldom told the truth. I still believe that telling the story from the beginning is the only way to do it.

Whether it is true or not, it is the only story I have.

My name is Flora. This book is my life.

CHAPTER 2

The Bambritch Book
Raining
144N

When I first arrived on Bambritch Island, I tried to arrive as a woman without a past. I didn't want to carry the stories and ghosts of everything I had said goodbye to in Jeff City, in Ommun, aboard the ship where I last saw Eddy. I wanted none of it to matter.

I wanted to be the Midwife and admit that what was gone could be buried, and what lay ahead was yet to be born. I wanted that to be true of me, most of all.

Now I see that if I do not carry my past with me, it will wrap itself around my ankles and drag me down. There is no living without it. There is no pretending I am not the sum of all these things.

I never told anyone here about Archie. I told them I was raised by a slaver and that I wouldn't keep people out who had done it at some point in their lives, so long as they didn't do it anymore. I didn't tell them by what means I came to understand how a slaver thinks or the way they live. I could compromise on that where the Midwife never would, where Eddy never could.

All these stories I have worked to preserve, and I have tried to erase Archie. He wasn't my father and he didn't cut me, but he made me who I am.

I never met my mother. Archie is where I begin.

Archie said he could remember the old world, but he must have lied. According to what's left of the Nowhere Codex and other books of history I have kept from Ommun, Shy, Demons, Niyok, and two nomadic tribes, it's just possible Archie was born before the end of the old world. But that would have meant he was over seventy summers old when I knew him—more if he were old enough to actually remember it. I've never known anyone who lived that long.

Most likely he was born to someone who did remember, a Mother or father who had lived in the old world and raised him on stories. He never told me who brought him up. He rejected the lies anyone else told him and replaced them with his own creations, always.

Here's what I can tell you about Archie without any doubt: he was an old man. Not as old as he said he was, but over fifty summers. Maybe fifty-five. He was older than my father, meaner and harder. It took me ages to trust my father, because Archie was the one I knew first. They were as different as night and day.

Archie's life had been hard and had left its tracks all over him. He was tall, but stooped from always carrying a heavy load as he fled from town to town. He was pale and pink-skinned, so the sun crisped and stripped him every year. He would sit in the firelight at night, rubbing himself with aloe or goose grease or whatever he could get, picking little crusty scales on his bare scalp and spotted shoulders.

He was bald from the day I knew him, but he wouldn't wear a hat unless he was freezing. One eye had been ruined in his youth, but he didn't cover it. He had one good blue eye, blazing and sharp on the right. His left was milky and deformed, with a divot that showed even when he closed the lid. He told me variously that it had been the casualty of a knife fight, clawed out by a woman, pecked out by a bird, and sacrificed to the god of some folk whom he offended in his youth. He liked that the eye scared people. He knew they would stare at it, and he took advantage of that fact.

He was scarred all over, but nothing as bad as the eye. I actually saw him get one of the scars, from a small shark he was trying to catch in Florda. He would exaggerate its size later, but he loved that story. The wound healed clean because he washed it in saltwater, but the scar was gnarled and noticeable. Little knife cuts and bites lined his arms and legs. More than once I saw a kid get a piece of him because Archie was just a little too slow. He would take swift and terrible revenge for those little crescents of tooth marks, but he respected the kids who fought just a little more.

He never respected me. I never fought.

My earliest memories are of being alone with Archie. We stayed in Florda for several years, in a little house on a beach. That was where the shark bit him. We fished every day, and where he went, I went. I learned how to bait a hook, gut a fish, watch the weather, and live with sand in my mouth and eyes. We bathed in the sea. We slept in the same bed, listening to the waves crashing.

Archie wasn't affectionate, but he did permit me to sleep against his back. It kept us both warmer, and made nightmares easier. Learning to sleep alone years later was agony for me.

I had no concept of where I came from. I didn't even know to ask until my time with Archie was nearing its end. I had no mother, no father. I was Archie's annoyance and his comfort. He told me I was a burden to him, but he taught me to read. He told me I was not a real girl and certainly not as good as one, but he called me one when he was inside me. I think he gave me my name.

I have no concept of a childhood without sex. It was explained to me as the reason for my existence. I have lived in places where children are protected, and I understand the importance of that, now. I have also seen children sold as I was sold to men who had no compunction about damaging a child beyond repair. Archie was never brutal to me, despite his constant use of my body. He told me again and again that consistent use was the greatest possible value for a body like mine, and so brutality was not to be tolerated. On the occasions when he rented me out, he made sure they understood I was not to be broken. At least, not in any obvious way.

"Break it tonight and you won't have it tomorrow." He said the same thing about tools, about toys. About me and the other children he bought and sold over those years.

We left Florda after a season of terrible storms. We were no strangers to the violent rains that crept up the beach at the onset of every summer, but one year the wind blew the roof off our house and the water rose to take the rest of it. We moved inland too late and too slowly. We both got sick and nearly died. People refugeed out of Florda, and we heard the king had passed.

"You were named in his honor," Archie told me as he squatted to shit out sickness for the fifteenth or twentieth time in a day.

"His name was Flora?"

"His name was Florda. But he said it was prettier for a girl if it was just Flora. Said it meant flowers."

"How did you know him?"

"I used to work for him," Archie said as he cleaned himself up. His eyes were rimmed with red and he was thin and haggard. I'm sure I looked no better, but I had no mirror in those days.

"Was he my father?"

I had never asked him directly about my parents before. I had only recently begun to realize that other people had parents. The question seemed terrible and forbidden, yet impossible to ignore. I quivered all over, saying the words aloud. I thought Archie would explode.

Instead he laughed.

"Definitely not, kid. Don't get ahead of yourself."

"Why did he say you should name me Flora, then?"

"He saw you, as a baby, fighting some other kid for her dress. You wouldn't let go. You were stubborn and wild, like the place. Like the king."

"What was my name before that?"

Archie stood and looked me over. "You didn't have one. I wasn't going to keep you."

"Why did you keep me?"

"You used to eat bugs. Nobody would feed you, so you would just feed yourself. Take what you needed. Walk right over somebody to get it. You were gonna live, I could see it. You were a fighter. I figured you'd be useful. Now, come on."

We kept moving all day that day. Sometimes we had a car or a truck, but they were hard to get and harder to keep. We'd run out of deez in a place where no one knew how to brew it and have to abandon another to the rust or the scavengers of the road. Archie mistrusted horses, though we met traders regularly. I'd pet their noses as their drivers told us how broken, how gentle the beasts were.

Sometimes I would think that Archie had picked up the horse traders' way of talking. He would offer up kids in terms of their brokenness, their gentleness. He'd pull down their lips to show their teeth. He would travel on the backs of girl children all his life, he said. But never on a horse.

I think he knew that horses could fight back when they didn't like their treatment.

We lived a long time in the high hills called Lachin, moving from town to town. The people there were isolated, hardly trading or passing news from one to the next. Later, I'd see the results of isolation in Ommun, with their number of redheads and albinos and a few with an extra finger or two. But I saw it first in those Lachin mountains, overrun with pale, spotty boys with double-jointed fingers and eyes that could look at today and tomorrow at the same time.

Archie traded first for coal, black and mined from the ground and able to burn longer than wood. It smudged everything it touched and smoked fit to kill us, but he loved it. When word got out that he carried old-world bullets for trade, that's when the folks who were willing to trade kids would appear.

Archie did not trade in grown girls or women. More than once, I saw him strip a girl to the waist and declare that her breasts had fallen and he would make no offer for her. By the time I was eight summers old, I could head off a deal at the door and keep him from getting angry about it.

"Take her home," I'd tell them. "She's too old for us."

Those girls would sell to someone else, without a doubt. Once the man holding her took it into his head to sell her, her age wouldn't be a problem for almost anyone else. Archie was peculiar. Most of the girls and women I saw locked down in harems and traveling in chains were old enough to breed; often they seemed pregnant, or the rare ones were nursing a child. I never saw anywhere else as lucky as Ommun on that score, but I like to think they're out there. After all, Ommun was hidden underground and I might never have known it was there if it hadn't been for Eddy. In the secret places, on the islands and in the dark recesses of the earth, who knows what goes on?

What went on in Archie's world was always the same. The seller would come after dark if we were near a town. Slavers would boldly show us their goods on the road or the path, but settled folk were always guilty about it. In towns where slaving was forbidden, almost every one of them would insist we leave straightaway so they could pretend the child had been stolen.

Archie would always agree, but with a warning. "If anyone from this town comes after me for child stealing or slaving, I'll tell them flat out that you made the deal."

They rarely changed their minds.

Sometimes the child would cry. If they were old enough to understand, if they hadn't been sold before, or if Archie was mean, there were tears.

Girls and boys alike would cry if they were older than four or five. They were rarely sold to Archie by their parents; most of them had been foundlings of one kind or another. The story would begin with goodness: *I kept my sister's son after she died* or *He was my neighbor's boy.* Archie would nod his head, listening to the justification despite the fact that he'd heard it all before.

Then, the denial. *I swore I would never do this* or *In better times I'd never have dreamed of selling the boy . . .* Archie clucked his tongue and murmured his agreement that their crop blight was rotten luck indeed, or that a sickly child would be no good at raising goats.

None of them ever asked what work Archie would sell the children into. Those who didn't immediately know had seen me at work, with Archie's sharp eye on me. I'd walk the edges of a lumberjacks' camp or visit a brewery and cast my eye on the loneliest-looking men. I'd walk the streets of a small town at dusk when every man with a family or a Hive would be long gone home to them, and only the men with no one would notice my existence. This work didn't bring in trade goods, but it brought daily necessities. I had a list of acceptable payments: cured meats, canned vegetables and fruits, dried tobacco, flour, well-made clothes. Archie would point me at a furrier or a bootmaker in season. Four or five nights' work would mean boots for Archie, or a fur hat and gloves for me.

Nobody would part with a baby. I shudder to think that I'd ever have been left in charge of a tiny child Archie had bought, but they were scarce everywhere. In the worst towns, in the midst of famine or in a slave-trading hub like Vana, babies were never for sale. A person with a baby believes in possibility. They carry the whole future in their hands.

A person with a small child is tired. A person left with a child not their own isn't connected in the same way, and the child is tiresome. Bratty. Whiny. Sickly.

A child who is not a girl is just another boy. Just another part of someone else's Hive. Easier to part with but harder to sell.

So Archie's favorites were difficult girls.

Rare as they were, I met a few girls that people couldn't wait to be rid of. There was Dinty, who was slow to learn and whined anytime the weather was hot or sticky. We picked her up in Vana, and Archie worked on her for over a moon while we traveled inland.

The weather down there is humid for the better part of the year, even after the storms pass. Dinty complained endlessly.

"My feet hurt. I'm sweating inside my boots. I've got blisters. Can we stop? When are we going to stop?"

"If you keep that up, Archie's going to give you something worse to whine about," I told her in my lowest voice. I knew he could hear us; my quiet was more a signal of obedience than a hope that I would go unheard. I knew better. Half-blind as he was, Archie could hear a pig rooting for acorns a mile away. Nothing got past his ears.

"I can't help it," she practically screeched. "I've never traveled this much. I can't just walk all day. I'm so tired." At this, she flopped herself down on a log that lay beside the road and sat, elbows on her knees, panting dramatically.

I looked her over. She was darker-skinned than me, but still got burned every day. She had beautiful hair, nut-brown with lighter streaks where the sun touched it. I had braided it for her before we got on the road. That was long before I learned the intricate braiding of the horse-women, but I wasn't bad. She had two tight braids that began at her hairline and neatly tucked all her hair in to hang in a couple of tails that touched her shoulder blades.

Dinty was skinny, as though she had had too much work and not enough food. She was old enough to get her blood, but the man who had sold her said it hadn't come upon her and he suspected she would never breed. She was built like a boy, but when Archie stripped her to examine, she had all the usual girl parts, except with a chest as flat as my own. She wasn't pretty in a way that made up for that lack, either. Her front teeth stuck out from her mouth, and there was a big gap between the front two. Her eyes were a little buggy, giving her a look of constant surprise. Her lips were full, but she never seemed to close her mouth. More than once I saw her run the back of her hand across the lower one to swipe away drool from her chin.

"She's no beauty," Archie had said, beginning to dicker for her price. "And she'll never breed. What's the use of her?"

Dinty had been putting her clothes back on slowly, staring at the floor while my keeper negotiated with hers, a short white man with a long beard.

"I figure she'll do fine in a harem. No breeding means someone could get a lot of use out of her, without any time off."

"Have you?" Archie stared at the man, his eyes flinty.

"Sure," the man said. "She's mine, ain't she?"

"Obedient, is she? Trained?"

The girl hurried to button up her top.

"Mostly." The man shrugged. "Worth what I'm asking for her, anyway."

Archie began to lament the price he had paid almost at once, I could tell. He preferred difficult girls, but he couldn't abide mouthy ones. I knew he would see to that immediately.

And then here he was, seeing to it.

He chewed his lip when he looked at her. I had tried to warn her, but she was as slow as could be. She could only learn this the hard way. I stepped away from her perch on the log and busied myself packing Archie's pipe. I thought maybe if I got it going for him, he'd cut this lesson short.

Archie walked calmly up to Dinty where she sat and hit her across the face with an open hand. She was so surprised that it knocked her to the ground, where she sprawled. I saw the line of drool from her mouth reach the dirt and turn red beneath her face.

She came up blinking, bewildered. "What was that—"

I wanted to tell her to stay down. Instead, I turned my back.

He hit her again, the sound of his hand against her face as flat as if he had hit her with a wooden plank.

"I can already tell that I paid too much for you, girl." He balled a fist and punched her in the stomach. I knew because I heard the air rush out of her mouth in a *whoof* sound.

He grabbed her by the hair and brought his mouth to her ear, though he did not lower his voice. "We stop when I say stop. You don't sit down until you're told. You don't eat, shit, sleep, or talk until you're told."

She was crying now, a high, keening sound like a baby.

"You shut your mouth and follow along, or I'll fix it so that your every step is agony. And you'll follow along anyway."

I packed the pipe with Archie's good tobacco, traded for in Vana and fresh in the leather sack. I tamped it down with my fingers and put the end of it in my mouth while I searched for his flint.

He yanked Dinty upright and whirled her around to face me. "Your situation in life has changed. I'm not that toothless old man who used to own you. I am a trader, and I am going to turn you into something valuable, something I can sell. The sooner you act like that one"—here he pointed to me, and I looked over at them as detachedly as I could— "the sooner you will live pain-free days. Do you understand?"

Dinty nodded her head, catching up at last.

I got the dry leaves burning and took half a drag for myself. A little tobacco at midday perked me up as a child, and I miss it now. But there is none growing near here, and perhaps that is for the best. In my experience, a crop that is grown for anything but food or clothing is a luxury, and luxury does not exist without slavery.

I held the pipe out to Archie and he took it from me, then patted my head. "That is how a good slave behaves," he said to her while looking at me. "Anticipating my needs and working to meet them." He patted my braids.

He was only ever affectionate to me in this way, to make someone else feel worse by comparison. This was the love that I got as a child. It took so long to learn to trust anything given to me by a caring hand.

Archie always wanted me in the morning. I think even then he was too old to rise more than once a day, and his once happened around sunup. When we were training a new slave, the process took much longer. Dinty resisted him so long that I began to think her former keeper had been lying about her use. Everything was new to her. She cried, she gagged, she wasted time saying no or begging to stop. It was weeks before she could successfully finish him off without my help.

I was already inured to it and businesslike about the process. I thought it would be easier for her since she was older; her body was better suited to the work and she might even enjoy it, as I saw older girls could sometimes do (or at least pretend). But she was terrible at it. She couldn't read the signs of arousal or progress. She had to be coached on what to say or how to hold herself. Archie had to physically take her hands away from her face, time and time again.

In the end, he knew she would fetch no great price. The best she could manage was grudging acquiescence or motionless vacancy. When we reached a fishing village along the coast, we met a group of men who spoke a strange, fluid language of which we didn't know a word. Through gesture and showing goods, Archie sold Dinty to a black-haired man who smelled like shrimp, and we left her there. She had been such a slow learner, I felt a terrible pang thinking how long it would be before she could make herself understood to them at all.

The story of my time with Archie is a series of tragedies like these, in which I only barely grasped what was tragic. Every life is a tragedy in progress, and I certainly knew no better. But now, I think of each of them as a story that might never be told. Who was Dinty? Who were her people? What did she hope to become? Did she turn that whole fishing village into her Hive after a few years, or was she sold again? Is she living in the belly of a whale somewhere?

Every child who passed through Archie's hands passed through mine as well. I didn't choose to become a slaver, but I was made one. By the time I had ten summers behind me, I knew the job well enough to do it on my own. I didn't know each of them was their own person, a soul, a being with its own destiny and desires, because I did not know that was true of myself.

It was only when I realized that I was a slave and not a slaver's apprentice that I understood that what Archie was doing was a great wrong. Right and wrong had no meaning in my life until I was almost a woman. I learned some of it from my father, but he was not a talkative man. I began to understand when I knew the horsewomen, but I could never see it the way they did. They didn't know what I knew.

Even when I met Eddy I still didn't really know. I had not yet made peace with what I had done, or what was done to me. Of course I can't think about the way I grew up without thinking about Connie. Every Mother I've ever met says they didn't understand their own Mother until they had a child of their own.

I didn't know what to do with that for a long time. Every woman says it, so it must have been true. For them. I had no Mother. Whenever I thought about having a child, I thought about that. Where would I learn it, the work of mothering? Mothers were everywhere in Ommun, and I learned some of it there. They were rare in Nowhere and everywhere else, and I saw how it changed people. They became fierce and fearful. They changed their entire being to exist for someone else. Or they didn't. They each came to understand that they were part of a line of women, back to the old world and whatever began it, of Mothers and daughters back to the first.

I came from no one and no line. I came from broken and unusual. I came from Archie and, later, my father. I learned how to cherish a child after I was too big to be held. What could I know?

But Connie wasn't a baby when they became my child. Maybe that's why it was so easy for us. I understood them. I loved them at once.

Here on Bambritch Island, all this seems like it happened to someone else. I can remember it; I can see how it made me into who I am. The line runs through me. If not straight to a living child, then to a circle of people here on Bambritch. I have a line the way the Midwife had a line: by making a safe place for people like me.

I can't stop thinking about this as the army approaches.

There is a sound, now, in the night. It whines like a mosquito, but it never comes near. Panic tells me it's the plane, flying through the night looking for the bright spots of fires. The Bambritch council got together and issued a blackout warning for the island. We decided not to tell people too much, not to panic them. Hortensia, the council's oldest member, agreed with me immediately. Zill and Eva almost always decide as one, and they were with me. Our planning has been slow—too slow. Carol is the youngest, the one most likely to believe. He believes they have a plane they can fly. He was most eager of all for a blackout rule, believing they might be able to see us from the sky.

I'm sure they can't drop bombs from a plane. I'm sure.

I've read about planes in many books. They used to be as common as sheep. People flew every day, covering distances I can't imagine in only a few hours. They used to ship food and goods through the sky. They used to wage war, dropping bombs and shooting guns from planes. There's no way to defend against that, if it's real. There's nowhere to run. We could maybe shoot it down, if we were lucky, but then it would have to fall somewhere. Maybe in the water, but maybe on our island. That's hardly better.

The mosquito sound drones louder, but nothing has been spotted. Watchers on the water are scanning the skies instead of netting the fish that are active only at night. They haven't seen it. Not yet.

The lookouts have passed the word that we have only a few more days before the army arrives. We're going to have to make some decisions, the council and the whole island. What we do will affect us all, and the five of us can't decide it for everyone.

I don't know that I have enough time to tell this story. We won't be able to gather until dawn, because of the blackout order. But I have only this time, and I cannot think of any better way to spend it.

I intend to write through most of the night. I couldn't sleep with this hanging over me, anyway.

CHAPTER 3

OMMUN

Alma was pregnant again.

This should not have been a surprise to anyone. Alma was continually pregnant, even as she was still nursing her triplets, born less than a year ago. She made the announcement with one of them suckling at her nipple, the rounded little face obscuring her pink areola with the fullness of her breast clear on all sides.

But the people of Nowhere who had refugeed to Ommun after the fall of Estiel had hardly seen any such thing. There had been one or two children born per year in Nowhere, and only in a good year. Mothers had been venerated all their lives for having borne a living child. Midwives had been trained for this, but many had only ever seen a handful of births.

Everyone out of Estiel was ragged and displaced. Nowhere was gone, burned to the ground by the late Lion of Estiel. Only a few had survived. Eddy had taken along the women and catamites of the city along with his own people. They had all suffered the same. Those who had lived in the Lion's harem had been driven back over the bumpy, broken roads and open fields only to discover there was no city where they were told they would be safe.

When the bus pulled up and they had all piled out, Flora hadn't known what to expect. There was nothing around, no sign of a city. Eddy had thrown off Kelda, his deerskin-clad companion from the fallen city of Womanhattan, and wouldn't even look at Flora. He had tried to shoot Flora's eye out only an hour before; Flora was not inclined to push. She waited. They all waited. There was nothing here, but nothing was better than where they had been.

Flora had seen Eddy take himself off and put on Etta. There were changes in the body: the slumping of shoulders, the dropping of chin. She watched Eddy drain out and Etta flow in like a change in the tide. She didn't know why this moment called for Etta and not Eddy, but she accepted it. Neither Etta nor Eddy welcomed questions about this aspect of themselves.

Etta had stomped around for a minute, then tapped on a hollow-sounding place in the ground and a hole had opened up. In small groups, they had been ferried deep below, to the strange subterranean metal halls of Ommun, secret city beneath the plains.

Alma, the Prophet and leader of the underground people of Ommun, had welcomed them all, ordered hot baths and hot meals, made sure everyone had a clean bed and a beeswax candle. Alice and Sylvia the Midwife had immediately begun to care for others, though they themselves were just as hurt, as sick, as tired. Alma's rabbity helperman, Neum, had recruited assistance from others and worked long into the night, bandaging wounds and dispensing the precious few drugs they had salvaged. Alice had nothing left of her own fantastic inventory, and the waste of it made her swear in frustration.

Ommun welcomed the catamites of Estiel, sharp-tongued feminine boys who did not understand what to do when separated from their city with its electric lights and powerful, demanding men. They settled uneasily in twos and threes.

It welcomed too the refugees who had hid in the tunnels beneath Nowhere. Tommy the bather had sounded the alarm first, saving most of the other bathers and his friends. The guards in the towers had been shot; only a dozen men had made it out of a city of over a hundred. Tommy's blond hair was full of dirt.

When that first, terrible night had come to an end, Flora had put a hand on the back of Alice's neck.

"Let's get you cleaned up and in bed."

Alice had nodded to Sylvia. "You, too." Sylvia had been almost too tired to hold up her head.

Etta had gone to sleep with Kelda early on that first night in Ommun. Etta's elderly mother, Ina, had sought out a solitary refuge, pushing a chair beneath the handle of her steel door before she had been able to relax and drift away. Sylvia knocked at a door and smiled weakly when Rob from Nowhere answered, putting an arm around her shoulders and pulling her in.

Flora and Alice took a room near the heart of Ommun, moving in as quietly as they knew how. Neum heard them nonetheless, and he appeared unobtrusively with hot water in a wide, flat basin, and clean clothes. These he dropped off with scarcely a word. Alma's directive had been very clear: no one was to ask anything of these people until she said otherwise.

When at last all had been quiet, slips of paper had begun to whisper beneath Alma's door. One of Alma's ladies collected them from her chair as she kept watch. The count came in: thirteen men, five women, six catamites, no children. Each with a number corresponding to what room they had taken in the vast, labyrinthine warren that was Ommun, each with the name of the person or persons with whom they shared that room.

Alma sat up in bed, knowing everything there was to know, passing what she knew on to the daughter who clung to her breast. The one she had named after Etta.

On the night that Alma welcomed them all and counted their official numbers, the room had been packed with refugees out of Nowhere, Estiel, and Jamestown. Their combined body heat and breath warmed the room, but the fireplace still blazed. Etta the elder stood with her back to the wall, knowing that the women of Nowhere were watching with their mouths agape, feeling what she had first felt when she had stumbled into the nursery in Ommun. Despite the horror of their recent days, they would see the magic that Alma housed in her body.

In their midst, she looked nothing less than magic. They all shared the haunted look of people who had recently seen the worst life had to offer, dark circles beneath their eyes, arms crossed or hanging listlessly at their sides. Sparks in their eyes, here and there, but otherwise indistinguishable from the recently dead.

Alma glowed like a candle in the center of the room. Her red-gold hair was loose tonight, cascading over her shoulders and falling in shining ripples to her feet. Her skin was rosy pink, flushed with good health and early pregnancy. Her bare feet were soft and peeped from beneath her clean white gown blamelessly, her toenails clipped and neat with the help of her attendants.

Her face was absolutely serene, green-blue eyes wide and untroubled as she spoke to them.

"I am so glad you are with us, Sisters and Brothers. I know that your journey has been perilous, and that you left the house of the Lion cast down in your wake. I gather that we have Etta to thank for that. Etta, whose arrival here was prophesied and came to pass. You'll all recall that I was given sight of these things before they came to be. That I sent Etta with the mish, that I knew she would bring great victory."

The people of Ommun clapped a little, but the air was solemn and they kept their hands quietly cupped.

Etta did not stir when her name was mentioned.

"Let us all go forth in one accord," Alma said as the child slackened at her breast, milk-drunk and asleep. She handed the baby off and tucked herself back into her clothes. "We have been given much, and so we must give. We have food storage and room enough for everyone who has come to us. We are blessed to add so many to our number, and we hope your bloodlines will strengthen and seed our own, until we are one people."

A few people shifted where they sat. Mother Ina's mouth compressed to a line.

Alma looked down, blinking in wonder. She looked up at them. "May Heavenly Mother guide me in my leadership so that I may unite us, build new families, and see to the births of many more living children."

Ina rose in front of her chair, looking around at the people from Nowhere. She seemed to seek their assent, one set of eyes to the next. She found that she had it, and turned back to Alma.

"Alma," she began.

The Prophet blanched. She was not accustomed to being addressed so informally. However, her brow uncreased as she smiled at the older woman.

"Alma, we are all thankful to be here, and we appreciate the safe place, the food, and the care we've been given. But I don't know that we're all planning to stay here and become a part of your city."

"But Heavenly Mother—"

Ina interrupted her so smoothly and so gently that those listening almost didn't notice. Alma did, and her eyes blazed quietly.

"I don't know that we all need you to speak over our destiny just now. Each of us must make her own choice. As a leader, I'm sure you know that."

"Of course I do," Alma said. "I just wanted you all to know that you're welcome here. Ommun has always welcomed refugees, as long as they bring loving hearts and contrite spirits. We know that many new-comers may not share our faith, but I believe that the seed of faith is in you. I know you don't bring a spirit of contention." Her eyes sharpened a little and she all but stared Ina down.

Ina nodded her head once, sinking into her chair. Alma's eyes did not leave her for a long moment.

"For today, I wish to dispense callings, for those who will accept them, and ask Ommun to stain those who will serve."

Silence greeted her.

"Alice, will you found a drugmaking center here in our city, and train at least one apprentice in your way?"

Alice nodded, smoothing her hair, ducking her head.

"Sylvia, will you consult with the Midwives of Ommun, to help them in their chronicling?"

Sylvia looked around, her blue eyes huge, searching the room. Lucy and a few others raised their hands to her.

"Sure . . . uh, sure." She nodded her head.

"Ina, will you work in the nursery? We have so very many babies this year, we could use another hand with them." Alma smiled sweetly, obviously thinking this the greatest of favors.

Ina sat silent for a moment. "I'll think about it."

Alma's smile faltered for a moment, but she picked it right back up. "Etta, will you join the mish and help bring more people to safety?"

Etta began to shake her head at once. "I decide where I go, and I go alone. I'm not interested in being sent or being part of a group."

The temperature in the big room was boiling with so many bodies crammed in next to one another. No one was turning on the big fans to ventilate it; they would clear the hot air after the meeting had ended. Even still, everything seemed to go cold.

"You're refusing your calling?"

Etta shrugged with the shoulder that was not pressed against the wall. "I don't believe you have any authority to call me to anything."

Alma's face went white and her eyes darkened. "Very well," she said flatly. "Sisters and Brothers, please stain these callings by raising your arm to the square."

Around the room, the people of Ommun made a swift gesture of raising their right hands, elbows sharply bent. Folks from elsewhere merely watched, bewildered.

A few people stepped forward to speak with the Prophet as the meeting broke up, but she swept from the room, her attendants in tow, carrying her babies.

Flora walked up to Etta, approaching her carefully. "She didn't call me to anything."

Etta snorted. "Good. Better that you don't fall into her hands." She sighed and ran her fingers over the short curls of her hair. "I know. I know she saved us. I know that we're lucky to be here. But I can't handle this at all. Fuck her for trying to tell anyone what to do right now. It's too soon."

"But—"

"What was that shit about adding to their bloodline? Does she have any idea . . ." Etta trailed off, watching the mish boys pair off and disappear. Some of the catamites cast lingering glances in their directions, but none of the local boys seemed to notice.

"Is that why she ignores me? Because she knows I'm not a breeder?" Flora spoke in a low, nervous tone. She glanced over her shoulder. She did not know if there were any women like her in this city underground, but she doubted it.

I hate feeling this way. I hate dreading people figuring me out, dreading what they'll say or do. I am exactly what I am and there is nothing wrong with me. So why am I worried that Alma knows what I've got between my legs? Why do I care what she makes of that?

Etta flinched a little at the word *breeder*. She raised a hand as if to lay it on Flora's shoulder, then flinched again and let it fall. "I'm sure that's not it. She called my mother to some bullshit, and Ina's clearly past breeding."

Flora watched the room empty out. She felt the air begin to lighten up as the fans stirred to life again. "I guess so."

Alice appeared, laying her hand in the small of Flora's back. "I'm done with today," she said. "And I have work to do tomorrow, it seems. You ready for bed?"

Flora nodded, looking to Etta's face for some trace of softness—some absolution or friendly farewell. There was none. Flora thought about the first time Eddy had put his hands on her and knew what she was, about the moment Etta had held a gun on her in the harem. She was never going to see acceptance in those dark-brown eyes again.

Maybe Eddy hates me for what I am. Maybe for what I did. Maybe because Alice still loves me.

Flora stared at Etta's back, trying to read her in the lines of her body. As always, the body was written in a language she couldn't read.

Etta's eyes had turned back to Alma's empty chair. She stared hard at the void there between the arms.

Disappointed, Flora walked away, holding Alice's hand.

CHAPTER 4

The Book of Flora
Ommun
Fall
Year 104, Nowhere Codex

It seems as though a place as safe as this should feel better.

Nobody has threatened me with a gun since we came here. No one has hurt me or told me how they'd like to hurt me. Nobody has used my body as though I weren't in it, or looked at me as though I were nothing at all.

We are free of the terrible stink of men and cats. We are out of the harem and away from that smelting city. Ommun might as well be another world.

But we are not free.

I don't know what it is. I know I could leave and nobody would stop me. But I'd have to go alone, because Alice isn't ready and Eddy wouldn't have me. Can you ever really be free if you need somebody?

And I need somebody. I always have. I can't sleep alone anymore. My own little house in Jeff City was one thing, though even then I found *someone to be with at least once a week. But these days I'm all nightmares and even my breath seems to have a cost.*

Ommun has soft beds and hot food, and women who act like they're everybody's Mother. They open their arms and let us inside, so what does that cost? Why does Eddy look at Alma like that? What does he know that I don't?

If Eddy's not free then I'm not free. If we're not free, then we're not really safe.

Ommun's strange words come stranger to me than ever, but they're not really new.

The Leaf: the young boys who do most of the manual labor, the ones who are too young to form the mish.

The mish: the older boys and young men who go out into the world to bring people back, or to raid like Eddy does. No girls leave Ommun.

Stain: to support people in their calling, and to show obedience to Alma and the order here in some larger sense (?).

Calling: whatever their job is. I remember in Jeff City, we all knew that what we did was important and that we all depended on each other, but there's nothing like feeling that you get your work in life decreed by God. Calling is like job + destiny = your whole life, as the Midwife might say.

The scripture (sometimes the triple): the book of stories they base their religion on. I've read some of it. It's much older than the Midwife's book, and a lot of it is fanciful. Things that couldn't have happened. They've also got one with a bunch of songs in it, this is also "scripture."

Spake: Alma uses this all the time when she just means "said." It's used all over their scripture book, I think she just phrases things that way to add weight to her words.

Heavenly Mother: their god. The book mostly says Heavenly Father. It's very old world. Fathers are everywhere; Mothers are special. I don't know when the switch happened, but Alma never refers to God as a man. I've seen religion in many forms in my travels, but living underground and focusing on a god who left you strict instructions on how to live makes it more intense here, I think. Everything the people of Ommun do is about this god, this tradition, this book.

They're very into books here in Ommun. Mostly old ones, but they have a good library and it keeps getting better. All the kids learn to read while they're still small, boys and girls alike.

Not much got out of Nowhere, but one thing that did is the Midwife's diaries. Someone cleaned out the shrine in time, got everything they could into the tunnels before it all burned. Ina's holding them now. I have Eddy's old copy, but it's not the complete book. Since I have no calling and nobody seems to need me, that's what I'm going to do. I'm going to read her story until I know what she would have done. She was built to survive. Like me.

I remember reading in the very beginning that she assessed the world, after the Dying, to decide what her purpose was. She wasn't a breeder. As much as she was a Midwife, she couldn't do that work for years of her life. I'm a silk thrower, but without a tree full of worms, that means nothing. I have been a slave more than I have been anything else. That is not my purpose. But I don't know what is.

Tomorrow, I go back to the beginning. To her beginning, to mine. Under the earth, I crack like a seed. Let's see what I can grow into, see how long it takes me to reach the light.

CHAPTER 5

OMMUN

Kelda, the last survivor of Womanhattan, wearing the deer-leather clothes she had made herself ten summers ago, slept with Etta every night that Etta would have her. Since their first night together, Kelda had practically worshipped her. They had found each other, saved each other, and Kelda was as attached to her as any person could be.

Kelda woke to the sound of Etta washing her face. She stretched her tanned, scarred hunter's arms and pulled her deerskin vest back on, began to lace it. The room smelled sour.

"I'll get you another basin," Etta said gruffly. "I've used both."

Kelda sat up slowly, extending her arms over her head and arching her back. "That's okay," she said, trying to hold back a yawn. "I can wait."

Etta dumped both basins into their private toilet, then went out the door to one of the centrally located taps in their corner of Ommun. The taps pulled water from deep underground sources. Etta had told Kelda that she had learned about it when they first came here. Ommun was built in the old world for people to shelter from storms or war. The many-leveled structure was connected to a deep hidden spring, and it had a network of cisterns that filtered rainwater as well. In the mornings, crews went to work lighting fires to pipe warm water to nearly all inhabited quarters so that everyone could get a wash.

Pump and pipe teams worked to maintain the vast plumbing throughout Ommun, making sure waste was safely flushed away to a dump spout downstream in the Misery, and that the clean water that came in wasn't contaminated.

When Etta came back with two more basins of warm water, Kelda washed her face. It was a marvel to her what advantages these people had in their underground city. It took a lot of people, but they had hot water, electric light, and enough food all year round. They were safe and secure and even happy. In their bathroom, a cake of lye soap sat, prettily golden and molded in the shape of a beehive. It smelled of honey and nut oil when she lathered her hands with it. This place was nothing like the twin cities in which she had grown up: one for men, one for women, and neither with wonders like these.

"This city is so rich," Kelda began, pulling on her deerskin clothes. They had lasted her through their time in Estiel. The women of Ommun had offered her a cotton gown, but she wouldn't accept. She checked that the laces of her vest were tightly gathered together, remembering how distraught they had seemed at even a hint of her brown breasts showing underneath without a baby attached to them.

"Guess so," Etta replied.

"So, if you're not going to go out with the mish, what are you going to do?"

Kelda tried to look preoccupied with lacing up her knee-high soft boots.

"Whatever I want." Etta wouldn't face her. She was standing with her back to Kelda, dressing quickly. She had slept in her long underwear, despite the warmth of the room and the deep, clean quilts on their bed. She had rebuffed any attempt Kelda made to get closer, but Kelda understood that. After Estiel, it might be a long time.

"What are you going to do?" Etta cast her a glance over one shoulder. Kelda popped up off the bed and set about making it.

"Well, she called me to work in the nursery."

"Why?"

Kelda laid the quilt down and smoothed it. "I don't know."

"You're a hunter." Etta shoved her guns home once she was dressed, setting them in their accustomed places. "You know how to tan hides and make bows and bowstrings. You can fish too, right?"

Kelda nodded. "Right. And make fishhooks. I've planted and reaped, too. And really, I'd prefer to be up top, in the sun."

"Why don't you tell her that?"

Kelda shrugged. "She didn't ask me what I prefer. She just gave me duties."

Etta sighed. "Like she knows. Don't go."

Kelda looked around at the little windowless room. "What else will I do?"

"Come with me."

The boys running the lift did not question them. The sun hit them like a physical weight, shining off their skin and narrowing their eyes. A fat rabbit ran past their feet as they walked away from Ommun, their backs to the river.

Kelda went ahead, stomping in her deerskin boots, flattening bushes and waving gnats away from her face. When she was hunting, Kelda could be silent. Today, however, she was not a hunter. Etta had told her what to look for. She even had a small hand-drawn picture of the two possibilities stuck into her pack, from Alice. But the woods here, near the bend in the Misery, were overgrown and lush. Bees hummed past them lazily in the thick, fragrant late-summer air. Kelda could smell the layers of rot in the forest floor, ripe with dead squirrels and sickly-sweet decaying berries. Conditions like these made it hard to focus on anything, especially as she kept catching the faint whiff of a predator somewhere not too far off.

Kelda was looking up at the trees. "You know, cats will lie up on tree branches. I've seen it, while hunting. Sometimes they'll drag a deer up there, eat it all day, and then drop what's left. Just raining dead deer. You ever see that?"

Etta picked through the bushes at the edge of the rough trail Kelda was blazing. "I've heard rock cats will do that. Never seen it, though."

She glanced up nervously, scanning the dark canopy of overlapping branches above their heads.

Etta could not stand still. She couldn't stay in Ommun and take on domestic work. Everyone there made her itch beneath her skin. Ina was not well. Her face had taken on a look like she was being pinched continually under her clothes. Her thinness was shockingly evident, with sharp angles jutting out everywhere around her battered wooden belly. Her eyes were too large, too dark. She had taken to working in the nursery over the last few months, spending all her time quieting crying babies and reading to the toddlers.

Even worse was Alma, who seemed to hover over Etta's shoulder at every turn, wanting to whisper something. Etta thought of her voice, saying that Etta was full of ghosts.

Shit, Etta thought. *I am now.*

Etta pushed forward, scanning over the riotous shrubs and vines and ferns that strangled one another for the dappled sunlight that barely shone through. She had not yet found what she was looking for.

She couldn't stand Alice, or Flora, or anyone who had known her at home. She couldn't stand Sheba, or any of the rescued women from the harem. Some of them had gathered to talk about what had happened, and to comfort one another and cry. Etta had not joined them.

Kelda had, and she had returned clearer eyed and with a weight visibly lifted from her. In the nights after they had returned to Ommun, she had sometimes held Etta when she couldn't sleep. When Kelda invariably dropped into a deep, seamless slumber, Etta had gotten up and paced the empty metal hallways of Ommun's underground city.

It had taken nearly a month after the escape from Estiel for anything to feel like normal life again. Ommun took in all refugees, gladly. The Leaf had been more than happy to adjust provisions and even break into storage to feed everyone.

Ommun was too large by far for the number of people in it. Empty rooms abounded, and everyone was settled into their own or a shared space. Ina was living alone again, but many of the women chose to room together. One by one they picked up work spinning or sewing or testing the water that flowed in. A few chose to go topside daily with the farmers.

Sheba, Etta's wordless, wantless rescue girl taken from slavers who had held her all her life had become another of Alma's attendants, to Etta's surprise. The girl had desired nothing after her rescue from Jamestown, not even a name. Her silence and her bearing had not changed, but her eyes followed Alma's glow and magisterial presence with awe verging on reverence.

Alma's triplets, including Etta's namesake, were flourishing. Each girl had dainty rolls of fat on her back and ringing her dimply thighs. They were always at Alma's breasts or in the arms of one of the many nursing women. Kelda had not believed in the multiple birth at first. She thought it was a story or some kind of metaphor. As the babies grew, their eerie similarity and identical faces did the work of convincing all the newcomers. The other twins running around Ommun did the rest.

People like Kelda, who rarely saw babies and had never seen multiples, were overwhelmed by the strangeness of Ommun. People like Sheba, who had come from nothing and less than nothing, were transported by the mere existence of this place.

But Etta could not help but compare it to Nowhere.

Nowhere had been better, hadn't it? Hadn't they been more free?

Not free, Etta thought. *Not free to live with Alice, or tell my mother that I loved her. Not free to be Eddy. And Tommy and the other fancy boys—were they free?*

Some of the catamites from Estiel had taken to living together in a block of adjoining rooms in Ommun. There were whispers about that already.

In her own mind, Etta had to admit that Ommun and Nowhere were very much alike, aside from the peculiar faith of the underground people and their uncanny fertility.

It's the same shit. Nobody likes what doesn't breed. Nobody wants to waste women. But if scarcity is the problem, why worry what the fancy boys are up to? Whose business is it? They can't all be making babies all the time.

Etta's fingers touched a fuzzy white clump of berries atop a tall, reedy bush. She stopped and stared at them a moment. She brought her face close and sniffed.

"Is that it? The plant you're looking for?" Kelda asked hopefully.

"No," Etta said, wiping her fingertips on the legs of her pants. "Close, but that's not it."

Kelda walked on dejectedly.

And anyhow, if they're so lucky in Ommun, why not let everybody be who they're going to be? It's not even a problem for them. They've got Alma having babies two and three at a time. What's a few women sleeping together beside that?

Etta thought of the faces at breakfast when she and Kelda showed up together. The way people from Ommun looked them over, as though they hadn't washed properly. It wasn't the same look they gave the other women who were rooming together. It was as if they could see her essential nature—the same way she and Kelda had first seen each other.

I know what you are.

Ghosts.

Kelda called back from farther ahead, behind a clump of moss-covered trees. "I think I've got something!"

Etta jogged to catch up, holding her pack so it didn't bounce the guns out of her waistband.

Kelda was holding one of Alice's drawings in her outstretched hand, looking at the plant that came up to her neck.

"That looks like this one, doesn't it?"

Etta frowned in concentration, comparing the two. She cut a tiny section of the hard, whitish berries with her thumbnail and sniffed.

"Bitter, just like Alice said. I think this might be it, Kelda."

"And this is the medicine?"

"Yes," Etta said, producing a knife and cutting the crowded heads off the plant, taking berries, stem, and leaf just to be sure.

"Well, we're not going to make it back to Ommun before dark," Kelda said, a slight whine in her voice.

"No, we won't."

"But we could go back to that little house we saw. The one from this morning?"

The little house Kelda was talking about had been a mostly stone cottage full of the metal skeletons of old-world furniture and almost entirely taken over by squirrels. Still, it had a stone fireplace and would keep them safer than sleeping in the open.

"Yeah, let's head back there."

Kelda took Etta's bow from her back and plucked at the string. "I'm going to shoot us something to eat."

"I'm not really hungry," Etta said. She was starving. They had walked all day and had eaten only a thin porridge with summer fruits that morning.

But Alice said that all these plants are basically poison, and the trick is to take just enough. So that means I'll probably end up shitting and puking, and I'd just as soon have a belly full of water as one full of hot fish or deer meat.

"Well, I am," Kelda laughed. She struck out again, her tread becoming surprisingly quiet as she made her way back in the direction of the old cottage. "I'm hoping for another rabbit. I'll eat two, if you won't have one."

"Fine," Etta said distractedly. She was looking over the plant matter in her hands.

Make tea. Pulverize the whole thing and steep in hot water, but don't boil it. It'll taste awful and bitter, so add honey if you have it. Drink as much as you can bear. If you don't feel sick, it's not enough. If you get too dizzy to stand, it's probably too much.

Alice's advice had come from diaries and distant memory. In her work in Nowhere, she had helped Midwives dose women who had begun to miscarry and wanted help, but no one had asked to be spared pregnancy altogether. There were stories from past Midwives where that had been the case, but the practice had become less and less common. There was only that one book from the old world where Alice had found the word for this procedure: *abortion*. It was a word neither one of them had ever said out loud.

Just enough poison to kill you but not me, little Lion.

Addressing herself to the parasite inside her, even for just a moment, made her weak and shaky with revulsion. Her body felt like an atlas of betrayal, swelling with treachery and planting sedition in her dreams. She felt like she was dragging an animal on a leash, but the animal was her. She could not exist in her body at all without knowing that although the Lion's leather straps were long gone from her wrists and ankles, his life was in her. His hope and his plans for the future lived on, eating her blood and her body to feed itself.

She stroked the poisonous berries and quickened her pace.

That ends tonight. It all ends tonight. If I could cut off the parts of me that keep you alive and leave them bleeding in this forest, I would. But this will have to be enough.

And how many more back in Ommun were infected with this same disease? How many of them carried Lion-seed in their bellies? How many little Paws would be born in the spring?

I can bring the poison cure back with me, Etta thought. *I can save them again.*

She groped for Eddy, her other self, her mirror. She remembered the feeling at last of being whole and perfect, working together as though she was his right hand and he was her left, united at last as *we* instead of *I*. But ever since the day she first woke to the nausea and sickening tenderness of this invader living inside her, Eddy had been nowhere to be found. He could not do this with her. He would not drag this animal body around as long as its doubled traitor heart kept beating.

She didn't blame him. And she could not wait to feel him return.

CHAPTER 6

OMMUN

Flora went to Alma first thing in the morning but found that she was out of her apartments already. Two women came out her door, carrying three tightly wrapped babies.

"Oh, isn't Alma here?" Flora smiled at the three and looked toward the door.

Eliza's black braid looked hastily done, and there were circles under her eyes. She held the child tighter. "The Prophet is out among the stake," she said very formally.

Lucy, her pink eyes shining in her pale face, reached out and put a hand on Eliza. She turned her kind face toward Flora. "Please don't mind my Sister. She's had a loss, and she's upset."

Eliza's mouth hardened. Flora dipped her head and looked at the floor.

"I'm so sorry to hear that."

"It's been a long time since anyone here has lost a child. The Prophet says it must be a sign."

Eliza busied herself with the children in her arms.

"Do you know where I might find her?"

Lucy nodded. "She went to find a medical laboratory somewhere in the unused spaces that Sister Alice can use to fulfill her calling. She says Heavenly Mother told her there would be one, but she must find it."

Flora nodded. "Which way to the unused spaces?"

Lucy explained which parts of Ommun's alphanumerical grid were uninhabited, and gave Flora an idea of which level Alma might be on now.

"Thank you," Flora said quietly. Eliza was staring daggers at her before she left. Flora pretended that she did not see.

Ommun spread out for miles beneath the earth, with a vaguely square shape. The grid helped by setting cardinal directions and establishing units of distance, and the coordinates were painted in fading old-world stencils at every corner. Even so, nothing could change the fact that they were in a dark burrow under the dirt.

The city had limited electricity, with scheduled days and times for most services. The corridors were always lit during daytime hours, but the uninhabited parts of the grid were disconnected to keep them from draining power. Flora hadn't thought about this until she realized she was getting deeper into darkness without any source of light. She had nothing on her that would help.

She peered into the brown dimness that faded to black and saw something glowing, off to the right, two junctions down.

She walked briskly toward it, trying not to be afraid. She rounded a corner and saw Alma, her hair in tight braids, a lantern held in a gloved hand.

"Prophet," Flora said in a low voice.

Alma turned and raised her lantern higher. "Flora. From Nowhere."

Flora smiled but shook her head. "Not really. From Jeff City."

Alma's face darkened somewhat, growing sad. "You were in Estiel."

"Yes, I was. Anyway, I was wondering if I could talk with you a bit."

Alma gestured with the lantern, and Flora caught up so they could walk together.

Some of the old steel doors were marked. The ones close to the main tunnel line had the same numbers that indicated living quarters elsewhere in Ommun. Others had designations that Flora had not seen before: "SEED REPOSITORY." "WOODWORKING SHOP." "WAR ROOM."

How much war fits in one room? Flora wondered. She thought of the harem in Estiel. *A lot, I guess.*

She realized Alma was not going to speak first.

"So, I was wondering why I didn't receive a calling, like everyone else." She looked sideways at Alma's serene and unlined face. "I thought maybe your argument with Eddy . . . Etta kept you from telling us the rest."

Alma chuckled. "Sister Etta didn't argue with me. She argued with Heavenly Mother. That's how you end up in the belly of a whale."

Flora didn't know what that meant, and so pressed on. "Well, I'm not here to argue. I would like to be useful. So I'd like a calling. I am trained as a weaver. There's no silkworms here, or I'd get back to throwing silk without a second thought. I've seen the spinning and weaving operation the Leaf has here in Ommun. I believe I could be of service."

Alma's face showed something Flora had never seen before. She looked uncomfortable.

"I'm not sure you'd work well with the Leaf." Alma was suddenly very interested in reading the labels on the doors as they walked.

"Alright. I'm not half bad at working with children. I can teach reading, and sewing. Wildcrafting, though I'm a little far from home."

Alma would not look at her. "Oh, the Sisters in the nursery and the school have all of that well in hand."

Flora gritted her teeth. She was beginning to see where this was going.

"Well, I know you don't like the idea of sending women out with the mish," she said. "But I can do that, too."

Alma sighed. "I just don't know who would be your companion. Who could be your helpmeet? Your partner. No one . . . no one here is like you."

Flora swallowed a lump in her throat and breathed carefully. For no reason at all, she thought of Archie. Archie: the only man who had ever owned her. The one who had taught her what partnership usually looks like.

"What about you?" She was relieved to find that her voice was steady.

"What?" Now Alma was looking at her.

"Well, Eddy told me about your magic. The way you know too much. The way you lay hands on people and change something inside their bodies."

Alma snorted. "That's my mantle. Those are the gifts Heavenly Mother gives me, so that I may serve my people. As she gives me the power to spake prophecy, and to birth healthy babies."

"So there's no one like you here, either. You're the only one of your kind. Yet you have a calling."

"Yes," Alma said at once, her eyes as narrow as blades. "A calling that came straight from Heavenly Mother, on the day that I was born. When I spake your name in prayer to Her, she answered me with silence. That's why you have no calling. She doesn't know who I'm talking about."

They came to a doorway that read "MEDICAL WEST 1." Alma stopped and laid her hands against it.

"Here it is. Just as Heavenly Mother said it would be."

She turned a beatific, satisfied smile to Flora.

And that's how she does it, Flora knew all at once. *She sees coincidences and seizes on them. She makes magic out of happenstance. She takes her lucky womb and her blue-gray-green eyes and makes them into miracles. Nobody else hears from her god, so who are we to argue?*

44

Alma seemed to physically shrink in her view. Her face looked puffier, less luminous. Flora could see the tiny fine lines slowly leaking out around her eyes and mouth, calling the eventual end to her impeccable youth. She saw how small and easily shaken, how petty Alma really could be.

In that timeless moment, Flora knew not to waste it. Not to applaud Alma's obvious triumph or even let her gaze stray to the door. She looked Alma straight in the eye.

"It's perfectly obvious that you don't want me here. You don't know what to do with me."

"Heavenly Mother—" Alma began, but Flora stopped her.

"I'm not interested in your special connection to someone no one else can see or hear. You can justify it any way you want. But I'm going to tell people that my calling is going out and raiding for books for Ommun's library. You can say whatever you like while I'm gone. But I want to be out on my own for a while. So I'm going."

Alma's mouth closed and her eyes took on that knowing, imperturbable look that usually accompanied a pronouncement of some kind.

"That sounds like an excellent idea."

"I notice that I'm the only woman here that you don't call *Sister*," Flora said quietly, turning to leave. "And while I'm gone, maybe you and your god can both learn my name."

CHAPTER 7

The Bambritch Book
Foggy moon
144N

Thinking of Ommun frustrates me so deeply now. They had a truly defensible city, hidden deep in the earth. Everything about an island makes it vulnerable except the isolation. We're open on every side; we don't have walls. Just the sea. Ommun had everything: old-world goods, more space and tools than they would ever need. Renewable power systems and weapons and resources I'd kill to have here.

We've built so much in the last decades. We have some working power, but we need a team of full-time raiders and another of smiths just to keep us in the necessary parts. We've never had a lot of weapons, and old-world weapons are dearer than ever. The army that approaches will find us armed with little more than sticks and stones.

I knew I couldn't stay in Ommun, no matter how safe and comfortable they made it. It's no wonder I had the urge to roam. I was reading the Midwife's book and thinking I could do the same that she did.

But her world wasn't my world. Bambritch isn't Nowhere. I'm not her. She was alone in a way that I never really have been. There was Archie. And Alice. And Connie. And Eddy.

Eddy. I thought he would teach me everything he knew about being on the road. I thought that I would join his line, and he would pass on what he had learned from Errol and Ricardo, that I would have a new place to say I began.

He was less enthused than I had hoped.

I remember how angry Eddy was when I told him I wanted to go raiding. I caught him just as he was coming back from some mysterious raiding trip with Kelda. They brought almost nothing back; I think they just wanted to get out of the Ommun hole for a while. He could still barely stand the sight of me after Estiel. We hadn't talked much, and he wouldn't look at me. But I wanted to get gone as soon as I could, and no one but he could tell me what I wanted to know.

Kelda saw me coming and found a way out as fast as she could.

"I've got to go and tell the nursery folks I'm sorry I didn't show up," she said, handing off her pack to Eddy.

He looked disgusted. "You don't owe them anything."

"I can't stand it," Kelda said, biting her lip and looking furtively toward me. I'm not sure which thing she couldn't stand: being rude or dealing with the awkward coldness between us. I think she loved us both. Truth be told, I think Kelda loved anyone who was kind to her.

Eddy sighed, taking Kelda's pack and shouldering his own. Neither looked heavy. He nodded. Kelda bolted like a deer.

I closed the distance between us. "Can I talk to you?"

He looked up at the ceiling. "Look," he said. "If you're coming to apologize again—"

"I'm not," I said quietly. "I need your advice. I have to leave. Tomorrow. Can I ask you some things about your travels?"

"Leave?" His eyes suddenly snapped to mine.

"I didn't think you'd care much," I said, trying to speak around the sudden tightening of my throat.

Eddy sighed. "Come in."

We found the door to his place with Kelda. He let me in and lit a lamp. The place smelled like unaired sickness. The fans that ventilated our rooms ran in succession throughout the day, with different sections getting attention at different times. The close sourness of the air made my mouth twist, and I tried to school my face.

"Where are you going?" He sat on the bed and gestured to a chair for me.

"Raiding for books," I said simply. "City of Demons is my goal."

He was already shaking his head. "If Alma sent you—"

"She didn't send me anywhere. I tried. I did ask. I made this one up on my own. I need to spend some time by myself. I'm always following someone, always waiting for someone to tell me what to do."

"The road is dangerous," he began. "More than you can imagine."

I felt my face go hot. "I'm pretty sure I can imagine," I said through my teeth. "I've been everywhere you've been. And a lot more than you, since I was a child."

He sighed. "I know that. I know. I just . . ."

"You just what? Would you even worry about me?"

He stood up suddenly. "Of course I'd worry," he said, staring down at me. "Why did we come here? Weren't we looking for safety?"

"We were, but it's not enough for me. I want to know what else is out there. I want to be somewhere that I'm not the only one like me. Did you ever think of that?"

He gave a dry little laugh. "No, I never think of that. Please tell me all about it."

I scowled up at him. "I'm going," I said. "With or without your help."

"And you won't even go as a man," he yelled, sitting down again and putting a hand to his forehead. The other hovered over his belly but did not quite touch. He laid them both on his thighs. "You'll be so much safer."

"I can't do that," I told him. "I am what I am."

"You won't be safe. You know that. There are men like the Lion absolutely everywhere." He pulled out the small pack he always wore and showed me his blurred and faded map. "Here. Here." He traced his fingers over the cities marked with manacles.

"You see this? You see? It's fucking everywhere. You'll never be free of it. You'll need to watch yourself constantly. You won't even take anyone with you?"

"You used to go alone all the time. To everywhere."

He nodded. "I paid for it. Over and over."

I sat down next to him. "Eddy, you look like you're sick."

He pulled away from me, though I did not reach for him. "I'm fine. And I'm not your owner. You do what you want."

"Are you really okay?"

Eddy nodded, but he clearly wasn't. "Let me show you on the map where to go. Places I know were mostly deserted, at least a few years ago." He put his dry, cracking hand to the map and showed me the way. "Don't go to Demons. I can't tell you anything about what's there."

The truth was I had already decided.

My father was a raider when he was young. He was an old man when he took me in. I was too old to have parents and he was too old to have children. We were a strange match. I was watchful. Furtive. More likely to steal something than to just ask for it. I assumed he had adopted me as a youthful outlet for his last few years of sexual function, but he really did just want a daughter.

He was white haired, with hands that were delicate and powerful. His knuckles were swollen and stiff most days, and he'd hold them to the outsides of the dyeing vats to warm them up.

He brewed a hot drink out of toasted dandelion roots every day. He knew every plant from root to flower, and how to use all of them. He rarely ate meat.

We got to know one another slowly. I kept waiting for him to slip into my bed in the night. When I got tired of waiting, I just made a move for it.

He was working, pulling silk off a drying line, looking to see if the color had taken evenly. I crept up behind him and laid my hand on his cock, over his pants.

"How's it turning out?" I asked him. I had seen fourteen summers.

He turned around slowly, gently. "I don't want you to do that," he said.

We had been sharing a home. He had fed me and given me new clothes. I didn't understand why he would do any of it.

"I don't mind," I told him. "I want to earn my keep." I was still looking at him and seeing Archie's face.

"You're going to do that," he said. "You're going to learn my trade. And keep me company. And maybe take care of me, if I get too old or sick to do it myself. But you're not going to touch me like that, ever again. Okay? That's not why you're here."

I shrugged. I wasn't disappointed, exactly. I just didn't know I could occupy any other space in the world than the one I had always known. Archie had taught me I had no needs of my own, only an endless responsibility for the needs of others. How was I to relate to a man like my father when that was the only road I knew to walk?

He saw that, or at least saw that I was unhappy.

"Can I show you something?" He nodded toward the house.

I nodded back and followed him in.

Father pulled a long trunk out from under his bed. "I was a raider," he said simply. "All through my youth. I didn't learn my trade until my beard was long. I came to Jeff City when I was thirty summers.

"I've seen all of this," he said, passing his hand over a wide expanse of the map marked GREAT PLAIN. "But when I came here," he said, his finger resting on a fat black dot marked DEMONS, "I saw something I had never seen before."

"What was it?"

He sighed and put the map back down. "A tribe of horsewomen."

I bit my lip. I knew that people talked about the horsewomen in Jeff City, but I didn't know what they meant.

His eyes grew dreamy as he looked through the wall and across to something I'd never be able to see.

"I knew a redheaded horsewoman once. A queen. She rode across the plains, from Shy to Peka. She was so beautifully and powerfully made. I loved her, but she was always too much for me."

He blinked and looked back to me. "But she had been a slave when she was a child. She fought to free herself, and so many others. She made me promise that I would do the same, if ever I got the chance."

"That's me?" I asked tonelessly. I don't know what I wanted from him. I wanted to be wanted, I suppose. And not because of some promise or some idea. I didn't understand him. It took me years until I did.

It was a few more months before he introduced me to the horsewomen of Jeff City. I had grown less shy with him. I'd answer his questions and he'd answer mine. He was teaching me to be a better cook. It turned out Archie had very different tastes in food than most.

Finally, the day came and he took me over to their collective home. They received him as a friend, all of them calling him Perry and many coming to plant kisses on his cheeks. I remember staring up at them, so beautiful with their complex braids and painted faces.

Father took my face in his hands and told me, "You'll come home every night. We'll have dinner together. But for the next few moons, you'll spend your days here."

I nodded. I wanted whatever it was they had.

The bathed me and braided my hair. They sang me songs and taught me to paint my face, then to make my own paints. I showed them some of what I had learned about dyes from Father, said it might work on hair. It did, but it worked best on the fair-haired and gray-haired.

They were young and old. They were from different places, though many told me they had come from around Demons, Shy, and Estiel. Many were cut, like me. Cut lips, cut balls, cut clits. Some ragged and some clean. Some breeders, some ruined. Many had been in harems, or sold as children.

It was the most beautiful time in my life. Maybe the only time when I really felt like a cherished child. They were just like me. They taught me things I could learn nowhere else.

They chose a full moon to show me the mystery of the pregnant mare. I know now from my reading that what they did is called an initiation. They prepared me and dressed me in a white gown. They put my hand to the belly of the horse and I felt the long bones of the foal inside her. They blindfolded me but I could still see the light of the moon, smell the horses. I could still feel their soft hands guiding me toward the circle.

In the light of torches, one of the older women took off my blindfold and showed me the long, shallow flats where the mare's urine was dried. It smelled strong and strange. It dried yellow, with tiny crystals along the edges. She led me to the workshops where the dried dregs were mixed with herbs and fat and made into the smooth cream they shared in clay pots, stamped in wax with a horse's head.

"This is ours," she told me, her papery hands wrapped around a jar. "Long ago, the first horsewomen made the same potion. It's been stronger and weaker, changing over hundreds of years. In the old world, it was stronger and they put it straight into their blood. They drank it and pressed it through their skin. Now we rub it all over ourselves, and we take in the power to make ourselves and become ourselves."

The old woman's eyes were huge and cloudy as a dream. Three women took my white gown away and rubbed me all over with the strange-smelling cream. I felt perfectly in myself, and yet very far away.

Looking back on all this, I wonder how many others have had experiences like mine. How many, throughout time, changed and transitioned and became and fragmented and all the other words I've heard used for it. How many through science and how many more through magic? I have an extensive library here in Bambritch, focusing particularly on the science of gender. I have had raiders bring me books from colleges I have found all over the map, painstakingly trying to put together the history of horsewomen, of transwomen, of nonbinary people like Connie, of transmen like Eddy, of people like the Midwife and like Kelda and like Alice.

We have always existed. Even the most ancient records hold that truth. And the horsewomen weren't lying—some form of that potion or that medicine from horses or from elsewhere has been created and used for almost as long.

When I look over the queer history of the world, I wonder if this isn't what humanity was always meant to be. The Dying broke up the expectation that everyone is one thing or the other, and that in perfect simplicity, two by two, we will live and love and reproduce. People talk long and loud about the natural way of things, or what we lost when the world changed. But I can no longer believe that such a world ever existed. We have always been too strange for things to work out so neatly.

So when I knew I was leaving Ommun, I wanted to find the places where the horsewomen said they had been captives and catamites and slaves. I wanted to find someone who was lost as I had been lost, and bring them home. Eddy understood that. It was why he brought back girls every year. I didn't yet understand that I was ready for a child, and that I was striking out into those places so that I could find someone to mother. It was the road that would lead me to Connie, though I did not dream of them yet.

I think about the lost ones who are still out there, each thinking that they are the only one of their kind. Somewhere, there is someone like me or Connie, being run out of town or left to starve because we're not the ones they think will save mankind. People abandon their babies because they want to make sure there are more babies. We are not a logical race.

I think about this army, marching north, burning towns, advancing always toward Bambritch. More reports coming in every day. More drawings from Speel and tales of burned towns, of a leader whom they leave behind to tell the tale. I look up at the moon and I count the days.

And I remember what things were like when I was out on the road.

CHAPTER 8

DEMONS

The old state highway was marked with cracked and faded signs that said *13* every couple of miles. In the predawn light, most of them were illegible. The original print was long faded, but people had added new information here and there, tying streamers to mark their way or define a path toward home. But Flora had been in and around Demons for a couple of weeks now, and she knew the way.

She was driving south across the great plains, a day outside of Demons. Demons was a big old-world city with almost no one in it, according to Eddy. Wind whistled through the punched-out holes in the tall, crumbling towers. She thought back on the long days in the ghostly remains of the city. The river was so teeming with fish that she could practically pluck her dinner out with one hand. New corn sprouted on every available stretch of earth, even the narrow bands between roads and in the garden boxes of the high, honeycombed dwellings of the old-world folk.

Flora hadn't trusted the emptiness of Demons. She had assumed there were people lying in wait, high above her or somehow below. She moved only at night. She never lit fires. Her night vision had gotten very good, but sleep was impossible.

Her truck was a crumbling, rusty wreck, borrowed from the mish in Ommun. They had lent her their oldest, least serviceable vehicle, and that fact had not escaped her. The floor would not take her weight in any place for too long, so she had labored to rebuild the frame and important places with planks of wood. She had had to reinforce the cargo area as well.

Flora was after books.

The main library in Demons was a fortress of shining, coppery stones. It was untouched by fire and still sealed up tight when she got there. Breaking in had taken a crowbar and a hammer. She had waited between blows, breathing quietly, to listen for someone who might approach from within or without.

Once inside, Flora decided she would need a light. She lit one of her torches and held it high.

It had been a long time since Flora had seen a place that was battened down during the Dying and had stayed closed. There were no crumbling skeletons here, no helter-skelter evidence of panic and chaos. Brittle, faded papers still hung on the walls telling children to come to the summer reading program or where to find books about the state of Iowa.

Iwa, Flora thought, looking up at them. *Same-same.*

She had a list of types of books she was looking for, but she couldn't get past the strangeness of the place. The smell of mice was present, but mild. The long windows still held their glass, made opaque by a thick coating of dirt on the outsides, where they had been carefully boarded over.

She crept behind desks and looked at the crumbling yellowed pages of desk blotters and tear-off calendars. She opened and closed old wooden drawers, looking with great interest at the dusty, ancient junk inside. She fingered a ring of keys and tucked pencils into her bag.

The plastic Dewey system signs were still readable, and Flora was beginning to know it by heart. She tracked down the books that Alma wanted: medicine, history, crafts. She moved on to the list from Alice, who had asked for books on local herbs and specifically books on poison and toxic plants. Flora also picked through books for children, choosing four large compendiums that might hold some stories the children of Ommun had not heard before.

Her bag full to bursting, she lifted her torch and headed back to the metal door she had broken through to enter. Near the front desk, she passed by a framed picture behind glass. The caption read, "Des Moines Public Library Staff and Volunteers, August 2021." She held the light a little closer, studying the faces and their old-world clothes.

Almost all of them were women. One older man loomed near the back of the group, arranged as they were under the shade of two spreading trees. Another younger man crouched in the front row, in the easy, loose-jointed manner of a teenager. All the others wore skirts and long hair, braids and jewelry, the telltale signs of womanhood from the old world.

They had kept the library. Flora wondered if that had always been the job of women.

Still wondering, she ground her torch out against the concrete floor in the entryway before squeezing back out into the night.

The wind whistled through the emptiness of Demons again, and the night had grown colder. Flora shivered, pulling her long silk garments and wool cloak closer to her body. She hurried back to her truck, cranked the engine, and got it going.

Out on old 13, she could see owls swooping at the periphery of her vision. The road was pitted and crumbling at the edges, so she had to drive down the center, spotting the near-invisible yellow dotted line that had once separated the two lanes.

She thought she might make it back to Ommun in two days. Her wooden wheels were in good shape, and she still had nearly half of her deez. She covered all but her eyes against the wind that cut through the hole where the windshield used to be. Clouds drifted across the stars. There was just enough light to see the green flash in the eyes of predators before they fled the roaring noise of the old truck.

Flora was out past the edge of Demons when she saw the remains of the camp. She might not have seen it at all; hanged bodies do not stay hanged. Cartilage breaks down and bones fall apart, leaving a nonsense ossuary and the frayed edges of rope. In this case, only a single horse skull still swung in the wind. Below, the long jaws of horses mixed with a pile of vertebrae, picked clean by birds and bugs, white turning to blue-gray in the starlit night. She missed the skull at first. She pulled over to see the sign.

The side of a half-collapsed building faced the road. Tacked to it were the stripped and shredded remains of a human hide. Beside that was painted one word, in letters taller than a man.

FRAGS

Flora stepped out of her car and looked around. There was no sound from any direction. The wind had picked up as the sun began to set, so the ropes that still hung from the trees swayed and swirled overhead. She saw the skull then, and looked below.

There had been many of them, she thought. Maybe fifty. She walked a little closer and tried to quell the panic rising in her chest like bats sensing the coming of night and making ready to bolt. She stepped on a long leg bone that might have been human or horse, she didn't know.

There was no proof these had been horsewomen, but she knew it as well as she knew anything. Why hang the horses, otherwise? She thought of the bizarre stirring sensation when she had felt the belly of the pregnant mare—had these been pregnant, too?

She looked again at the painted word. FRAGS. She had never heard it before, but that was no surprise. Every little town had its own vocabulary and peculiar names for things. Was this a name for horse-women here? Or was this the triumphant announcement of those who had killed them?

Flora had chosen Demons because of those stories she had heard. There might be more like her here. She might trace the line of horse-women across the plains, finding more and more of them and knowing that she was not alone. She thought of Alma telling her that her god did not know Flora's name.

Is there a god of horsewomen? Are our names spoken somewhere else?

There was nothing here, not even a story. Just death and that one meaningless word.

Flora got back to her truck and leaned against it. She wanted to say something. She searched herself for a benediction. A vow that she could make this right. A way to tell the dead that she was going on and so they weren't the end of the line. But no words came. The sadness of it fought with the fright in her until she slipped back into her seat and shut the door. She sped off as quick as the ruin of the road could accommodate her wooden wheels. She did not look back.

She couldn't hear the other car over her own engine. Neither car had any working electrical, so neither gave off any light. Flora's had a mounted lantern she could light if she chose, but she was wary of attracting attention. The two cars were nearly upon each other when both drivers applied the brake, screeching to a halt.

The other car was smaller, not a truck. Its windshield was made of long, thin strips of wood. Only a couple of lengthwise slits opened to allow the driver to see what was ahead. It was dirty all over, with mud spatters.

Maybe came up from the south, but where? The Misery? Crossed some little creek?

Flora stared and waited. She felt exposed on every side in the old truck, which had no doors. It was a rickety old cage with an engine running beneath it. It offered no more protection than a bicycle would have.

This other car was built for action. Looking it over, getting used to it, Flora could see it had pikes mounted along its hood, with the longest ones along the bottom as if the driver might spear a rabbit as they drove. The sides were enclosed with what looked like wood and leather. Fuel tanks were lashed to the roof.

She tried to stare in through the slits in the windshield, but all was blackness within. She wasn't even sure she would see movement if there was any.

Flora had not seen another person since she had left Ommun. She so seldom saw any deez-powered vehicles on the road that this one gave her serious pause.

Just because they have deez does not mean they came from Estiel. They don't have to be Paws of the Lion. They could be anybody.

But her body would not listen to reason. It was all animal, thinking only of diving through the door and running away, truck be damned.

You've seen worse and weirder than this, she reminded herself, trying to soothe the urge. *Far worse and far weirder.*

The two drivers sat on the road, facing each other, neither one giving a sign. Flora thought once of calling out, or waving. Just to see what might happen.

It might be another woman, she thought. *Who else would go to all that trouble to avoid being seen?*

But it also might not be. And she could not take the risk.

A night bird screeched somewhere overhead and the moment broke like a fever. The enclosed car began to shift to the right, moving to get around Flora's truck. Flora snapped to action, shifting the gears and moving to avoid the car, to pass it on the other side.

She had one fleeting glance of a few shreds of dark cloth whipping out behind the other car as it sped away into the night.

There are too many things in this world that I will never know, to get all wound up about one car on the highway in the night.

But when dawn came and she tried to bed down in an old gas station, sleep would not come. She opened a book and tried to unwind. She thought of the car. She thought of the hanged horses. The sun was high in the sky before she slept.

The wooden car's engine did not wake her as it rolled up beside her truck, three hours later.

CHAPTER 9

OMMUN

Ommun's single classroom was a riot of children from the ages of six to sixteen, milling and trying to get their supplies for the day. They squabbled over chalk and slates, the latter chipped with age, and pulled chairs noisily away from their desks.

Oliver lifted the small brass bell and rang it. The high-pitched sound cut through the roar.

"Good morning, class."

"Good morning, Brother Oliver," they chorused together.

"Good morning, class." Alice was still getting the hang of their very formal schooling structure. She had not been a teacher in Nowhere, but even if she had, it would not have prepared her for this.

"Good morning, Sister Alice."

"Bow your heads for the blessing, children." Oliver bowed his own head and they followed.

They always did as they were told. Alice folded her arms but kept her head up and her eyes open.

Oliver's voice rose and fell in a rushed uneven cadence that started off fast and strong before dying away at the end of each sentence. "Dear most gracious Heavenly Mother. We thank you for this day, and for the opportunity to learn. We thank you for sending Sister Alice to us, that she may strengthen our people with her special knowledge. We ask you to bless us and our lessons, that they may enlighten us and keep us safe. We pray these things in the name of thy children. Amen."

"Amen," came the answer.

"We're going to have a science lesson first thing today," Oliver announced. "Please split into your groups."

Alice got the kids ten and over—the ones to whom all chemistry was new but accessible. The children of Ommun had previously had some instruction in practical biology, derived from farming and husbandry. They had also had cooking lessons, which gave her some scaffolding on which to build their knowledge of basic reactions. However, she had come to understand that beyond midwifery, the underground city had almost no medical profession. The old and sick simply died, and often without the comfort of good drugs. Alice could train a chemist, but she had to start with the basics.

Across the room, Oliver was showing the different parts of a flower to the under-tens, who were getting a more detailed version of biology than had previously been in their curriculum. Alice had worried that Oliver would balk at her suggestions, but he took them as "wise counsel" and began immediately to work it into his lesson plan.

Alice had been overwhelmed when she had first come back from Estiel, over a month ago. She had endured imprisonment and torture there until Etta had killed the Lion and destroyed his house to free Alice and the other women he was holding there. To get past her own grief and to adjust to her new surroundings, she had accepted work as soon as she was able, and had thrown herself into her calling.

But there were things she had to know. She had gone first to see the kitchens where the delicious food she had been eating was made. After that, she had wanted to know where all of it was grown. Gabriel and Rei had taken her up the lift to peer out of one of the secret doors and shown her a field of potatoes, with baby goats in the distance.

When she asked whether they'd ever had a doctor or a drugmaker, she was met with sad reluctance to answer.

Gabriel had pushed his long golden hair out of his face. "We have no drugs here, Sister. And no doctor to speak of."

"What do you do when someone breaks a bone?"

Gabriel shrugged, looking to Rei. "Get it set by someone who wants to try. Bite down hard on something. Mostly, it won't ever heal right and it'll always give you trouble."

Rei had smiled a little. "That hardly ever happens, though. We're blessed and anointed, you see."

"I see."

More anointing followed when Alma sent word that a laboratory had been found for Alice. Neum was terribly pleased to deliver the news, but he had no details to share.

"Is it in working shape?" Alice asked. "Can I take my students there?"

Neum's ratty little eyes had darted around. "I haven't seen it, Sister. I'm not sure."

Alice stalked off to the location he had given her. The door was locked and she had to go back and track down someone who could break in; the keys were long gone. Once inside, Alice sighed heavily. This was going to be a lot of work, even before the real work could begin.

There was an inch of dirt on absolutely everything, and the evidence of chaos was on each visible surface. Broken glass lay all around, like dead teeth furred with dust. The cabinets yawned open, emptied of anything useful. She found the remains of old glass syringes and rolls of rotted gauze in the corners. She tied up her hair and covered her face, then set about making sense of the space.

It took the better part of two days, but it was worth it. Underneath it all, there were stainless-steel instruments from the old world as well as a handful of reference books that were mostly whole.

And water ran through the pipes in here. She had no kettle or fire to heat it, but she could clean up enough once it ran clear. Alice busied herself scooping up the broken glass and setting bundles of garbage out in the hallway. Ommun had a patrol of boys who were in charge of refuse. Where it went, she didn't know, but on the second day she found that the first day's garbage had disappeared.

Under a mountain of decayed boxes, Alice unearthed an examination table and lovingly wiped it down. She missed her house and her herb garden terribly, but she was beginning to see the possibilities here. She could bring her students here and begin their real education, moving them toward the kind of work she had always done.

"Needs a greenhouse. But it's not so bad, is it?" Her voice sounded small to herself. She sent a messenger with a hand-drawn map so that the older children could meet her here for their next session.

"This will be good," she said, and she tried to believe it. She wrapped her arms around herself.

Her words hung in the empty air. She wanted Flora to come home. She wanted Etta. Etta was nowhere to be found.

CHAPTER 10

DEMONS TO SHY

Flora knew there was someone in the room with her before she woke up. The truth of it wound itself into her dreams and alerted her that she should wake up slowly, carefully. She slit her eyes against the midday light, trying to hide her state. She kept her breathing low and slow.

A figure sat across the room, legs splayed out and back to the wall. Through the thickness of her lashes, Flora couldn't make out much. Their clothes were slick and a little shiny. Leather armor, she supposed. Their boots were the moccasin type that Kelda wore, stitched up the side with long strips of rawhide.

She flared her nostrils unconsciously, trying to pick up the scent of the other body in the room. She could not smell anything but the dirt and herself.

"Quit acting like you're not awake," a voice said. "I can see it."

The voice was unmistakably female.

Flora opened her eyes slowly, but did not stir her limbs. She was wrapped in the long loops of silk clothing she had made for herself, warm and secure and utterly covered.

The woman who sat across from her was indeed in leather armor, but her arms were bare. Flora could see the definition of her muscles, with long lines of stick-poke tattooing marching up and down. Her head was shaved. Her lips were thin, a disapproving cut in a hard face. Her eyes were brown and flinty. Her eyebrows were shaved, as well.

"What's in your pack?" she asked. Flora could see her shift a lump of something between her bottom lip and her teeth.

Flora sat up slowly, with balance and grace. She tucked her hands into the deep and secret folds of her silk clothes.

"Careful there," the bald woman said, moving her hand to the grip of a knife in her belt.

Flora relaxed and showed her hands again. "My pack is full of books. I raided an old library last night."

"Why?"

"Because I'm trying to learn about medicine." Flora had spoken to some of the mish in Ommun. They told her never to reveal that she came from a city full of people. Always pretend to be alone, to protect those behind. Eddy said the same thing.

"Medicine?"

"Yeah. You know, what plants can be used to—"

"I know what medicine is," the woman said, spitting a stream of dark juice from her jutting jaw. "No weapons?"

Flora shrugged. "I'm not much good with them." She had two guns on her body, but it wasn't a lie. Her training had been brief, and even at this range she doubted her accuracy. She had never used them, even to catch food. She hoped she'd never have to.

"Why are you out here all by yourself? Where's your keeper?"

"I have no keeper," Flora said quickly. *Not for a while now, anyway.* "I'm free and I belong to myself. My name is Flora."

The bald woman looked her over, considering. "My name's Can."

"Can? Like 'Yes I can'?"

"Yeah," the woman said shortly. "Because I always can."

"Alright. Good to meet you, Can. Why'd you sneak in here while I was asleep?"

Can shrugged her shoulders, relaxing a bit. "I saw you on the road last night, in that open truck of yours. I'm out this way an awful lot, and I've never seen a woman on her own. I couldn't believe it. Where did you come from?"

"Jeff City," Flora said.

"You're a ways from home."

Flora shrugged back, mirroring Can's loose, slack posture. "Things weren't so good there. Had trouble with a guy who called himself the Lion."

"Called?" Can's eyes were suddenly sharp. "He change his name?"

"He's dead," Flora said. "You know him?"

"Everybody knows him. He's a slaver. The slaver king."

Flora sighed. "Well, he's not anymore. There was an uprising in his own harem. He's dead, most of the Paws are dead. That's all over now."

Can looked shrewdly at Flora, clearly not believing.

"So are you headed home to Jeff City now?"

Flora shrugged again, trying out her slow smile. "Not yet. Summer's not over, and I have plenty of deez. I'm going to keep raiding for a bit."

"You're not afraid?"

Flora laid her hands on her thighs and smiled a little wider. She was seeing a small gleam in Can's eye now. "Afraid of what? I've been a slave. I can survive anything but death, and if I'm dead, I've got nothing to worry about."

Can smiled back, the gleam becoming more evident. "No, not if you think about it that way."

"What are you doing out here? Where are you from?" Flora tossed the questions back, seeing the sudden warming in the woman's face.

"I'm from Shy, and I'm out here looking for you." Her smile was speculative, almost flirtatious.

Flora's smile turned full on. "Now there's one I haven't heard yet. Where's Shy?"

"East of here. Big place. Women only. We've been planning to kill the Lion for over a year now. I know people who would feast you well to hear the story of how it happened. Would you come?"

"How far east?"

"A ways," Can said, looking in the direction of the long-gone dawn. "You don't have to come. But I think you'd like it. I've never brought a woman home who didn't."

"I have people waiting for me," Flora began.

"Of course you do. We all do. We won't keep you. But all the same. Flora." Can said her name deliciously, like it was a slice of new fruit she was rolling over her tongue. "Come for just a few days, get some more deez, and go home with a story. What do you say?"

It's a waste of fuel to drive the truck out there, Flora thought. *But if I leave it here, it might disappear. Or I might not be able to find this place again.*

"What about my truck?"

"I can tow it," Can said, pushing herself up with one fist against the floor. "Save you the fuel. Then you have it when you want it."

Flora stood with her, uncertain. She watched Can closely for a long moment. In the end, her curiosity won out.

But her truck was too heavy for Can's car to pull, so they had to leave it. Can helped her push it to a culvert and cover it with brush.

"It should be safe here," Can said decisively.

Flora felt better when it was hidden. Settled. She was glad to be with someone, even if it scared her.

"Women only. The whole town?"

Can nodded, sliding into the dark cab of her car. The interior was well preserved, with padding on the seats and much of the plastic intact. Flora ran a hand over the smoothness of it, sighing.

"You like that old-world feel, huh?"

"It's soft," she said. "Comforting."

Can winked at her in the semidarkness. "If you like comfort, you're going to love Shy."

Flora was nauseated when the car started to move. She fought back the memory of the bus out of Estiel, the long dark road to Ommun. She felt that she couldn't breathe in the closed-in, chugging coffin of the car.

Can saw her distress and popped open a wooden louver that brought fresh air into the cabin. "Can't keep that open all the time. But if you feel like you're gonna yak, get a few breaths in, then shut it again."

Flora nodded, pressing her face close to the intake point for new air. She gulped and gulped. When she felt she could, she closed the slats. Can nodded.

"Were you born there? In Shy?"

"No," Can said. "I was liberated from a slaver somewhere in Iwa, not far from where I found you."

"Demons."

"When I was just a kid."

Flora nodded, not sure if Can could see her. "Me too. Liberated. When I was a kid. I came to Jeff City from someplace far, far away."

"Have you always been a raider?"

Flora laughed a little. "No. No, I have friends who are raiders. But I throw silk." She held out one arm to let Can feel the material.

"Whoa, how do you make that?"

"With worms," Flora said, grinning.

"Ick. Never mind. I'll stick to leather."

"If you've been wearing it all summer, I'll bet that leather sticks to you."

Can laughed. "It is good to have company. I haven't seen a woman or a girl on the road all this long summer. I guess that's thanks to who-ever killed the Lion."

Flora wanted badly to tell her it had been Eddy, brave Eddy, killer of men and freer of slaves. *Keep everyone safe. Don't tell anyone who's at home.*

But I'm going to have to tell them something.

Wait. Wait and see what kind of people they are, then decide what to tell them. They'll let you know what they like.

By the end of that first day, Flora knew that Can liked to answer questions about herself, and would always turn them back on Flora. She knew that Can drove with a careful alertness that Flora lacked in herself. She knew that Can did not drink enough water and scoffed at the idea that it was bad for her.

"Just means stopping more times to piss," she said ruefully.

When they did stop, Flora took care to get far, far away from Can before squatting down to piss carefully, concealed under many layers of silk.

Three days later, she knew Can snored when she slept and sang in a terrible, tuneless voice. She knew that Shy was not far away then, and that Can brightened little by little as they approached. She knew that Can was an experienced raider, able to navigate by the stars and avoid the worst parts of the road through a combination of feeling and memory.

What Flora did not know and could not tell was whether Can was a horsewoman, like her.

There's no way there is a city of all women and none of them are like me. Some of them must be.

She looked Can over constantly, tracing the line of her jaw and lingering on the defined muscles in her arms, the thick curly hair in her armpits. She smelled her. She listened carefully to the sound of her voice.

Horsewoman. No, not like me. Yes, she is. No, she isn't. Maybe she came from those horsewomen in Demons. Frags. Maybe she knew them.

Can did not mention her blood, nor did she obviously carry rags or a moon cup like Eddy had.

But that might just be timing, Flora thought desperately.

They gave each other privacy. Neither one of them ever disrobed, or washed more than face and hands. They talked little. Can preferred to watch the road with total concentration. Flora read books from her bag, sunlight slanting yellow through the slats of the car's armor. They rolled into Shy on the fourth day at midmorning.

When Flora saw the size of the city, she gasped out loud.

CHAPTER 11

The Book of Flora
Shy
Hot and sticky
104N

After the emptiness of Demons, Shy is so incredibly full and loud. I've never seen a city this big. Can says there are a thousand or more here. There are no men, but not like that split city that Kelda comes from. They never let men in, not for any reason. I asked what happened if someone gave birth to a boy, but I didn't get an answer.

Much of the old city still stands here. It is as big as any I've seen, even when I was traveling with Archie. The towers sag against the sky, some with great rusty blades punching outward and upward from them. Shy women don't live in any of the tall buildings, but they use them for lookout and some for farming.

The city sits upon a river, and they row and pole boats with the current to move goods and to travel. The river meets the sea to the east, through narrow channels and a long journey. They have more fresh fish and mussels

than they can eat, and that fish ink that Ina loves so much, and they tell
stories of towns under the water.

I wish I had brought silk to trade, because none of them have ever seen
it before. Someone asks to touch my clothes three times a day, but at least
they ask.

They have a good library here. I have come to measure every town and
village by whether they keep books and how well they keep them. Shy mea-
sures like a giant any way I look at it.

They also brew beer here, raise goats and cattle and pigs, weave wool,
and tan good leather. I will likely trade one of my guns for a good pair of
boots. I lost my last good pair in Estiel, and the old-world boots I've been
wearing are cracking and will not keep out water.

No one in Shy knows that Ommun exists. Living below ground is
the ultimate advantage, it seems. They know of Jeff City, of Nowhere and
Jamestown and Womanhattan and places I've never heard of. Their maps
are better than Eddy's. I could put my finger on one and show Can the place
where I was born. She asked me if I ever wanted to go back there. I told her
there were trees full of big orange fruits that tasted like sunshine when you
bit them, but there were also monsters in the water and sickness on the air.
She laughed and told me I couldn't have come from a place like that, but
I'm all those things, too. She just doesn't know that yet.

I wonder what Father would have thought of a place like this. He
loved that so many in Jeff City went as women in the street. He loved the
horsewomen and the little boys dressed as girls. He always said he wished
he could live in a city of nothing but women, but he figured that must be
what comes after death. What could be better?

I don't know if Shy is where I'd like to go when I die. I don't think
you go anywhere but into the ground or up in smoke. But there's something
about this place I like better than Ommun. Ommun always makes me feel
like I'm holding my breath and waiting for something to happen. Shy just
feels like everything is alive and I'm allowed to be part of it.

I'd love to bring Alice here. Or Eddy, if he would . . . I don't know if he would. Could. I couldn't ask.

I intend to head back before it gets much colder. I wouldn't want to be caught out in the snow. It's terribly windy here, and the cold off the water bites at night. I can't be long now.

Tomorrow, I'm to tell the story of the Lion to an assembly. Can and her friends are passing the word and inviting everyone. After that, I'll be on my way. Can has the location of my truck marked on her map. I'll go home to Alice with stories to tell.

CHAPTER 12

The Bambritch Book
No fog now
144N

Refugees came in yesterday and this morning. I know we won't get many. You need a boat to reach the island, and we don't make it easy. With the blackout in effect, it's difficult to spot a landing, unless you arrive in broad daylight, and many won't take that risk.

Raiders tell me that there are dozens coming into Settle, maybe hundreds. The few who came to Bambritch have pieces of the story, so I've worked to spend some time with each of them. The vast majority cannot read or write, so I'm recording here. The Midwife did this, too. I tried to show some of them, to explain that I'm keeping up her work.

I wish Eddy was here to see it. Eddy would understand. I wonder where he is now. I think about him carrying the gun that belonged to the Unnamed Midwife, carrying her book after we left Ommun for good. Entrusting the books to me.

In the end, almost none of them saw the value. They're all so concerned with survival that the spirit in Nowhere that guarded their history is extinct. I told them I was keeping a record so that those who come after us can learn from what we've already done. They are all convinced that there will be no one after us. Too many of them came from cities where there were no babies last year or the year before that. They're all just living day-to-day, wearing rags and eating what they can find. Almost none of them brings a valuable skill.

The few of us who first came to this island, we promised we wouldn't let ourselves get that way. We were a strange bunch, motley outcasts from Settle and other villages, but not for things we had done. People who had left places like Ommun, for the same reason we walked away from safety. Because safety is sometimes a cage. I remember when we first founded Bambritch, we used to talk about a test. Hortensia had these ideas. We would ask people if they had ever sold a slave or bought one. We talked about barring anyone who had a mark that meant they were an exile. We argued into the night, trying to decide how we'd keep bad people out.

Alice was pregnant then, and she kept having the same nightmare. She dreamt that the Lion wasn't dead, that he had grown to three times the height of the giant he once was, and that he was coming for us, walking straight across the water toward the island, unstoppable.

She had dark circles under her eyes and she looked so thin it made me guilty just to glance at her collarbones. We had plenty to eat, even in those days. I couldn't understand how she was diminishing even as her child grew.

"We have to keep out people who might turn out to be like him," she said, choking back sobs. "We have to. After all we've been through, I think you, of all people, should know that."

I tried to address everyone, but ended up looking mostly at her. "I know you're just trying to protect yourself and your child," I said. I had to gulp water. My throat wanted to close like a cave-in. "But if we're going to keep out anyone who's ever dealt in slaves, then I'll have to leave."

Alice blinked, her thin, birdlike arms crossed over her belly. "But you were just a child," she began. "That's—"

"It's always going to be something," I said. "Some reason. Some circumstance. Some way that they didn't know how bad what they were doing really was. We have to give people a chance to show us who they are now. Some people will have nothing to do with slavery, if it isn't common around them."

"No," Connie said quietly.

"What?"

"You're wrong, Flora. They're still the same person, even if they never have the opportunity. They still don't understand what it means to be a person, even if they don't have a chance to take that from anybody."

Connie never liked to talk in front of a crowd, and they reddened as all eyes turned to them. Hortensia was smiling behind her hand.

"You don't have to ask whether they have or whether they will. You just have to ask them whether they think it can be justified. If they say yes and start to give reasons, they can't come. If they say no, they probably can."

That still ruled me out, but I couldn't say that to my only living child, who had seen through a lie of their existence and found a way to cut it clean in two.

Connie was so much like Eddy. I used to imagine the two of them together, Eddy teaching Connie how to handle a gun or gut a fish. I used to imagine a third between them, a little shadow of a person. The person Eddy's child might have grown to be.

But I haven't dreamed that way in a long time. What is, is. What time we have is all that we have. Everything comes to an end eventually. Eddy did. Connie did.

I remember thinking in those days that Connie would grow up to be a leader, take my place on the council, and I would teach them to braid their hair.

What we want for our children and what they want for themselves are so different, I don't know how two such animals live together. They chafe against one another like a fox in a dark henhouse. Feathers fly. Everyone bleeds. And in the end, one of them is lost forever.

Connie. My Connie. I wish you were in this book more often.

Alice is still here with me. She has her own house and a Hive so big I can't keep track of it. We haven't been together like we were in the old days for a long time. Years, now. She's off the council, twenty summers gone by. Forty that we've been here. We're old women now. She's too busy teaching the raiders to gather and sketch wild herbs. Her students have a greenhouse that keeps us all out of pain.

I hope it's still here, come spring.

After Alice left the council, we were four. Even numbers deadlock, so we had to choose a replacement.

Eva was young in those days, her hair still mostly black and with no cane at her side. She had come from Cruises, just south of where the Midwife had begun her journey. She had lived among free women, in old houses that sat between the forest and the sea. They had all taken ill, and she and her daughter had had to move on. Eva carried baby Wallis north for many months, finding no one and afraid of slavers. They had come to Settle before following the salmon and the stories to Bambritch.

I've read her book. It is a tale of loneliness and persistence. I helped teach Wallis to read myself.

It was Eva's idea that the council should include a man.

"Most of the island is men," Eva reminded us, her voice patient and sweet as always. "They deserve a voice on the council."

"Men cannot be trusted to rule," Hortensia insisted. I remember thinking she was the oldest woman I'd ever seen, and that was years ago. She's likely to outlive us all. She dries and braids lavender in huge bunches every year. She has no lovers. She lived and still lives alone.

"They can be taught not to stare. Not to touch. Not to interrupt. But they cannot overcome their predilection to violence. I don't want to be ruled by someone who thirsts for blood."

"Calm down, you baying old hound," said Zill. "You're talking about men of your generation, not mine."

Zill reminds me of Eddy, when almost no one else here does. Zill shaves her reddish hair down to an inch of fuzz. Her skin isn't nearly as dark as Eddy's, but she's dusky. She speaks hard and fast, and she seems like she's always spoiling for a fight. She was raised by fishermen, but she's a raider (what else?).

"I've never had a man interrupt me in my life. And most of them thirst for blood far less than I do."

Hortensia did not argue, but she pulled her lips in tight, like the rim of a drawstring purse. "Well, we can vote on it, I suppose. But we're four, and we might not get an answer."

"Let's try it," I told them.

Zill and I voted for, Hortensia raised her hand stubbornly against. Eva didn't vote at all.

"You're abstaining?"

Eva looked around the room, anxious. "It depends on the man," she said. "Can't we talk about an individual, rather than some general idea?"

I smiled at her. "You're right. Does anyone have a nomination?"

Zill perked right up. "Yeah! I nominate Carol, son of Alice."

Alice had been the first one to attempt to continue Nowhere's system of identifying children by their Mothers' names, and she's so popular that it actually caught on here.

"Carol is only, what, sixteen summers? Seventeen?"

"About that," Zill said, still grinning. "What difference does it make? He's a well-trained healer. And working as a builder. He's clear-headed and decisive, but he's also a careful listener."

Eva was nodding, looking fairly persuaded.

Hortensia had pulled a knitting project out of her basket and was studiedly not looking at Zill. "Does he have any children?"

Zill shrugged. "He's a member of two Hives that have children. Nothing obvious."

Hortensia nodded to her knitting. "Does he act like a father? Or like a child, who competes for attention?"

Zill looked at me. I shrugged. "I don't know."

Hortensia nodded again. "Show me a man who isn't a child in his Hive, and you'll have my vote."

So we had to go and watch Carol interact with his Hive kids and the women in his life, under some pretense. We had to satisfy our elder to get our youngest member. But we did it.

Hortensia is always like that. She wants proof. She has to lay her hands on it, or she won't believe that it's real.

She's still like that today. When raiders started talking about this army, she didn't believe them.

"There's no way they can get those old war machines moving," she said, shaking her head. Her white hair is so thin now I can see her scalp.

The raiders showed her their drawings of a huge, boxy car that crawled along the ground on treads, not wheels. They showed her the tracks it made in the mud. We sent a boy to the library to look it up. A tank.

They showed us drawings of guns longer than a person and trucks carrying too many people, all armed.

"The sound," I pleaded with her. "That awful sound like a mosquito in the night."

Still, Hortensia was not convinced. "I don't hear it," she said stubbornly.

"You don't hear anything."

It was only a few days ago, when the refugees came in, that Hortensia really believed. I could see it in her eyes when those boys and their mother climbed out of the boat that had landed in the dark before false dawn.

"More behind me," the woman said. The edges of her hair were burnt. "I don't know how many, but more are coming."

"Where is the army now?" asked Zill. "Where did you come from? Settle?"

"Coma," the woman said, glancing over her shoulder. "They were headed for Settle. We had to come up all the way around the other islands. There's nobody else out there."

"How did you know we were here?" Hortensia asked.

Eva frowned at her. "Everyone knows we're here. We trade with every town for miles."

Hortensia frowned right back. It was too late or too early to argue.

The refugee woman held her little boy's head to her chest. They were barefoot.

Zill looked her over and realized we were interrogating the wrong person. "Come on, I'll take you somewhere you can get warm and rest. Somewhere safe."

The family followed Zill. The rest of the council waited on the shore for signs of another boat.

Carol joined us, sleep crusting his eyes. He was shirtless, with gooseflesh all over his chest.

They landed far away from us, near the oyster beds. We followed the sound of yelling.

This was a larger boat, filled with men. They'd been fighting; they all smelled like smoke and many were wounded.

"We have to take them to the Midwives," Hortensia exclaimed. Now that she believed, she could catch up to the rest of us in our panic.

Some had to be carried. We moved slowly, like a long, limping centipede. The Midwives got word and streamed out to help us, bringing people into the infirmary and triaging at once.

I sat with a middle-aged man who looked scared but mostly unhurt. Someone brought us tea.

"Can you tell me anything about them?"

The night was warm, but he shivered. He looked up, so I looked up, too. Low gray raggedy clouds slid between us and the stars.

"They have terrible weapons."

I nodded. I took a sip of my tea, hoping he'd do the same. He just held it.

"They destroyed our village so quickly. Nowhere to hide. We ran for the boats, but they fired on us as we ran. On defenseless people."

"Did they ask for anything? Did you refuse them women?"

He shook his head. "They kept asking for frags. I don't even know what that means. Their leader was so angry that we didn't understand."

I sat with him as long as I could. I patted him on the shoulder before walking away. He still hadn't touched his tea.

I pulled the council members away for a meeting. We were far from the council house, so I led them toward one of the shelters where oysters are sorted. The smell off their beds was salty and lively. I could hear the water lapping gently against the rocks.

"We may not have a chance to negotiate with them," I said. "The raiders and the refugees say the same thing: the army asks for frags. They're after something that doesn't exist."

Hortensia's mouth flattened to a line. "Nonsense. Absolute nonsense. They may as well ask for a baby that shits honey. They can't get that monster machine across the water to us. The tank. The big guns. They don't have a boat big enough."

"We don't know that," Zill moaned. "We don't know if it can swim, either."

Carol was shaking his head. "I read that war machine book longer than anybody. That machine can't swim. Those guns are too heavy. They're going to attack us with people and guns, but likely nothing more."

"What if the plane is real?" Eva looked suddenly terrified. "What if they can attack us from above?"

Hortensia turned on her. "If the plane was real, they would have used it already. The raiders would have seen it. The refugees would tell us that the fire came from above."

Eva nodded but did not look comforted.

"We have to pull all the boats on the Settle side to the island," Carol said. "Don't leave them anything. Coma is gone, but they're probably going to launch the attack from Settle."

I thought about the rest of the towns around us. He was more than likely right. No other port was as big, and Bambritch is visible from Settle.

"Can we get a crew together to do that now, before dawn?"

Carol was already moving. "What we can't bring this way, we'll burn."

That made my jaw ache. Building boats was hard work, and we have only a few who know how. But better to lose boats than suffer the same fate as Coma, or the other towns the army has come through.

When Carol had left us, we three women closed our circle in tighter.

"What do they want?"

"They can't want to just kill." Eva was chewing her lip raw.

"What if we offer to host the army? Round up all the willing women we have and fuck them weak?" Hortensia never talked about sex, so her frankness shocked me.

"Do you think that would work?"

Her gaze was as level as a stone. "Do you think there's a man alive who wouldn't consider it?"

I thought about the population of the island. I knew almost everyone. "I think we could get ten volunteers."

"I think that number will be better tomorrow, when more have seen the refugees. Plus catamites." Eva was calmer now, doing the math.

I nodded.

I gathered them closer, lowering my head. "That's not what they're after, though. It might work, but I keep hearing that the commander of the army is looking for frags."

Eva scoffed. "Frags? They're not real."

Hortensia shrugged her thin shoulders. "Yes, we all know that. But they're serious, and they're willing to kill over it."

"Can we fake it?"

Zill looked around, angrily chewing her lip. "How? Hand over a pregnant woman and say she did it to herself? What would convince them?"

I shook my head. "We're not doing that. But maybe we could get them to believe we know that frags are real, and send them off on some errand to find them."

"They'd only return angry when they figured it out," said Zill.

"That's not the immediate problem," Eva said. "The first thing we need to worry about is those guns. They might just kill us all."

I was silently wondering what the range on those guns could be. If they could stand on the shore in Settle and shoot at boats, or even at the island. If they could kill us without ever so much as seeing our faces. If our offer of flesh would be one they never heard. If they'd be willing to talk about the question of frags, and if we could convince them to look elsewhere and leave us alone.

Out loud I said, "That's almost a plan. Call a town meeting. We need everyone to know what is going to happen, and what we're planning to do."

Hortensia and Eva broke in two different directions, away from the oyster house. Zill headed up the road to pass the word that we would meet. I walked to the oyster bed and pulled a bivalve up out of the mud. I shucked it open with one of my knives and ate it while it lived.

How many oysters will be left when we are all gone?

CHAPTER 13

SHY

Early in the morning, Can came to the rooms where Flora was staying. Flora was carefully shaving her face and neck in the gorgeous large mirror that hung on the wall. It was an old-world treasure, only cracked in the upper corner and hardly cloudy. Flora had not seen so much of herself at once in a long time, unless she could count the distorted image of herself in a pool of water. She took her time, braiding her hair in the best style she had learned from the other horsewomen and hiding her darkened roots beneath her work. She lined her eyes with her own preparation of charcoal in oil, working the black solution into her brows and eyelashes as well.

She had been without the marin the horsewomen made in Jeff City for a long time now. She had not gone home, and no one in Ommun knew the practice of drying out mare's urine and purifying it into ointment. She felt the loss of it, and she tried hard to compensate. As she heard the knock on the door, she nicked the very corner of her chin with her sharp razor, and a thin line of blood ran down her pale neck.

"Damn it," she swore to herself. "Who's there?" she called aloud.

"Can." The visitor did not offer any further information.

Flora pressed a tiny square of cloth to the cut on her face and went to the door. She opened it.

Can stood there in her everyday leather armor, her arms crossed over her chest. She looked bored.

"What is it?"

"You said you wanted to see a brewery," Can said. "Came to take you."

Flora nodded, glancing surreptitiously at the dot of blood on her cloth. "I'll be right with you. Come on in."

Can strolled in and flopped down on Flora's neatly made bed. "Cut yourself shaving, huh?"

Flora looked back over her shoulder, alarmed. "Yes." She began to pack her shaving things, wiping every piece clean first.

"Lots of the older women here have whiskers that make the spotters up on top of the gates look twice," Can said with a grin. "Can't blame them for not going to the trouble, but I like a smooth chin myself."

"Me too," Flora said quietly. "Where I come from, some women shave all over."

"All?"

Flora looked back again and saw Can's eyebrow was up and she was smiling.

"All."

Can grinned a little wider. "I'd like to see that." She put a hand up and rubbed the close-cropped fuzz on her own head, showing a lusty thatch of hair in her underarm.

Flora smiled to herself but did not answer. She finished stowing her gear and made sure everything was neat behind her.

"Alright, show me to the brewery."

Can popped up, leather creaking. She led the way.

The brewery Can chose to show Flora was in a huge open building. Women wove through a complicated maze of steel and copper drums, carrying baskets of wheat, hops, and fruits. The whole place smelled like steamed yeast, and Flora tried to control the look of disgust on her face until she got used to it.

A short woman with black hair cut straight across her forehead came to them, bringing samples poured off a barrel into glass jars. The beer was dark, thick, and bitter smelling. Can downed hers at once, seeming to swallow it all in one go. Flora took a sip and found it objectionably thick, sour, and foamy. She coughed and blew suds off her lips.

Can laughed a little and pounded her on the back. "That's alright. You're not used to it."

They gave their glasses back and passed through, looking over the clean brewing equipment.

Can looked sideways at Flora. "I thought you'd enjoy this. You said you'd never seen one."

Flora shrugged. "I haven't. But I don't have a taste for it, I guess."

"What do you have a taste for?"

Flora tucked her arms into the long folds of her elaborate silk wrappings. "Weaving and books."

"You've seen the library?"

"Oh yes," Flora breathed. "You have a great one here."

"Girls here can study anything they want," Can said with pride. "We have some who study the stars. Some who write stories. Some who put together dancing and singing shows. There will be a show tonight, at the gathering. Since you're entertaining us, the mayor thought we should entertain you, too."

"I don't know that my story will be all that entertaining," Flora began. "It was mostly just—"

"No, don't give it away!" Can's eyes were shining. "I've been wanting to run a raid through Estiel since I was a kid. I want to wait and hear your story properly."

Flora sighed. "There are places just like Estiel. And worse. You'll get another chance. There's always another man like the Lion."

Can actually licked her lips. "I know it."

The tour of Shy's industries dragged on, but Flora could barely pay attention to any of it.

They want me to tell the story in front of everyone so they can feel like they lived it. Who would want to live that? How can I tell it so that they believe me, but I can stand to go through it again? Will they think I was weak for serving the Lion instead of defying him? For feeding his slaves instead of freeing them? Will they hate me like Eddy did? Will someone try to shoot out my eye?

Around midday, Flora pleaded hunger and headed back to her borrowed room. She didn't eat, instead flopping herself down on the bed and screaming into the down-filled pad there. She would not cry. Would not. The heat in her eyes and the fist in her throat could push all they wanted to; she would not give in.

Crying brought the memory of Archie as nothing else did. If she let even a single tear leak out, he'd be there. Sitting on the edge of her bed, a cigarette in his hand. His yellow skin hanging from his jowls and making loops across the long bones of his arms.

"I don't know what you're crying for. You're lucky to be alive. I don't have to keep you around. I got ten more just like you, you know that?"

Flora breathed in slowly, out slowly. She did not cry. She did not answer Archie. He wasn't really there, and she would not let him come.

She thought again about standing up in front of the people in Shy, telling her story. She breathed in long and slow, pulling hot air through the layers of bedding where she had crushed her face.

When she was a little girl, Flora had learned from water. She had watched the swelling floods across the south. She had ridden on the white waters of surging rivers, Archie leading his ragtag bunch of orphans ever onward toward some imagined place. She had learned how to be water, and she became water now.

Her feet were dissolving into water, trickling like rain down the side of a house. Her calves were water, running like the rivulets into a puddle. Her root was water, clear in a bowl like collected rain. Her chest was water, deep as a lake, her heart a fish. Her arms were water, icicles melting into the floe that made way for the spring. Her neck and head were water, surges of rain falling from a gray-black sky.

Water was everything: life and death. It could be hard or soft; it could take any shape. It could wear away stone, like that secret place Eddy had shown her. It could drown a man, or save him.

Flora was water, soaking her bed and dripping to the floor beneath it. She was nothing, wanting nothing and feeling nothing. Through that afternoon, she slept.

The woman who woke her was not Can. When Flora opened the door, she saw a tall woman in a long green dress that laced up the front. She had curly golden hair that had been brushed out and lay in long coils. She had used berries to stain her lips and pinked her cheeks. Flora looked over the woman's carefully lined eyes, seeing how the blue she used brought out the blue-green irises.

She smiled as Flora appeared, puffy with sleep and creased across her face. "I'm Benny. I'm here to take you to the big gathering." She was missing her two front teeth.

Flora smiled and tried to pat down her red hair. "Just give me one second."

She primped a little, relining her eyes in charcoal and tucking a few loose strands back into her braids. Behind her, the blonde woman sidled in the door and looked around.

"What do you do here, Benny?"

"I plan gatherings," Benny said airily. "When there aren't many, I grow potatoes and make really good chips. You'll have some tonight, at the mayor's table."

"Chips?"

Benny smiled. "You'll see."

Flora left her bed unmade and followed Benny out into the street.

"Shy has several large theaters along the waterfront," Benny was saying as they followed the streams of people flowing through the streets. "They're all from the old world, but we've kept them up over the years. Tonight, we'll be at Madam Barbara's. It's not the biggest, but it is the nicest. She keeps that place shined up like new fruit."

As they neared the waterfront, Flora began to smell hot foods of all kinds. A block outside the theater, stations sat on every corner with women handing out scoops of different treats. People shook out old-world plastic bowls and sacks and boxes, ready to receive. Flora frowned that she hadn't known well enough to bring one of her empty leather sacks, but Benny produced a tall plastic box with a scalloped edge.

"Here," she said, handing it over. "But make your choices wisely, because you can only fill it once."

Flora went recklessly to the stands and kiosks, taking scoops of hot salted nuts, sweet popcorn, fried pork cracklings, and dried fruits. She was disappointed at how rapidly her little box had filled, but she ate a large handful of popcorn as she walked, thinking she could at least make some room.

It would never be enough. The next belt of stands offered falafel, which Flora had never seen or even heard of before. She took one hotly into her hand, with a generous dollop of hummus on top to cool it down.

"What is this?" she asked with her mouth full.

Benny ate one too, slowly and waiting to swallow before she spoke. "It's all made of beans. You wouldn't believe it. There's a whole section of the city where they make it. I trade for it all the time."

At the mention of trade, Flora stopped to wipe grease from her mouth. "Why is this all given away? Why no trade?"

"It's a gift to the mayor," Benny said, shrugging. "On show nights, if your number comes up you have to help feed the crowd."

"What do you get in return?"

"The mayor keeps the peace in the marketplace. Arranges the raids and protects the city."

Flora looked around at the seemingly endless food, the thousands of hands reaching out to take.

"This city is rich," she said to Benny.

"You have no idea."

If Flora had regretted her choices when she saw the first falafel, she was deeply unhappy when she met the chip vendors. Hot potatoes in every shape: spears and wedges and corkscrews came bubbling up from pots of lard on every side, smelling like heaven. They were fat and thin, crispy and soft, browned and briskly seasoned. She saw dippers of meat gravy, tomato sauce, and thick white egg dressing poured and spooned on top of mound after mound of hot, starchy, spongy potatoes.

She looked at Benny, stricken. Benny laughed.

"The mayor will have hot chips at her table." Seeing the look on Flora's face, she went on. "I promise. They're her absolute favorite. You will get some."

Flora cracked a few nuts between her teeth, watching the crowd. "Does everyone come for show night?"

"Oh, no," Benny said, gesturing toward the wide staircase that would lead them to the cavernous theater doors. "There are always people who have other work that won't wait. Guarding. Tending to the sick. Watching the children who are too young to come to something like this."

Benny's gait became stiff and awkward as she started up the stairs. Flora looked her over.

"Are you alright?"

Benny grimaced. "I was injured three winters ago. The nurses set the bone, but climbing always hurts."

"I'm sorry that happened to you," Flora said.

Benny shrugged. "It's not that bad, considering how it might have turned out."

They went up haltingly, headed toward the far left side of the entrance.

The woman guarding that door was muscular and broad, with her head shaved like Can. She wore three guns.

"Yes?"

Benny gestured to Flora, a little out of breath.

"This is the visitor. Flora. Going to sit. With the mayor."

The guard nodded, stepping aside. "Please go right ahead. Madam Mayor is expecting you."

Benny did not follow.

The theater was lit inside with torches affixed to the walls. Flora could see where old smoke marks had been scrubbed and scraped away, but the fires of all the years had stained the stone. The vaulted ceilings above were too dark for her to do anything but imagine them—likely packed with bats who would take wing as the sun continued to set.

All around her, Flora heard the people of Shy murmuring and talking, laughing and jostling one another. She heard three or four languages in the crowd, something she had not experienced since she was a child. Most cities had only one language, but when she had traveled with Archie she had been in places big enough to hold enclaves where other tongues were spoken. The effect was disorienting and wonderful at the same time.

She came to a narrow hallway without further direction or an escort, so she pushed through. At the end, she parted a set of heavy, plush blue curtains.

After the dark passage, the light of the theater was overwhelming. The whole place glowed like a bonfire, with torches and footlights and candles at every table. Candles glowed in the aisles between seats, each of them placed safely into a glass of some shape and shining through.

The table before her was overloaded with the foods she had seen on her way in and more: roast birds and fresh bread, butter and vegetables and fruits of every color. Flora saw a large bowl of honey beside a pot of hot pine-needle tea, and a bowl of cream next to dark bottles of what she assumed would be wine. Hot chips in several shapes were heaped upon silver plates, with every manner of sauce and dressing in silver bowls ringing around them. Despite the handfuls of snacks she had eaten on the way, her mouth watered. Flora had never seen a feast like this, not even in Ommun. Nobody ate this well.

And then she saw her hostess.

Mayor Max was a large woman. She spread out to preside over her table, taking up one side of it to herself. She wore a voluminous old-world gown of bright red that had been carefully hemmed to keep it from raveling. Flora's keen weaver's eye could see the skill that had been applied to preserving the garment. Chestnut-brown hair was swept into braids and whirls, with some wavy sections lying upon Max's broad shoulders. The arms that came from under the short sleeves of her dress were like smooth, peeled birch branches with spotted white skin and a thickness of both muscle and fat that rippled as she reached for objects across the table.

When she saw Flora, Mayor Max stood, her body regal and imposing, and reached for her instead.

Flora reached too and found her dainty hand dwarfed in Max's substantial grip.

"Madam Max, mayor of Shy. You must be Flora." The woman's voice was rich and round, like a mouthful of cream that would coat your throat as you swallowed.

"That's right," Flora squeaked back.

"I'm so glad that you're with us tonight. I can't wait to hear your tale. Please join me and eat as much of this food as you can, while it's still good and hot."

Mayor Max bumped her soft, luxurious belly on the edge of the table as she sat back down, but did not seem to notice.

"This is Anya," Max said, gesturing to one of her companions. Anya had a lovely round face, which she had painted a fair bit, to Flora's practiced eye. "And this is Yon." Yon was as black as Eddy, but wore her hair in long, even braids ending in gold beads.

Flora nodded to both of them, seeing how each attended to Max. Anya ran a fingertip softly over Max's forearm as the larger woman poured something golden out of one of the dark bottles and into a glass. Yon leaned forward and whispered in the mayor's ear, prompting a little blush on the wide expanse of cheek below.

Harem? Flora looked them over for the signs of world-weariness or distress and found none. She took them in from head to foot, noting their straight backs and languid, relaxed legs. They were dressed beautifully and without bruises or scrapes. They were well rested and well fed.

Doesn't mean they're not a harem, she thought. *But if they are, it's a damned nice one.*

"Drink with us?" Max was offering the bottle.

"What is it?"

The mayor took the cup from in front of Flora and filled it with the warm yellow liquid. "Mead. Made from honey. You'll love it."

Flora took a swallow and found it sour-sweet and a little off-putting.

Max laughed deep in her throat. "It takes a little getting used to. Have as much as you like."

Flora took that to include everything, not just the mead. She made a daunting pile of chips and took from every pot of sauce. Some were sweet and some were smoky, but the best one by far was the white, eggy sauce that was so thick that it sat up in peaks where it had been spooned.

"What do you call this?" Flora asked, showing a chip well covered in the stuff.

Anya laughed. "Mayo. Maxi puts it on everything."

Mayor Max smiled and chucked Anya's chin. "I'm gonna put it on you."

Anya smiled wickedly and leaned in to kiss the mayor. Flora could not help but stare. Yon reached over and put a hand on Max's massive thigh, watching the other two with frank hunger.

Not a harem. A Hive.

Flora put that thought away for later consideration and tucked back into the food. She had an ache in her belly before long, but she still struggled to make herself stop.

Chips. Chips and mayo. I have to learn how both of these are made before I go back. There's no two ways about it.

A loud, high popping noise came from the stage. A thin woman was cracking a whip in the air. She stepped close to the footlights and spoke loud and clear, quieting the room. The mayor and her ladies looked up from their close vantage point, mouths full.

"My dear gentlewomen of Shy! Welcome to the gathering! *Marhabaan bikum!* We have a special treat tonight. In addition to our annual children's pageant, we have a guest who will tell us the story of the defeat of the Lion of Estiel!"

Applause and cheers rocked the house, and Flora was shocked by how quickly Mayor Max had reached around the table, snatched up her hand, and raised it clasped in her own.

"First, a song and dance while you enjoy your feast! Second, our visitor will tell her tale! And finally, the glorious history of the city of Shy! Who's ready for that?"

Another cheer went up and Max let go, sinking back into her chair and drinking more mead. She filled Flora's glass as well.

"Courage," she said, somewhere beneath the din. She winked. Flora drank.

The woman with the whip put a cupped hand behind her ear and leaned forward at the waist. "Was that all of you? I don't think that was all of you. Who's ready for that?"

The crowd was thunderous, stomping their feet in the upper balconies and making Flora cringe.

"That's better! We're ready for you, Shy! Take it away, Gran!"

A stunning woman strode to the middle of the stage. Beneath, from the orchestra pit, Flora heard a fiddle and drums begin to play, joined by some instruments she couldn't name. She gulped mead. Gran began to dance sinuously. Flora scooted her chair closer to Mayor Max, penned out as she was on this side by Yon.

"Mayor Max," Flora began urgently. "I don't know how to tell this story. Not to so many people."

Max smiled widely, showing perfect teeth. "Just be sure to speak up nice and loud."

"No, I mean—"

Flora was drowned out by whistles and whoops on all sides. Onstage, Gran had thrown off one of her many veils, displaying her left breast as she whirled.

Max's own whistle was just subsiding. Yon looked down at Flora, her perfect nose twitching in her dark, beautiful face. "Are you afraid of standing in front of a crowd?"

"Not exactly . . ." Flora began again, but the whistling redoubled.

Yon rolled her eyes. "You'd think they'd never seen a pair of tits before." She turned her attention back to Flora. "You were there, weren't you?"

Flora nodded, looking at her hands.

"Then just tell us how it really was." Yon's voice had softened now.

"What if it was terrible? What if the truth is an awful thing that no one wants to hear while they eat a delicious fallfall?"

"Falafel," Yon said kindly. "Don't worry. We've heard it all here. A woman gave us a story once of a slaver who tried to breed little girls before their blood. Then, Can came out onstage wearing the skin she'd just cut him out of. Did a little dance, then threw what was left of his penis to the second balcony. There's nothing you could do to shock this crowd."

Flora drew back a little, blinking.

Well hell.

She looked up at Yon, feeling sick and sweaty.

"Are you going to make it? Do you need me to whisper in Max's ear? I can do that, if you really need it."

Well hell, Flora thought again. *What do I have to lose?*

The thought would not materialize wholly, but she knew what she had to lose. She forbade herself to even think it.

I'm just like them. They've already confirmed it and they know it and I belong here.

But Eddy's cavern sprang to her mind and she had to swallow big mouthfuls of mead to send him away.

Tell the truth. Be the truth. You were there. That's all.

On the stage, Gran was nearly nude now, holding the last scrap of her costume modestly between her legs as she rather immodestly pantomimed fucking the air around her.

"So coy!" Mayor Max's voice was thick with drink. "Show me! Show me!"

Gran blew a kiss down to Max with her free hand, then shook her head. She gathered the fabric between her hands and ran it slowly up and back, teasing the view but never giving it away.

"She'll never show us," Anya pouted. "I've heard rumors about what she's got, but I'll never know."

"That's the beauty of the mystery, pet." Max ran a plump rosy hand over the tops of Anya's breasts, coming to rest at the woman's thick waistline.

"But you've seen all my mysteries," Anya said, turning her pout into a caricature of itself.

"Seen and better than seen," Max said, giving her a squeeze. "Onstage, a mystery is fine. Here, I want to know everything."

Yon leaned forward and nibbled Max's ear. Max turned toward her.

"I haven't forgotten you either, my doe." She settled her wide jaw into the crook of Yon's neck and kissed her there. Yon sighed.

"Max, not so soon. We'll miss the rest of the show. Just like last time."

"Mmmm," Max moaned from her hidden place. She sighed, pulling back. "Oh, alright. Alright."

Flora looked away from them, transfixed by Gran. The dancer had tied that final piece of her costume delicately between her legs and over one of her hips. As she bent to pick up her discarded costume, Flora watched her intently.

I'm just like them. One and the same. I can do what Gran does. I can hold them and give nothing away.

Gran came to the edge of the stage and locked eyes with Flora. The dancer winked. The weaver blushed. Gran was clearing the stage and the whip-thin woman was back. She held up both hands, waiting for the noise in the house to die down. A footlight fizzled and went out. Flora saw a young girl pop up at once from beneath the stage in heavy gloves and coax the flame back to life again. The thin mistress of ceremonies grinned.

"I don't need that girl to light me up," she boomed to the crowd with her tongue between her teeth and her finger pointed down toward the pit. "Gran did that job just fine." She laid her long-fingered hands over the crotch of her tight pants and spanked there lightly.

The crowd's reaction was thunderous; they were good and lit, too. Flora swallowed hard.

They're not expecting me. They're having a good time. I can't do this. I can't just spin it around and make them angry, make them sad.

But the emcee was striding over to their side of the stage already, priming to introduce her. Flora patted her silks and smoothed her hair. She put up one of the long loops that covered her head.

Like Archie said. Always have something to reveal. Always have a secret.

"Tonight we have a special visitor, here as a guest of our fine mayor, Madam Max!"

On cue, Max rose and waved to the crowd, throwing kisses to the balconies. Women whistled and stomped. Yon and Anya dimpled on either side of her, preening to be seen as well.

The emcee went on and Max sank back down, her hand sliding into Yon's skirts to slip between her thighs.

"Tonight's guest comes from another town. Somewhere not as grand as Shy, but there is no city in this blighted world as grand as Shy, is there?"

The cries of *No no no* came from all around. The emcee held her arms out.

"This stranger comes from a city of brave fighters. She herself was one of them. She herself was part of the battle that killed the Lion of Estiel."

The crowed hissed and Flora could feel their collective energy contracting and going colder. She watched the emcee with awe. This woman knew what she was doing.

"This stranger helped rid the world of one of its great monsters. Slavers. Killers. And tonight, she has agreed to tell us the tale. Shy women, I ask you to welcome Flora of Jeff City!"

The emcee reached out her hand and Flora took it, coming up the four steep stairs that led from the mayor's private table to the stage.

Flora's heart pounded in her chest. For an instant, she could see eyes all over the room, taking her in as a stranger. She felt them look her over, make their decisions about her. She heard the rush of polite, encouraging applause.

She faced out, still holding the emcee's hand. The taller woman bowed and slipped away, leaving her alone.

In the glare of the long flames, Flora floated alone on an island of light. She felt like she was behind a white wall, like a clean sheet of silk hung up for her privacy.

Good. That's perfect.

She reached up and pulled back her hood, showing her intricately braided hair. She heard a few gasps and it made her smile. She held up her hands.

"Good women of Shy! Thank you for having me here tonight—"

"Louder!"

"Speak up!"

The voices came from the upper balconies and the far back. Flora swallowed and began again, speaking from her belly and pushing her voice to the rafters.

"Good women of Shy!"

Cries of approbation answered her, then died down.

"Thank you for welcoming me to your city tonight. Thank you, Mayor Max, for your hospitality. Thank you, Can, for bringing me here."

She cleared her throat and laid her shaking hands on her hips, trying to look confident.

I have faced people who wanted to eat me alive. Surely I can do this.

"I come from Jeff City, a small town formerly in tribute to the Lion of Estiel. We sent him all kinds of tribute. Weaving, like my own work. Crops and bullets and arrows. But most of all, his tribute was women and girls."

Flora took a few steps forward, lifting her head. "Paws of the Lion would come to Jeff City whenever they wished and take whatever they wished. We didn't fight them because they would have killed us all. They burned other villages that didn't give him tribute. They burned down Nowhere, the village my friend Edd—Etta came from.

"We brought him trade of strange drugs. Etta's lover Alice is a skilled drugmaker. She distilled milk from flowers that can make a person sleep through sickness. She is so clever, she has saved many lives. But that was not enough for the Lion. He stole Alice. And Etta. And me. We were all part of his harem."

Flora dropped her head for a moment, trying to remember enough of the story to make it feel real, but not so much that she could not escape her memory.

"Go on," chanted a few women in the front row. The chant picked up and echoed throughout the house. "Go. On. Go. On. Go On."

It gathered strength and so did Flora. She held up her hands.

"Thank you. So, we were in his harem. There were women from all over, women from places I'd never heard of. Little girls, some still babies. The Lion kept killer cats, bigger than a man. He kept Paws all around him at all times, so he was never alone. He kept Etta in his own apartments and tried to make her tell him all she knew. Etta is a great raider, and she knows where weapons are hidden all over around the Misery.

"Etta is the strongest, cleverest person I've ever known. She stood up to things that would kill most people. She endured and she fought. When she had an opportunity, she fought the Lion, hand to hand. I didn't see it happen, but I heard she put a knife here—"

Flora thrust a hand hard into her own armpit to show them. She became the Lion, staggering a little. She stalked to the far end of the stage, grasping for invisible weapons.

"And still he fought. He sent his great cats to kill her. She killed them instead."

Now she was Etta, crouched low, hands out before her like a set of claws.

"She killed him with a thousand wounds. She cut him and bit him and stabbed him and shot him. She skinned him and took his hair for a trophy on her belt. She lit his house on fire. She made sure he would rise no more.

"The Paws tried to stop her, but she killed them as she went, stealing guns and cutting them down without a look."

Flora strode back to the center of the stage, both hands raised in finger guns, thumbs acting like hammers, her mouth set in a line.

"She came to the harem. She said, 'Come with me, for we are free and no man owns us.'"

She also tried to put a bullet in my eye and called me traitor, Flora thought.

"And she gathered us up. Her mother and me and all the women she did not know. She found the boys who were kept as catamites and brought them, too. She saved us all and took us to Ommun, a secret place. She was following her hero, the Unnamed. Do you all know the Unnamed?"

"No!" A few scattered cries. Mostly silence. She held them in her hand.

"The Unnamed lived through the Dying. She kept a chronicle of all her days, from the old world to this one. She founded Nowhere and made the place safe for women. Her story should be in the library here. Maybe you have a story of someone who helped to build Shy? Someone who was a hero to heroes like Etta? I hope that you do. Stories like that one teach us how to be."

Flora settled at the center of the stage. She put her hands together in front of her, modestly. "I didn't kill the Lion. But I know that he is dead and his power is gone. I saw the end. He will trouble people no more. There are other men like him, but at least that one is gone. Thank you."

She bowed slightly at the waist, dropping her head down.

The applause started slowly, but it gained enthusiasm and swelled. Flora began to leave the stage.

The emcee skipped up to meet her, putting a hand on her shoulder. "Thank you, Flora. Thank you. How long will you be with us?"

"I leave tomorrow," Flora said, forgetting to tell the house and just answering the other woman. Remembering, she turned her face out to the crowd. "I leave tomorrow! I have enjoyed my time here!"

The emcee put a thin, light hand between Flora's shoulder blades. "Please take our thanks and our love with you. Give it to Alice and Etta and all your people. Tell them what they have done affects us all. Will you do that?"

Flora nodded. The thin woman swept her into a spidery hug before pushing her out at arm's length and holding her there. "Flora! Shy women, give your thanks to Flora!"

Flora used the renewed applause as cover to leave the stage. As she walked down the steps, her legs wobbled and threatened to give her up.

Mayor Max had refilled a glass with golden mead and was pushing it at her the instant she rejoined them.

"Excellent tale," Max said richly. "Truly excellent."

Flora ducked her head and drank. She struggled to get her breath back as the next act took the stage. Children and teens seemed to stream up the stairs on all sides but the mayor's private one. More came from backstage until they crowded to the footlights, ranged out in radiating lines like a fan.

The emcee raised both hands. "Shy women, this is your story. This is the story of Shy!" She bowed and stepped nimbly backstage, disappearing in a flash of long legs and strip-skirt flaring.

Four girls sat down immediately in front of the footlights, their faces bathed in the firelight. Each pulled a drum on a strap from her back to her front and sat it in the space she made between her crossed legs. Flora saw that two of the drums were newly made from wood and animal skins, while the other two were made from old-world metal. The four girls banged the drums with their hands, making the warm sound of skin on skin spiked with the colder, harder sound of bones finding metal. Flora jumped a little on the downbeat.

The drummers moved their hands from center to rim, following each hard beat with a tapping of their fingers. A girl with long braids strode out from the rows to center herself between the drummers. Her voice was low and powerful and carried across the theater, which was now as silent as hundreds of breathing bodies can be.

"The world was dying but Shy didn't die."

Flora was certain that the girl's well-pitched voice could be heard by all assembled, but the entire group on stage repeated it, word for word, in the rumbling, excited tone of thunder anxious to catch up with the lightning as the storm rushes in.

"The world was dying but Shy didn't die."

The girls on the stage moved as one, couples joining arm in arm the way that drops of water join together. They swirled two by two, serpentine around one another.

One by one, the dancers began to drop. The ones that remained upright stepped over the dead.

"The world was killing, but Shy didn't kill."

The dancers repeated the narrator's words again, and began to catch one another in headlocks, shoot one another with finger guns. Flora saw one grab her partner and perfectly pantomime slitting her throat. The girl dropped.

When only a few were still standing, they stopped. They looked around. The narrator did not turn to see them.

"The world was falling. Shy did not fall."

The dead began to rise. The girls began to climb on top of one another. The biggest and most muscular knelt on the stage, boosting smaller girls onto their knees, holding and anchoring them by the hand. Other girls climbed on to that second row, balancing on shoulders and reaching back to pull up smaller and smaller still. One tiny girl climbed up the tower of bodies without fear, coming to the very top as though she were climbing a tree. They held her aloft, shaking a little but perfectly solid. She raised her arms and held them there.

On the far side of the stage, Flora saw an identical tower taking shape. Arranged in just the same way, the girls lifted one another up and built the structure. However, as the girls climbed, they pinched one another. They withdrew their hands and wobbled one another on purpose. Girls tripped and fell. The little ones scrambled over one another, trying to rise to the top first, to secure the ultimate position.

"Shy did not fall. Shy did not fall. Shy did not fall." The cant rose between them.

On the far side of the stage, the tower began to collapse. Destabilized girls fell out of place clumsily, kicking one another as they came down. Flora saw one girl catch a bare heel full in the mouth and was surprised to see her spit a little blood after the offending foot. Bodies hit the floorboards with bangs and thumps. Girls landed on top of one another, slapping the stage with their hands to take the impact. Skillfully, they tumbled to hit the ground without real injury.

"Shy did not fall. Shy did not fall. Shy did not fall."

On Flora's side, the tower stood steadfast. The girls holding the littlest in her place moved their hands to her knees and the small of her back. They lifted and flipped her suddenly, sending her high into the air and catching her in a basket made of their arms. No sooner had she landed than they tossed her again, catching her this time on a single leg, the other raised up to her head and held there in her small, strong fist. The projectile girl grinned, then fell backward, twisting again into their arms.

The tower of girls began to carefully sort themselves into another shape, coming down into a wide ring, arms crossed over arms.

On the other side, the pile of disorganized and fallen children had begun to fight one another, pulling hair and elbowing to prevent one another from rising. Anyone who got up past her knees was fairly tackled and dragged back into the writhing mass.

The girls in the ring began to lean side to side, their ringed arms forming a pulsing snake, rising and falling in smooth undulations. The drummers changed their beat again, surging in a round from left to right, making the room pulse like a heart.

"Why did the world die?"

The girls in the ring did not echo the speaker; their heads were bowed together. Instead, the girls in the roiling pile echoed her, calling out in distress. "Why did the world die? Why did the world die? Why did the world die?"

Flora felt the energy thrumming across the whole theater. The crowd was part of the show; this had become less spectacle and more ritual. The mayor and her women were swept up in it, their hands still on each other, their eyes closed in rapture. Flora could see the mayor's wide, pillowy breasts rising and falling rapidly in her tight gown as she gasped along with the chant.

The caller spread her arms wide and the chant changed. "Men. Men. Men. MEN. MEN. MEN."

The mayor's fist came down on the table as the chant spread across the theater. "Men," she cried. "Men. Men. Men."

The words came apart from one another, beads on a string with too much room between them. Interspersing the shouts of *MEN MEN MEN*, the caller interjected.

"They kidnap. They rape. They slave. They steal. Rape boys. Rape girls. Rape the world. Kill the world. Killed the world. Made guns. Made plague. Made sick. Made death. Killed the world. Killed it dead. Killed us all. But we rise. Yes we rise. Rise again. Rise in Shy. Rise and shine. Rising Shy."

The girls began to rise again, building one huge structure of their bodies, its base wide and its upper level so high that Flora had to tip her head all the way back to follow. On top, smaller girls were launched high into the air and caught, over and over and over.

The caller stalked the front of the stage, reaching out her hands to the house. "Women build. Women make. Women birth. Women keep."

The orchestra struck up a wheezing but spirited song. Everyone in the theater not already on her feet leapt to them, and the anthem of Shy rang out to the rafters.

Flora didn't know the words or the tune, but she found it stirred something in her heart. She was choked up, caught in the wave of shared feeling in that place.

As the song ended, the wave began to dissipate. People settled down.

The mayor sank back into her chair, clucking her tongue to her two attendants.

"Is there anything left in that bottle? Have it this way?"

Flora passed it over. "Is that the end of the show?"

Mayor Max laughed a little. "What could possibly follow that?"

Flora could say nothing back. As the crowd began to thin, she gathered herself, looping her silks around her head again.

"Thank you for having me as your guest," she offered to the mayor by way of parting. "It was an honor."

Max reached out and took Flora's wrist, looking her over. "It wasn't an honor; I wanted to get to know the mysterious stranger I was promised. I see now that there wasn't much chance for that here."

Flora looked down at her. "I have to be on my way soon. I am expected home."

Mayor Max nodded. "Tomorrow, then. Meet me at the baths. I start in the early morning and spend most of the day."

"I don't—"

"Don't worry. I won't bite." Max bared her teeth as though giving away her lie already.

Flora started to object again, but the woman was moving quickly now, extricating her large body and even larger skirts from her position on the far side of the table. Her ladies followed her a few paces behind, bustling away toward their own private exit.

Flora stared after them.

A few minutes later, Can appeared. "Could I walk you back to your room?"

Flora nodded, wrapping her silks tighter.

Can got them clear of the building, but the crowd was thick. The night was warm and humid, and Flora could smell the river. Lamps were lit on the tall posts that lined the street, and the odor of burning animal fat added another sickening layer to the night.

Flora knew well the humidity of summer nights, having lived her life in warm, wet places. But she felt as ill as if she had never breathed air this heavy before in her life.

"Did you eat too much? That mayor sets quite a table." Can was lighting a fat cigar that smelled of herbs and sour, spoiled tobacco.

Flora fought the urge to retch. "No . . . no, I just need some fresh air."

"Oh, let's go through the park, then."

Can cut them a path toward a dimmer space: a flat area between the buildings that held rusty, ancient playground equipment. Flora saw that some of the pieces had been welded and others built up with wood. It was quieter here, and a little easier to breathe.

"Mayor Max invited me to the baths tomorrow."

Can smiled, her fat cigar clenched between her teeth. "The baths are lovely. You may have baths back home, but nothing like this. There's a whole guild who just takes care of these. The old mayor, Ang. She decreed it. Greatest idea of my lifetime."

Flora looked over at Can, who had oiled her biceps and shone in the city's cast-off light. "Where I come from, most people bathe alone. Some of my friends come from a city where there are bathers, who help with combing and shaving and delousing. But I'm . . . I'm somewhat shy. About being naked. With people I don't know."

"You're shy in Shy," Can smiled. "Do you have scars? Moles? Pox?"

Flora shook her head. "Just shy."

Can reached out and put a hand on Flora's shoulder gently. Flora looked up and saw a tiny cloud drift in front of the moon.

"I've seen it all. The mayor's seen it all. Stripes from birth, and stripes from slavers. My old aunt had the stump of a hand. Saw a girl once who was webbed between her toes like a bullfrog. No shame in it."

Flora shook her head. She felt the same exposure as when she had stood on the stage. She would choke if she didn't say it.

Just say it. Just say it and get it over with. Isn't it always worse if it's a surprise?

"Have you ever seen a girl with a cock?" Her voice was lighter than she thought it would be. Too light for a word with so much weight.

Can smiled wryly. "Only every time I take my pants off. Is that what you're worried about?"

Flora looked at Can, unable to close her mouth. "I thought men killed the world."

Can laughed. "They did. That's why there are no men here." She saw the look on Flora's face and shook her head. "You worry too much, stranger."

The shortcut brought them back to Flora's little room faster than walking the street would have.

Can put a brisk, friendly kiss on Flora's cheek. "Rest easy, silkworm. Come to the baths and have a good time. Tell the mayor a story; she likes that. And then come get me and I'll take you back to Demons. Alright?"

"Alright," Flora said softly.

She locked the door behind her. She combed out her hair. She rubbed goose fat from a small pot into her dry elbows. It was too hot to sleep in anything but herself, so that was what she did.

CHAPTER 14

The Bambritch Book
Fog back in
144N

I remember Shy looking just like the books say heaven was supposed to be. I thought about never going back, just letting the folks in Ommun worry a little while and then forget about me. What was there? Eddy didn't want me. Alice could have anything she wanted, so she'd get over it fast. Alma didn't trust me or like me, so what could the future hold in that city under the earth?

In the awful, unrelenting heat of the night in places like that, there is no sleep. I remember when I first came here, how blessedly cool it always seemed. I loved the rain just as much as I loved coming out of it and warming myself by the fire. I learned from the folks who were holding Bambritch how to live on the island. They were old and childless. Just a handful of them, Gilly and Fred and Walker and John, and Hortensia. They taught me to dig clams and oysters and geos out of the wet sand, how to make a feast of them and the small potatoes they grew and herbs and goat butter. It reminded me of the rich food I had loved in Shy, and how I was tempted to stay.

My time with Archie had inured me to slavery. I could accept it until I could not. Out of Estiel, everything was different. I was coming around to Eddy's way of seeing things in black and white. I don't know if that's just the result of getting older, or if the world was changing, or if what I saw changed me. Maybe it was all three of those things. But once I knew, I couldn't unknow. I had to leave Shy.

Can came to me in the heat of that night. I was naked and alone, oiled up and covered in my own sweat, trying to think of anything that would lull me to sleep. She knocked at the door and I wrapped myself in a sheet. She took my hand and led me out into the night.

There was this lush field off the end of the block. It was hopping and singing with bugs, and the moon was so clear. I was shy about being naked out of doors, and then much more so when I realized there were others out there. Half of Shy was out there, fucking in the heat of the night. The rising and falling rhythmic sound of sex was everywhere, though the grass was too tall to see much of anything. I caught a flash of Max, her hair tossing in the windless green, riding someone with a deep, throaty chuckle. It could only be her.

Can dragged me down. I had not been with a woman like her—a woman like me—since the horsewomen of Jeff City. It was strange and familiar, like singing a song I remembered from long ago. She was hot and soft and sticky and insatiable. She whispered that she wanted to eat every piece of me. I gave in. I was eaten.

She thrashed and moaned to be taken, so I took her. She bit my shoulder and came like the bursting of a berry, so very sweet. It is a fine thing to take and be taken and belong only to yourself. Can was brief and bright, but she understood that. I will never see her again, anywhere in this wide and strange world. But I'd be glad if I did.

Everything seemed to die down like a round, each completing verse and chorus in its own time until the last notes rang out among the bugsong. I was wet and dirty, Can was too. She asked me back to her place.

In her house, she had built a wide, flat reservoir on the roof that gathered water and kept it, with an opening above the tile enclosure of her shower. The water that poured down was not cold or warm, but somehow just silky streams that passed over the skin, leaving nothing behind. She washed me first, petting her rough hands down along the length of my body.

"You don't grow any hair," she said, not really asking.

"A little," I said. "I still have to shave, a bit. It's because I was cut so young."

"You're beautiful," she said low, planting a kiss in the dip below my hipbone. I smiled down at her as she worked the mud from my feet.

She stood and I washed her too, taking just a little of her precious soap. It was expensive in Shy, and she used it like a thing that could not be replaced. When we ran out of water, she brought me a clean, rough sheet to dry myself. I was wrapped in it and feeling very relaxed when a little boy opened the door and crept in.

"Hello?" I was startled, but the kid didn't even notice. He dipped his head without speaking and began to crawl across the floor.

"That's Tatty," Can said dismissively. "Don't mind him. He's just here for the laundry."

"Oh," I said, watching the child gather the dirty sheets from the bed and use them to make a parcel of Can's rumpled clothes in the hamper.

"What do you pay him?" I asked. Laundry is an arduous task, and the boy was so small. He was rail thin, with every rib visible in his bare chest as he bent and worked.

"Nothing," Can said in the same tone, clearly not thinking that this was worth talking about.

"Oh, do you trade?" I looked over the skinny kid again, growing concerned. "Do you feed him?"

"No, his keeper feeds him."

Tatty was quick and silent. He slipped out the door without a word to or from Can. I got the feeling that if I had not been there, Can would not have acknowledged that the child was in the room.

"Who's his keeper?"

"I dunno," she said lightly. "One of them."

I sat down on her bed and looked around. "I need you to tell me how this works. I don't understand."

Can was toweling her bald head and searching for clean clothes. "How what works?"

"Why do you have children who work for you, but you pay them nothing? Does everyone in Shy have that?"

She sighed and sat down beside me. "There is so much work that needs to be done, every day," she began. "Nobody can do it all for themselves. I don't want to have to grind my own flour, gather my own eggs, trade for my own sugar. So I concentrate on doing what I do best, and other people do their part."

I nodded, frustrated. I understood the way cities divided labor, but I didn't want to tell her I wasn't stupid. I just let her talk.

"There are a lot of small jobs that keep Shy running that children can do. So the kids who haven't become women yet are put to work, when they're old enough. They all report to a keeper, who's responsible for feeding and boarding them. They're cared for, and they see their parents regularly. But they have to earn their keep, just like everyone else."

"When do they become women?"

"When did you?"

I pressed my lips together. "I've always known who I was," I said, finally.

Can smiled. "Well, most of us have to decide. I became a woman during my twelfth summer. I was stubborn and I wanted to believe there were some good men, somewhere. When I was apprenticed to a raider who would train me, I learned the truth. I became a woman as soon as I came home."

I thought for a long time before speaking again. "So these children are slaves," I said. "They aren't paid, and they have no other choice."

"Well, you don't have to put it like that," Can said, with a clear scoff in her voice. "Nobody hurts them. Nobody fucks them. They're safe and they're taken care of. What more is there to childhood, anyway?"

I couldn't answer her then, and I cannot now. In my travels, I have learned the same lesson again and again; every city as rich as Shy has that same flaw at its heart.

The life I live now is beautiful, but no one on Bambritch is entitled to the labor or the body of another. That is our one unshakable rule.

When I think about what may be lost if this advancing army overtakes us, I feel a cold so deep that my bones are above it. Reports still say they're three days away, but what if that plane can fly? What if they have old-world weapons capable of leveling cities or poisoning the water around us? What if my Connie ran off to join the fight against them and . . . I can't even write the rest of that sentence. I won't. They have to be safe. They must be. They are.

CHAPTER 15

OMMUN

Etta followed Alice down a series of almost unused hallways. The emptiness rang around them, echoing their footsteps on the metal walkway. Etta put her fingertips against the warm metal, dragging them as she walked.

"Wait until you see it," Alice was saying. "It's maybe the best old-world laboratory I've ever seen. Glass and syringes and steel tools. Good steel. No pits, no rust. How they weren't using it, I'll never know."

"They don't know any better," Etta muttered.

"What?"

Alice didn't look behind her; she was too focused on her goal.

"Nothing," Etta said.

Alice found her door and pushed it open.

The space was well lit and immaculately clean. Alice had begun her work already, hanging up drying bundles of plant matter and beginning the tricky processes of refining and purifying with heat. A low flame burned below a flask of cloudy yellow liquid. Etta could see three pots of poppies drying around the room.

Alice patted a freckled hand on a steel exam table. "Hop up," she said.

"I don't want to do this," Etta said, her voice like a croak.

Alice came forward and took Etta's hand. "I know you don't, okay? I know that. But you have some decisions to make, and I want them to be yours rather than time's. Do you get that? I want to help you."

Etta nodded numbly. She pushed herself up onto the table with her palms and sat there, not moving.

Gingerly, with infinite care, Alice put her hands on Etta's belly.

Etta let out a long, shaky breath.

Alice felt around, her thin lips flattened to a white line. She looked nowhere, seeing only with her fingers.

"You're further along than I thought. Three, maybe four moons."

Etta made no sound.

"It's not too late, if you want to call it. I have everything here that you would need. I would help you. But it's late enough that it won't be easy."

Etta sat silent, looking at the floor.

"Is this . . . is this the first time that—" Alice broke off, awkward, not wanting to say it.

"No," Etta said flatly.

"How did it go last time?" Alice's voice was soft.

"Not well. But I didn't have to call it. It took care of itself." Etta folded her arms over her middle. She was wearing her shirt pulled out of her pants and loose, hiding the bulge there that would soon be too much to hide.

"Well," Alice began carefully, "if that were going to happen again this time, it would probably be soon. By this point, the stickers have stuck. You're going to have something. Maybe a baby, maybe not. But chances are good."

Etta snorted. "Good."

Alice put her hands on Etta's face, not a professional anymore but a friend and lover. She kissed Etta's cheek up high, just below her eye. Her lips dampened.

"Let me get Sylvia. I'm no Midwife, not really. Let's get someone who knows what she's doing."

"No," Etta said, her voice breaking. "I can't even look at Sylvia. Or Ani. Or her girls. It's my fault, what happened to them. To all of you."

Alice tried to lift Etta's face and found she could not. "That's not true at all! We would have eventually come to the Lion's notice. You might as well say it was my fault. It was my drugs that made him come to us. It was me and Flora who told him where the city was."

Etta did look at her then, her eyes blazing. Alice put her hand on Etta's head, the low, close curls just growing in there. Etta hadn't shaved in months. "It wasn't your fault. Or Flora's. I just . . ."

"You just think you can fix everything. You just think you should have broken the world with two hands and remade it for us."

Etta laughed a little jaggedly, on the edge of crying. "Only that."

"We have all done what we had to do. Your mother. My mother. The little ones. Shit, even Alma. She does what she has to."

At the mention of the Prophet's name, Etta sighed hard. "She's going to be weird about this when she finds out."

"Everyone is," Alice agreed. "Is there any way to tell them it wasn't the Lion? Was there anybody here in Ommun who might have done it, before?"

Etta shook her head slowly. "I don't know what to do."

Alice let go of her and walked a few steps away. "You told me you wanted to find the carry berries and have done with it. I told you what to look for, and you went out to find it. What happened?"

Etta sighed. "I don't know. I wanted to do it. I think of this thing as a parasite and I want it gone. But I couldn't kill it. I had everything I needed, and I couldn't do it."

"Did you bring any back?" asked Alice, always eager to keep up her supplies.

"In my pack," Etta said listlessly. "I'll dig it out."

She rummaged. Alice watched her carefully. "I'll make it for you, now. I'll stay with you until it runs its course. I can put you out, if you want that. I have enough som—"

"No," Etta said, pulling a cloth bundle of berries out of her bag.

Alice put her hand on top of Etta's. "If you're sure. But you're going to pass the point of no return. Soon."

Etta said nothing, not even nodding. She slid off the shiny metal table and Alice heard her boot heels hit the floor.

"Who else knows?" Alice looked away, pretending to straighten something.

"Kelda. She's been staying with me."

Alice swallowed. "Your mother?"

Etta shook her head.

"Will you let Sylvia look at you?"

"Not yet." Etta looked at the floor. "Not yet."

Alice watched her. "Okay. That's up to you. But I'm going to keep asking. I don't know how this will go for you, but I don't want you dead. You've got a better chance of coming through this if you have some help."

"I know that." Etta's voice was small. She was pulling her pack onto her shoulders, already aiming for the door. "I keep thinking I can kill him again, if I kill what's his."

Alice didn't ask what she meant. She knew.

"But I'd be killing me, too. Something in me that wants to live. Anything that can live, should live. Shouldn't it? Like Sheba?"

Blinking, Alice thought a minute. "That skinny girl who doesn't talk? Sheba? What's she got to do with anything?"

Etta sighed. "Like Chloe. Like Flora. The ones that lived through it all."

"Like you."

Etta looked up at Alice then, her clear brown eyes like something trapped in a cage.

"You did that, too," Alice said. "You've lived through it all. You ought to tell your whole story. Write your book, like the Unnamed."

"You sound like my mother."

"It's good to leave behind your understanding. Other people can learn from it."

Etta's hand came to settle on her low belly. "I wish my whole life wasn't filled with people asking me what I was going to leave behind. Can I just fucking live?"

Alice had no answer for that. Etta slipped out, and the drugmaker worked to process the berries while they were still bruised and fresh. She might need them sometime soon.

CHAPTER 16

SHY

The baths smelled like bad eggs. Flora pulled her silk to her nose as she approached the old building. There was no guard or attendant at the door, so she went in.

She followed the sound of voices, down and down old stone stairs. On the bottom level, the staircase opened up and spilled into a huge room full of pools lit by torches, where the egg smell was stronger still. One long pool filled the middle of the space, with smaller ones ringed all around.

A voice rang in the cavernous space as Mayor Max called out to her. "Flora! So good of you to join us. Slip out of all that wrap and get into this lovely water. It's nice and hot today!"

Flora saw the woman's large pink arm waving to her. She walked quickly in that direction.

Most of the pools were empty at this still-early hour. She could see a few women quietly enjoying the stillness, ignoring the mayor.

Max was surrounded in her small pool by four other women. Flora recognized two of them from the theater the other night.

"Shuck all that off, dearie," said a red-haired woman on Max's right. "And if your hair color happens the same way mine does, you'll want to pin it up and keep it out of the water. You have pins?"

"I have ties," Flora said, already tucking up her braids into each other and getting her hair off her neck. "Thank you for the warning."

"This water will suck the color right out," the woman said. She had a strange accent that Flora had never heard before. "Also, if you're wearing any jewelry, take it off and stow it. The water will ruin that, too."

Flora didn't wear any metal, but thanked the woman anyway. "I'm Flora," she said, smiling shyly.

"Greta," the other redhead said. "And this is my sister, Ann. We're both visiting from Niagra."

"Where's that?"

"North," said the woman with the strange accent.

"Land of frags," Max said in her teasing voice.

"We are *not*," Ann said, a little too forcefully for a tease.

"Oh, don't be like that," Max said, pouting. "There's no such thing. I just like making you angry. You're so pretty when you're mad."

Flora looked around, bewildered. She'd been about to ask about frags, but another conversation had already begun. She wanted to undress without being watched, so she took the opportunity and began to slowly unwrap her silks.

"How can you stand to wear all that when it's so sticky out?" Ann was watching her disrobe.

Flora froze. *Not distracted enough.* "I'm just used to it. Also, I'm a bit shy, if you wouldn't mind."

Flora heard them fall into conversation behind her. She pulled off layer after layer, carefully bundling her clothes and putting them up on a bench where they wouldn't get wet. She came down to her smallclothes— the layers that rarely left her skin. She took a deep breath.

"Come along now, love." Max's voice boomed again. "I want to hear more of your story. Get in already."

Flora peeled off her inner layers, noting that they'd need a wash soon. She laid her hand modestly over her pudenda, arm crossing her nipples, and stepped nimbly into the water. She didn't exhale until she had sunk in nearly to her chin.

The water was very hot and stung the bare flesh of her back. The smell seemed to have faded, however, and it was pleasantly milky when she looked down. She couldn't see anyone's body below the waterline.

No one said anything about her body, not even so much as a raised eyebrow.

"What part of my story can I tell you?" Flora asked Max after a few breaths to acclimate herself to the heat.

"Well, hold on," Max said, her full lips dimpling her cheeks and chin. "Greta was in the middle of hers, I think. I just got excited when I saw you come in."

Flora felt sweat begin to bead on her forehead and upper lip. She dipped her face to rid herself of the tickle.

Greta smiled, showing bad teeth. "I was long in the trade, as I was saying, Madam Mayor. I'm not as young as I look."

Max grinned at her, reaching out to rub one slick finger under her chin. "Never tell anyone your real age, sweet Greta."

"What trade was that?" Flora asked politely.

"Sugarcane," Greta said blithely. "There are islands to the south where it grows easily. You've never tasted anything so sweet in your life. Sweeter than honey by far."

"I've eaten raw sugarcane," Flora said, smiling and feeling the muscles in her back relax. "I came from Florda. Not those islands, but close. Everyone trades it. It grows there, too."

"You're from Florda!" Ann was the first to exclaim and reach out across the water, not quite touching Flora. "How did you end up here?"

"Oh, adventures. Misadventures. You know."

"No, we don't know," Max said demurely. "That's the point."

An attendant came by with small, delicate old-world glasses of some amber liquid. Each woman took one, but only Flora thanked the person who had brought them.

The liquid was sticky-sweet, but quite alcoholic.

"What is that?" she asked.

"Honeysuckle cordial," Ann said dismissively. "And not a great one. Do go on."

Flora drank the rest of hers, thinking it was delicious and not worth complaint.

"I was the apprentice of a slaver for a long time. A man named Archie. I would help train new slaves when he picked them up, get them trained and ready to be sold. He bought me in Florda, but we traveled a great deal in the trade."

"You were a slaver?" Ann was aghast.

"She was a child," Greta said immediately. "She didn't choose that life." She turned to Flora. "You're not still in the trade?"

"No, of course not," Flora said quickly. "I told you my story about the Lion. I've seen awful things, and I've helped end them where I could."

The women nodded as they settled down.

Greta resumed her story when the mood had shifted. "I've grown very rich with the help of people like Mayor Max, here, who run an orderly city and make trade safe. I can come to Shy with goods of worth any time of year and never worry I will find the city wiped out, burned down, or in chaos. The places I know like that, I can count on one hand."

She held up her left hand and Flora saw that the last knuckle of her smallest finger had been cut off with some clean, sharp instrument.

Max reached out and laced her fingers through Greta's. She sighed and looked toward Flora.

"What happened to Archie?"

Flora swallowed. "He bought me from the king of Florda when he was already an old man. He kept me for a number of years, then sold me to my father in Jeff City. He couldn't have lived long after that."

Greta clucked her tongue. "The king of Florda! That's something I haven't heard in a long time."

"No?"

Greta shook her head and Ann laughed a little. Ann's hair was so pale it was nearly white, and when she tucked a loose strand behind her ear, the water made it seem translucent. "There were four or five people calling themselves king down there. Each of them in a pink palace surrounded by oranges and caimans. Each of them with a harem and some weapons, some kind of claim. Then they all started building armies to outdo one another, to be the only king of Florda. Naturally, they're all dead. Because the only thing that sort of life buys is death."

She smiled smugly. "There's only a handful of villages along the coast down there now. They didn't build. They got the sweats and the flux and died off where war didn't do it. They didn't learn to be women."

Flora felt a small, strange loss. It had been her home, though she hadn't really known it. It was good to think of kings losing their harems and people getting free, but not of everyone dying of sickness and never building anything that could last. It was like loneliness, combined with a wound to a half-felt hometown pride. Flora felt it sink through her. She had to concentrate hard to rejoin the conversation in the pool.

". . . wouldn't live there if I were king of it," Max was saying, rubbing her nose against her shoulder to scratch it. "Too hot, too humid. Too easy to get sick. The snows save us every year."

Everyone nodded as if this were a very wise thing to say and not an obvious truth.

"So, what are you doing in our neck of the woods?" Max asked Flora.

"Can found me in Demons. I've been raiding libraries for some specific stuff, and that library is almost untouched. If you're interested. Good books on drugmaking, and I couldn't take them all."

Max laughed a little. "Shy has one of the finest libraries in existence, that I can promise you. You should see it before you go. But I warn you: no raiding."

Flora smiled. "Of course not. Never steal from the living. And I've seen your library."

"Smart woman," Max said, draining her tiny glass. "Let's get some breakfast."

Dried off and dressed, the women made an unhurried party toward Max's garden. It was laid beneath sheltering trees before an imposing, well-kept house. Max sat at the head of the table. Flora settled on her left.

Breakfast was another astonishing spread. Flora stared in amazement at the beautiful table laid under the shade of a low, spreading tree. Breads of all kinds, cheese and jam, meats she couldn't identify mixed with partridges and late-summer fruits. She was hungry, so she ate well.

I could get used to this, she thought. They ate well in Ommun but simply. It seemed that the Leaf prepared food in a utilitarian manner, rather than one meant to increase anyone's enjoyment. Flora often found the food bland and underspiced or undersalted. She had overheard a few people from Nowhere grumbling about what their raiders used to bring in. How they missed it.

The thought of those grumbling voices brought her the memory of Alice, first and most sharply. Then Eddy and Kelda.

Home.

Ommun was not home, any more than Jeff City had been. But she knew where her heart was, while she was here.

Flora made her excuses about staying for dinner. About staying another minute.

Max just wants to be entertained, she thought, watching yet another knot of beautiful women wind in around the mayor and vie for her attention. *She doesn't need me for that. When does she ever work?*

Flora, with her bag in hand, hair dry and braided tight, found Can. They walked together to Can's car.

"Can you take me back to my truck?" she asked, biting her lip. "I really must be getting home."

Can nodded, a small smile on her face. "Not tempted to stay in the city of women?"

Flora smiled back, her face broadening as she thought of an answer. "Every woman in the world isn't enough to make up for the ones you really want."

"You've got that right," Can said, adjusting the pikes on her car and settling in the low bucket seat behind the wheel. "Give us a crank?"

Flora started the engine. They got on the road before midday. Flora saw the gates of the city in full daylight for the first time. She saw hanged bodies displayed there, flyblown and jaws agape. She didn't look long. Some of them were hardly more than boys.

Executed for being men. Was that really their only crime?

Flora knew better than to start the conversation while Can could still see Shy in the mirror that pointed out through the rear slits. She waited until she knew she could run if Can pulled over, or at least until Can couldn't get reinforcements immediately. They crawled away from the city on the crumbling road, more like gravel than the smooth asphalt it had been laid to be. Grass and yellow flowers grew up and impeded their wooden wheels as they made their way back toward Demons.

The sun had begun to set before Flora cleared her throat to say what she had been rehearsing in her head for hours now.

"So why is everyone in Shy a woman?"

Can grinned and shot a thin stream of brown juice neatly through a knothole in her door. "You finally just coming around to talking to me about this?"

Flora settled deeper into her seat. The humor in Can's voice put her somewhat at ease.

"I try to work things out on my own first. It saves me a lot of embarrassment. And worse."

Can nodded and tucked her wad of tobacco deeper into her lip. "You were there, in the theater. You heard the story. Even if you didn't hear it there, you gotta know it. Men killed the world. And now, they're the most dangerous thing in it."

Flora nodded. "Sure. Sure. But most of the people in Shy were born men, right?"

"Nobody is born a man," Can said, tucking her face to her shoulder as if to look at her, but keeping her eyes on the road. "You're born a baby. You're born naked. Everything after that is something that you learn to do."

"I guess," Flora said. "But women and men can do different things."

"Can they? Or is that just something we decide?"

Flora scoffed. "Well, I mean have babies. Make babies."

"Except that lots of people can't do either. What are they?"

Flora sat silent. "But their bodies."

Can shrugged. "Every body is different. What does it matter who has a cock?"

Flora had nothing to say to that.

"Anybody can hurt you," Can said, her voice softer and slightly gentler. "There was a woman in Shy, years ago, who raped other women with a cock made of wood. Nobody could stop her. She'd catch them on the upper floors of the farm towers, where nobody could hear them calling for help. She would wait by the well and get someone all alone at night. She had become a man."

Flora sat with that, feeling the weight of another story sink into her.

"And we kill men in Shy. That's all there is to it. You choose to be a woman, or you choose not to be."

"So she was hanged at the gates? With those other men?"

"Sure." Can's whole body was relaxed, almost negligent. She radiated a lack of concern.

"What if someone was just a man, but didn't do any harm?" Flora was trying not to be too keen, looking at a swirling bit of dust instead of at Can's face. "Could they live?"

"Not in Shy. Eventually, it would come to that. It always does."

"So some you just send away?"

Can shifted her posture. "Mostly they leave on their own. If it's that important to you to be a man, you can do that anywhere. Just not in Shy. It's not worth it, with the world full of slavers like it is."

"Some of those slavers are women," Flora said mildly.

"What's your point?" Can fixed her with a hard look.

"Nowhere was like that. Executions to keep things safe."

"Nowhere?" Can spat again.

Flora shook her head. "A village. A town. The place where my Eddy came from. They didn't kill all men, and they weren't all women. But they killed slavers and rapists, always."

"Eddy? Didn't you say 'Etta' when you were on the stage? Was that the one in your story? With the Lion?"

"Yes," Flora said. "But he's a man. He chooses to be a man. Lots of men do, you know. And they're safe and they can live in cities with women and not hurt them."

"I've seen places like that," Can admitted. "But they're just delaying what's inevitable. You're a raider; you must have seen it everywhere. Men eventually get the idea that they should be in charge. Then they back each other up. Then you get problems like the Lion."

"What about the woman with the wooden cock?"

"Nobody followed her. No woman saw that happening and thought it seemed like a good idea and wanted to join in. Because women don't do shit like that. Women don't keep slaves. A woman here and there, but not women as a kind."

Flora sat in silence and digested that. *You do. You just don't call it that.*

The sun sank lower and the light began to blind them on the westward road. Can slit her eyes and dipped her head a little. The orange light made a band across the bridge of her nose.

"I thought you were scared. You looked scared most of the time that you were there. I should have told you it was alright sooner, but

I kind of like seeing the look on an outsider's face when they realize what we are."

Flora huffed a little air to blow a hair off her face before turning sideways to look at Can while she spoke. "My town was full of horse-women like me. I've seen places like that, but no place where everyone just called themselves women as if there was no difference."

"What's a horsewoman?"

"What I am. What you are. A woman who was born with a cock. Where I'm from, we take horse medicine to help us look more womanly. I don't need it as much, since I was cut as a baby. Some need it far more."

"Horse medicine?"

"It sounds confusing," Flora said. "But it makes shaving easier. Some horsewomen say their voices get higher, or their chests a little softer. I don't know if it's medicine or magic, but it has always helped me."

Can was nodding. "Shaving is awful," she said. "For a while in Shy there were some women with beards, but it made it really hard for them to make friends. Nobody wants to be seen with that."

"Why does it matter?" Flora asked. "When everybody's a woman and a cock doesn't matter, why does a beard matter? Or hair on your chest?"

"I don't know," Can said. "Just not what women prefer, I guess."

Flora thought of the men of Ommun with their carefully groomed beards and the coarse hair on their arms. She didn't like it, but the women of Ommun sure seemed to.

Do we decide what we like? Is it born in us, or is it different if you have seen different things? Do we like what we saw growing up? What our mothers liked? Is there a day that comes and goes when we decide what we like, now and forever?

Flora thought back to the work she did for Archie, for the things she had pretended to like and had eventually learned to enjoy.

I always knew what I wanted. But I taught myself to like things I didn't want. Am I the only one? Are harems all over full of women who learn to like what they've got, because they've never had anything else?

She thought of Sheba, and the thought died cold and alone in her head. Sheba had never learned to like anything.

And the men who had her, what they liked was to take everything from her and those other girls. Everything. Even their names.

"You alright? You're shrinking."

Flora realized she was tight all over, turning herself into something small and very guarded. "I'm fine," she said, making the effort to expand and relax a little. "Just thinking about old times."

"So, where you're from, it's not safe to be a woman. Is it?"

Flora sighed. "It's complicated. It's safe to be a woman if you were born to be one. I was safer in Jeff City, where horsewomen were normal. The Lion ignored us to search for breeders. We were better off. It's not safe where it's not understood, or part of everyday life. People sometimes feel tricked . . . or think you're trying to upset the order of life."

She thought of Eddy, when he had first felt her body in that strange, deep, salty cave. The terrible betrayal in his voice. Tears pricked her eyes as she tried to forget how cruel he had been.

"Why?" Can asked. "Every town, every village needs more women. What part of life has any order, anyway? Women like us are the solution."

"Breeders are the solution," Flora said softly. "We're something else."

Can sighed. "Maybe. Still, I think we've got it right in Shy. Nobody checks what's under your skirt unless they're about to lick it. Nobody thinks of it as her business. We're all women, and so we're all free. What's better than that?"

Flora was quiet for a while. "Can?"

"Yeah?"

"Do you know what frags are?"

Can laughed a little. "Of course I do. I mean, they're just a story. They're not real. You know that, right?"

"What are they, though?"

"A rumor. Women who can impregnate themselves. Who don't need a man. Can you imagine that? We could do away with them

131

altogether, if that were true. You hear stories that there's frags up in Niagra, or down in the jungles. It's just stories for kids."

"Just women?" Flora asked.

"You know any men who get pregnant?"

Flora thought of Eddy. Flora did not know how to define anything anymore. She thought of the horsewomen dead beside that word.

That can't be real. I never read it in any book. I never heard of one in Jeff City, or Florda, or Niyok. But I've seen so many things I never knew existed.

What would it mean if it were real? Would they be as revered as Mothers, or endangered because of the threat they represent?

She thought about Alma smugly pregnant forever and ever, needing no man to seed her. All those towns with carefully regimented rules about breeding, done. Slavers out of business. She imagined Kelda, holding a baby that was hers and only hers, gotten on her own terms. She imagined herself, weighted down in the center and impatient for her own child to be born. The feeling that whipped through her body was a mixture of terror and longing and confusion. She had never let herself want that before, because it hadn't been possible.

What is possibility? The world might be new again tomorrow.

When they stopped for the night, they were cold and lit a fire. Can asked quietly and gently if she could hold Flora as the slept, just for warmth and togetherness, nothing more.

Flora said yes, and that's all that it was. Can curled behind her and Flora pulled Can's big, rough hands to her belly and rested them there. And it was good.

CHAPTER 17

The Bambritch Book
Rain
144N

I've been interviewing survivors, whose stories I'll keep beside the record I've been making here on the island. I think about my little trunk, the one I'm going to hide this book in to see it through. I can fit everything that matters to me into a box the size of my body. That's rather fitting. If there's to be nothing left of us, then so be it. I'd rather take the chance that I can't get at my own books than that they'll be destroyed. If we're still here in a season, I'll begin to write again.

Most of the survivors cannot read or write. I think those skills are often quite rare, and I got used to an unusual number of people who had them because of Nowhere and Ommun. Everyone born in Bambritch is taught as a child. So I've been scribing these newcomers' stories as best I can, as the Midwife sometimes did. My story contains theirs, as packed and as jeweled within as a split pomegranate.

The Book of Ichabod, as scribed by Flora

Ichabod has a thin frame and bad eyesight. Comes from a place called Kloma and worked with cattle, milking and slaughtering. Twenty-five summers or so.

"The army done run us out. I heard they run out people all over Tehas, too. They marching all over, trying to find some fool thing. They got an airplane and they make noise with it, but it don't do nothing. The guns, now, they do a lot. Big guns, like to blow up a whole house or a whole church. People stop fighting when they see that, they just lay right down. We done gave up. Anybody would.

"Looking for frags, they said. Ain't none of us know what that is, so they roust people, start asking questions that don't make no sense. 'How'd you get pregnant?' At the dance, how else does a body get pregnant? 'Whose child is this?' Everybody's child; we're a family. We were real smart until they started killing women and children right in the face. They weren't kidding.

"The commander? Funny looking. Long hair and a face like a gent. Kinda purty. Cold, though. Army's huge. Come from all over, all colors and all kinds. Some of them speaking tongues I ain't never heard before. Some Spaniel, too. They got trained hounds, set them on my cattle. I never cried so hard. Them baby calves.

"Killed pregnant women. Yeah, they did. Kept asking how'd it happen, how'd it happen. I ain't never seen anybody do that. With babies so few and so hard to come by. Acted like it wasn't even nothing. Just with a gun, just real quick. But still. Asking all these questions, asking for frags. I guess we ain't have no frags.

"Here? Because they told us to. Yeah, they said if we stopped or settled anywhere else, they'd kill us. Told us where to go and the name of the island and all. Loads never made it. Died on the road or else gave up and went to settle somewhere hid. I don't know why they sent us here. I don't understand it. You folks have a nice little town up here in the cold and the wet, but why here? The commander knows you, you know. Told us to ask for you. To ask for Flora.

"Y'all got any rules about courting around here? Yeah, I know we might could die, but until then what's life for? I see. I see."

◆ ◆ ◆

The Book of Uni, as scribed by Flora

Uni is very young, maybe sixteen summers. Long black hair. Lots of scars, nervous.

"I was in Pediex most of my life. I don't remember anything before that. I was sold when I was little, but I grew up and figured out how to sell it myself, it's not hard. It beats the shit out of trapping nutria. They're mean, you know.

"The army didn't come through Pediex. We got refugees, though. From weed country. We figured they were coming our way. I was headed to Settle, but I met up with some people who were coming here. They all said the army is looking for frags, but frags aren't even real. This is like that story about saying 'Bloody Mary' to your reflection on the water when the full moon is out and getting a child from her. Kids' stuff. Stupid.

"No, I've never been pregnant. First of all, you can sell it in all kinds of ways. Most guys have had other guys more than you think. You do like they do, you don't worry about it. Second, you take herbs that close up the womb. Yeah, they're real. I got them from a witch in Pediex. You have them up here, too. I've seen them. Sure, I can show somebody.

"You got queers here? No kidding. Someone told me that, but I didn't believe them. No, I don't have any problem with that. I can sell it to women, too. Another way to not get pregnant and dead. No, we didn't have any in Pediex. Nobody would have put up with that.

"No, we didn't have anyone in charge, exactly. There were some trade groups up and down the river who made contracts for business and a few older folks who would settle disputes. Mob justice, couple of hangings for rapists. Girls like me never bothered, always paid. I liked Pediex. It was my home. I'll probably go back, once all this blows over.

"Will they? I don't know. They can't be everywhere. They're a big army, but still just one army. And they keep pushing north, so why would they double back down? It's my city. There's pink flower trees by the river. There's fish all year round. It's green like here, but not so cold."

◆ ◆ ◆

The Book of Fa, as scribed by Flora

Fa is older, white haired, quite twitchy. Smells abominably of deez.

"I've been making fuel since I was a child. Can't smoke around me at all. Grew up in some desert, I don't know the name. Drier every year. We moved toward the woods north of Pediex, made good deals there. Everybody needs deez.

"No idea about the frags. Yeah, I heard the army is looking for them. Mostly slavers are looking for girls, right? Yeah, no idea.

"The future? I'd like to settle down somewhere they need deez. No trucks on this island, are there? Settle, though. Looks like a good-size town. Bet I could catch right on there. Oh, it's nothing. Always something to move you along. Not enough rain, too much rain. Fever. Fire. One place is like another. This island is like other islands. I bet some of your boats run on deez. Where do you get it? Ah, yes, Settle. Settle sounds right."

◆ ◆ ◆

The Book of Cat, as scribed by Flora

Cat is a young child with tip-tilted black eyes and a burn scar over most of her left arm.

"I came in with my mother. I'm always with her. Yes, the army was scary. Big, big guns. They were so loud and I just wanted to run away.

"I know about frags. Yes, I do. They come from the water. They look like seals but then they peel their skin off and look like girls. Then they make a baby but take it back to the ocean to see if it can swim. If it can't, then too bad. That's too sad.

"Of course they're real."

CHAPTER 18

OMMUN

Alice put away yet another bottle of som. She kept telling herself that she was trying to make enough to supply the people of Ommun when she was gone, but she didn't know where she was going.

"Have you thought about how long you want to stay here?" she asked Kelda, who was assisting her in the lab today.

"What do you mean?" Kelda asked, looking up from her work separating dried herbs from one another.

"I keep trying to think of what will be enough to get them going. The people of Ommun. But that thought only comes because I'm already planning to leave."

"Where would you go?" Kelda asked. Her face showed concern that was rapidly edging into panic. "Nowhere is gone. Burned to the ground. Womanhattan was destroyed. We have no other home but Ommun, and they're good to us here."

Alice rolled her eyes and capped the vial she had been filling. "Good enough, yes. Better than some places."

They did not usually speak of Estiel, when it was just the two of them. Neither one of them liked to say the name out loud.

"But I can't stay here forever. I can't stand living underground, for one thing. They whisper about us, for another. Are you happy here?"

Kelda shrugged. "I'm safe. I'm not hungry. For the first time in my life, I'm not forced to take part in breeding. Not any part of it, not even providing release. I like it here, Alice. I thought you did, too."

"Don't you miss the sun? Don't you wish you could roam?"

"I do roam," Kelda insisted. "Just the other day, I took Etta into the woods."

"Sure," Alice said. "After you got help with the lift. What if you wanted to leave without getting help or permission?"

"I'd make the climb," Kelda countered. "Anybody is allowed to make the climb, anytime they want."

Frustrated, Alice clinked two pieces of glassware together just a little too hard. "I'm not saying there's anything wrong here. It's just . . . It's a lot of little things. I don't feel that I belong."

"You could belong anywhere you chose to," Kelda said, her chin jutting forward as she swept broken bits of leaves from the countertop and into a compost bin. "With your skills, anybody would have you. You're just choosing not to belong here."

"And you," Alice said, turning her back on the younger woman, "are just settling for a place that makes you feel protected. That could be anyplace too, until it isn't."

Kelda bit her lip and didn't say anything.

Alice softened and came to Kelda, sliding an arm around her waist. "I'm not angry with you. I just feel . . . trapped. Not like we were before. A much nicer trap. A soft cage with plenty of food. But a cage still. You understand?"

Kelda shook her head. "I don't. I grew up in a place where I had to ask permission to speak. I showed you, our language of signs? I had to ask permission to use my voice. I could never leave. I could never just wake up in the morning and do as I pleased with the day. I had to tell someone where I was going, who I was with, when I would be back. I had to take off all my leathers once a month and let a doctor touch me all over. I have my freedom here. I don't care that it's below ground, or that the prophet is a strange woman, or that the mish has a bunch of guns. Nobody makes me feel like I am less than they are. It's not a trap, Alice. It's a home."

Alice sighed and laid her palm against Kelda's cheek. "I'm sorry, love. Your life has been so different from mine. It makes us want different things. That's all."

"Are you going to leave without me?" Kelda's voice was very small.

"Where would I go?" Alice smiled and tossed one of her golden braids back over her shoulder.

Kelda brightened and went back to her work. It did not occur to her that Alice had not answered.

The laboratory was deep in the uninhabited section of Ommun. In the main halls, bells and calls were repeated by all who could hear them, passing the word that the dinner hour had come, or that there was danger afoot. As far out as they were, Alice could just barely hear an echo of their nearest neighbor's bell.

"That's dinner," Kelda said, putting down her work at once and moving to wash her hands.

Alice watched her approvingly, noting that Kelda was a quick study and made her practices into habit neatly and without complaint. Alice washed up too and they began to walk.

After a few minutes, they began to see other people. Men from the mish immediately cleared their pathway, allowing the two women to go first.

"After you, Sister Alice. Sister Kelda."

Kelda rewarded the men with a broad grin. Alice ducked her head and smiled a little, not wanting to encourage anyone in particular. None of the men had ever approached either of them. They found out after they had been in Ommun for a month that Alma the Prophet had forbidden any man to court any of the new women until it was known whether any of them were with child. She had told the men of her underground city sternly and in no uncertain terms that these women were off-limits.

Alice counted it up in her head. She figured they had four or five months before the issue would come up. Etta would be one of the last.

Then we'll see how free we really are, she thought. The smell of rich vegetable stew came to her then and she inhaled deeply, pushing the thought away.

The people of Nowhere had not really integrated into Ommun. They clustered together in their quarters and tabled together at mealtimes. Alice saw that most of them kept their eyes open during prayer, though they folded their arms and bowed their heads respectfully.

Alma sees it too, Alice thought as she watched the Prophet's eyes linger on their group a little long. Alma was still nursing her triplets, keeping the men of Ommun at bay. No nursing woman was available for courting, either. Between the courting prohibitions on the refugees of Estiel and on the Prophet herself, the men of Ommun were working with a worse temptation than ever.

It shows. Alice saw the young men, always in pairs, always working. They knew better than to stare, but still they lingered and tried to help where it was obvious they weren't needed.

Looking over her shoulder just then, she caught a longing look cast at her back by a kid with a black beard.

And then there are the ones who don't look. She spotted Gabriel and Rei sitting together, splitting a hot roll between the two of them. They spoke in low voices to one another, their foreheads almost touching. *There is no one else in this room for them.* Looking at her own table, she saw Tommy and Heath. Heath had been badly burned trying to rescue friends in Nowhere, and Tommy took painstaking care of his burns every day. He had come to Alice for remedies and painkillers, asking her advice about treating Heath so that his scars would not be too severe.

She thought of Errol and Ricardo, the two raiders from Nowhere whom she knew only from Etta's stories. They had trained Etta to be a raider when she was little more than a child.

Alice could picture Etta trailing always behind them, long limbed and gawky in girlhood, demanding always that they tell her more stories of the road. More stories about what she could expect, and how it would be. Etta had lost them as soon as she had just begun to discover herself, alone out on the road.

Etta. Alice spotted her at once, sitting beside her mother. She made her way over to them and sat close. Ina was gray and terribly small without her wooden belly. Beside Etta's glowing, thickening frame, she looked like something that had been dried to last through the winter.

Alice watched Ina carefully, trying to discern whether the old woman had guessed what was plain to Alice's own eyes. But Etta and her mother both ate with their eyes downcast, not speaking at all.

"Where did you go?" Kelda asked, nudging Alice to accept the bread basket.

"Just thinking," Alice said lightly. She popped the bread in her mouth to keep Kelda from asking her more. Kelda, never skilled at reading anyone, asked anyway.

"Thinking about what?"

Alice didn't have to answer because the door to the dining room opened decorously and Flora ducked inside. She came quickly to sit with the three of them at their table, and two boys from the mish set a place for her immediately. She had washed from the road, but she had obviously been traveling for some time.

"Sorry I'm late for dinner," she said.

Alice reached an arm around her waist and Kelda put a hand on her shoulder. "So glad you're back!" Kelda's grin was wide.

"I'll greet you all properly later," Flora said, smiling. "For now, I'm just very hungry." She set to the food in front of her and ate steadily. The Leaf boys saw her in action and brought her a second bowl of stew without a word.

Midmeal, Etta pushed her half-full bowl Flora's way. She patted Flora's silken arm. "It is good to see you."

Flora smiled up at her. "I have stories from the road."

Etta smiled back, lips barely curving. "Good." She touched Flora's elbow briefly as she rose from the table.

"Flora." Alma's voice floated over them warmly as she made her way to them. With two babies slung and seemingly endlessly nursing at her breasts, she was too wide for the aisle and a little awkward. Still, her hair hung in shining ripples and she seemed to give off the warm glow of health. "So good to have you back."

Behind her, Sister Joan had her hands pressed together. "Please say you've got good news."

Flora swallowed a large mouthful. "My bag is filled to bursting. The library in Demons is in really good shape."

Joan's blue eyes lit up and she clapped her hands. "I'll come and get them tonight!"

Flora nodded, tucking back in.

"Flora, may I speak with you after you've had your honeycake?" Alma's voice was thick and self-satisfied as silk.

As if on cue, a plate of dripping honeycake was set before her by a redheaded boy, who was gone before Flora could say thanks. It was a generously cut piece.

"Of course. Where should I meet you?"

"The library," Alma said breezily. Her skirts whispered against the floor as she walked away.

Alice looked at Flora, her unasked question clear on her face. What could Alma want with Flora that had to be discussed in private? Flora shrugged and ate her cake in a few large, rapturous bites.

"Should we set up the fireside?" Kelda was inching closer to Alice, but Alice held her a little away.

"Yeah, that probably won't take long." But as she watched Flora go, she wondered.

There were three firesides in Ommun. The largest and best was, of course, Alma's alone. It was a large-enough room that everyone could gather there, with a brown dais two steps up and a fireplace that a full-grown man could stand in. A few times a year, Alma would seat herself in the enormous, throne-like leather chair there and tell stories, coming around eventually to their meaning for the community. After the fall of Estiel, she had held one.

It had been Ina who had explained this ritual to the refugees.

"It's their religion," she had said, her voice forever coarsened from her ordeal in Estiel. "It's in the Book of the Unnamed, remember? The same folks. The Mormons. These are just more of them."

That was generally accepted among those who knew the story of Jodi and Honus, but Ina was not done.

"They tell old stories as a way to make sense of what's happening now. We don't have their stories, but we have ours. We should do the same thing."

Ina was the oldest person who had made it out of Nowhere. Her suggestion was taken as a directive.

The second fireside belonged to the Leaf. They used it to tell stories and give guidelines to the men of Ommun. Alma was careful to allow no man power over the whole community or over the children, but over one another she declared it fitting and fair for them to have their own order. Tommy and Heath had found the little room and asked the Leaf if there was another.

"There's the one in the east wing," a Leaf member had told them. "But like most of the east wing, it's a mess."

With general enthusiasm and many hands to make light work, the fireside had come together in no time. The leather chair was cracked and peeling apart, but it had been patiently re-covered in fabric and sewn back into shape. The chimney was cleared, and preliminary tests showed the smoke would travel safely up through and out of Ommun.

Kelda led Ina to the east fireside now, holding her hand when they were in the seldom-used and dark east hallways. The rest of the loyal Nowhere contingent followed soon after, building the fire and lighting candles, setting the room.

"I don't know why Alma only does this sometimes," Kelda said as the room began to warm up with the golden firelight. "Now that we've got the idea, we do it all the time."

"We're not like them," Alice said absently. "We do most things differently."

"I'm not one of your *we*," Kelda said absentmindedly. "But I'm also not one of them."

Alice reached out and touched Kelda's shoulder. "You're like me. That's enough."

Ina was the first to settle into one of the old high-backed chairs near the fire. Alice saw how stiffly she moved, how carefully she settled herself. She went and sat on a low cushion at the older woman's feet.

"Mother Ina, would you like me to rub your hands for you?"

Ina sighed. "No, child. But thank you."

Alice lowered her voice somewhat. "I can help you, if you're in pain. Or if you have trouble sleeping."

"Don't you?" Ina fixed Alice with a frank eye.

Alice winced. "Sometimes. It helps to have someone there."

Ina's eyes flicked over to Kelda and back again. "I suppose it does."

"Didn't any of your Hive make it?" Ina's Hive had been vast; Alice couldn't recall any specific members.

"Sure, a few. I don't want them, though. I don't want anything, child. Truth told, I can't seem to really want a goddamned thing. Mostly, I want to be left alone, for quiet, and to not be cold."

Alice reached over and patted the top of Ina's foot, wanting to comfort her without invading her space.

"I understand that. It'll be a long time before I want a man again, I think."

Ina looked at Kelda again. "Mmhmm."

Alice fell silent. People gathered and waited. The room grew warmer as they fell to talking in small groups.

Everyone's attention seemed to turn to Ina at once. There was no signal, no calling. It just shifted, and she knew it was time.

She moved from her place at the fire to the big chair they had remade for her. Carefully, she settled herself down.

"I've known most of you all your lives," she began. "Some of you I remember the day you were born. I know a lot of your stories and some of you know mine."

She reached up as if to tap her fingers on her belly, but found it wasn't there. Ina had worn the wooden shell to mark her as the Mother of a living child ever since Etta was born. She still felt herself incomplete without it. Her fingers moved through the empty air to her own small belly. Her face crumpled.

"I know my belly made it here from Estiel," she said distractedly. "But I don't know where it got to. If anyone knows, please get it back to me."

She wove her fingers together and began again. "As I was saying, we know each other's stories. But more than that, we share a history. We share the story of the Unnamed, and everyone who was with her at the beginning in Nowhere. I've thought a lot about the way the people of Ommun do this, the way they take old stories and apply them to their lives today. I think we can do that, too."

All around the room, people nodded. They were spellbound. Alice laid her head on Kelda's shoulder. "Does this make you feel bad?" she whispered. "More like an outsider?"

Kelda shook her head. "I am always happy to hear an elder Mother speak," she whispered back.

Ina held her chin high and spoke to the room. "I have been teaching the story of the Unnamed for many years now. I have shown generations of boys how to copy her story and keep it with us, so that we never forget who we are, or how we began with her.

"When I was younger, I used to take pride in the idea that we were all her children, though she had no children of her body. It made me feel better, because back then I had none either. When I had my living child, I put that thought aside. I decided that somehow, other connections were less real than that.

"Children, I was wrong. We've all seen so much that no one else has seen. We share stories that no one else knows. We are bound together as a people by what we do, not how we happen to be born, or to whom. Birth is an accident, and believe me when I say that. It nearly killed me; it is something that happened to me and my living child both. Neither of us would have chosen each other.

"But we chose each other after that. We're choosing each other now. We're choosing people from Jamestown and Estiel and Ommun. We have to make this choice every day, because that's how we decide who we are. Because the choosing never ends. The work never ends. I know that now. Nothing is settled and nothing is won. The Lion won't stay dead, because men like him always rise. We don't stay free because of something we did once. We stay free because we fight our way free every day.

"It's tiring, my children, I know. I'm *tired*," she said, leaning into the last word with every one of her years. "But I've got to do it anyway, and so do you. That's what I learned from the Unnamed. She never stopped. She never quit watching for a baby to be born. She never quit writing in her book. And neither can we."

From her place in the back of the room, Etta began to applaud. Ina looked straight to her as others began to join in. It wasn't an uplifting speech, exactly, but it was true. And that was good enough.

CHAPTER 19

OMMUN

Ommun's library was a thing of beauty. The mish had worked for years to pack it with books from far away. They had specific instructions on what to bring back so that the collection was full of highly useful nonfiction about husbandry, farming, cloth weaving, and other vital skills. They also collected fiction, but Alma had insisted that it be of the highest spiritual caliber, so many books were rejected upon arrival.

Still, Flora thought as she looked around. *They've done very well. I'd never run out of things to read here.*

Since reading the Books of the Unnamed, Flora had become obsessed with diaries. The mish here in Ommun were required to keep them, but many of the others did as well. The result of that custom was that after a few generations in the underground city, journals had their own section in the library; the journals of Ommun were catalogued by year and placed in alphabetical order. Alma was often seen reading the books of the prophets before her, reflecting on their experience.

She was there now, sitting in a straight-backed chair with a book in her hand. Her babies had been passed off, to nurse with another woman or to be put down to sleep for a while. She looked up as Flora walked in.

"Flora." She smiled warmly.

Flora did not often have the full force of Alma's charm turned on her, and her knees nearly buckled at the effect. She had heard people say that the Prophet's eyes were sometimes blue, other times green. Flora saw in the dim light of the library that they were a muddled hazel-gray, and could likely change depending on how you saw her.

It might not be magic, but she is still beautiful.

Alma's entire being was lush and rosy with health, and generously proportioned along her tall frame. Even at the end of a long day, as this had been, she had an air of careless freshness about her.

Flora looked her over, drinking her in.

"What can I do for you, Alma?"

Alma stood and turned her back to Flora, looking up at the shelves, then turned and faced her again. "I wanted to thank you for bringing the additions to the library from Demons. Sister Alice said you brought some on drugmaking that will be most helpful."

"Oh, you're welcome. It was a good trip. I ended up—"

"And you don't feel too run down, I see. You came straight to dinner, instead of taking to your bed."

Flora noticed the interruption and slowed her speech down. *She's building to something. Give her room to run.* "That's right."

"You seem to be doing well. Settled. Finding a place for yourself."

Flora walked a few paces away and wrapped her arms across her chest. "I don't know if I've found my place, exactly. But I like to be useful. And I can't throw silk here."

Alma was nodding. "I wonder if you'd be open to courtship, in that case. I know it's soon and I made everyone wait. But I thought I'd ask some of the women who definitely aren't pregnant, just to ease some of the tension around here. It's driving the menfolk crazy."

Flora looked around the room, trying to find a way out. "Alma, I'm . . . I'm surprised that you'd ask me that. You know what I am."

Alma came forward, reaching for Flora's hand. She laid it lightly on her own chest, above one heavy, milk-full breast. "Your body is valuable in other ways. There is so much you can do with it, even if you cannot breed. You can become part of Ommun."

Eddy told me about this. This is how she does her magic, whatever it is. She lays her hands on you and changes you. She changed Eddy. How will she change me?

But nothing happened except that Flora's hand and then her face grew suddenly warm.

"I don't think you mean that," Flora told her. "You call every other woman *Sister*, but not me. Would you be alright with me adopting a child, to raise as my own?"

Alma swallowed, pushing Flora's hand away. "I don't think that would be good for a child. I wouldn't want them to stumble in their understanding. But you can be useful to a man. You're almost a woman."

"I am a woman," Flora said. "And I am not yours to give. I don't lie with men, anyhow. Not unless I have to. I've only ever loved women. Well, and Eddy."

Alma's cheeks flushed and she looked away. "Impossible."

"I'm not the only one," Flora said softly. "You can't make me into some kind of example for those who don't fit the way you want us to."

"Who else?" Alma asked at once, all gentleness gone from her voice.

Flora shrugged. "I'm not going to tell you. And you'll never know, not unless you pull everyone apart and force them to be with men, like the Lion would do."

Alma gave a little gasp. "That isn't . . . I'm not . . ."

"If you are brokering who should breed and at what time and with whom, you are. That is exactly what he would do. Making people into a harem can look a lot of different ways, Alma."

Alma swallowed, composing herself. "You've certainly given me a lot to think about, Flora. I thank you for being so forthright. Now I must say good night."

She swept from the room majestically, as she always moved. Flora did not turn to see her go.

I cannot stay here. I wasn't sure before, but now I am.

But will anyone go with me?

◆ ◆ ◆

Flora did not sleep well. She had not since leaving Estiel, and she had noticed that many others who had escaped the harem suffered the same. She would awaken disoriented, sensing dawn but never able to see it. In the Lion's high-rise the windows had been blocked and boarded, allowing only slits and pinpoints of light to let them know when the sun had come up, but at least there had been those hints of brightness. Shy had been like a dream between then and now. Deep under the earth, Ommun had no such luck. The electric lights were timed to turn on at full dawn, when the generator crew went to work. It wasn't dawn down here until Alma said so.

Flora would creep through the nightlight-illuminated metal hallways, coming upon some other refugee in the night. Often it was Etta, who would leave Kelda blissfully passed out to prowl and pace, guns worn in plain sight. Other times, it was Mother Ina haunting the nursery, holding a doll or hovering over an empty crib.

Once or twice, Flora had tried to talk to Ina in the semidarkness. Once or twice, Ina had answered her.

Ina had been somewhat vague since the harem. Flora had come to look on her as a source of support, of unflagging strength and nonjudgmental love. Where Eddy had blamed Flora for her cooperation, Ina sympathized. They had all been induced to perform labor in support of the Lion's household; Flora was no different. Ina had understood.

However, since the night of their escape, that strength had deserted Ina. She had begun to show her wounds, and seemed to be aging faster than ever. Flora had first known Ina as a vigorous older woman. Now she seemed withered, bent, and ready to die.

She would respond to Flora's gentle questions with vague nonanswers.

"Trouble sleeping?"

"Trouble living."

"Doing okay?"

"Still here. Still here."

The old woman's smile was sunken. Her hands had turned into claws. She had no Hive. She slept alone.

This night, Flora did not find Ina, nor Eddy. She ran into Tommy and his two bather boys, Clay and Fio.

Tommy was a slight man, long in the torso with muscles like wiry little tree branches. His hair was fair and his face was boyish. Flora could see that he shaved every day. Fio was shorter, dark skinned, with a high forehead that made him look like a giant baby. Clay was bigger, bearded, with a hooded look to his eyes. They made an unlikely trio, but walked always hand in hand, or with arms around one another's waists. Heath was not with them tonight.

She ran into them as they came away from the section of Ommun populated by the mish who were still at home. They stopped in their tracks when they saw her.

"Good woman," said Tommy deferentially. "What brings you out in the early hours like this?"

"Same as you," Flora said.

"Doubt that," said Fio, stifling a laugh.

"You don't know," Tommy countered playfully. "There are enough boys back there that are awfully curious about Flora's potential Hive."

The three men laughed. Flora blanched a little.

"Oh, I didn't mean anything by it," Tommy said coyly. "I'm just like you."

Flora stared at him.

"You know. Fancy." He shot his hip to the side to affect a more feminine stance. "I mean, we all are. But some of us still prefer to act like men." His smirk was incandescent in the dim light.

"That's not what I am," Flora said.

Clay gave her a hard look. "We know that, good woman. But you're not really one of them, are you?"

Flora shrugged. "Maybe I'm not up for the same reasons as you. I just couldn't sleep."

"Who could sleep with the boys of Ommun right next door?" said Fio, pulling the other two around Flora and down the hallway. She let them pass.

She walked past the doors from which they had come, hearing furtive whispers and the susurrations of bedclothes rubbing against one another. She walked down to Alice's laboratory and found her lover exactly where she thought she would be.

Alice was distilling something, watching the steam collect in a broad-bellied glass vessel and drip into the next. Alice's hair was tied up in a messy bun, curls falling out to frame her face. She was lovely in the firelight, the freckles on her nose and cheeks fading as she lived more and more of her life out of the sun. She wore one of the long cotton gowns that the women of Ommun slept in. Flora had hand-washed her own silks and kept exclusively to them, despite the fact that she knew they made her look foreign.

Or maybe because they do, she thought.

Alice did not look up as Flora came through the door. Flora sidled up behind her and put an arm around her waist, pulling her back and smelling the nape of her neck.

"I couldn't sleep, either," she whispered.

"It's never really night here," Alice said softly back. "I used to paint half my room with glow-paint, but even that would fade after a few hours. These nightlights and candles drive me crazy. It's never dark. I miss the stars. I miss my house. I even miss my mother."

Carla had been killed when Nowhere was taken. One of the many casualties of that day.

Alice turned and took Flora in her arms. "What do you miss?"

"My father," Flora said. "Though he's been gone for years. My silkworms." She thought a minute, biting her lip before going on. "I miss Eddy," she said finally.

Alice, ever immune to jealousy, was not upset. "Etta's right here," she said. "We didn't lose her."

"We did," Flora said. "We lost him. I did, anyway. I love him, and he thinks I betrayed him."

Alice sighed. "Nobody can love Etta the way she wants to be loved. She wants too much. She wants to own somebody but tell them that they're free."

Eddy would hate hearing that.

"He's not himself lately."

Alice scoffed. "Of course she's not," she said, leaning into the pronoun. "She's pregnant."

Flora pulled back and looked at Alice, shocked. "What?"

Alice made a face and looked away. "I shouldn't have told you. I shouldn't tell anybody. But she needs to come to a decision, and she's making me very nervous by waiting this long."

Flora blinked and blinked again. She shook her head. "It's the Lion's, isn't it?"

Alice bit her lip. "I think so. If she was raped by anyone else, she didn't tell me that. I don't suppose it matters."

Flora thought hard, pushing herself past the places she kept out of her own memory, recalling Eddy helpless, chained, kept. "I don't think anyone else had access to him," Flora said. "Has to be."

"So she wants to kill it, because it's his. And she wants to keep it, because it's hers. And pretty soon it won't be up to her at all."

Flora had a sudden physical craving so strong that her abdominal muscles nearly cramped with it. Her arms ached as if they were not holding Alice, as if they had never held anything at all. Her chest tingled. She had wanted a child before, but never like this. She had felt a pull in her heart, a sympathy for lost children. She had taken care of the younger kids Archie had taken on, tried to teach them and protect them where she could. She had felt the normal human pull toward babies, taking communal responsibility for them and pleasure in their coos and cries.

But never had it roosted in her body with such force. If her belly had had hands, it would have snatched the unwanted child out of Eddy and put it into herself, without hesitation.

She laid her head on Alice's shoulder and said nothing.

"What are you brewing now?"

"That's the stuff," Alice whispered. "I'm brewing poison and death. That's the smell of the end of a pregnancy."

Flora sniffed the air. It was a little acid, like sour fruit. A little rotten, like wet fallen leaves. And yes, underneath it, there was the metallic smell of blood, the spill when it was all over and hope was gone.

"For Eddy?"

"She's not the only one."

Flora crept quietly out of the lab. She needed to think.

Dinner was subdued the next night. Flora answered questions about Shy for the mish, who had heard stories about it but had never gone themselves.

"Look, you really shouldn't plan to stop by there. I mean it. I don't think it's safe for you." She didn't mention the casual slavery of Shy, or

155

the execution of men. She still did not know what should be done about it, or what could be.

"No place is safe for you," Gabriel said, looking into Flora's eyes. "Yet you go."

Flora swallowed a mouthful of cornbread. "I don't go where I know for sure I'm not safe," she said in her low voice. "I do sometimes end up there by accident."

She looked over to Etta for her support. She often weighed in on subjects of raiding. Tonight, she was absent from conversation. She had barely touched her plate. She was staring at Alma.

"You can't eat her," Ina said next to her living child's ear.

"What?" Etta turned to her, her eyes wide.

Ina pointed her chin down and looked up at Etta sternly, her forehead a stack of wrinkles. "You can't eat Alma, so I don't know why you're looking at her right now. You can eat this pile of good food on your plate. That's what you need to be doing."

Etta looked down at her cold food and stabbed a fork into a serving of iron-dark greens. Her expression was sour, but she said nothing.

"I could live in a city of nothing but women," Ina said, looking down the table. "After this life I've had. Sounds like a great idea."

"Me too," said Kelda, smiling. "What a lucky life."

"Not me," Alice said. "I like having men around." She smiled at one of the young men who was eavesdropping from another table, and he blushed from his collar to his hairline before looking away.

Flora was looking at Etta. *How does it feel to know all the people closest to you want to go somewhere you couldn't be?*

She saw Etta flinch and put a hand to her belly.

Oh. Oh, shit.

Flora glanced from Alice to Kelda. They both looked away. They knew.

Flora looked again at Etta's untouched plate. Etta caught her staring and looked at her with sick, sunken eyes.

Ommun had a wealth of berries in the summer, and dessert saw everyone with their own small bowl. Flora watched Gabriel and Rei smear the red juice on their lips, laughing, staring at one another. She saw Kelda tip her bowl into her mouth and crush them all at once between her teeth. She saw Etta eat a small handful before passing the rest off to one of the catamites, who was doing the same trick with his lips, trying to get Gabriel's attention. Gabe pushed his long golden hair off his shoulders and ignored the boy. Rei looked up and smirked.

Etta was one of the first to get up. The people of Nowhere had a hard time adjusting to the rotating groups of boys and young men of the Leaf Society who served food and cleared plates. They typically stacked and gathered and began to clear their own places, and the boys would have to shuffle in and remind them to leave the dirty dishes where they lay. Flora saw Etta take advantage of this and go. She followed her out.

She was not headed toward the east-side quarters she shared with Kelda. She walked toward the library and pushed open the unlocked door. Flora slipped in behind her.

"You brought back a lot of new books," Etta said as Flora joined her in the darkened room. Her voice didn't echo; it was swallowed in the rows of shelves stuffed with pulp and paper.

"I certainly tried to. And I told the mish that there's plenty more to raid in Demons, and the city is abandoned."

"Do you ever think of going to one of those empty old-world cities and just starting over? Just build your own town, with your own rules?" Etta's face was invisible to Flora, but her tone sounded dreamy. Musing.

"You mean like the Lion?"

Flora felt Etta turn, felt the change in the air in the room. "No, not like the fucking Lion. Like the Unnamed."

"Oh. I never had thought of that, no. It's an awful lot of work to start from the ground up. And you've got to have people to do it with you. The first twenty years are probably hard, lonely labor."

"Sure," Etta said. "But then nobody can tell you who you are."

"Do you want to do that?"

Etta's breath hitched and she made a short grunting sound. "I don't know what I want to do."

"Are you sick?"

"No," Etta said much too quickly.

"You barely ate at dinner."

"What are you, my mother?" Another low grunt, almost long enough to be a groan.

Flora took a step toward the slight shape of Etta, the sound of her voice. "I'm someone who loves you. Same as always. Even though you tried to shoot me in the face." She smiled as though she could see her.

"I was out of my mind," Etta said. "I . . . had been through a lot. I'm glad my mother stopped me."

"Me too."

Flora put a hesitant hand on Etta's shoulder. Etta did not flinch.

"Really, are you okay? Do you need to go see Alice?"

Etta groaned for real this time. "No, Alice can't help me. It's happening."

"What's happening?" Flora smelled blood when she inhaled, unbidden and absent from the breath before it.

"The same thing that happened before." Etta doubled over and began to moan.

Flora managed to get Etta back to her own quarters with a minimum of people seeing them. She put a long, thin piece of silk beneath her right shoe and swept it along behind them as they walked slowly, cleaning up the trickle of blood coming off the back of Etta's right heel.

The room that Flora shared with Alice sometimes was empty; Alice was elsewhere. Flora helped Etta get out of her pants and shoes, but she would not take her shirt off. She lowered herself into the tub and sat there, looking dazed.

Flora had already used her allotment of power for the day, so she couldn't run the small electric coil that would have heated water for the tub.

"I could ask someone—"

"No," Etta told her, bearing down.

"Your mother—"

"Especially not her. Just sit with me, okay? Please just sit with me. It won't take long."

Flora sat on the rim of the tub. Etta reached up and took her hands. "Okay?"

Flora nodded.

Etta put her teeth together and bore down. She took long breaths, held them, and bore down again.

Flora saw sweat bead on Etta's forehead, despite the cold of the cast-iron bathtub beneath her. "It's okay," she whispered.

"I know. I know. I know. I know." Under Etta, a thick river of blood streamed toward the drain.

"What if you bleed to death?" Flora's eyes were wide as she watched the blood river widen and swirl around the drain.

"I won't," Etta said shortly, then grimaced again. "There it is. There it is."

She reached between her legs and pushed forward a shapeless, clotted mass. It was dark as liver and the size of her fist. It was life and it was death. She sagged backward in the tub. She dropped Flora's other hand.

"That's the worst of it. The rest is just bleeding."

"How do you know?"

"I've done this before," Etta said, not opening her eyes.

Flora did not want to look at the lump of flesh but found that she could look nowhere else. "What should we . . . what do we do?"

Etta sighed. "Fuck, I don't know. Take it out and bury it, I guess."

Flora was up and nodding, grateful to have something to do. She took one of Alice's precious jars, the glass without a chip and the lid in perfect shape. As she walked back into the room, the smell hit her in the face again.

It was the smell of the sea, from when she was a child. It was childbirth upside down: no milk and no tears. It was the smell of a pack of dogs in heat, yelping as they passed in the night.

Etta saw what she had and held out her hands for it. She pushed the lump into the jar and shut the lid, smearing bloody handprints all around the glass. Flora took it from her, hands shaking, and rinsed the outside in the cold water in her sink.

"You have to get cleaned up," Flora said. "Are you sure you don't want help?"

"I'm fine," Etta said in a ragged but forceful voice. She turned on the cold tap and began rinsing the bottom of the tub. Flora turned and left the room, carrying the jar.

Where do I put this until tomorrow? On the nightstand, where I can stare at it all night? Do I hide it in a drawer? Will he want to see it? What will it do while we dream? Did it ever have dreams of its own?

Flora looked up when Eddy emerged from the bathroom, naked from the waist down and shivering. He had bound himself, despite the pain he must be in and how tender his breasts must be. Flora saw the change all over him, the shift in his posture and the width of his stance. Even through the agony of labor, Eddy's presence was as clear as the sun breaking through clouds. In the midst of miscarriage, Flora could see the relief all over him. He was himself again, alone in his body, sovereign. She put the jar on the dresser and forgot about it. It no longer mattered. Eddy mattered, and she didn't want to leave him standing there, bleeding and cold. She wrapped Eddy in the clean sheets the people of Ommun had given her. His teeth clacked together as he shivered.

Flora looked into his red-rimmed eyes. "Eddy?"

"Yeah," he said at once. He nodded, swallowing. He looked back at her. "Yeah. Can you . . . I need . . . my moon cup. It's in my pack. Can you go get it?"

Flora nodded. "You need to lie down."

"Get that first." Eddy stood sagging in the doorway, bloodied but whole.

Flora went on feet that barely touched the floor. Kelda was reading in bed and started when Flora burst in without knocking.

"I need Eddy's bag."

"Why, what's wrong? Is she taking off? Is she leaving? Is she?" Kelda had stepped out of bed and Flora saw that she was naked, her muscular body oiled and completely shaved, like Eddy's.

"No, he's not leaving. I'm sorry, I can't tell you any more. Just trust me, okay? Where's the bag?"

Kelda went with wide eyes to the closet and brought out the dusty, careworn backpack. She handed it over.

Flora tried to smile at her. "Don't worry. You'll see him in the morning."

Kelda nodded and watched Flora go, shutting the door behind her.

Flora found Eddy curled up in her bed, tight as a pill bug, fast asleep. She put the bag on his side of the feather-stuffed mattress, where his hand would find it if he reached out. Under the blankets, Flora shored him up on both sides with a towel and a sheet, trying to contain the blood that would likely flow all night.

She lay rigid beside him, listening to him breathe. *He might develop fever. He might die. You can die of this. He might be very cold. I covered him up. Is he covered enough? Would he like to be held? I probably shouldn't. I don't know what he's feeling right now.*

She awakened from a thin sleep hours later, her hand on Eddy's shoulder.

"Don't touch me," he mumbled. She withdrew.

Sometime before dawn, he inched across the bed and curled against her back. They awoke together later, separate and whole, covered in Eddy's blood. Wordlessly, Flora got up and began to heat some water. Eddy did not move until she told him the tub was warm.

CHAPTER 20

The Book of Flora
Ommun, where the sun never rises and there is no weather
104N

The minute I saw Alma, I knew she was up to something.

Alma always dresses like a person who has no labor to perform, though that isn't true at all. She works constantly, in supervision and assignment of tasks. People seek her out daily for judgments and advice. Her word is the last in any dispute, and the people of Ommun trust her to literally speak for God Herself. I've seen her nursing two babies, obviously exhausted, pregnant, and listening patiently to a group of mish who wanted to know whether they could bring back someone who wanted to help farm sweet potatoes, but would only agree to live on the surface and not in the city below. I've seen her use reason and divine revelation in her own strange braid of leadership, making it nearly impossible to tell what is her own opinion and what is the word from their final authority.

She works hard, and maintaining that image is an obvious part of the work. She has to look larger than life so that they will believe in something larger than life. So every day, she wears one of her long, white, gauzy dresses. I've touched it—it's just woven cotton. My fingers itch sometimes for my old silk tools. I could make her something that would convince people that she is God, rather than just speaking for Her.

But tonight she was wearing her whitest, most otherworldly gown, with old-world threads of some shimmery golden stuff worked through it so that it caught the light when she moved. She had had someone dress her hair into intricate braids that piled on either side of her head, with loose escaped curls draped down in front of and behind her shoulders. No one in Ommun paints their face, but I think Alma has a secret stash because her lips looked berried and her eyelids seemed yellow-gold like she used crushed flower petals. Just looking at her tonight in her braids and her regal mien made me miss the horsewomen so much that my throat closed up.

But once I got past it all—her beauty and her power and being awe-struck by her—I realized that it's never just pageantry with someone like her. It's politics. I suppose the way we present ourselves always is, but for leaders it's even more important. I know before she says anything that she's got something to say.

It's the usual feeling when Alma says we all need to join her at her fireside. The people from Ommun are excited and everyone else is wary. But we go, and we sit and stand all around the room and wait. Alice sits beside me on cushions on the floor. I can see Eddy and Kelda, standing beside a column, half-hidden, across the room.

Alma stands before us, beaming. There's no fire lit; it's too warm this time of year. Instead, someone has filled the fireplace with tallow candles, and their glow lights up the translucent material of Alma's gown. She raises her hands for quiet.

"As you all know, I am expecting once again. Though it is tradition for us not to reveal who a seeder is until a child is born, I have received a revelation that this time, I may share that with you all early. My seeder was Neum."

She reaches a hand out to the short man. He rises, looking around the room with a shy smile. The women of Ommun take note.

Alice's voice is in my ear. "That's a reward."

"What?" I keep my voice low and try not to turn toward her too obviously.

She does the same, ducking her head a little to speak toward my ear alone.

"She can't know. I've heard she takes a different lover every night, and then just names a seeder that she's pleased with. She's naming him so that he can be put out for stud now, instead of in a couple of months. That's a reward. She's paying him for something."

Neum is beaming at the attention he's getting all over the room. I remember the last seeder she named—Shemnon, I think. He's young and very good looking, with a deep, muscular chest from working the lift most of his life. Neum is the opposite: a small, round man, bald on top. He fetches and carries for Alma—Eddy told me that Neum tended to him when he first washed up here.

Neum is the kind of man who needs this sort of boost in order to be considered at all for breeding—even in a place as lucky as Ommun. They have more women than most, but even still, many men are left out. The women choose the same men over and over, the proven ones and the ones they just want to be with.

The stir dies down and Neum sits. Alma's hands go to her belly.

"With great joy, I share with you that my child or children will not be the only ones to be born in the spring. I have been shown wondrous things by our Heavenly Mother. Revelation has been given to me that many of the women of Nowhere have returned from their trial in Estiel with their wombs quickened."

Silence in the room. Candles flicker and no one moves.

"And luckier still," Alma says, her smile never faltering, "one of the women from Jamestown, our own beautiful Sheba, has been blessed!"

Sheba doesn't move. I can't see her well, but from here her face looks a little swollen. She's early yet.

"Shit," Alice says. "I didn't know. I could have offered her some . . . help. Some care."

Alma's full lips press into a line. "I thought that you ladies would be moved by pride to share your good news with us. But I see that your meekness is great. I'll have to call you by name."

Silence still reigns. Some of the women in the room look around nervously.

Alma raises her hands again. "Sylvia. Bronwen. Jenn. And Sister Etta." She spreads her arms out to the congregation, motioning for them to stand and receive their due. No one moves or speaks for a long moment.

Finally, Bronwen stands. She's older, the Mother of a living child already. Gray is shot through her hair and she keeps a hand in the small of her back as if it pains her to stand. "Alma, I am pregnant. But I don't see why that's anyone's business but mine. I don't want to talk about it with the whole village. I'm seeing a Midwife."

At the word Midwife, *Sylvia stands up. "She is. It's between her and me. Can we drop this?"*

Alma is beaming. "Why wouldn't you want to share this glorious news? This is the day that the Mother hath made! We should all rejoice and be glad in it."

Sylvia weaves her fingers together and shoots a look at Eddy. "Alma, we were not, uh . . . seeded under joyful circumstances. This is a painful subject. And a private one."

"But if joy comes from pain, we should focus on the good in it," Alma explains. "And it's not a burden you must bear alone. We will come together, as a stake, to care for you and your children. They will come to the nursery and be loved by every woman in Ommun. They will be consecrated to us, so that every child knows the love of the entire stake. This is a gift."

Bronwen's brow knits up tight. "It isn't a gift. I paid for it. And I'll pay again, maybe with my life."

Alma scoffs. "No one has died in childbed in Ommun since before my time. We are blessed by our covenant."

"But those women were all born here," Sylvia says patiently. "Women still die giving birth in other places. They did in Nowhere. Janet died in Estiel, when she was in perfect health. Her girl died, too. There are pieces to this that you don't understand."

Ina, in a front row, bows her head, her hands going to her chest. I can see her shrinking.

It's the first time anyone has said Janet's name out loud, in front of so many people. I wasn't in the harem when she died. By the time I got back, she was a bloodstain and a name no one could say. There was no baby left behind, and I couldn't help but wonder if someone had smothered the child rather than let it grow up in captivity. The women of Nowhere are like that. Like Eddy. They might have done that, but I'll never know.

"But that is the past," Alma says impatiently. "You are part of us now. Your children will be born under the protection of Ommun."

I am staring at Eddy. Eddy, whose child has already died under the protection of Ommun. He's staring at the floor. Kelda puts an arm on his shoulder and I see him shrug it off.

Alma tries again. "We have been blessed. Sister Sylvia, I know it's not ideal circumstances, but you might never have had a child at all. Right? Midwives do not become Mothers among your people. The Law of Emma?"

"Emily," Sylvia says. "And I'm keeping to that law. I'm not pregnant."

Alma's eyes dart to Neum. Just for the briefest of moments, but it's there.

"But your moon blood has not come since you returned from Estiel. It's been four, almost five—"

"I was pregnant," Sylvia breaks in. "Now I'm not."

Jenn stands. She is far too thin, and her scalp shows through her hair. "I'm not pregnant anymore, either."

Lucy's mouth is open, pulling down at the corners. She's standing just behind Alma. "How . . . how is this possible? Both of them lost? How could Heavenly Mother allow this?"

Alice begins to rise beside me and I put my hand on her knee. "Don't," *I say, low and pleading.* "Please."

Alice stands as if she did not hear me. "We have ways of ending a pregnancy. To save the woman. I have learned it from old books and the Unnamed herself. I helped them do it."

There is a gasp that comes from everywhere at once. I see Lucy put her stone-white hand over her mouth. Eliza covers the eyes of the child in her lap, then thinks better of it and covers the kid's ears instead. The room ripples.

"You helped them do what?" *Alma's face is blotchy red, her serenity and composure gone.*

"End it," *Alice says simply and without malice.* "It was theirs to end."

"It was not." *Alma's voice hits like a slap in the face.* "It was NOT. Those children belonged to all of us. To all womankind. To Heavenly Mother. And you killed them."

"They were never alive," *Alice says patiently.* "They were never meant to be. They were pain made flesh."

"They were hope made flesh, you mean." *Alma advances toward Alice, quivering with rage now.* "You witch. You have committed a grievous sin."

"I'm not pregnant anymore, either," *Eddy calls from across the room.* "Alice helped me, too."

Alma's head whips toward him. "You. I might have expected this from you. You, all full of rebellion and ghosts. You have defied the will of Heavenly Mother at every turn. You're stiff-necked and disobedient." *She takes a few steps toward Eddy, and I can feel the deep unrest in the room. This could get ugly—very quickly.*

"We are not yours, Alma." *Alice is reaching for her, trying to form a connection.* "We weren't his and we aren't yours. We are our own. If we cannot decide what happens inside us, we are slaves. Do you allow men to rape here in Ommun?"

"No good man does that," *Alma says.*

"We have not been among good men. A man can force a woman to bear. A woman must protect herself any way she can. That's all we have done. Protect ourselves from pain and death and sorrow. Each woman must decide for herself."

"No," Alma says at once. "No. No. You have decided for us all. Life must renew itself. We must go on." She turns to Bronwen. "You did not do this terrible thing. This witchcraft. You must have known, in your heart, that it was wrong. This sorceress offered you a choice and still you chose the right." She walks toward Bronwen, hands outstretched. "Surely, you can tell these women that they chose wrong."

Bronwen folds her arms above her belly. "I can only choose for me, not for them. I don't want anyone choosing for me. Just like I don't appreciate you announcing to everyone that I'm pregnant. I am not a thing. I don't belong to anyone but myself."

"We must all belong to each other," Alma wails, her lower lip quivering. I can see the shine in her eyes—tears or merely excitement, I cannot tell. "This is how we remake the world. This is how we undo the Dying. We are the givers of life."

She's never had anyone argue with her like this. On something so fundamental. She doesn't even know where to start. Her desperation scares me. I have seen this kind of rage before, when someone disagrees with reality and cannot accept it. Nothing good comes of that.

"It's not a gift if you have to pay for it," Jenn says, echoing Bronwen. "It isn't magic. It's blood and terror. I understand it's always been easy for you, but that's not the same for everyone."

Ina stands and turns to face Alma. She's going to try to be kind, I can already tell. "I nearly died to have my living child. I've seen many women who did. Most of them take the child with them. Life is not always increased by birth. I just think . . . I think no one should have to face that. It's a hard decision, but no woman can be forced to bear. If we do that, we're no better than slavers."

"That's right," Alice calls out.

Alma ignores them, turning to the crowd and spreading her hands wide. "People of Ommun. These strangers are lost and we must show them the way. We must turn to our scripture, to find the truth. We must remember that Heavenly Mother knows each and every one of us as we are formed in the womb. Before we are born, she knows us. We are precious to her long before we are precious to anyone else." Milk leaks from her and stains her gown, as if she called it forth on purpose.

Gabe stands, holding one of the great thick books they study from. "Prophet? Isn't this thing spoken of in Numbers?"

"What?" Alma is not quite steady. Her loose curls are frizzing, rubbing against the skin of her neck. She focuses on Gabe like she could kill him with her eyes. "What is spoken of in Numbers?"

"When a woman is defiled, and a priest gives her bitter water that causes her womb to rot?" Gabe is breathing hard and swallowing fast. His voice starts strong and sure, but grows higher the longer he speaks. He is losing ground, quickly. "Isn't it saying that a woman can—"

"That is a story for the old world," Alma snaps. "Not this one, where children are so hard to come by."

They're always doing that, the folk in Ommun. Trying to argue from storybooks about how things are supposed to go. I hardly follow it. I've tried reading their books, but the language is so strange that I find it hard to understand. They're all raised on it, so they're no good at answering questions. They act as though we were all born knowing.

Alma takes a deep breath and smiles. It doesn't quite fit her face. She's still red all over and she can't stand still. Her wet gown clings to her breasts. "Sister Bronwen, I will be so pleased to welcome your child to our stake."

She walks back over to her big chair beside the fireplace and takes in the room. I try to imagine what we look like to her. I can see her struggling to decide what she's going to do now.

"The rest of you, I'm going to need to pray about. Heavenly Mother will show me the way between mercy and justice."

Her face closes like a fist. She turns to Mack, a young woman who is holding one of her babies. She tucks the child in her arms and rises to leave. That's it.

The people from Ommun rise to follow her, but the rest of us are left looking around at each other.

"She wouldn't kick us all out over this," I say to Alice.

"Maybe just the guilty ones. Witches like me." Alice is chewing her lip and staring at Eddy. He's making his way over to us through the streams of people. Kelda is, as always, in his wake.

Alice spits out her lip, red in a drawn-down crescent. "Why did you—"

Eddy cuts off Alice with a look. "I'm not waiting on any kind of decision from her. Has it occurred to you that she thinks we kill children? She might have us murdered in our sleep, to set an example. I'm leaving before dawn. Anyone who wants to come with me is welcome."

"You really shouldn't travel yet." Alice tries again. Eddy's look could freeze a river in June.

"Pass the word," Eddy says curtly.

We're good at whispering in the shadows, at least. We've been good at it since Estiel. But it doesn't matter. Because when Eddy goes to say goodbye to his mother, she's dead.

CHAPTER 21

The Bambritch Book
Fall, cold
144N

It was Ina's death, as much as anything, that made it so that we had to leave Ommun.

The fight was life and death. It was whether we lived or died, and how we did either. Eddy couldn't bear to live there, and after Ina, none of us wanted to die there.

Well, almost none of us.

Looking back at my book, I see that I wrote almost none of this. How could I have? It's a wonder I wrote anything down. We were always leaving somewhere and losing someone.

I remember hearing Eddy coming back down the hall too fast. I was up, packed, and ready to leave. Alice was with us. A handful of others from Nowhere wanted us to knock on their doors and we would leave together, greet the sunrise.

Eddy was still bleeding and exhausted but couldn't really sleep. Kelda told me later that he lay uneasy in their bed for about two hours before getting up and being done with it. It was still full dark, but I couldn't sleep, either. I was ready.

I wasn't ready at all.

Eddy didn't go back to Kelda. He came to Alice and me. He was as pale as I had ever seen him, almost gray. For a moment, I thought his bleeding had worsened and he was going to die.

His mouth opened, but no sound came out. His jaw worked a minute. Alice went to him and put her hands on his shoulders.

"Ina?" Alice asked.

"She's gone."

"She left without us?" I was so stupid when I was young.

He looked at me over Alice's shoulder. "She died."

He sank, knees buckling, the rod of his spine becoming a rope. Alice caught his sagging body on top of hers and shuffled them awkwardly toward the bed. Eddy lay down, his feet still on the floor.

"You're sure?"

"I know what dead looks like, Alice."

Alice bit her lips over and over. I remember the blood draining out of them and rushing back in the candlelight, pink and white and pink and white.

"I'll be back," she said. She went straight out the door.

I sat down with Eddy. I knew better than to touch him when he was upset. Alice might get away with that, but I never would.

He wasn't crying. He just looked to be in shock.

I didn't say anything. Everything that came to mind to say was a platitude, or irrelevant, or a question he couldn't possibly answer.

Alice came back, walking fast and talking faster. "Etta, I'm sorry. You were right, your mother is gone. We need to get to work now, okay? Okay?"

Eddy didn't move.

Alice went to her bags and started gathering supplies. When she came up empty on a few things, she headed for Ommun's storehouse. And, of course, that brought questions.

Some kid, might have been Ammon or Shemnon or Nephi—who knew anymore—followed Alice back, demanding to know what she wanted the supplies for. She wouldn't answer him. I met the kid at the door.

"Mother Ina has died. Now is not a good time for a lot of questions."

I don't remember his name, but I do remember how his face fell. So young.

"I am sorry, I didn't mean to upset any of you ladies. I will let the women know."

"Let them know what?"

"You'll need help," he said gently. "I want to make sure that you get it."

I went to Eddy, but he didn't want me. He didn't want anyone. He had thrown his arm over his eyes and would barely speak. So I went with Alice.

She was so incredibly tender with Ina's body that her smallest movements choked me with tears. She undressed the body and washed her all over, lovingly, with a basin of warm water. She mixed beeswax with dried herbs and rubbed down Ina's hands, face, chest, and feet. The color clung to her skin, making everything a little yellow. I helped her move and arrange the body, but I found myself shrinking from touching her.

I had seen death before. I had seen it come, red and violent. It came into children and adults and animals, and I had dealt it with my own hands. But Ina was so peaceful, the lines of her face relaxed and everything seemingly let go. I was spooked by it. I think she was the first person I ever knew who really and truly died of old age.

Alice dressed Ina in a clean shift and laid her hands on Ina's flat belly.

"Her baby belly should be here. Right here." Her face crumpled and red rushed to the center, burning beneath her freckles. "My mother should be here. The old women. Her friends."

She had not talked about Carla much since we'd left Estiel. Bronwen had seen Alice's mother cut down in the fight for Nowhere, and brought the truth of it to the daughter. There had been no time to mourn then.

Alice took her time now. She held Ina's hand, sobbing and sniffling. That was the moment when I realized that every new death in my life was like a new link in an old chain. They connect, and you run your hands over all the ones that come before it. It is never new. It is never just one death.

"My father died years ago. I was grown, but it still hurt me."

Alice looked up, wiping her eyes. "How?"

"Twister," I said. "You got those around Nowhere, right?"

She nodded. "There hasn't been a big one in a long time."

"This one wasn't that bad," I said. "Just bad enough. He was hit by a flying piece of wood, just straight to the temple. He didn't even look that different. But I was angry for a long time, that he didn't take shelter with me. When he told me to." I sighed. "At least there's no reason to be angry with her." I gestured to the body, cool but still pliant.

"Oh, I don't know. Etta gets mad at everything. She's probably thinking right now that our time in Estiel shortened Ina's natural life."

I looked down at my hands. "Maybe it did. For all of us."

Alice wiped her nose. "Well, if my mother was here," she said, suddenly resolute. She began to gather the sheet beneath Ina and untuck it from her mattress. "She'd tell me to be about my business. This kind of thing won't wait, and crying won't bring anything back."

I nodded and stood, trying to mirror her actions on my side of Ina's bed. Alice gathered the edges of the sheet together and began to sew a shroud.

When she was nearly done, she told me to go ask Eddy if he wanted to say goodbye.

I walked back to the room where I had left him, but he was gone.

Three young men—Aarons, Alma always called them—arrived and helped us carry her off the bed and out. When we came to the split in the main hall, we moved to head for the lift, but the boys took the body the other way.

"Hey," I said, pointing down the dim line toward the way out. "We need to head up."

One of them, a blond, shook his head at me. "We have to take her to the mourning room. Alma is waiting."

"Alma? What does she have to do with this?"

"She performs funerals, as Prophet."

They were off again without a word, as if nothing we could say would change their plans. As if she were theirs.

I had never seen the mourning room before. It was clearly shut up and used for nothing else. The Leaf boys were still dusting when we got there. Alma was puffy-faced, not ready to be awake and yet serving. She greeted the body with a sad smile.

"Dear Sister Ina. She lived a long and fruitful life. As a Mother, first of all. She fulfilled her purpose." She gestured to a pine box on a low table. The wood was raw, but old. She saw us staring.

"Our wise founders, those who built Ommun, provided for us in every way they could. There are enough coffins in one of the lower storage levels to last us many generations. I had this one brought up for her."

Alma had a way of stating the facts as if everything that occurred was a gift especially from her.

"We need to pass the word," Alice told her urgently. "Everyone from Nowhere will want to say goodbye."

"The news has already gone out to all the people of Ommun," Alma said smoothly. "We will all be part of her funeral."

This was clearly a well-rehearsed set of steps. Fresh wildflowers appeared at once and went into built-in vases all around the white room, along with fresh water. A long table was set with milk and juice and bread. People began to join us in the room, sleepy and stunned. Some were still in their pajamas. The children did not appear.

Tommy was hot-eyed and upset, going straight to Alice. "Where's Etta?"

Alice shook her head, looking around. "I don't know. She discovered the body, and then I lost track of her."

The room began to fill with the low, murmuring sound of everyone passing the news and catching up. Chairs scraped against the floor. Alma, ever the veteran reader of the room, began to gather herself.

"Brothers and Sisters," she began. "We come together today to celebrate the life of one of our own. Mother Ina was a recent addition to our stake, one of the many refugees from Nowhere and the destruction of Estiel. She was nonetheless one of our own Sisters, and we loved her as we love any Mother of a living child."

Alice caught Bronwen's eye across the room. Tommy glanced between them both. They had all caught it: Alma was adopting language from Nowhere to describe Ina's life.

"Ina became a Mother late in her life, despite wanting and trying for many years to have a child. She knew that it was her destiny and her highest good to bring another life into this world. She valued that life above all others, even risking her own to bring Sister Etta into this world."

"You didn't know her." The voice came from the back of the room. People turned.

There stood Eddy, his pack on his shoulder like he was already on his way out the door. He was. We all were.

He carried in his hands Ina's wooden baby belly. He had found it in one of Ommun's laundries, discarded with the unsalvageable clothes some of them had worn in from Estiel. No one in Ommun had known what it meant, and so it had not made its way back to its rightful owner.

Until now.

He came up the aisle, laying his bag beside Alice as he went. He was dressed in all dark clothes, a dark man in that white room. It was as if all our eyes lent him weight, making him more than what he was. He took on gravity as he came up and stood before Alma.

"This isn't your story," he said to her beatific face. "It never was, but that didn't stop you from telling it."

Alma didn't flinch. "This is my place," she said. "I lead Ommun. I speak to Heavenly Mother, and she speaks to me. You need to sit down."

Instead, Eddy turned around to face us.

"I won't be told how to live. And I won't be told how to die, either. Most of all, I'm not going to stand and hear my mother's fucking life story from someone who barely knew her."

Alma was nearly blocked by Eddy's body, so she took a step to the side to continue addressing us. "Sister Etta, you are prostrate with grief. You can feel your sorrow without sharpening it to hurt those around you."

Eddy did not turn to look at her. "I am here to feel my sorrow, and yours. I am here to say goodbye to my mother. I am here to mourn the others who should be with us right now, who knew her even longer than I did, those who were lost in Nowhere and Estiel."

Alma opened her mouth as if to speak, but Eddy cut her off.

"Ina, daughter of Maude, had not always wanted to be a Mother. She was glad that it happened, but she was other things, too. She was trained as a Midwife and would have been one her whole life if not for the Law of Emily."

Heads nodded around the room.

"She was a teacher. She taught scribes to copy books, and then taught them how to write their own. She was a fierce fighter for the history of Nowhere, and wanted to make sure that it included everyone."

Eddy was catching his rhythm now. He moved his feet farther apart. He looked up from the corpse.

"She was funny. Smart. Wicked. She would always call people on their shit. Me, most of all. She had one of the biggest Hives in Nowhere. She lived in the House of Mothers for as long as she could stand it, but they drove her crazy. When she had her own house, there were maybe thirty men in and out of there? Forty? All ages, all kinds. She was always with somebody. She was never lonely, but she belonged only to herself.

"She was a good Mother to me. Good woman, good Mother. She took care of me, made sure I was able to stand on my own and find myself. When I got my first blood, she led me through the strangeness of it. When I told her I wanted to be a raider, she accepted it. She gave me my first gun, the same gun I carry now, the same gun that had belonged to the Unnamed.

"There were parts of herself she never shared with me. I don't know much about her life before I came. Her old friends, Carla, Ash, and Shannon, are gone now. Only the youngest of her Hive are still with us. Parts of her will always be a mystery to me, but maybe that's how it's meant to be. She's not mine. She never belonged to anyone but herself."

Alma finally got the bit back between her teeth and stepped down off the dais to stand beside Eddy.

"She was all of ours," she broke in smoothly. "She belonged to everyone around her, as part of a community. As each of us does. That's why I have decided to decree that the next child born in Ommun will bear her name. The next Ina—"

"Will you fucking stop?" Eddy turned and spoke straight into Alma's face. For once, Alma actually flinched.

"Stop. Stop trying to give and take names. Stop trying to connect things so that life makes sense. Stop trying to tie everything together where it doesn't fit. If the child doesn't come out of you, you're not naming it."

Lucy stood up, quivering with rage. "The Prophet names and blesses every child. That's her right, and you need to respect it. Our names come straight from Heavenly Mother. This is an honor she's doing for Ina, just as she did for you. You should be grateful. You people are never grateful."

"Sister Lucy, your faith shines right through you." Alma smiled.

"No," Bronwen said, rising out of her seat. "Unless someone is holding on to a real big secret, the next child born here will be mine. I've already picked a name. I don't want to be told who my child will be."

"But Sister Bronwen," Alma said, coming forward. "Remember when I blessed your child? I laid my hands on you and gave my matriarchal blessing. Told you all that would come to pass."

Bronwen shrank a little, putting her hands over her belly. "What are you saying?"

"Blessings come to those who obey," Alma said. It wasn't quite a threat. Not really.

"And blessings can be taken away, right?" Eddy was blazing all over. "At your pleasure. By your decision. Based on what you think."

Alma looked him up and down. "You do this to yourself. You have no faith. Your body is corrupt. Haunted."

Eddy gave a small, mirthless laugh. He stepped forward one more time. He laid the wooden belly against his dead mother's body.

"I know exactly who I am. I won myself, in fight after fight. On the road. In Nowhere. In Estiel. With every lost girl I brought home. Every time I refused to be someone I'm not. I'm sorry I never told my mother my name. I waited too long. But I am not waiting another minute."

He looked up over his mother's body and addressed everyone in the room. His eyes were dry.

"My name is Eddy. I am the living child of my mother, Ina, who lies dead here today. I was trained as a raider by Errol and Ricardo, my good friends. I killed the Lion of Estiel. I have saved girls and women all my life. I have fought slavers wherever I have met them. I have loved only women in my life, and I will keep right on doing that. I am leaving

Ommun today, because I will not be told how to live, love, or die. I will take as many with me as will go."

His words rang out in the room like music. For a moment, no one spoke.

"I named a daughter after you," Alma spat, red in the face.

"You named your daughter after someone who doesn't exist anymore."

Eddy turned his back to her and slipped his arms beneath his mother's shroud. He lifted her body without a struggle.

Alice picked up Eddy's pack and shouldered it. We went back to gather our things. Bronwen met us there.

"I can't go," she said with tears in her eyes. "I understand why you're leaving, but I just can't. Not while I'm facing childbirth. It's so dangerous already. I—"

"It's alright," Alice told her. "You'll be safer here. I know why you're staying. I get it." She patted the other woman's cheek. "I hope it goes well for you."

Bronwen wiped her eyes. "I know what I'm giving up. Come back someday, if you can. You know she'll let you come back. If you just . . . you know."

"I know," I told her.

The rush was on. Little by little, the people who were going to follow us gathered in the hallway, milling and talking. They had all packed. Not everyone had boots, which I immediately began to worry about.

And then I asked the question nobody had put into words yet.

"Where are we going to go?"

"Back to Nowhere." Tommy spoke up like there had never been a question at all. "That's our home. We can rebuild. We can replant the fields. Where else would we go?"

I didn't know. It made sense that they all planned for that, but they had so much work ahead of them. There was almost nothing left of Nowhere.

"We won't be far," Sylvia said. "I can come back in a year or two and see if Bronwen wants to come home. Or . . . anyone." She glanced around, not sure who was with us and who wasn't.

That was when I spotted Rei and Gabe.

Gabe ducked his head, tucking a loose lock of his long hair back into the braid at his neck. "I don't know who to ask," he said. "But we want to come along. Ett—uh, Eddy said anyone who wanted to follow. That's us." He shot a look over at Tommy, and I got it.

"You two are coming together," I said, nodding to Rei.

Gabe nodded, and Rei reached over and took his hand. "We're companions. Always have been."

I nodded back. Nowhere was not mine to give or withhold, but I knew that Eddy would welcome them.

Alice stepped up, and in that moment I believed she would lead Nowhere. "Of course you are coming together." She raised her voice a little, but kept her gaze on the two men. "For a long time, it was hard in Nowhere for people like you . . . and me. People who weren't breeders. But we've seen where that kind of thinking leads. And it's time to let people be who they are."

Kelda appeared with her leather bag and leather clothes just in time for that. I saw her fix her bow on her shoulder and smile a little.

I knew, even then, Alice would have to say it over and over, everywhere she went. This stuff is complicated. And people forget. And people make sacrifices so that children will be born. But we all believed her in that moment. It was real, and Nowhere became somewhere new before any ground was broken.

We waited for Eddy, but he didn't come to us. So we headed to the lift.

Alma was there, arms crossed over her leaking breasts, face like a storm cloud in red. She is still the most beautiful woman I've ever seen, but it was hard to remember that when she was so angry.

"I forbid you to leave," she said, her voice ringing mightily through the halls. "You were promised to us. All of you."

Bronwen had followed to see us off. She approached the Prophet, her face soft, her hand laid against her belly.

"Don't make it any harder for them," she said. "Let's have peace between our people."

"We are one people," Alma insisted. "We can't afford to be stiff-necked about this." I could see that beneath her exhortations, she was terrified. Maybe she had never lost people like that before. Maybe we really were the first break in her peace. She just didn't know how to take this break, and I felt sorry for her. She stood there streaming milk, thinking she could mother us all forever.

But she could not, and it was time.

Alice shook her head. "No, Alma. We're going. You can't stop us."

Alma held up one hand, pointing her out. "You may go. You're a witch. You kill children. You led these people astray. But no one else."

Tommy came forward, with Rei and Gabe behind him. Alma's eyes widened. "If we didn't believe that when the Lion said it, what makes you think we'd believe you?" Tommy's voice was clear and carried across the crowd.

Alma's face twisted from rage to sorrow and back again. Betrayal was as clear on her face as if we had sold her to a passing slaver. "Brother Rei. Brother Gabe. How can you leave us? What of your calling? Your mish?"

They couldn't look at her. They looked anywhere else.

Alma grew redder still. "I won't have this. I won't order the Leaf to raise the lift. You will not leave."

"Then we'll make the climb," Kelda said, tiredly. "We'd better get started."

The only other way out of Ommun was a long climb, hand over hand, up a ladder in a steep tunnel to the surface. I looked around, making sure everyone who was with us could make it. We were in good shape. I decided we could.

It took much longer than any of us thought. A few minutes in the lift translated to hours on the metal rungs. My arms got tired first, the muscles in my biceps and shoulders shuddering and seizing. I had to loop my arms through the rungs and hang there, trying to stretch them out and bring them back around. There was nowhere to really rest. It was agonizing within the first hour.

Soon thereafter, my thighs began to quiver, the breadth of muscle there taxed beyond anything I had ever asked of my body. My calves cramped twice and I had to push my toes up against the ladder, hanging my body weight against it to stretch them out. This put strain on my ankles, which ached fiercely. By the time I could see the hatch up top, my feet felt like something had taken bites out of their soles. My hands were raw and red, the creases looking like cuts.

And isn't escape always like that? Isn't it always something you carry on your body, something that makes it impossible to pretend it wasn't real? It wasn't like Estiel, but it was an escape.

When we finally made it to the surface, we could still hear Alma shouting at us up the tube. We couldn't make out her words through the echo. She was just a booming bunch of nonsense coming up from below.

That was the last time I saw Ommun.

Eddy was already on the ground. He had carried his mother's body the whole way up, somehow. Maybe he strapped her to his back. While we had made our sorry goodbyes, he had built her a funeral pyre and laid her tenderly upon it. Her wooden baby belly made a mound over her shroud, and Eddy laid his hand on it for one last moment. He drummed his fingers the way she used to do, making the little hollow tap-tap sound like a drum from the emptiness within.

I wondered if I would ever see another woman wear that symbol; if anywhere would ever be like Nowhere again. Almost free. All those women living somewhere that they were so close to free.

We stood with him as the sun finally pulled itself from the horizon. He struck flint to steel and Ina freed herself, too.

CHAPTER 22

The Book of Flora
Nowhere
Fall, in ash and ruin
104N

We're leaving Nowhere tomorrow. We're headed after Errol and Ricardo.
Eventually, we'll go my way and toward the Midwife's home, way out west
somewhere in the unknown.

There really is nothing here. The Paws made sure of that. There are
two structures standing, and both are badly burned. One of them used
to be the House of Mothers. The boys have decided to settle there, until
they can build up something better. They have a moon or two before it's
too cold or too wet.

The tunnels are still in good shape, though moles and every manner of
creeping thing have moved into them. The land takes things back so fast.
There's bear shit out near where they used to bake bread. That made us all
pretty nervous.

The Book of Flora

It's hard to be back here for me, so I can't even imagine what it's like for everyone else. Eddy is barely speaking, but what else is new? Alice, on the other hand, is falling apart.

She started crying at the gates and hasn't stopped. She made her way out to her old place and cried over her garden, her greenhouse, her breezy little home that she loved so much. I loved it too, but I couldn't take up her time or space with my small grief when hers is so large it's swallowing her whole. I didn't know whether to leave her alone there, but I couldn't join her when she lay down in the dirt and cried over her plants.

"I raised them from seeds. From cuttings. Some of them were very rare. This is years of work. My whole life, really. I never, never should have left. I don't know what I was thinking." *She laid her face in the charred stems and sobbed.*

I know what she'd been thinking. I know what we'd been trying to do. I guess none of it seems like it was worth it now. Where am I supposed to go with that? Does she blame me for it? It was she who talked me into going to the Lion, not the other way around.

It didn't save us. It probably just hastened the inevitable.

Tommy tells me the baths are gone, but there's a basement to that building that may be salvageable.

"It's all steel and tile. Nothing to burn. It stinks, and it's full of ashes and charred timbers. But I think we can clean it out, and start the pump up again. There's still water in the cisterns, and we can haul up more from the creek if it runs out before the rains. With nobody here to use it, though, we should be all set."

He stands with his hands on his hips, looking around.

"Are you okay, being back?"

He squints at me. "I don't know. Not really. But I'd rather be here than in Ommun."

As if they heard their names, Gabe and Rei appear. Have I ever seen one of them without the other? Anyway, they're obvious now. All over each other, always hand in hand. I guess they've been waiting a long time to do that. Tommy gives them a lot of sidelong looks. I wonder how that's going to go, when it's just them.

How does it always go? Someone gets frozen out. Eddy curls up against Kelda's back at night, and Alice curls up against his.

I've been cold before.

I don't want to stay here, but I don't know about going out on my own. No horses. No trucks. Nobody to walk with me. If they stay, I stay.

I don't know what I want. Yes, I do. I know exactly what I want, but I can't let myself want it. Not when it hurts like this.

I'll go where Eddy goes, for as long as he'll let me. I'd have taken care of his baby, if he had wanted me to. I'd never have told him he had to birth it, but he could have left it with me forever, and it would have been my own.

What do you call it when you wish you could take someone else's problem? Not only to help them, but to help yourself. I don't think there is such a word.

We've been here six days and we have an accord, as Alma would say.

Eddy finally starts to talk. He says, "I'm going east. I'm going to follow Errol and Ricardo's route, the two men who taught me to be a raider. They gave me their map. They had seen so much more of this world than I have. I have to see if there's anyone out there. Going to live like a raider and travel every day. Anyone who wants to follow me needs to keep up."

I know he wants Kelda and Alice to follow, but I don't care. I stand right up. "I'm coming."

Eddy nods. Not going to give me any more than that, I guess.

Alice doesn't stand, but sighs. "I'm going where you go. It's too sad here. I'd rather try something new than deal with all that's lost here." She wipes her nose.

Kelda looks at her shoes. "I don't know if I can leave here," she says.

Eddy nods at that, too. "It's okay, Kelda. I can understand . . ."

He looks away, shifting his weight from one hip to the other.

"I don't trust what's out there," Kelda says, and her voice quivers. "I want to go where you go, but leaving home has not led me to good places. I . . . I want to know if there's anyone left in Womanhattan. I might . . . I might go back to Ommun."

Eddy sets his jaw. I can tell he hates that idea, but he doesn't want to say it.

Gabe says it for him. "There's nothing back there for people like us. Just a more comfortable cage. I'll take you to Womanhattan—I know the way. But don't do that. Don't give up who you are for a soft bed."

Kelda's whole heart is always on her face. She can't help it. She looks at Gabe now with a child's trust, the way she looks at Eddy. "Thank you," she says.

Tommy half smiles at Eddy. "You know I'm staying," he says. "I wish I could set you on the road freshly shaved, like you like. But my tools are gone."

Eddy smiles back. "I'll come back with new tools. Sharp and rust-free. You'll see."

Tommy holds out his arms and Eddy goes to him. They have an easy intimacy; Tommy never asks for anything, and Eddy never assumes the worst in him. I'm sorry that they're going to lose each other.

All we do is lose. I badly want to have someone in my life whom I never have to lose. Never have to say goodbye to and mean it. Never have to take one last look, not knowing whether it really is the last.

Is that even possible? It isn't. We're all going to leave and die. But does it always have to be so soon?

CHAPTER 23

ON THE ROAD

Every day, Eddy would carefully lay out Errol and Ricardo's maps. He would trace his finger along the routes, murmuring to himself about where he had already been. Sometimes, Alice could get him talking about the two men who had trained him when he was young.

Errol was the quiet one, the good planner. He saw the road ahead and knew exactly what was needed, what they would have to pack and what they could find along the way. Errol was never caught unprepared.

Ricardo, Eddy laughed about constantly. The adventurer. The trickster. He was useless until there was a crisis, and then he was the best man you could have along. And there was always a crisis, eventually.

Eddy had not seen them since he was a young man, but they were with him in spirit every time he set foot on the road, every time he checked his map.

The weather had become unbearably muggy, and they had taken to sheltering during the hottest part of the day, doing their traveling in the early morning and evening.

They camped along a crumbling old-world road, spread out from one another and testy. Alice was scowling over Eddy's shoulder, looking down at his marked-up map. "Why count places you've already been?"

Eddy shrugged. "If they were there when I was in town, I'd know it. Besides, they told me where they were headed."

"And where is that?" Alice laid her head to the side, against her own shoulder. The heavy air had frizzed her curls, making her look harried and irrational. But she wouldn't let Flora braid it, or even put it up. It just grew and grew until she was a blonde shrub. She finger-combed it when she bathed, which was not often.

Eddy ran his finger along the coastline between the Republic of Charles and Niyok. "Somewhere here."

Alice rolled her eyes. "Don't be ridiculous. That's too much territory. How would you have any idea how to find them, if they're even still out there?"

Eddy laid his palm flat against the soft paper, trying to get a hold of himself. "Because they have signs that they left," he said through his teeth. "They taught me."

"Have you been leaving signs?" Alice looked around, her palms turned up to the rotting ceiling of the old-world building that shaded them. "Because I haven't noticed you leaving any."

Eddy looked away. "I don't want to be tracked," he said.

"Exactly," Alice said, stalking off. "You don't have a plan. We left Ommun like you had a plan. We left Nowhere like you had a plan. You're just doing what you always do: raiding until you find an excuse to stop. Why? What is the point?"

Flora was sitting with her back against the spongy wall, wrists crossed over her drawn-up knees. "What's the point of anything we do, Alice? Why did you come along in the first place? You could have stayed anywhere you wanted, with your skills."

Alice swallowed. "Do you have any water left?"

What water they had gathered was swarming with bugs. It all had to be boiled and filtered, and the work was constant. Still, Flora offered her canteen without protest. Alice took it from her outstretched hand and drank without sparing. She looked down at the empty bottle when she had finished.

"I don't know. I wanted something else. I thought we were on our way toward something." Alice licked her lips.

"We are," Flora said. "We just don't know what it is."

The air was too heavy to take in and push out fast enough to fight. Limp as a rag, Alice sank beside Flora and sat with her back to the wall. It was too hot to touch one another.

"I just hate that she always acts like she knows what she's doing," she said in an undertone to Flora.

"He," Flora said back, insistently.

Alice looked away.

When night was falling and they should have been on their way, Eddy made no move to marshal them. Flora went out at twilight and wove a basket of reeds with the skill of a weaver. She pushed the basket into a narrow space between stones in a stream and waited. She did not have to wait long. She came back with a half dozen shiny silver fish, built a fire, and began to roast them.

Alice said nothing but brought her wild mustard seed and precious salt to season them with. She dug from her pack a small sack of flour and mixed it with water and salt. She baked them flat, unleavened bread on a stone she pulled close to the fire. Eddy came to the smell of the food and looked them both over.

"This is much better than being on my own," he said, smiling. "I'm glad you're both with me."

Flora grinned up at him. It had been a long time since he had said anything to make her feel as though her existence was anything but an inconvenience to him.

The roof was rotten enough that Flora built the fire inside, positioning it below a hole that she thought would vent the room. The three of them clustered around it, passing tin plates and hot bread and the fish, sharing and looking one another in the eye for the first time in a long time.

Flora smiled as she watched the other two eat. It always pleased her to see someone happy with what she had made. She used to love clothing people, seeing them draped in her silk, delighting in the feel of it on their skin and the way it was like nothing else. Worm-wool, Eddy had called it. Feeding people was not so different from that. She gave them something that they could use, something that made them happy. She was always weaving the threads together, and sometimes it brought the pieces of her heart closer to one another. Sometimes she could feel it starting to heal itself.

This must be what mothering is like, she thought to herself. *Always giving like this. Thinking of their needs. Showing them the world, because it's always going to be new.*

But it was Eddy who had shown her the newness of the world. It was Eddy who had taken her into the cave, away from Jeff City, back into a life on the road that she had nearly forgotten. It was Alice who had shown her the hips on a rosebush, or the seeds in a pod on the roadside, or the bark on a tree that would cure a headache.

So we are all Mother to one another, she mused. The fish in her mouth had a hot, crisp skin that was much improved by Alice's share of her precious spices. *I suppose we are father as well.* But that made her think of her own father, and Archie, and her mouth puckered.

I cannot say that I was made wrong or raised wrong, she thought, trying to weave the threads of past and present. *Only that I was made. So if I were to mother someone, could I do better? Could I keep any child safe? Surely I could do better than was done to me.*

But I have had almost no example. Except moments like these.

She thought of Ina while she watched Eddy eat. *Ina might not have known Eddy perfectly, or understood him. But she loved him. He came into the world knowing he was wanted and would not be sold. Maybe that's enough.*

Alice put a bite of hot bread into Eddy's mouth and he smiled. The two of them seemed very close together all of a sudden. Alice smiled at Flora over Eddy's shoulder.

I was not wanted, and I was sold. And yet I am myself, Flora thought with a sudden stab of jealous need. *And I may have to sleep out in the grass tonight, damn it.*

The space was wide, but there was no division in it for privacy. Flora ate faster, already planning how she would slip away. She stood up, gathering her tin plate and fish bones, pivoting toward the door.

Alice reached out and caught her hand. Alice's gleaming eyes stared up at her, enormous in the gloom and framed by her mane of untamed hair. "Hey," she said. "Don't go."

Flora slid into Alice's arms almost helplessly, melting into the gut-clench of being wanted and suddenly allowed to want. Alice kissed her, and Flora moaned against her lips, unable to stop herself. Alice turned to kiss Eddy, and Flora dropped her mouth to Alice's freckled neck, moving her hair away and bringing her teeth against Alice's skin.

Eddy was not relaxed, not yet. Flora could feel his tension on the other side of the wall of Alice's body. Still, he was incapable of resisting Alice.

Who could say no to that, Flora wondered as she saw Eddy's long fingers spread over Alice's breasts to squeeze them through her cotton Ommun-made gown.

"That's it," Alice sighed. "That's exactly what I want."

Alice got what she wanted, over and over. Eddy and Flora worked carefully around one another, pleasuring Alice and bringing forth her laughing, gasping climaxes in a torrent that never seemed to stop.

Alice took a minute to catch her breath and push her abundant curly hair off her forehead before rolling toward Eddy. "Alright, then, now you."

Flora froze, unsure of what she should do. Curled against Alice's back, she merely watched.

But Eddy did not want this. Alice tried to slip her hands beneath Eddy's tight binder, but he gently and implacably pushed her away. She smirked and moved her hands to undo his trousers, but he stopped her there as well.

"It's okay," Alice breathed. "You're safe here. All that's passed. It's just us."

Eddy wouldn't speak. He was trembling, growing smaller. Flora saw him receding, saw herself reflected in his dark eyes. She knew with the instinct of a thousand assignations that he was not able to say what he wanted. It was not her job to divine it, but she knew she could. She knew.

She reached over Alice's body to touch Eddy gently on his still-clothed hip. "Lie back?"

Eddy looked at her. What she saw there was some noxious cocktail of fear and desire, and it almost felt like home to her.

"I know what you need," she said in her most soothing voice. "It's okay."

Eddy did lie back, slowly. Flora put her mouth to Alice's ear. "Tell him you're going to straddle his cock. Ask him if that's alright."

Alice turned to look at her.

Please don't say anything, Flora begged silently. *Please just try to get this.*

Alice smiled and lifted a shoulder, then turned to Eddy. "Sweet Eddy, can I straddle your cock?"

Something flashed in Eddy's face, some combination of shock and recognition as if he had seen something he had only dreamed was real. "Yes," he breathed, almost involuntarily. "Yes, you can."

Alice was fully nude, having stripped off every stitch in her long moment of doubled adoration. Gracefully, she came up on her knees and split herself across Eddy's lap. Eddy drew his knees up and Alice settled down, root to root, exactly where she was supposed to be.

Flora heard her sigh as she slid down Eddy's cock and knew she could do this. This wasn't new to her, after all. Alice began to ride and Eddy's hands came automatically to her hips, beginning the push and pull that created the delicious friction of this act. Flora came up on her knees behind Alice, biting and sucking at the back of her neck, reaching around to cup and squeeze at her freckled breasts.

"Just like that," she breathed in Alice's ear. "Can't you see what you're doing to him? That's it. That's my girl."

Alice's breath hitched in her throat as Eddy thrust upward beneath her, bouncing her whole body with his fucking.

"Tell him," Flora said, sliding her gaze over Alice's pale shoulder and locking eyes with Eddy at last. There he was. Right there. "Tell him how good his cock feels inside you. Tell him how beautiful he is. Tell him he should come inside you and be part of you, forever. Lose himself."

Eddy gazed back at Flora with an intensity she found she could barely stand. Alice brought one hand down to her own clit and worked it quickly, sharply, rocking with Eddy as he worked himself into a fever. With the other, she reached behind her and pawed her way through Flora's silks. Flora groaned as Alice's fingers found her, slick and rampant, and slid right in.

It was all of them at once. It was the storm so near that the lightning and thunder and rain all crash into one another in the same instant. They howled together like a pack of wolves, their heads tilted up toward the moon. Their breath became a single hot rush, their sweat a single salty river.

"We are so lucky," Alice whispered, collapsing onto Eddy's chest. "This is something only women can do."

Flora and Eddy stared at one another as only women can do. They shared this moment, not arguing with Alice about what they really were. Eddy reached out his hand and their fingers twined together, locked in the perfect understanding that only lovers can share. He sank his other hand into the chaos of Alice's hair and sighed.

CHAPTER 24

The Book of Flora
On the road
Cooling, winter coming
104N

We've been on the road for months now. I keep reading the Midwife whenever we're at rest and the three of us aren't fucking. So much of her story is just her and the road. She was alone so much of the time. I can't imagine her heartbreak every time she thought she had someone and had to lose them. How could she stand it?

We travel south and it gets more humid and more desolate. We haven't seen anyone in over a moon, but we've avoided anything that looked like it was once a city.

Eddy pores over his map and makes notes. He doesn't write. Alice collects plants, takes cuttings, gathers up what she can. Eddy and I hunt and we eat. There are deer everywhere. Muskrats. Geese. Wild horses and cattle, now and again. We've heard rock cats in the night and huddled away from their awful screams. We've been lucky. I hope we stay that way. I think of the horses Eddy and I lost to the wolves. I'll never forget the sound of their teeth scraping the bones.

Alice tries to talk to Eddy, but she goes about it all wrong. How is it that they've known each other all their lives and she can't read him at all? Alice, he doesn't want to talk about Estiel. Ever. He doesn't want to talk about Ina. He barely wants to talk about Nowhere. His whole body says No whenever she starts. Alice, my darling, he really doesn't want to talk about being pregnant. That happened to somebody else.

And if it had happened to me? I'll never know what that's like. I wonder if I could stand it. If I could get pregnant the way she did and endure it, bring a child into this world knowing it was conceived in horror and might mean the death of me? Could I stand any of that? I have accustomed myself to letting someone else have the use of my body; surely a child inside can't be much worse.

I'm not jealous, and I try not to measure anything I have against any other woman's body. But I do wonder what it is like to live with that possibility. I imagine there is good and bad to it.

We're going to reach the sea soon. We've all started to smell it, but I can feel it. There's almost nothing left around here that will tell us where we are. Signs are overgrown and rusted and faded beyond all recognition. There's hardly a road, and we've been on foot. Eddy reads the stars and says we're headed east and south.

And still Alice doesn't let up. She wants to know, would Eddy ever want to have a child? What would he name it? Would he want a kid to grow up and be like him? I try to jump in and change the subject, or answer for myself. But she won't let it go. Maybe she wants something badly herself and can't say it. Maybe she's thinking of all the people back in Ommun who will or won't have a child come next spring.

I think about Eliza miscarrying back in Ommun and having to share her news with Alma, who always seemed pregnant or nursing or both. How differently that goes, depending on what you wanted. Maybe wanting is the real mistake.

Two moons on the road and we're headed into the city called Vana. I remember it, a little. Vana's signs are new, painted in white and blue, and the road is in good shape. We catch a truck headed for the fish market and ride behind an old man named Darius. He seems a little too eager to give us a lift, and would not accept a trade. But I'm so glad to be off my feet and bouncing over this road I can't care about it. I sit between Alice and Eddy to keep them from talking, but I needn't have bothered. The roar of the truck drowns us out. I take my pack off my shoulders and Alice rubs the sore spots for me. Eddy doesn't take his off. He never does.

CHAPTER 25

VANA

The driver dropped them on the south side of town, and they began to walk toward smoke up ahead. He didn't say much to them as he sped away, and they weren't sure why he had stopped there. He kept driving in the same direction they had been headed.

"Vana is a slave-trading city," Flora told them. "I've been there more times than I can count."

"It's not marked on the map," Eddy said again, tapping his finger on the little dot on the coast. "Maybe it used to be a slaver city, but it isn't anymore."

Flora shrugged as they walked on. "The road looks good and the signs look new. There will be some kind of trade there."

Alice jogged ahead, spotting a plant along the path that caught her interest. "I'm excited to be headed into another town," she said. "It's about time we saw some new people. And that fellow who picked us up seemed fine."

"I don't know why he wouldn't take a trade," Flora said, her brow lowering. "Doesn't make any sense."

Alice plucked some little purple flowers and held them up for inspection. "Who cares," she said.

Flora and Eddy exchanged a look. Alice was much too carefree when they let her be the center of their attention too often.

As if coming a thousand times were any kind of proof against danger, Flora thought. She watched Alice decide the flower was not as useful as it might have been and thread it into her curls.

Vana was spread out on a long grid, with crumbling houses and ancient trees that dripped to the ground with the moss that was slowly killing them. Most of the population seemed packed along the sea, and the three of them headed toward the most concentrated areas of smoke they could see.

They came to a series of squares that thronged with people, where meat was smoking in a succession of grills and metal enclosures. The whole of the area smelled like food, and they all saw each other licking their lips.

Eddy caught up to Alice and put a hand on the small of her back, checking out the crowd. Flora closed in behind them.

Everyone they could see was a man.

This was not without precedent. Many cities held at least some manner of segregation, or women were more likely to group themselves indoors while men were outside. But it put all of them on guard.

"That's them," a man's voice called out. "That's the three of 'em. I told you."

Flora looked toward the sound. It was the man who had given them their ride almost into town.

Eddy looked sick. He reached for his guns, but it was already too late. The crowd was upon them, running them toward a pink stone building, pushing them through the doors. They pulled the three of them apart, putting Alice and Flora into a wooden enclosure on one side of the large room and holding them there at the point of a rifle.

Eddy they pushed roughly toward a raised box at the front, holding several guns on him as well. Eddy kept his hands off his weapons. He watched. He waited.

Flora put her hand to the bump of one of her guns hidden in the folds of her silk and thought carefully, meticulously about how to free it.

Can we shoot our way out of here? Can I cover Alice, who has no gun on her?

Silently, Flora and Eddy had this conversation across the room.

"Who'll start the bidding?" the bearded man who had driven them in called out.

"Wait," Eddy said. "Just wait."

But he was drowned out at once by offers: Rifles. A boat. Someone offered horses, but everyone around him laughed. The room was in total chaos.

Flora watched. She watched attention swirl and move throughout the room. She watched Eddy's eyes darting, calculating. She watched the laughter and the ribbing and saw that they were becoming something much less than real to these men.

They have no idea we're armed. She turned the thought over and over in her mind.

"Oughta undress her," yelled a man who had just wagered a boat and two goats. "Just to be certain of what we're getting. These are good goats."

Another laugh followed, and Flora saw the rifle that was pointed toward her list away and droop toward the ground.

"I'll do it," called out a clean-shaven man who was close to where Eddy was standing. "Don't you bite me, now. The wild ones, they like to bite."

He turned toward the crowd to accept their laughter and in that instant, Flora's and Eddy's eyes locked. This was the moment and they both knew it. Time dilated, and everything seemed to move as slowly as sap down a tree. Eddy had his gun out first, but Flora was right behind.

Despite her lack of training and shaking hands, Flora found she could pull the trigger at the critical moment. She shot the man who was just turning back to Eddy. Her shot tore through his neck and he stood a moment, spraying blood over those nearest him.

Eddy shot the man holding the rifle on Flora and Alice, who had not yet reacted to the sudden change. Alice dropped when she heard the first shot, hands over her head.

Good, Flora thought. *Stay down.*

Eddy got his second gun free and unloaded it into the crowd. Flora emptied one before shoving it back into the folds of her silk and withdrawing the other. She was watching for more armed men.

She held her loaded pistol out before her and reached for Alice's hand. Alice took it, standing slowly.

Eddy clambered down and joined them, and together they began to walk toward the door.

Flora faced the men, Eddy faced the way out. His gun was empty, but he held it in front of him as though it were not.

"Nobody needs to follow us," Flora was saying. "We clearly ended up here by mistake."

Nobody moved. The shock in the room was absolute. The dead and wounded lay untouched, and the survivors did not run. Their eyes followed the three women leaving the building as if they were seeing horses dance or fish fly.

Outside, Eddy pulled the other two into a carriage that had been tied to a post. He untied it and tapped the reins against the backs of the two horses, unsure of whether they'd respond.

They set off at a leisurely pace and Flora sat up on her knees, keeping watch behind them.

Within moments, there were two riders after them.

"Eddy," she said in a warning tone.

"I know," he said. "I hear them."

"Go faster," Flora said. "Hit the horses harder, they'll run."

"Where the fuck are we going to go?"

Alice had one hand digging into Eddy's arm and the other into Flora's leg. "Head for the water," she yelled. "Maybe we can get to a boat."

"They'll just follow us there, too."

"What else can we do?"

"Shoot them," Eddy yelled back, pulling the coach around a sharp corner.

Flora took aim at one rider, but between his movement in the saddle and her own in the bouncing carriage, the shot went wild. Alice screamed when the gun went off.

"Shit," Eddy said, seeing that the road came to a dead end ahead of them. "Shit, shit, shit."

Now would be a bad time to say I told you so, Flora thought, taking aim at the rider again. She didn't want to waste another shot, but he wouldn't know that. She thought she saw him slow up a little.

Eddy pulled around the next corner and Alice yelled, "There! That boat there!"

They pelted down the cobbled slope toward the waterfront. The riders were close behind, but Eddy pulled the horses to a stop and jumped out anyway. Flora got out behind him and he snatched the gun from her hand in an instant.

He took aim at the nearest rider and put a bullet through his shoulder. The man fell from his mount messily, bellowing. They turned and ran for the boat.

It was long and slim, built for speed. It had two masts and looked well cared for. Eddy found its mooring rope and threw it onto the deck. "Come on!"

Flora and Alice climbed over, Alice wobbling and nearly falling. Flora caught her.

Eddy stood on the dock a moment longer and took a shot at the next rider who appeared. He missed. He vaulted over the edge of the dock into the ship, which had begun to drift just a little. He found a pole on board and used it to push them away from the edge, trying to make it too far for a man to jump.

When the man came up from below decks, throwing open the hatch and yelling, Eddy nearly shot him just for startling them.

"What is all this?" yelled the grizzled old sailor, looking around at the three of them. His face was as creased as a dried apple, but he was muscular and hale. His age was impossible to guess.

"Sail this thing," Eddy roared at him. "We need to get out of here!"

The man opened his mouth to protest just as a bullet buried itself in one of the masts of his ship. Eddy looked back and returned fire into a knot of four men on the dock. They scattered.

The old sailor was already hauling up his sheets. They pulled away from Vana and out into the tides smoothly, quickly.

When they were far enough away to feel safe, Eddy aimed his gun at the sailor.

"Are you a slaver?"

"No," said the man, seemingly unimpressed to be held at gunpoint.

"What were you doing in Vana?"

"Trading rum," he said.

"What do you call yourself?"

"Bodie."

Eddy nodded. "Well, Bodie, you've got yourself some passengers. We'll work out a trade, we'll pay you."

Bodie nodded. "Fine by me."

"We need to sail north," Eddy said.

"Nope," Bodie said simply. "My route goes south."

Eddy set his jaw. "Fine."

Flora and Alice made their way over and introduced themselves. Bodie's eyes were immediately glued to Alice. Alice took notice and smiled at him.

And now we are four, Flora thought, seeing how Eddy already hated the look the other two had shared. *As simple and as complicated as that number always is.*

They looked back on the coast of Vana as it receded. Eddy took out his map and marked the city with a pair of black manacles. He carefully folded the paper and put it away.

CHAPTER 26

The Bambritch Book
Fog rolling out
144N

Raiders from here in Bambritch tell me that they've heard stories about this army combing through towns and villages as far east as Demons, but it's so hard to know what's true and what's being exaggerated by people swapping stories.

They say the army moves mostly on foot, led by a commander in a tank. Reports vary on how many tanks they have, how many guns. Terror fuels memory like nothing else, but it also fuels invention. The commander has become a figure of legend: sometimes a woman, sometimes a man. Always tall and imposing, always said to be dressed in black with a red sash or a scarf or something. I doubt it's a single person. More like a handful of leaders taking turns playing figurehead.

Always, always people tell us they have a plane. No one has seen it take to the sky, but they say it looks good. Not much rust, wings on straight. No one knows what to ask; none of us has ever seen a plane fly. We wouldn't know by looking whether it was skyworthy or not, so we ask the questions we would of a boat, of the wheels on a truck. It can't be the same.

My thinking is that if they could fly it, they would.

They collect women, that much seems clear. They have gathered up women and girls from every town they have wiped out, but the reports on that don't make sense, either. They will also take men, and they have a reputation for killing anyone they find pregnant. But others say that pregnant women are taken up and kept. The reports fall apart, they contradict each other.

The commander or commanders don't answer questions. They ask for one thing, over and over again. Frags. Fragging. I have only heard or seen that word a handful of times in my life. I don't think frags exist. I think about the people I've known and all the things they believed about childbirth. I remember hazily from childhood that Archie took me into a village once where they thought children came from the moon. People will believe anything if you don't teach them how to reason for themselves.

They must be after something that doesn't exist. That's the only explanation for the scale of destruction they're bringing into the world. What do you do with a desire that can never be satisfied?

I cannot sleep. I pace my library and think of what will be lost if we lose Bambritch. I think of Eddy, out there somewhere, my opposite and my twin upon the sea. Is his home safe? Can someone keep telling the story? Can one story-keeper make it out alive?

If fragging was real, then Connie could have been mine. But they never were. Never could be. Never will be again.

CHAPTER 27

The Book of Flora
Florda
Warm winter sunshine
104N

*Florda is almost exactly as I remember it, but wilder than I knew it then.
There are wrecked towns everywhere along the river, some abandoned for
years but many more freshly burned. Several times a day we pass hanged
men, flyblown and rotting, twisting in the wind, strung from metal posts.*

*The sea has risen over much of what used to be forest and jungle and
beach. Caimans are everywhere, lurking like logs and waiting to strike. I see
long, thick snakes in the shallow water, hunting fish and beavers. Falling in
would mean death by teeth long before drowning.*

*Bodie says he doesn't worry about caimans anymore. He's covered in
scars. Now that it's hot, he's nearly naked all the time. (Alice loves that.)
He's all toothmarks and old gashes in his brown, leathery skin. This
morning he's got the sails furled up and we're poling through the shallows.
He's wiping sweat off in little rivers, cursing. He curses even more than*

Eddy, and that's saying something. Some of the words he uses are ones that Eddy didn't even know, but he's now taking to them like they were always his. "Cunting," for example. "Sonofabitching."

"Caimans aincher problem," *Bodie says through clenched teeth. He's got a lump of chaw tucked under his lip. (How Alice deals with the stench of that in his mouth I'll never know.) "I've seen the thing the caimans fear. Deadlier by far, and there are so many now. We'll see them soon. It's not their territory yet."*

Bodie spits into the sea. His muscles ripple and shake as he poles us through what used to be a place for children to play. A huge metal wheel stands rusty in the water, the bent struts reaching up toward the sky. His slender boat, the Ursula, *is responsive to him. Their relationship is intimate and clearly long-lived.*

"What are they?" I ask. "What does a caiman fear?" I've seen their teeth. I've had nightmares of them since I was a child. It doesn't seem to me that anything could frighten them, though we've seen huge snakes wrap around them as they thrash.

"Hippos," he says darkly over his shoulder to me. Eddy, poling on the other side, looks up.

"Hippos?"

"Si," Bodie says.

"I've seen those in books," Eddy says, clearly not believing. "They're round all over, with tiny little ears. They don't look scary."

"They're round all over and full of tusks," Bodie says. "You'll see." He taps the end of the pole against the metal plating around the base of his ship. "They're why I have these. Them and the makos. The sea is nothing but teeth out this way. Warmer the water, the worser it gets."

Eddy doesn't answer him about the sea's teeth. More and more, he's quiet these days.

It takes the rest of the day to reach Tona, and to find a safe place to moor the boat. Bodie doesn't leave the boat, not ever. Alice and I talked about this when we first sailed with him.

"Someone has to stay with Bodie," I told her.

"So he doesn't take off without us?" Alice was sunburned after only a few days on the sea. She puts on a jelly at night that's supposed to help her skin, but she's turning brown where she used to be freckled cream, and red where she was white.

"That's it," I told her. "We can take turns with who has to do it, but we can't risk not getting back on board. How would we get home?"

Alice cocked her eyebrow at me, a little smile on her lips. "And where is home, again?"

Eddy snorted a short, sharp breath, like a horse getting ready to charge.

We can't go back to Ommun. Nowhere is gone. Where Eddy wants to go is so far away, Bodie says we may never see it at all.

"I don't know," I told her. "But I want to choose where I get stuck. Don't you?"

Alice nodded. Eddy stalked off to be alone somewhere. Back then, Alice was still sleeping with me, curled up in a hammock below the deck. She tried spending some nights with Eddy, but he was sullen and sent her away. Nobody wants to talk about that at all.

I want us all in one bed. I want the comfort of it and the security. I want things the way they had been before Eddy knew what I was. I want a place where we all accept and love each other. Hell, even Bodie could come.

But now Alice sleeps only with Bodie. I've crept up on deck and seen them, sweating even in sleep, the moon shining on their wet skin. His arm is always over her, like she's something he's afraid will be stolen. I've seen him boil water for her to wash her moon cup, proud as a parrot to have a woman on board who bleeds. Eddy washes his alone.

We're all tired when we get to Tona, and Alice volunteers to stay with Bodie. Bodie squeezes her hip, obviously pleased she's going to stay. Eddy and I wade through the shallows toward Tona. The village is busy in the twilight and stinks of fish. Every house seems to have fish hanging to dry, fish guts poured out in buckets at the back doors of kitchens. A tall, crumbling building has snakeskins tacked out to dry, fires at their base, triangular heads fifteen windows up.

"What do you think you'll find here?" Eddy asks me tersely. "Nobody here will know you. Nobody will remember Archie. Why come back here? What do you have to hope for?"

"Why go anywhere?" I shoot back. "Why do anything? Isn't it all meaningless? What does it matter where we start or where we end up? Why did we leave Ommun?"

That shuts him up.

He won't let me touch him. I know we could heal this thing between us if he'd let me be sweet to him. It wouldn't even have to be sex. I could hold him, I could help him shave. Anything. He's like a stone. To Alice, too. Now.

Tona is clearly a trading city. Boats moored all over, some of them long-legged, as Bodie calls them. Big, tall sails and huge rudders. There are enormous houses and halls, all lit up, trading fish stew and bread and drinks.

Eddy looks over at a man in the street who's calling off the menu to passersby.

"Let's get something to eat, huh?" He doesn't wait for me to answer.

I catch up with him at the doorway of one of the loudest places. He is already halfway in.

"You have to ask," I remind him.

He rolls his eyes at me.

"You have to ask," I repeat. "We need to know, to be safe. Come on."

He stomps back to the barker. "Are there women for sale here?" he grumbles.

The barker looks me over. "Yes, sir, but it seems you're already provisioned."

"I mean," Eddy says, perking up a little, "can I buy slaves here? Women or girls? Catamites?"

The barker shakes his head, his lips pursed. "No, sir. There's a parlor on the fourth floor where you can pay by the hour. No slave markets in Tona. King of Florda won't have it."

My stomach flips over when he mentions the king of Florda. "What king is that?"

"King Valencia, these last seventeen seasons," the barker says. "Long may she reign."

I nod to him. Eddy is already headed inside.

I can see at once that Tona isn't a slaving city. There's security to check anyone going up the four flights of stairs, to make sure they have something to trade and that they aren't too drunk to stand. There are at least five women in the room, all lounging in the company of men who can look nowhere else. There's a desperation about slaving cities—a dullness in women's eyes and a mean-dog look about the men. Tona feels free.

Eddy trades Alice's toothache paste for bowls of fish stew for the both of us. The broth is red, and peppers and onions swim up from the bottom. It's delicious, but I haven't had spice like this in years and my eyes water up. I see Eddy wipe his nose a few times.

The man who slides between us takes this as his opening. He offers Eddy a fresh cotton cloth, putting his elbow on the table. "I heard you're in the market for a catamite."

Eddy looks over his shoulder and back down at his stew, avoiding the man's gaze. "You heard wrong."

"I thought Tona wasn't a slaving city," I tell the man, putting my spoon down.

Eddy doesn't take the cloth, wipes his nose with his fingers again. "Fuck off."

The man turns to me. His face is handsome. He's smiling. "Not a slave. Just a boy for sale."

"As a catamite?"

He shakes his head. "Doesn't matter what you want him for. We just want his kind out of Tona."

"What kind is that?"

"The kind that pretend to be girls." He puts down the cloth on the table and pushes himself off. "Daybreak tomorrow. There's only two of them. They'll go quick."

Eddy doesn't want to stay, but I convince him. We fight about it, hammock to hammock, back on the boat.

"This obviously isn't the place where we want to stay."

"I know that. I know. But let's go and see in the morning."

"If that kid is for sale, then we're both in danger here. This is not better than Ommun. Or any of the places we've seen and couldn't stay."

"No place is going to be Nowhere, Eddy."

Eddy sighs. He hates when I even bring it up. But it's not an angry sigh; there's no edge on it.

"I wish I had spent more time at home. When my mother was alive. When I could have been with Alice. It wasn't perfect, but it was good. I was so anxious to be away. So sure there was something better."

"There is." *I think about the horsewomen in Jeff City, the Hives we had seen out on their own. The women in Shy.* "There's better. But maybe better is always paid for by someone else. Maybe there's no comfort without somebody in pain."

Eddy is silent for a long time. "I don't think that's true."

"I only know what I've seen," *I tell him.*

"That's the problem."

The harbor ripples through the night and I can hear the screaming of the birds that don't sleep but hunt all night. I hunt with them.

In the morning, Eddy won't go with me. Time was, I would have begged. I begged in Ommun and Nowhere. I have begged on this ship more times than I can count. Today it's too much and I just turn my back on him. If it surprises him, I can't tell. He's always closed off to me, but today is the first time I close in response.

I walk to the public house where we heard about the boys for sale. It's just before dawn, and not many are awake. I see people up feeding their chickens, checking their nets. There's no smoke in the morning, and everything smells like fish and the sea. We haven't been here long enough for the smell to fade. I remember this from when I was a child, the wet air redolent of rotten fruit and bog and fish. The villages Archie dragged me through were smaller than Tona, for the most part. Archie shied away from bigger trading cities, unless he had to go there. He was convinced he'd be shot and hung up as an example in one of them.

"They'd do the same to you," he'd tell me darkly. "Once they knew what you were."

His warning is with me this morning. It's always with me. There are places that punish men like Eddy for being what he is. There are places that are dangerous to women like Kelda, surely. Alice is welcome wherever we go; that is her magic. I'm always the one they worry about.

It's no great crime to live as a man. Men are plentiful and everyone understands why you do it. Women lying with women is a waste, but you'll hardly get killed for it. Living as a woman without being one is the thing that always stirs hate and violence. As if there is some great deception in it. As if it is the worst kind of fraud. Yet a woman who cannot breed or will not try is never the same sort of problem. And women past the end of their blood are no threat. I am no different from them.

These boys have committed the crime that is a crime almost everywhere we go. The crime that Ommun could not accept. The crime that Shy was built on. The crime that I am.

I find them by the crowd. I trade a pair of leather sandals I made on the ship for a big basket of fresh cornbread and salt fish I can take back to the ship. It's a better deal for the woman who sells it to me, and she knows it. She makes some sort of sign and says I'll be "blessed by the mouse." I don't ask.

The two slaves are hauled up on the stage at first light. The handsome man I met last night holds the taller one by the back of the neck. The other is younger, smaller, and more easily cowed.

Rage roils in me and I can barely keep still. They're girls. They're both obviously girls, with the truth in every line of how they stand and the way they look out over the crowd without hope.

The man begins to speak and I panic. They have another tongue here. I've heard it before, must have been while I was a child here in Florda. It's fast and rhythmic and every sentence seems to rhyme with the next.

I cast my eyes about the crowd and find the woman who sold me my breakfast. She's showing the shoes to some man. I put a hand on her forearm.

"You speak this tongue," I ask her, nodding to the platform.

She nods. "Of course. Everyone in the marketplace speaks Spaniel."

"I need your help."

By the time she understands me fully, the younger girl has been sold. She's shuffled off and into the arms of a short woman.

"That's his mother," my translator says softly in my ear. "She bought him back."

"Who was selling the child, then?"

"Must be his father. She'll have to leave Tona. She can't stay here with that. They're trying to make sure no more are born."

The auctioneer pushes the older girl forward and begins to call out again.

"Is that child's parents in the crowd? Are they bidding?"

My translator shakes her head. "This one has no family. They died of a fever. He's alone."

I tell her to start bidding on my behalf. I have silk, but she tells me there's no interest in that. "What's that word he keeps using? Is that the word for pretending to be a girl?"

I remembered the disorientation I felt after Jeff City, trying to explain what it meant to be a horsewoman. We are everywhere, but the word is always different. Sometimes it's a word we choose and sometimes it's not.

"Guevedoces," says my translator. "They are born girls, but then they turn into boys after they are twelve or thirteen summers old."

"Turn into boys?" I stare at her. She watches the auction, waiting for an opening. I tell her to bid metal tools. Nobody flinches. Knives and tools are common here. Damn.

"Si, everything comes at once. The bird, the eggs. One day a girl, the next day a boy. Big disappointment."

"How?"

"Nobody knows how, but it keeps happening. The king wants all gue-vedoces cut and moved far away. Sent out, or sold to travelers."

"Have they been cut already?"

She shrugs. "Maybe it is for the buyer to do. I don't know."

I tell her to switch to som and the crowd goes silent around us.

I am watching the slave. We lock eyes and I see pure shock there. Total disbelief that I am willing to pay what I am.

The auctioneer accepts far less som than I would have paid. We have paid more for ink. I go to the platform and pass off the two pots, taking care never to touch his hand. He pushes my purchase at me, and I try to catch the child without grabbing at a body that is not mine to touch.

I thank my translator as we pass her. The child follows me without a word. The crowd begins to break up, moving to greet the dawn.

When we reach an open space beneath tall palms, I turn to the child.

"My name is Flora. You're not a slave. I paid for you, but you belong to yourself. Do you understand?"

"Si," the child says sullenly. The eyes don't look away from me, but there is no trust in them yet. Why should there be?

"What's your name?"

Brown eyes are so soft, so sad. Mouth in a line and trying to look tough. "Concepcion. Connie. But I guess I have to change that."

"Why? It's yours. You can have any name you want."

The kid crosses arms across a skinny chest. "I'm Connie. That's my name."

"Then that's what I'll call you. And is it he or she?"

Connie shrugs. "I don't care."

"I care," I say softly. "It matters to me. Which feels right to you?"

"Nothing," Connie says immediately. "Neither." Shining black braids flash in the sun as the kid turns away from me.

"Neither, then. That's alright. Connie, I want to take you away from here. I know it's your home, but I think it's best if we go. This was once my home, too. Will you come with me?"

"What other choice do I have?" They bite their lip and I can see their struggle not to cry. Not that grown-up. Not yet.

I set the basket of food on the ground. I pull a knife out of my belt and throw it in. From my back, I take my other light cloak and lay it over the top.

"You can go on your own, to wherever you wish. This isn't much to start with, but it's something. It's more than many people have when they take to the road. There are good places and good people out there, but also a great deal of danger. I'm not telling you that to frighten you. I'm telling you because it's true."

They look down at it, blinking. "It's not enough."

I shrug. "It never is. If you wait until you're ready, you'll never go."

"Where will I go with you?"

I look out toward the harbor. "On a boat, with some friends of mine. On the sea, for a long time. We're looking for something."

"What are you looking for?"

I don't even know how to say it. None of us does. It's too big to be spoken. It would never fit through my mouth.

"Somewhere where it is safe to be who we are. We are tired of being in danger because of how we were born."

Their eyes widen. Of course that makes sense to them. What else has their life been but a long setup for a bad joke?

"Where is the place?"

"We don't know yet. That's why it's going to take so long."

"But it's real?" They push their hair behind their ear. There's something so indefinable about them. Not boy, not girl. Something else.

"I believe it is real. And I want to take you with me. Will you come?"

They look at the basket again, and for a moment I'm sure I've lost them. I'll see their back as they sprint away toward whatever they can wrest from life on their own.

"I'm coming. I don't know what else to do. I can't stay here. And I'm afraid to go alone."

I nod to them. "Come with me, then, Connie." I pick up my things and we go together.

I bring Connie to the boat. I wish they didn't have to watch me explain. Eddy isn't happy. Eddy is never happy. Bodie doesn't care at all, merely shrugs and tells me there are four more hammocks in the hold and I need to rig one up.

Alice, as usual, tries too hard and does too much. She doesn't touch the child without asking (at least folks in Nowhere had good rules about that—nobody in Ommun could ever figure it out). But she comes close and talks too much.

"What a beautiful living child you are! I'm so glad you've come to join us. What's your name?"

"Connie," they tell her, barely meeting her eye.

"Connie," Alice repeats. "I have some books, if you find yourself bored on board." She smiles a little at her own joke. "Of course, I've read everything we have at least twice."

"I can't read," Connie says tonelessly.

Florda is a hard place for books. They bloom and rot if they're not kept carefully, so many villages have none at all, or just a few. I'm not surprised they can't read, but it does hurt me a little.

"Well, then, I know what we'll be doing at sea." Alice smiles.

Connie scowls in response.

I take them down into the hold with me and search for those other hammocks. That's no problem, but there is a shortage of pegs and nails where a hammock can hang. I string one end for them on the same nail as mine, but run it in the opposite direction. On the other side, I pause for a minute to figure it out.

Eddy comes tromping down the steps. "Help you with that?"

I turn around. "I wouldn't think you'd want to."

He looks at Connie a little guiltily. "I was hasty. I just worry. Of course I want to."

He helps me tie some knots, since we lack the hardware. I think it will work.

"Hop on in," I tell Connie. "I'll hold it still."

They don't trust me. They still don't know what to make of us, or what to expect. But they let me steady it. They climb in. And it holds.

Florda is swamp to the sea in every direction. There are islands now where there was solid coastline. Sailors we encounter say that no map works and they redraw what they know of fishing villages every season. We know when we make the Gulf because the current resumes.

No one packed anything for them. Not a change of clothes, not a little bread. They were turned out as though they were nothing.

I ask them later how that could be. They won't even look at me.

CHAPTER 28

THE *URSULA*

The small boat bobbed through choppy waters, leaving a rippling wake as it passed.

Connie walked the length and breadth of the ship. It wasn't much, and it was already feeling cramped with five people on board. They found that they loved the crow's nest, once they had made the climb. They hunkered down belowdecks only when tired or cold; they preferred the open air and the view whenever they could get it. This occasionally meant getting run off by Bodie or Alice when the pair wanted privacy. Connie didn't mind, for the most part. They found their own ways to pass the time.

In Connie's former life, they had hoarded art supplies. There had been a few precious old-world tools in their collection, a trio of paintbrushes, tied together with a little yarn. A dip-pen, though Connie had made their own ink, experimenting with berries and leaves, never really achieving anything they thought was worthwhile. Paper was hardly made at all in Florda, so Connie drew on walls and stones and anything they could.

They did the same aboard the *Ursula*, though they had lost their tools in another life. Connie began with small burnt sticks, sketching in the dark belly of the ship by the light of a little candle. They drew pieces of their old life, caimans and people they had known. They scratched the moon as it changed and the fish they saw at sea.

Flora found these later, brushing some of them into black smudge with her shoulder without realizing what they were. When she looked closely and saw that they were drawings, she knew at once they would be Connie's work. Eddy had never drawn and would barely write in his book. Alice could sketch botanicals but did so in a cursory manner, as part of her own record-keeping. Flora inspected Connie's drawings carefully, noting the grace and lifelike qualities of the living figures. She copied a few into her book, determined to preserve them but saddened by what they lost in translation.

Connie resisted all clear attempts at conversation, preferring their own company at all times. When Flora found the game on board, she felt an idea come into being.

She took the cloth sack with the pieces to Bodie.

"Bodie. Hey, Bodie."

Bodie looked up from his maps of the coastline, where he was making corrections.

"Mmm?"

"This is a game, right?"

Bodie's weathered face scrunched and worked as he focused on the bag. "Aye, that's a game. Picked it up in trade years ago. Haven't played it in the longest."

"Do you still know how?"

Bodie sighed. There was never enough to do on board, and he couldn't fault Flora for idleness. Games and books were the best for boredom, and he knew that better than any of them. He set loose the tiller and walked over to her.

"Aye, I remember. I'll show you."

The game was very simple. The board was wood, with depressions carved into it in two long rows. The pieces were shiny little stones, colorful and clear, smooth to the touch. Flora thought they looked like jewels.

"Here, it's simple." Bodie began to show Flora the movements of the game. "You can play it with someone who shares no language. It's that simple." Once Flora grasped the mechanics and knew the object, she saw how that could be true.

She looked up to tell Bodie she got it, but she saw the genuine pleasure in his face. He was having a good time.

She picked up her jewel-pieces and played him back. They were both grinning before long. They played it through to the end, and Flora beat him, but just barely. One last bright-red stone remained, as she had cleared her lane completely. He beamed at her.

"You've got it!"

"I'm going to teach it to Connie, but you ought to teach Alice, too. It's a good one."

"I have some others, as well," Bodie said, smiling still. "Fancied them more when I was a younger man. But I've not had this many passengers in a long time. Good time to remember. You're right, of course."

Flora neatly tipped the board back into the sack and the pieces rained down softly into its folds. She tucked it under her arm and went to find Connie.

Connie was in their hammock, working hard at reading a book for children, brow furrowed.

"You'd do better with that on deck, in the light," Flora said.

"I'm fine," Connie gave back in a bored monotone.

"Want to take a break? I found a game."

Connie turned their head to look. "What game?" Suspicious.

"It's called jewels," Flora decided. "I'll show you, if you'd like."

As before, Flora set the game before her on the boards of the lower deck. In the low light, the stones were not as beautiful but instead looked like flawed secrets. She put the stones where they belonged. She waited.

Connie came at last, sinking to the floor with their book still in hand, as if they did not want to commit to playing. "How does it go?"

Flora led them through the moves of the game, taking care to explain what the object of it all was.

Connie watched carefully, nodding, picking up the steps.

"So the last jewel has to go here?" They pointed to the well nearest to themselves.

"That's it. So if I do this . . ." Flora pulled a handful of jewels from a divot and dropped one in each that she passed, bringing the last one home to her base. "Then I did it right, and I get to go again."

Connie nodded again, focused solely on this one thing.

Flora won the first game, and the second. By the third, Connie was ready.

"Watch this. Watch." Connie reached out and made a perfectly effortless first move. Then a second and a third. Before long, they had cleaned out the entire board, leaving nothing for Flora and not letting her move once.

Connie looked up, beaming. "There's an order to it. A way to do it perfectly, so that you never lose."

Flora sat stunned. "You're right. As long as you go first, you can't lose."

Connie nodded, looking back down at the board. They looked back up, stricken. "I guess it's not much fun this way."

Flora smiled encouragingly. "It was fun to figure out. How about we work on reading for a bit?"

Connie was agreeable in that way that children are when they realize they've annoyed a good and generous caretaker, and they want back into good graces. They sat with heads together over a thin children's book with gold foil peeling off the spine. Painfully, slowly, Connie began to sound out each word. Patiently, lovingly, Flora helped them put it together into meaning.

The sea rocked the two of them, alone in the belly of the ship.

CHAPTER 29

The Book of Flora
The Ursula
Fall on the sea
104N

I have been trying to get Connie to tell me more of their story. Some of it they'll tell me with no problem. Other things are more delicate.

They remember their parents, before they died. They can tell me that their father helped them learn to tie a knot, or that their mother never wore skirts if she could help it.

"Did your mother teach you about getting your blood?" I ask, trying to gently get at the time when Connie was raised as a girl.

"She mentioned it," they tell me, already dodging away from the question. "I didn't really expect it to happen. It didn't seem like a real thing."

"It is, though. Alice deals with it all the time."

At the mention of Alice, Connie pressed their lips together. They have quite the little fire simmering for her, and they don't want me to know about it.

"Well, what about Tona? What was it like there?"

Connie shrugs. "I got work cutting cane or picking oranges. It was always hot and there were always bugs. I didn't like it there, but I had never been anywhere else."

"Were you hungry? Lonely?"

"Sure," they say, picking up a piece of charcoal and making hash marks against the hull of the ship. They don't elaborate, and I don't know how to push it without them pulling away.

"Did your parents call you 'she'?"

"Yeah, of course they did. They thought they had a girl."

"Did it happen all at once? The change?"

They don't want to look at me. They turned their back, but they keep talking. "Overnight," they say, in almost a whisper.

"Did they see?" I ask. "Or did you have to tell them?"

"I told my mother," they say. "I didn't understand what was happening. She had told me so many times I was going to go through changes and become a woman, so I thought I had. I hadn't ever seen a man naked. I didn't know."

"How did she react?"

They don't answer me. I can guess not well.

I drop the subject. They keep sketching hash marks, closer and blacker, resembling nothing at all.

I think about the Midwife and the curious way that she wrote in her book. I've read many other diaries, and hers is still peculiar among them. She omits all kinds of words from her sentences, but I still understand what she means. I sometimes look at the way she writes and think that it's so much easier to talk without articles or pronouns, because it takes the question of whether she's being a man or a woman, whether she's talking about a man or a woman, out of my head entirely. Why should it matter?

I try to show this to Connie, to talk to them about being a they *instead of a he or a she, and how freeing I think that is. They won't talk to me about that at all. Instead, they want to know about the Midwife.*

"So she was like me?" they ask. "A girl until she became a boy?"

"Not exactly," I say. "She was more like Eddy."

They look up at me, not understanding. "Isn't Eddy like me?"

"Not exactly," I say again. "There are lots of ways this can happen."

They cock their head like a puppy and I smile at them. "I've never known anyone like you," I tell them.

"Have you ever known any frags?" they ask.

I shake my head. "I think they're only a legend," I say. "I don't think people can do that."

"But you don't know," they insist. "Just like you didn't know that a guevedoces could exist until you met me."

I nod slowly. "That's true. It's a strange world. There are plenty of things in it I don't know much about or understand."

They seem satisfied with that. I feel a little closer to them every time we talk like this, even as they resist me.

CHAPTER 30

THE *URSULA*

They had been nearly a moon upon the choppy, shallow seas around Florda as it gave way to the Gulf. They had seen sharks and beaver. They had gone ashore and gathered fruits: coconuts and funny hand-shaped citrons, as well as the fat oranges that grew everywhere.

"I remember these from when I was little," Flora said, licking the juice as it dripped down her wrist.

Connie silently ate two in a row, staring out at the lapping waves.

Alice scratched at the citrus fruits' skins. "I could extract oil from these. With enough time and the right tools. My lab . . ."

She trailed off, clearly frustrated without the lost wonders of her labs, both in Nowhere and in Ommun. No one offered her any comfort on that subject. They had none to give.

Eddy pulled the fruit into sections with quick fingers. "It's so sweet. Tastes like sunshine. Can we dry it and keep it?"

Flora shook her head. "It doesn't dry well. It rots. You've got to eat it fresh or make jam. That's all there is. You can dry the peels, if you hang them up. They smell nice, and you can throw them in tea."

Eddy smiled a wry smile. "Like my mother did with dried peaches. She loved that peach mint tea."

Connie's head came up at that. "What was your mother like?"

Eddy looked the child over. "She was old when she had me. Almost too old. She had given up hope of ever having a living child and was studying to become a Midwife. I was a surprise."

Connie did not ask for more, but their face was so hungry that they didn't need to.

"She was forthright. Never got around the truth if she could tell it instead. Very strong, and a good teacher. Never let me get away with shit. She had a huge Hive, her whole life long. Always wanted to have her options. Have her choice."

"And she loved you?" Connie asked this as if it were the detail on which hung all others.

Eddy sat silent for a moment. "More than I deserved. Isn't that what Mothers do?"

Connie nodded but said nothing. "Did you know your father?"

Eddy shrugged. "Who cares? Any man can father a child."

Connie looked down a moment before stalking away and climbing back up into the crow's nest.

It was Connie who saw the ship first, but they didn't know what they were seeing, or that there was cause to raise an alarm.

They only said something out of surprise, blurting, "Oh."

Bodie's head jerked up, knowing the importance of surprise. His eyes tracked the movement on the horizon, and for a moment he just stared.

"Get belowdecks," he said to Alice. Then he looked around. "You, too. Both of you. All of you. Get below."

Flora's eyes widened. "What is it?"

"Slave ship," Bodie said, his mouth settling into a line. "Get below and don't make a sound. Boy! Get down here."

"Call them Connie," Flora said urgently, stepping forward to take Bodie's arm.

He waved her off. "Not today we don't. Today he's boy, and he's the only other person on this ship besides me, you got it?"

Connie climbed down swiftly, hard with new muscle.

"Where do you want to be?" Flora searched their face with her eyes. She didn't want them in danger, but they knew how much moments of choice like these might mean to the child.

Connie looked at the ship that approached them. They licked their wind-chapped lips. "I'll hide."

Flora patted them gently on their shoulder. Alice reached out and did the same. Connie put their hand on top of Alice's small freckled one.

The three of them slipped belowdecks. They had talked about this before, all of them knowing that there must always be a place that women can hide.

Eddy stayed on deck. "I've dealt with slavers before." He checked his guns and touched his binder.

Once it had been spotted, the ship took forever to approach. It was bigger than it had first seemed, looming larger and larger as it came fully into view.

Men swarmed the deck in every direction, pulling the sails and climbing the rigging to get a better look at the small craft as they closed in. It was impossible to count how many, silhouetted as they were against the sunset. They were man-shaped black holes against the sky, each bearded face lifted at the angle of a predator as it scents prey and searches for its weakest point.

Bodie pulled up both poles and oars. He let his sheets hang slack. The ship drifted sideways, unmoored and without propulsion. He did not drop anchor.

"Allo there! Qui qui?" The brass-voiced call came from the prow of the larger ship.

Bodie held very still. He assumed the caller had a spyglass on him, though he could not see it.

"Soy Bodie. Ma ship Ursula. Sans cargo. Sans crew. Solamente me, et first mate Eddy. Sans mujeres. Savvy?"

He spread his arms wide as if to expose himself and invite scrutiny of the women he did not hold in his pockets.

Eddy lifted his chin behind its balaclava. He counted men on the ship, counted bullets and how long it would take to reload each time. There was no land in sight. Swimming was not an option, but failure was all but assured.

"Pare to be boarded," came the reply.

Bodie ground his jaw. He trudged to the anchor and threw the crank, letting out the chain.

Eddy looked up. "You're just going to let them come aboard?"

"They could outrun us. Plow right through us. Might have long guns aboard. This isn't up to me."

Eddy touched his gun again. "What do they want?"

"Never can tell," Bodie said, spitting on the deck of his ship.

The slave ship came alongside them, turning broadside before dropping its anchor. Planks and ladders dropped from above, connecting one deck to another. Bodie blanched, but smiled afterward, his weathered brow making an attempt at serenity.

A short black man came down unsteadily, cursing under his breath. He stepped to Eddy first. "Capitán."

Eddy shook his head and pointed to Bodie.

"Désolée. First mate." He clasped Eddy's forearms in a two-handed grip. Eddy fumbled to return the greeting.

The man walked over to Bodie. "Capitán."

Bodie took his arms and nodded. "Y tu?" The strange sea-patois was delivered lazy-mouthed, bored. Eddy had no other languages but his own and could not entirely follow, despite the sounds being familiar.

"Sylvain."

Bodie nodded. "Qu'est ce-que tu business?"

"Mujeres. For sale. Savvy?"

"Savvy. Not buying, though."

Sylvain's big, bloodshot eyes slid from Bodie to Eddy and back again. "Dos hommes solamente. No use for mujeres? Perhaps you hold secret mujeres?"

"Sans mujeres," Bodie said smoothly. "Sans trade. Poverty, savvy?"

Sylvain smiled wide. "Primero, the prices. Si?"

Thumping above as more feet started down the ladder. Three women laid their bare feet on the deck of the *Ursula*, one after the other. Each was dark skinned, clean, and well fed. All three wore their long black hair loose.

Eddy stepped forward, looking at their faces. They showed no signs of being drugged or beaten. They shared close resemblance in their faces. He looked over to Sylvain.

"They're all from the same family? Sisters?"

"Aye, sisters. De la jungle, las tribes to the south."

The women were naked to the waist, wearing only loose skirts of rough cotton weave. Sylvain walked over casually and seized one of their breasts, squeezing to show its resiliency.

"Breeders, savvy? Quality bon." He flicked a nipple with one finger. The girl gave a small, closed-mouthed whimper. She did not shift her body away from him, but it was clear she wanted to.

Eddy spoke up fast. "Trade fish. Fresh fish."

Sylvain made a face. "The fuck tu savvy we sail upon?"

"Corn flour," he offered, flatly.

Sylvain pointed at Eddy's chest. "Bullshit, homme. Bullets. Pistolets. Mira la shine leagues away."

Eddy grasped his bandolier reflexively. He hadn't thought about the fact that he was wearing his wealth across his chest.

"Ruined," Bodie said swiftly, cutting across the tension. "Soaked in seawater. Solamente for show." He shrugged. "Little man. Sans pistolets. Showbiz."

Sylvain grimaced. "Rico. Pense que rico." He spat. He tapped his foot at the three girls, who immediately turned to climb back to their own ship.

"Désolée," Bodie said lazily.

"How many? On your ship, how many?" Eddy was watching a girl climb the rickety, shaking ladder.

"Crew is forty-two."

"He means cargo." Bodie offered this helpful translation while looking at nothing at all. Especially not the hidden door to the hold. His eyes touched everywhere, resting nowhere.

"Cargo is dozen. Touts fine. Touts de la jungle. Mas rico por toi."

Bodie nodded. "Mas rico. Désolée."

The ladder slackened as the final girl removed her weight from it.

"Where will you take them?" Eddy kept his voice steady. Tried to feign disinterest.

"A la mer. Where else?"

"Are there enough men at sea to sell them?"

"Toujours." Sylvain looked them over once more. "Sans mujeres?"

"Si," Eddy said shortly. He started a moment later when Bodie slung a sinewy arm around his shoulders.

"San mujeres, parce que best mates."

Sylvain sighed. "Mariposa."

Bodie grinned, showing his very white teeth. "Si."

Behind his balaclava, Eddy grimaced. After a moment, when he had control of his face, he pulled the cloth down to show his beardless chin. He reached down and grabbed a handful of Bodie, squeezing playfully.

It worked. Sylvain looked away, marking his upward route of escape. "Avwa, mariposas."

"Avwa." Bodie grinned.

Eddy let go of him, wiping his hand on his leather trousers.

They said nothing as the larger ship made ready to depart. They didn't stir and didn't stare. They made no move to crank up the anchor or make fast the sails. They waited until the men on the deck were only shapes again, against the now-purpling sky.

When they were long gone, when they were sure they were alone, Bodie let go of Eddy. Eddy drew a long, shaking breath.

"Twelve women who will never go home."

"Nobody goes home," Bodie said, turning the anchor crank alone.

"They'll be sold to men who don't speak their language."

Bodie pulled a sheet and tapped his foot on the door of the hold. Alice popped up from beneath the door at once.

"I met a woman once who had been sold as a girl. Kicked her buyer off his own ship into rough seas and took to the sea on her own. Don't underestimate a wild-caught slave."

Eddy set his jaw, but said nothing more.

Flora came up behind Alice, blinking in the faded light. "Oh, it's already dark."

Connie shoved up resentfully, striding about the deck again. They looked out over the sea, after the ship.

"Those ships used to come to Tona," they said. "Bringing girls from nobody knows where. They speak some other tongue. They all seem to be breeders. When they get pregnant, they disappear."

"Where do they go?"

"Nobody knows."

The passing of the slave ship upset them all, soured the evening. The night was cloudless and the stars came out unwaveringly one by one.

"I didn't need to hide belowdecks," Connie said to Flora, their jaw tight.

"No, you didn't. But you haven't cut your hair. And you haven't changed your style of dress. I didn't want you to be manhandled and stripped so they could figure you out. I don't want that for you any more than I do for me."

"So what? I can survive that. I've had it enough."

"You can survive nearly anything. Doesn't mean you should invite it." Connie made a scoffing noise.

"And if they're looking for catamites . . ." Flora didn't want to scare Connie, but it had to be said.

Connie blanched at the word.

"Then it doesn't matter. It didn't matter for me. I ended up in a harem." Flora set her mouth, trying to seem like she was long over what had happened in Estiel.

"Me too," Eddy said softly from a few feet off. He was watching the moon rise above the water.

"Me too," Alice said with a false bright-eyed cheer. "But I guess I'm not a surprise."

"I am," Connie said softly. "No matter what, I'm a surprise."

"Exactly," said Flora. "That's enough. It's not just women who have to worry. It's anyone who isn't a man."

The sky blackened, remaining deep blue only at the rim of the sky. They all slept on deck that night. In the morning, they landed in the wreck of an old-world city and had to take to the road in order to find somewhere to barter for supplies the sea could not provide. They didn't know how far they would go, without a port city in view, so everyone came along.

Bodie moored the ship, running it partially aground in a secluded cove that had easy-looking high-tide marks. He hid their belongings and supplies under the hidden trapdoor in the deck, then kicked handfuls of sand over the opening to obscure the cracks. He dropped the anchor and worked to make the boat look abandoned, stripping fronds from trees and throwing them all over the deck. Wading waist-deep in the water, he rubbed his bare, leathery hands against the anchor chain, then smeared the rust across the hull of the ship. He collected sea stars and plastered them against the metal at the waterline. When he was finished, the ship looked as though it had been there for months.

Flora still thought it looked ready to be stolen, but it would take skill to get it out of the sand and back to the sea.

"I've done it before. Hundred times." Bodie kept his teeth clamped shut as he walked away from the *Ursula*. "She'll be here when I get back."

Eddy spat. "Get out of the shallows. I see eyes."

"Caimans," Flora said at once. "Just like in Florda. They're all over. Probably snakes, too."

"I wanted to fish some shrimp. Or those little mud bugs." Bodie sounded deflated.

"You'll get another shot at it," Alice said. "It's all bog and stream around here, it seems like."

Connie kicked at a puddle, trying to get up to where there was dry ground. "I hate that I can't see to the bottom. The water in Tona is cleaner than this."

"Goodbye, my girl." Bodie kissed his fingertips and flung the gesture over his shoulder as the *Ursula* went out of sight.

Connie looked up sharply, then away.

"Why are ships female?" Alice threaded her arm through Bodie's and helped him up through the mud. He was shoeless.

"Because you can get inside them."

"You can do that with anybody," Connie muttered.

Bodie cast an eye their way. "Also because her wheel is covered in hidden blades, and if a man touches her the wrong way, she'll take his fingers." He grinned, showing his gray front tooth.

"Me too," Eddy said.

Connie gave Eddy a rare smile. They shouldered their pack. "Where are we headed?"

Bodie pulled a brass spyglass from beneath his shirt where it hung on a chain. He scanned the horizon.

"Think that's smoke, off in the west. Let's head that way."

CHAPTER 31

The Book of Flora
Gulf Coast
Winter
104N

We walk inland from the sea for nearly two days before we reach the village where we saw smoke coming up. We hit the outskirts of an old-world city and we assume the people who built those fires would be there, but the city is deserted. Wild dogs run through the streets and birds nest in the buildings.

Connie doesn't trust me yet, but they stay close to me. Eddy scans the branches of trees and the rooftops, convinced we are being watched. We are watched only by the birds. I am sure of that.

I watch Alice as she clings to Bodie like she can't walk on her own. What makes her act that way around men? Like she needs something only they can give her? I don't know the answer, but I know that men grow taller in her presence. They respond to it, every time, even if there's no chance to sleep with her. It's just her way. Her power.

For a moment, I wonder what it would be like to have that power for myself. But it doesn't keep her safe. And it means every man's eyes go straight to her. I remember when we were taken to the Lion. It's always that same sinking feeling. They go to her like water flows downhill. There's no way to say no to it.

Every place brings us that wanting. Wanting brings us closer to danger. It's not that the women in Shy didn't want anything, but they built a city free from it. Nowhere was free from it, too. Different. Ommun was different, too. Controlled. I don't know. I'm just jumpy. I know we need to trade to make our way, but I wish we didn't have to seek out other people. Maybe ever.

CHAPTER 32

GULF COAST

They were no more than huts, the little circle of dwellings in the clearing. Each had a single door facing the center of the small field, where a communal fire burned low. Each hut gave off its own little snake of smoke in the wet air.

"Eleven houses, figure two or three in each," Eddy said, low. "Not too many."

"Unless there's another clearing nearby," Bodie said. "This is just what we can see."

Eddy scanned the tree line.

"Why are we doing this?" Connie's whisper hissed in Flora's ear, their voice ragged with worry. "Why take the risk?"

"Because we need to trade," Flora said calmly.

"For what? We can hunt meat on our own. We can tan skins."

"Or we can make a trade with people who've already done all that, and save ourselves a lot of time and trouble. Hunting is dangerous. Picking berries and mushrooms in a place you don't know is dangerous.

Each place has its own perils." *Its own Lions,* Flora thought but did not say.

"This is stupid," Connie said sullenly. "What do we even have to trade?"

Flora looked them over, suddenly very tender. "Not you. We don't do that."

Connie gave her a look of disgust.

If they think that's why I bought them, they're never going to trust me. Why did I? What can I tell them?

They moved as far away from Flora as they dared.

Alice stepped out, standing up straight. "Hello?"

Bodie made no move. Eddy went to grab her arm, but Alice put him off.

"We're already in the open," Alice said. "Let's get it over with."

Eddy put an easy hand on his gun.

The door to one of the huts swung open, smacking smartly against the outside wall. A short black man came out, dressed in reptile-skin pants, boots, and vest. His head was shaved, and he wore long knives hanging from his belt on both sides.

He scanned them and then addressed himself to Eddy.

"Papa! Traveler? Trader?"

"Trader," said Eddy levelly.

"Traders!" The man cupped his hand around his mouth and yelled it again. "Traders! Traders!"

Hut doors opened all around the clearing. Men hustled out of every door with crates and boxes, one with big glass bottles. A young boy scurried out of the woods, his hands red and covered in bee stings. He came up heedless to Connie, his grin wide and front teeth gone.

"Honey? Trade honey? Best honey! Gathered fresh today! A treat! A slice!"

Quick as a spider, the boy twisted to pull his pack in front of him. He opened the flap and a captive bee escaped lazily, ascending through the muggy air. The boy produced a tiny curved knife and whipped it inside the bag. He came up with a piece of dripping honeycomb, proffered toward Connie's face.

"Taste! Taste for nothing! Then we trade." The kid's excitement was infectious. Connie smiled a little, taking the sticky lump uncertainly. They put it in their mouth and their eyes rolled back in their head.

"Best, see?" The kid exploded with glee, swinging his bag back behind him. "We trade! We trade!" He turned around to shout at the adults behind him. "I trade first!"

The man with the long knives smiled at the kid, showing that he too had no front teeth. "Right, Rocky. Right."

Turning back to Eddy, he sobered his face. "What we trade?"

"Drugs," Eddy said. "For pain, for itch."

"Books," said Flora. She noted that no one looked at her when she spoke. *Maybe they can't read. Eddy's already shortening and simplifying his language like they can't. Maybe he reads people better than I do. Maybe that's the better thing to read, anyway.*

"Fish," Bodie piped up. "Have some fresh deep-ocean fish, fat in the belly. Ink bearers. Cuttle and squid."

The man with the knives tapped his chest. "Papa Croc. Trade pelt. Beaver, bear. Deerskin. Trade meat. Possum, deer today."

He pointed around the circle. "Tools. Wood and metal. Shoes. Good ones! Ink marks, if you want forever. Fortunes told. Him? Blow your dick off. And honey, if you trade with Rocky. Fruits for free, this season. Point you to them myself." Each man waved or tapped his own chest in turn.

Eddy and Flora nodded to one another, splitting up at once. Eddy dealt with Papa Croc, trading for meat. Flora spoke to the man who made shoes, who showed her at once how he chewed the leather to make it soft. Connie needed good shoes, and these would make an excellent gift. She showed the man lengths of silk, to his immediate delight.

Nearly running out, she thought. *Who knows if there will ever be more?*

Bodie traded away all his fresh fish for a new, very sharp axe and a clay jar full of fermenting cabbage.

"Can open it in one summer, five summers. Still good!" Bodie, who had learned from his father the importance of vegetables and fruits at sea, was pleased by the tight wax seal on the jar.

Alice got busy at once pulling a bad tooth and looking at an infected bite. She dug deep into her kit to clean and stitch up her patients.

"Nobody want their dick blown off?" Standing over near the coals of the fire, the man was clearly disappointed. He had gone into his hut and changed into a deerskin dress. His long hair was greasy but brushed out and lying on his shoulders. Enormous grapefruits filled out the front of the dress, and he had circled his mouth hugely in red with some kind of shiny, fatty berry mixture.

Alice smiled and looked around at her party. "I think we're all okay with our dicks. Thank you."

The man with the grapefruits stalked back into his hut.

"Don't be shy," Papa Croc said. "You knock on his door if you need to."

Trading done, they stood awkwardly, trying to decide how best to move on.

"You stay," Papa Croc declared broadly. "Stay and trade stories." He lowered his chin and raised his eyebrows at Eddy.

Eddy shrugged. "Gotta make camp somewhere."

Papa Croc grinned and told Rocky to bank the fire.

The sun set long and late, stretching out the shadows of trees and making the day seem to last forever. A tripod made of iron appeared and two men hung a huge iron pot. Other men brought saltwater in buckets, followed by squirming sea bugs in baskets and nets. The man with the grapefruits had taken off his costume and rubbed the paint from his face, but a pink stain remained around his mouth. He sat by the pot with a long metal spoon, fishing out the curled red carapaces and piling them on wooden plates. He scowled into the steam of the pot, speaking to no one.

Another black man proffered a leather sack that turned out to be full of sauce made with sea salt and red chilies. Eddy tried a bite and coughed long and hard, with Alice pounding him on the back.

They all ate until there was a huge pile of shells in front of each of them. The bugs were labor intensive, having to be broken in half, the meat sucked out, the head full of juices and the tail only a mouthful of meat at best. Still, they were plentiful and delicious. The chili sauce, when used with caution, brightened them considerably.

"What did you mean by marks?" asked Bodie, patting his full belly. "Forever marks, you said."

A bearded man stood on the other side of the fire, smiling the same missing-tooth grin the rest of them had. He rolled up his deerskin pants to show a tattoo, black and grainy, on the side of one tanned calf. It was the image of a wild boar, its tusks heavily exaggerated. "Marks! To show a story of when you were brave. Forever! With needle and ash."

Papa Croc stood at once. "I will tell our best story. The story of how I killed a god. The god whose skins I wear now, as my mark."

He walked close to the fire so that the orange light lit his face from below. He spread his arms wide and began. "In the old time, when women still walked the earth, they called them *crocodile*."

"Caimans," Flora muttered under her breath.

"When women walked the earth," Connie whispered back, puzzled.

"Crocodile were small then. People kept them in their homes. They taught them to play games and eat from their hands."

"Corruption!" A man yelled from the far side of the fire; Flora could not see his face.

"We live not in the shadow of corruption," Rocky piped up in response.

"Exactly," Papa Croc went on, smoothly. "In the corruption, croc was everywhere. Small and insidious, under your beds. Then, when women leave the earth, crocs grow large. They eat up men. They eat up corruption. They eat up old world until nothing left. They grow big so they can rule. This was in my father's father's father's time.

"Then came the god. The god's name was Attila, and she was bigger than big. Big as a tree! She'd lay her eggs and wait for us. Wait for Dellacraw. She swallow up children, she swallow up men. Her nest full of eggs of gods, someday as big as she.

"Dellacraw was a young boy. Young like Rocky. He go to Attila, with his knives."

Croc pulled his long knives from their leather sheaths and showed their finely honed edges. "Dellacraw say, come get me. And Attila, she come. He stab her in the mouth!"

Croc illustrated this by thrusting his long knife up into the air, its blade reflecting firelight as it quivered in his sinewy arm.

"But Attila smart. Attila roll and roll. Dellacraw hold on. Dellacraw wait until she roll over, and put his other knife in her belly. Dellacraw pull his knife up, spilling Attila guts in the mud. He slay Attila the wicked, and dead men spill from her guts. Dellacraw free them in her death. He take her skin. He guard her eggs until they hatch. He make the next god, Camilla, who grow as big as her mother. He become Papa Croc, and lead his people."

Croc puffed up his chest at this, putting both hands across his wide pecs.

"Forever with the skull of Attila!" the yell came from one, then from many.

Alice laughed and stood. "Wonderful story! But tell me, why do you speak of the time when women walked the earth? Women still do."

Eddy shot her a look, but she did not sit down.

Flora arose as well. "Surely, each of you had a mother. You know women walk the earth."

Laughter rose up like embers from the fire. "I am born of crocodile egg," Papa Croc said.

"I am born from bees!" Rocky's voice was always tuned to pure joy.

"No, but . . ." Alice glanced around. "Really, though. You came from a Mother and a father. A man and a woman."

"No women," Papa Croc said almost dismissively. "No more."

Alice began to unbutton her cotton shirt, dingy now, but new from Ommun. She was still laughing. "No, really. Maybe it's been a long time since you've seen one."

Eddy stood up. "Alice, don't."

Alice shrugged, pulling her shirt open and exposing her freckled breasts. Bodie smiled in open admiration.

"See?"

Papa Croc laughed, scoffing. "Not real."

"Big deal," said the grapefruit man. "Anyone can have those."

Alice looked around at him. "What?"

"Not real woman. Never real woman."

Flora looked around at her company. "What's a real woman?"

General laughter greeted her question.

"A real woman. One who can do it. Give life."

Alice and Flora looked at each other.

"How do you know one of us can't do it?" Alice's smile was faltering. Flora looked into the fire.

"Do it!" Papa Croc stood, chest forward. "Show us you can do it. Then, you are woman."

"No one here has ever seen a child born?" Alice looked around the circle again. She tried to meet Flora's eye, but Flora would not look up from the heart of the fire.

"Never. No women left. No one can do it."

"How do you know I've never done it before?" Bodie put his hand on her, but Alice stepped away, letting it fall.

"Show us the mark!" This came from the man who made marks, who carried his tool over his shoulder even now. "Your forever mark, that shows you gave life."

"What mark?" Alice pulled at her skirt a little. "You mean—?"

"Your lightning," Papa Croc crowed. He clawed his fingers across his own belly, scratching zigzags over his skin. He held out his hand to a man at his right, who put a tiny wooden carving into his dark palm.

"Here," he said. Alice looked down. Flora came a little closer to see the small effigy. It was the body of a woman, with heavy breasts and a pregnant belly as round as the full moon. The belly was shot all over with tiny, intricate stretch marks, white in the pale wood. The body had the tooth-ridged head of a crocodile.

"No lightning, no baby. No baby, no woman." Croc folded his arms, turning away from her and ending the discussion. "A story! A story of bravery!"

"Ah," Bodie said, standing. Alice sat down in his place, buttoning her shirt. "I've been brave so many times. If I had a mark like yours, I would need more than one. A mark of an octopus. And a shark. And a storm. And monsters. And a great many men."

Papa Croc laughed loudly at this, with the other men joining in after him. "So brave," he said. "Tell us a story!"

Bodie cleared his throat. "Alright, alright. Once, I was on the deck of my ship. The *Ursula*. It was a gray day, and the air was heavy. I was alone. I could feel that the sea was uneasy, like a man spoiling for a fight. I turned around to look behind me, where I had come from, and a tentacle shot up out of the sea. It wrapped itself around me and pulled me into the water. It was the most terrifying creature the sea has to offer: the giant squid."

He put his scarred arms into the air, showing how the tentacles fought him, wrapping around his body and dragging him into the deep.

"I pulled the knife from my boot," he said, doing so and showing it to them in the firelight. It was shorter than Papa Croc's but viciously sharp and with a set of teeth down low, near the handle.

"The beast pulled me close and made to eat me, but I plunged this into its eye. Its black-blue blood dribbled out into the water, and it dropped me. I had won, but I was lost.

"I fought to swim instead of drowning, but the current took me away from my boat. I wrecked on a beach and my boat did, too. I coughed up bloody water, but I was alive."

Eyes grew big all around the fire. He had them spellbound.

There's no way that happened, Flora thought. *But what if Eddy told his story? What if he talked about killing the Lion's lion? Who would believe that? Or if I told them I came from women who whisper to pregnant horses and make boys into women with their magic?*

Flora schooled her face. She listened.

Why don't we tell? I've sat in these circles so many times. It is always the men who tell. There are women in these stories. There have to be. But I never hear it from them.

Bodie was crouched down now, showing how he woke up afraid. "I awoke on the beach of a great city. It had shining towers and flying machines. And the king of that place found me, and I told him I had killed a sea monster. So he told me that a terrible monster was attacking his city at night. It was as tall as three men. And it ate babies. And no one could defeat it. So I spent the night in his house. I met his beautiful wife."

"Not real," said the grapefruit man, dismissively. "The wife was not real."

"What?" Bodie asked, derailed.

Papa Croc was sucking the meat out of one last cold bug. "Was she big in the belly? Did you see her give life?"

"No," Bodie said uncertainly.

"She was a man," Croc said, throwing the shell into the fire. "King had a husband."

Bodie shrugged. "She looked like a woman to me. Anyway, I met the monster that very night. He was huge!" Bodie bent backward, looking up as if meeting the eye line of the towering monster. "His teeth were the size of my hand, and dripping with red blood. I stuck him in the leg with my knife, but he didn't even feel it. The blade was trapped in the bone and I was defenseless. He swiped his big hands after me, but he was slow. I ran between his legs. I dodged and jumped and ran. Then I picked up a stone from the ground. I used my belt and I slung it up at him. The stone hit him in the eye, and just like the squid, black blood came pouring out. He was a monster too, but on the land instead of in the sea."

Bodie bent forward and put his hands on his knees. "The king thanked me. The people wanted to make me their new king. The king's wife came to me and . . . uh . . ." He glanced at the grapefruit man. "She blew my dick off," he said.

A cheer went up around the fire, accompanied by a number of unmistakable gestures.

That got them going, Flora mused.

"But I couldn't stay. I went back to my boat and made repairs and sailed away. And that was the story of how I became a monster-killer."

There was applause and some hooting and stomping. Papa Croc stood up and pounded Bodie on the back with affection.

Bodie held up his hands for them to stop. "Alright, alright. Trade. Someone else has to tell a story."

Papa Croc looked over his shoulder, fast, whipping his head as though he heard something in the gathering gloom.

"Hunters," someone else said. "Back early."

Flora heard them then, a group of men in soft deerskin boots, good at being silent but picking up speed as they homed in toward the fire.

They were ragtag and bloody, carrying several boars tied to spears, swinging with their skins split and their guts missing. The men parted to welcome them, and they ranged in, chests out, proud of their kill.

One of them stared at the visitors a little longer and more intently than the others. He was middle-aged, with gray hairs in his rough beard and dry rivulets in the skin around his eyes. His once-black hair grew wild and long under his raccoon cap, and it was braided with crow feathers.

Alice moved closer to Bodie, instinctively shielding herself from his gaze. Flora stood. Eddy ignored them.

"Etta? Is that you?"

Eddy looked up and squinted at the man with the feathers in his hair. "Who the hell?" He stood up, still straining to see.

"It's me, Etta. It's Errol."

Eddy went around the fire to look the older man in the face. It took him a long minute.

"What did you give me when you left Nowhere?" Eddy stared the man down.

The man gave a short laugh. "My map. And every fucking thing I knew."

"Oh, shit."

"It's me!" Errol was fairly crowing now. "It's you! I never thought I'd see you again!"

They caught each other up in a fierce, tight hug. Flora watched them through the heat shimmer of the fire.

Coincidence, she thought. *The things we see too many times, and the things we only see once. That's what we make into religion. Those are the things we have to struggle to explain, so we make something up.*

Even from where she stood, Flora could see the plain wonder in Eddy's relaxing face. He looked younger, wilder.

Alice had detached herself from Bodie and slunk closer to them. "Errol? Really? Where's Ricardo?"

"Alice," Errol said, his voice full of plain awe. "Daughter of Carla. Last time I saw you, you didn't have any front teeth!" His smile faded a little. "Ricardo's been gone four summers now. Snakebite."

Alice hugged him suddenly, and Eddy wrapped his arms around them both. It was a little knot of Nowhere, made up of loose threads. There was nothing for the rest of them to do but stare.

"I don't understand," Connie whispered to Flora. "They used to know each other?"

"A long time ago," Flora said in a low voice. "Errol helped train Eddy to be a raider. They lived together in Nowhere."

Connie nodded, remembering only the stories they had heard about Nowhere. "Should we leave them alone?"

"Maybe," Flora said. "But I really don't want to."

"Come on back to my place," Errol was saying with a broad gesture. "We'll catch up."

The walk was short, and frogsong carried them there.

Alice introduced Flora, Connie, and Bodie as they settled in Errol's hut.

Flora put her hand against the curved wall of the simple little house, looking around at its humble dimensions. It was framed with sticks, she saw, and filled in with mud and grasses.

Must have been built in the summertime. And you're out of luck if it rains at all. Why would you do this? There are brick houses not far from here that are safe to live in.

She pushed against the wall and felt its uncertain give. She tried not to show the distaste she felt for sitting on the dirt floor.

Why be indoors at all? It's like being outside.

Errol was smiling at her. "Yeah, I know. It's not much. I miss the big houses back in Nowhere sometimes, too."

Flora blushed a little, taking her hand away from the wall. "It's just . . . why? There are houses all over the coast, nice ones. Enough for everybody and then some. Why build like this?"

Errol sank down easily, long accustomed to the hard earthen floor. He crossed his legs and comfortably pulled one bare heel up high onto his thigh. Out of the corner of her eye, Flora saw Connie attempting to do the same.

"It's the way here. Papa Croc and the ones before him. They decided that living in the bones of the old world means that we can't grow a new one. They tell each other ghost stories. Say that the old places are haunted, filled with the spirits of the dead. They scared each other out of the old towns, and said it was better to start over clean. New."

Eddy was still standing. "Isn't it cold? Rainy? What about when it snows?"

Errol shrugged. "We have skins. Deer and boar. Some of us have taken a bear. We get together, and we manage."

Eddy did not sit, but he looked down at Errol, shaking his head slowly. "What happened to you? Why didn't you ever come back?"

Errol shrugged. "Since then? So much. I've seen things you wouldn't believe. I've done some things I can barely understand. And . . . I couldn't go back. You know that, right?"

Alice blinked. "What do you mean, you couldn't?"

He tossed the black feathers back off his shoulders. "We couldn't go back because we were tired of pretending like we weren't in love. Ricardo and I. We just wanted to be together. And they made it impossible for us."

"Who did?" Alice fairly demanded.

"You know who. You can't tell me you never had this problem with your mother. Did she know about you?"

Eddy was shaking his head harder. "There were people like us in Nowhere. Fancy boys. Me and Alice. They didn't like it, but they tolerated us. We just didn't talk about it. It wasn't anybody's business."

Errol chuckled a little. "They tolerated *you*. Because we left. We fixed that for you."

Eddy did sit then, slinking to the floor. "Were there others?"

He was nodding. They were locked eye to eye now. "Every raider who left and didn't come back, basically. Some of the guys who trained me. It was like this piece of us that we couldn't put anywhere. So many places have . . . rules about it. Laws."

Connie was red in the face already. "Well, they have to! Everybody wants to have new babies, and there's only one way to get them. So they have to have laws about . . . unnatural things."

Flora looked over and saw they were fuming. Shaking.

"You don't have to justify what they did to you," she said gently.

That was the wrong thing to say.

Connie stood up, stormy and ready to run out the door.

"I wouldn't," Errol said. "We get wolves after dark."

Connie stood with their back to the earthen wall, arms crossed.

"You're right, kid. Every place is out to ensure that babies are born. But there's never enough women. So how bad can it be if a couple of guys pair up?"

"That just leaves women to deal with this," Alice said tiredly. "I can't even count the number of times I've had this fight. If women are obligated to have children, then we may as well be in chains."

"I don't understand," Flora spoke up. She was digging one of her books out of her bag. "The Midwife. She was like us. And there were others in Nowhere, at the very beginning. Breezy! Don't you know about Breezy? How could Nowhere turn you out when it was founded by someone who accepted this?"

Eddy sighed. "Those books. They change all the time. Ina used to call the short version 'the canon.' They'd leave out all the stuff where the Midwife fucked women, or wanted to. They'd definitely leave out Breezy."

"Who was Breezy?" Connie was interested in the book, but their reading skills weren't yet up to the task of the diary.

Errol sighed. "I haven't thought of her in a long time. Breezy was a boy who became a girl."

"Breezy was always a girl," Flora said. "Maybe that was just the time that she was safe enough to show it."

"I didn't know that could happen," Connie said.

Errol stretched his legs in front of him and grabbed his toes. "Well, you've probably heard that the men around here don't even believe in women. I'm guessing they made the three of you feel pretty out of place."

Alice nodded. "Their definition is hard to swallow."

"They all are," Flora said.

Eddy was rolling his eyes. "Can we ever talk about anything else? Where have you traveled? How did you get here?"

"Oh boy," Errol said. "I've seen everything. Ricardo and I went back to Niyok and saw the glass towers. The water has risen every year, and even the boat people are gone now. It was totally deserted the last time we went through there."

Eddy began to smile. "I remember you talking about Niyok. Where else?"

"We traveled by boat for a long time, just out on the sea. There's more sea than I could have imagined, back when I lived in Nowhere. There are people in boats out there who speak languages we couldn't figure out. They traded us strange goods: coconuts and pineapples and cocoa nibs. They had little brown boys on board rather than women. They brewed liquor out of anything they could get their hands on, all of it sticky-sweet. Some of them wanted to fight. Some of them we had to fight, because they were slavers. We used to take rescued women down to the Republic of Charles. That town was bright and fat. Probably because we brought them so many women."

Connie's eyes were shining now. "What is it like there?"

"They grow tobacco everywhere. Everyone rolls it and smokes it. The whole place stinks. There was a slaver running the place for a long time, but he was overthrown by an uprising of women. Last I saw, there was a council of old women running the whole place. Trading at the port, sending out killers like Etta, here."

He smiled at his former pupil, who did not smile back.

"Eddy."

He looked Eddy over quickly, getting a feel for every eye on him. "I taught you this act. I know what you're doing."

Eddy dropped his head to his chest, putting a hand on the back of his neck. It made Flora ache to see him like that.

"No. You don't."

Alice saw the tension and sought to break it. "So, are you going to stay here? Is this it for you, or do you still go raiding?"

Errol folded his legs again. "I'm not young anymore. The road is dangerous. I think this might be it. I like these guys. And what else is there?"

What else is there? Flora thought. *What a question.*

They talked long into the night. Errol wanted to know about Estiel, which he had seen, and Ommun, which he had not. Flora told about Jeff City, and Bodie told more stories about life on the sea, some that seemed true and some that did not.

When everyone was settling down, Flora saw Connie with the Midwife's book. They were working to sound out the words, finger traveling along below the lines. Their brow was furrowed and they were hunched around it, like it needed protection.

She decided not to ask for it back, though she preferred to sleep with her bag fully packed. In the morning, Connie had packed it into their own.

The minute Flora saw Errol and Eddy, she knew they had stayed up most of the night talking. They were both soft around the eyes, puffy in the face.

She walked over quietly. "There's dandelion, if anyone wants it." The drink, made of toasted flower roots, was a favorite in many of the villages they had seen.

Errol shook his head. "I drink pressed apple in the morning. Sometimes fresh, sometimes funky. Depends on the morning."

Flora smiled. "What kind of morning is it?"

He looked Eddy over as they both stood. "Funky."

The three of them drank from the body of a dried gourd, once Errol had pulled the cork from its belly. The drink was hot in the mouth, funky as promised, and immediately went to Flora's head.

"How long do you ferment that?"

Errol pulled the gourd back and looked at it. "It's young. Maybe a moon? It goes bad fast in the summer."

Eddy took a pull and grimaced. "How can you do this for breakfast?"

He grinned. "Remember the time Ricardo and I found that wine cellar? We brought back all those bottles."

Eddy's grimace only deepened. "Most of it was sour. Gone over. Not fit for pickling in."

Errol nodded, looking down at his gourds and bottles. "Yeah, but the stuff that was good was *incredible*. I never forgot it. I keep looking in burned-out basements, hoping for more. But that hardly ever happens anymore."

"Why not make wine?" Flora asked.

Errol shrugged. "Grapes grow where it's warmer and drier. Out west."

Flora nodded. "That's the way we're headed."

He looked between Flora and Eddy, his brow lowering. "Why? What for?"

"To go back to the beginning," Flora said.

"To see the Midwife's city," Eddy added. "Maybe find some people there who were like her."

Errol was already shaking his head. "We were there. Ricardo and I. There's nothing. I mean, there's people. But they're barely human. Chanting and drumming in the hills. Burned bodies hung on poles. The whole place was a bad dream. I couldn't wait to get out of there."

Eddy looked at him in disbelief. "That can't be everywhere. The map says there's days and days of coastline. Did you give up after just seeing one place?"

"You don't understand," Errol said, taking a step toward his former apprentice. "It's the weather out there. It's awful. Hot and wet, with water flooding the old cities. Storms. Earthquakes. Bugs. It's worse than Florda ever was. It doesn't ease up until you get way up north. I can show you some nice spots, if you want to go west. Don't go to Midwife's Bay. I'm begging you."

Eddy and Flora looked at each other. When they had left Ommun, this had been the one thing they could agree on. They didn't know where they were going, but they both thought that would be the right place to figure it out. They both wanted to see what the Midwife saw when she set out. They wanted to find the people there, to see if things were better. Freer. Different.

Errol was still shaking his head. "You've never once taken my advice," he said to Eddy. "Why would you start now?"

They left him at his hut, with no promises they'd ever see each other again. Nowhere was a memory they held between them, but Errol would not follow where they were going.

The travelers bartered a little with Papa Croc and his people. Alice traded medicines, and Bodie helped out with some boat repair. Flora was just about out of silk, and Eddy hadn't much to trade these days. The two of them sat with Connie.

"We're going to head back to the ship soon," Flora told Connie. "We're going south so that we can go west."

Connie nodded. "Why not stay here?"

Flora looked around. "Do you like it that much?"

Connie shrugged. "I kind of like the way they look at things. I mean, things would be better if women didn't exist. We wouldn't all fight over it so much."

Flora looked them over. "You really think that?"

Connie looked away. "I don't know. It doesn't matter. It's just . . . it's like they're right, you know?"

"What do you mean?"

Connie looked from Eddy to Flora and back again. "Well, it's like you two. Eddy, you're a woman. Except you're not. Because you decided you're not."

Eddy stiffened and Flora saw him clench his fists. But he didn't say anything.

"And Flora, you're a woman because you say so. Because you're cut. Because whatever."

"That's not exactly it," Flora said gently.

"Yeah, okay, everybody says it's complicated. And I was a woman, until I wasn't. Because there aren't actually any rules, and none of this matters. The only thing that matters is who can bear. And if not one of the three of us can, then nobody here is a woman, are they?"

The three of them sat in silence while the trading carried on.

CHAPTER 33

The Book of Flora
Somewhere
Cold rain
104N

I don't know how to help Connie finish growing up. I think about what Father did for me, but he mostly just put me with people like me so I could learn from them. He made me feel safe, made me get a trade, made me think about respect. But I was already me before then.

There is nobody like Connie. The people in Florda said this happens sometimes, but I've never heard of it before. There aren't any horsepeople for this. I don't know how to help them become a person that is neither woman nor man. I don't know how to tell them that their way of looking at this is narrow. Cruel, even. That this is the kind of thinking that allows men like the Lion to exist.

Can a thought do so much? It must. Thoughts do everything, in the end.

I watch Errol and Eddy say goodbye. Eddy seems so softened, so saddened by this meeting. It's like he lost something rather than gained it back.

Errol did nothing to connect him to the man he wants to be; he was a sad reminder of all that is lost. We didn't even really talk about bringing him along with us.

Eddy has nothing to tie himself to, no way to define himself. He's lost. I remember that feeling, after my father died. Like the earth has shifted beneath your feet and there's no safe place to stand. I hate seeing him suffer. I hate seeing the way Connie confuses him. Even hurts him. I don't think they're good for each other. I don't know who is good for Connie. They look up to Bodie, at least a little. I think I've seen them looking at Alice the way I look at Alice. I don't love that.

The more people in a group, the more complicated things become. There's no way around that, it seems. We did it wrong in Jeff City, they did it wrong in Nowhere. They're doing it wrong in Ommun, and all over the world, I'm sure. Maybe there is no right way to do it. Maybe this is just what we are.

We're back on the sea, heading south. Bodie says that this time of year, we might be able to cross something he calls the narrow jungle sea. If not, we'll be another couple of moons headed south, toward terrible cold, before we can cut up north toward Midwife's Bay. We hope that the water is high.

Bodie's maps make no sense at all. They're fragmentary, taking in only those towns on the edge of the sea. He has long paths marked off for sharks, others for slavers and something he calls "bad rivers." He says he can navigate by the stars, but when Connie asked to be shown, he said he didn't know how to explain it.

I watch Connie try on each of us in turn. They stand like Alice, hip cocked to the side, chest forward, lithe and loose in the neck as she stares up at Bodie as if he were the sea and not a man upon it. They always shake this pose off as if it were a chill.

They fall right in behind Bodie; Bodie the utterly oblivious sees nothing. He teaches them to steer the boat, to work the sails, or to read the sea. He notices not at all when their eyes fill up with admiration, their mouth

*softens and smiles for him. He treats them like something between an incon-
venience and a pack animal. They adore him for it.*

*I watch them try to become Eddy, box up their shoulders, and help him
haul a net full of fish on board. Watch them become neat-handed with a
knife, following Eddy's gruff instruction and building up thumb calluses.
I see them throw Eddy off like a coat that's heavy with rain. Take a deep
breath. They never mirror Eddy for long.*

*It's hard to know when they're mimicking me. I've heard them pick up
words from me, especially as they learn how to read. I see contempt on their
face when we both piss over the side of the boat. For me or for themselves,
I'm not sure. They clearly think I am something lesser, something unreal
beside Alice's legitimacy or Eddy's strength.*

*They don't love me. I suppose that was too much to hope for. I've
invested in Connie all the things that went unloved in my younger self. I've
given them my orphan sadness and tried to show them the same kindness
my father showed me. I gave that man reasons to love me, but he did it
up front, like a credit. I've given the same to Connie, but they don't know
how to accept it. Maybe that will never change. It would be enough if they
trusted me, but we're not there yet. I don't know what it will take.*

*So they bounce around between us. I try to remember that it has noth-
ing to do with me. They're not doing it to hurt me. They're just figuring
themselves out.*

*There's only so many examples of how to be a person on this boat. I hope
that when we find someplace to settle, they have more choices. There are a
thousand ways to be themselves, but they have to find their own.*

CHAPTER 34

The Bambritch Book
No more fog, late fruits in
144N

The council met today to discuss what we are going to do when the army reaches the island. If they don't stop, it will be tomorrow.

We sat down at the big round table, Zill holding her head, I think with hangover. She drinks her own honey mead whenever she's alone—and she's been alone too much lately.

Hortensia turned her back almost entirely toward Zill, pointedly ignoring her. Hortensia thinks that Bambritch should outlaw everything: old-world drugs, pipeweed, drinking, everything. We've talked about it, and drunkenness certainly contributes to a little bit of chaos around here. But time and again we come back to the question of whether we can attempt to control anything people do with their own bodies that doesn't hurt anyone else. So we do not, and Zill drinks on.

Eva has clearly gone without sleep these last few days. She's been caring for refugees with Wallis in tow, and the thin skin beneath her round brown eyes is dark as a bruise. She holds her chin in her hands and stares at me.

Alice came in late, as usual. She was still as beautiful as ever, her freckles as perfect in her skin as stars in the night sky. Her ringlets she had tied back, working as hard as she was to secure her vault full of emergency drugs and her precious recipes against whatever might come. She told me she had lost twenty years' worth of work in the wreck of Nowhere and would not lose it again. She buries everything now, carefully sealed and daubed with wax. If the whole place burned down, she could always go back and dig. Or tell someone else where to find it.

Alice has been my love all these years, though it has changed shape in that time. Like a child, our relationship was small and fragile in the beginning. It grew up, developed a mind of its own, changed into something we could not predict. She keeps a Hive of men and women both to rival the size of any here on Bambritch—it might be the biggest. She has had three living children. She is beautifully generous with her whole being, and I cannot help but worship her still.

She sat next to me, letting her long-fingered hand slip over my knee for just a moment before she settled in.

"Speel said they do have an airplane," she said without preamble.

Zill's head came up. Hortensia sat bolt upright in her chair.

"What?" Eva's eyes were already bright with tears.

Alice nodded. "They didn't see it in the air, but it's moving with the army. They're towing it behind a truck. Sometimes they start its engine. That's that whining noise. They're running it to scare us. So that we know they're coming."

I turned to Zill. "Are all the boats moved out?"

She nodded miserably. "And the bridge is ready to blow. We will probably never be able to rebuild it, but I don't care."

"Did Speel say whether they sent a messenger ahead?"

Alice shook her head, looking down. "They looked for one, but there was nobody out there. No rider, no bicycle. The other towns . . ." She cleared her throat a moment.

Eva broke in. "The other towns reported no messenger. No message. They have no demands."

"That doesn't make any sense," I said. "They must want something."

I stared at the wood-grain patterns in the table. They looked like long, stretched-out faces, screaming in torment. "They must want something," I said again.

"We need to talk about plans to refugee," Alice said flatly. "We can move people toward Torie."

"And then what?" Zill asked. Her breath was like bile. "We can't get more than a little head start. They'll just follow. They're cutting up every little town in their way. Where can we go?"

"Okay, then we'll just stay here and die," Alice said. "Is that your plan?"

"We have weapons," Hortensia offered up. "We can arm a reasonable number of people."

"With handguns," Eva said. "Rifles. Bows. They've got so much more than that." She put her hands down on Speel's drawings of the advancing army. "And there's no way that we're better armed than every other town they've put down. They've faced armed resistance before."

"Then what is there left to do?" Zill said. "Surrender?"

I shrugged. "We could try talking to them."

Hortensia and Zill both rolled their eyes. I wish they knew how alike they really are.

"What good is that going to do?"

I shrugged again. "It's worked for me before. I don't see that we have a lot of options. Those who want to refugee should do so. Eva, can you lead that? Make sure Mothers and children get the first spots on boats."

Eva nodded, already gathering up to leave.

"Hortensia, Zill, will you figure out who all has guns and get them to high places in time for the arrival? If we're going to have a shoot-out, let's claim the advantage early."

They turned toward each other and began arguing at once.

I turned to Alice. "Is your vault ready?"

"Ready as it'll ever be. And there's enough space to hide me in it."

I put my hand on her hair and looked into her eyes. "That's my girl. Looking out for herself to the very end. Who's got the boy?"

Her youngest living child, Calyx, was only ten.

"He's with Shannon. She'll go to Torie, I bet."

"Make sure we find out." I loved that kid, the little cross-eyed boy who called us both Mom. Nobody had ever done that, not even Connie.

"I will, of course." Alice kissed me on the cheek with dry lips.

When the coast was clear, I went to my own vault. I hadn't told anyone about it, and now I don't know why. There's a small trapdoor in the room where I have my office in the council building. The space beneath is short, so that I have to stoop when I stand. There was an old chest down here when I found it. Inside, there were a few century-old bottles of whiskey, a rusted metal can of coffee, a Bible, and some capsules marked with the old-world symbol for poison. The coffee was stale and useless; I added it to my compost. I've read about it, but I don't think I'll ever taste any in my life. The whiskey I've still got. I'm saving it for a very bad day. We've got Bibles far beyond what we need in the Bambritch library, and this one was unremarkable. The chest was in good shape, though.

I've got the Books of the Unnamed. Some of what we brought out of Nowhere were her originals, others were scribed copies. I think the whole thing is here. Those go down first. I have the collection of Eddy's that he left with me, and those I have to let my hands linger over for just a minute. It's been so long since he's been gone, I don't understand how it can still dig at me so. Then, the few books I've gathered here; the stories I've scribed from others who've come through Bambritch and some from those who've stayed.

On top of these I will lay my books, tomorrow before the army gets here. I'll seal the chest and lay the rug on top of the trapdoor. If they burn the office down, the chest will survive. I've made sure of that. The Bambritch library may not be so lucky.

I can scarcely go there anymore. It makes me think of Eddy.

CHAPTER 35

The Book of Flora
The Ursula
Cold rain at sea, winter
104N

The coast of California drifts by slowly. The currents are sluggish and the wind is nonexistent. We barely go ashore. We find oranges, sometimes. Smaller than what we saw in Florda. We see no people.

There are ruins of huge buildings, all crumbling into the sea. We harvest oysters and clams from their overflowing beds in the mud, sitting and feasting on them on the deck of the ship. Connie insists on roasting theirs over a small brazier, holding the half shell between metal tongs.

"Perfect waste of a good oyster," says Bodie, who eats the bivalves live as fast as he can pop them open with his short knife. He shows the trick to Alice, who is neat-handed. Eddy manages on his own, shredding the shells and cursing to himself.

I cut myself once, wrap my hand in silk, and go again. I've about got the hang of it now. Each oyster is like a whole sea made miniature in the mouth.

Connie makes a face as I gulp another. "They're like when you've got a cough that brings up snot out of your chest."

Bodie laughs. "They're like a mouthful of cunt, boy."

"I'm not a boy," Connie shoots back, but they're blushing.

I never considered that before, but as Bodie says it I can tell what he means. It's the same kind of briny satisfaction and slippery wonder. Alice smiles sweetly at him and Eddy stares at them both like looks could kill. I hope we meet some other people here, soon.

Night on the coast is anything but silent. Close to the shore, there is the chattering of a thousand kinds of night bird. The evening is warm and they're all about their business of fucking and squawking. Insects sing in the grasses and in the trees, too. Bats and owls overhead, after everything that crawls. If there were people here, it makes sense that they'd be active at night. But there are no fires, and no sound of humans.

We throw the anchor out a mile away from the shore and we can hear the strange songs of the whales that swim below us.

Connie comes to me, wide eyed and shaking. "What is that?"

I open my eyes, knowing I was hearing the sound already in my dreams. Eddy is up too, his hand on the inside of the hull.

"It's an animal. In the water."

I nod.

The three of us head up top and interrupt Bodie at the business of pleasuring Alice. Alice looks up alarmed, pats him on his bare shoulder. He comes up, his face shining, wiping his chin as though he's been eating fruit.

"What is it?"

Connie's face is purple in the dim moonlight. "What's that sound?"

As they speak, it comes again. It's so low I can feel it vibrating in my chest, the sound cresting to a shimmer and then changing to the rain-lapping sound of spray.

"*There!*" *Eddy is pointing just off the aft.*

"*Whales,*" *Bodie says. "Just a pod of whales passing by. They sing to one another.*"

We follow Eddy's pointing arm and see them. They're impossibly huge in the water, their backs breaching in sections so long and wide that they seem like islands being born in the moonlight. The spray from their blowholes mists back slowly to the sea, fine as fog.

Connie's close to me all at once, wrapping both their arms around my one. I pull it out slowly, gently, and feel them pull away. I wrap it around their shoulders and bring them back close.

"*It's okay,*" *I whisper. "They don't care about us at all. They're here for each other, just passing us by.*"

"*One of them could swallow me whole,*" *they whisper.*

"*I don't think they do that,*" *I tell them, though I am not sure.*

Bodie strolls up behind us, with Alice in tow. "It's true. They're not like sharks. They've no interest in men."

Connie relaxes a little but stays close to me.

There are so many of them, passing by us in the night. We see their shining skins and spumes pass for what seems like hours. None of us can sleep. The night is too alive.

Bodie lights a little fire in the brazier. We don't need it for warmth, but it's nice to see each other's faces.

"*My mother used to dive into the water with the whales,*" *he says. "We had them in the cold north, too. Different kinds. Orcas, in black and white, and they will eat a man. Or a woman. She was mad for them. She painted the sides of her boat with whales and dolphins and all manner of sea creatures. She made the best paints and the best pictures.*"

Alice sits beside him with her head on his shoulder, but I can see that she's holding Eddy's hand on the other side. "Were you her only living child?"

He shakes his head. "No, she was strong. She had four. Died with the last one, my little sister. Sister died that winter. Sickly. We put them both out on the ice."

Alice sighs. "My mother had two. My brother and me. Julian. I don't know what happened to him. And my mother died defending Nowhere. Which is exactly how she would have wanted to go."

"Your mother was an iron-willed woman," Eddy says. "She had no love for me, but I respected her. Tough."

Alice nods. "I still can barely think about it. With all that happened, she's like an afterthought. I forget that she's not there, still waiting for me."

"She must have been mad as hell when you set out for Estiel." Eddy has not talked about this at all before. I tense up all over. Connie feels it and tenses, too.

"Probably," Alice says, a little guilt creeping into her voice. "I thought I could help. I thought I could be like you."

"I didn't talk her out of it," I say, rushing to say something. "I knew it was a terrible idea. I knew she'd never pass."

Eddy looks up at me, his eyes like dark holes beneath his brow in the firelight. He shakes his head. "I'm not still holding that against you, Flora. I know you were trying to do the brave thing. I know . . ." He looks away, out over the sea. He looks up and I can see his eyes again. "I know you did what you could. It wasn't your fault. My mother helped me see that. I can let it go."

I nod, gratitude squeezing my throat. "We all got out of there because of you. Including your mother. All those kids."

Bodie is following this quietly. If he knows the story, it's because Alice told him. The three of us have not spoken it out loud to one another.

"I told the story to the women in Shy," I tell him, trying to smile. "They were all so grateful that someone had taken him and his cats down. They were living in the shadow of Estiel, just as much as everyone else."

"What's Shy?" Connie asks, huddling closer to me as if they were cold.

So I tell them. I tell the whole story, out of Estiel and back to Ommun. I can't ever tell them how I came to be who I am, but I can tell the stories. I can show them the scars. I can explain what I have seen in the world, and *how strange it is. And then it will become part of them. Isn't that what all Mothers do?*

The sky is tinged with green before I come to the end. Dawn is on its way.

"I was my mother's only living child," Connie says softly. "If she'd had another, it might have been easier for her to deal with me. With what I am."

"She died of fever, right? That's what they said at the auction."

They nod against me. "Not long after I got my eggs. She and my father both. I got the fever too, but I didn't die. She loved me, though. I know she did. She was just disappointed with the way things turned out."

"My parents sold me," I say. "I don't remember them at all. Just my keeper, and then my father."

Connie looks up at that. "Really?"

"Really. I never met my mother at all."

They put their head back down, then look up again at Alice. "Why don't you have a child?"

Alice shrugged. "Just lucky, I guess."

"But you could," Connie pushes forward. "If you wanted."

"It's not exactly up to me," Alice says with a little half smile.

"What do you mean?" Connie's brow is furrowed.

"It's not like you make a decision and then it happens," Alice says, rolling her eyes a little. "There are herbs you can take to keep from catching pregnant, but they don't always work. There's nothing I can take that will make sure the kid catches life. Or saves mine."

"But you're doing the thing? The thing that makes babies?" Their eyes dart between Eddy, Bodie, and Alice in a tight triangle.

"That isn't really something you have a right to ask me about," Alice said.

There's a little bit of silence. We can all hear the waves lapping against the sides of the Ursula.

"I disappointed the living fuck out of my mother," Eddy says ruefully, bringing the conversation back from the dead. "We got better, but she always wanted me to have a living child. Keep my book. Leave something behind."

"Will you?" Connie is young enough to still ask questions as guileless as this one.

"Will anyone?" Eddy gestures toward the bridge in the distance, just starting to glint in the rising sun. "What lasts?"

Nobody has an answer for that. We all go back to bed. We pick up the habit of sleeping in the day and moving northward up the coast at night. There are more whales, and countless dolphins and seals. There are shooting stars above us in the cloudless sky. There is a reason people like Bodie keep to the sea, as it rocks us, night after night, in our cradle of strange and home-brewed love.

CHAPTER 36

THE *URSULA*

There were reefs and shipwrecks all along the way toward Midwife's Bay. Bodie's maps marked some of the older ones; others cost them course corrections and lost time. They weren't in any hurry, but Bodie hated to go around anything.

Flora sat on the other side of the ship, working a skein of wool off and back onto her drop spindle. She hadn't made anything new in ages and her hands fought their idleness. Her braids had grown ever more elaborate. She washed her hair in collected rainwater and dried it in the sun. Her red tint had not had any maintenance in a long time and she could see silvery threads of white making their inroads along her dark brown. The sea air and sun were showing gold and red highlights, and it was pretty in its own way.

Eddy had been long without a razor and had taken to twisting his kinky curls into short, stubby locked knots that he could toss around when he shook his head. Flora thought he had never looked stranger to her. Eddy was eating a mango with great gusto, the juice dripping down his elbow. He caught Alice watching and gave her a wink.

Alice too was looking restless. Flora knew that without her work she was often at loose ends. There was no medicine to make upon the sea. None of them had been ill, and there was nothing to do but pick whom to sleep with at any given moment and count the days. Bodie had taught her how to make combs out of the shells of turtles they found on the beach and she worked at that, off and on. He told her his own mother had had a set she used both to detangle her own hair and to hold it out of her face. He pulled Alice's blonde curls back from her face, pinning them with his thick, leathery fingers. "Just so," he said, smiling in his weather-beaten face.

Alice gave him a devastating smile and went back to work with one of his files on the turtle shell. As she worked, Bodie reached out and cupped a hand against her low belly, as if confirming something there. His hand made a small mound below her navel, and all at once Flora knew.

She looked at Eddy. Eddy had seen. Flora saw Alice meet Eddy's eye and shrug before looking sheepishly back down. Alice put a hand over Bodie's, leaving her filing for a moment. The circle they made was perfect, and everyone on the outside of it knew themselves superfluous. Everyone but Connie.

Connie spotted something in the distance that made them yelp. "What is that?"

Eddy's head snapped up. He saw a tall, shimmering fall of something silvery, moving ceaselessly in the breeze. It undulated like water, stretching up high into the sky, catching the sunlight in winking bright lights.

Bodie stepped to the bow and pulled his spyglass. "It's for birds," he said. "I've seen one before. It keeps them away from a fishery, or something else that they want."

"Can we get closer?" Flora asked. "There must be people."

Bodie consulted his map and looked out over the water. "It's plenty deep enough here. I can get close. You'll have to take the dinghy if you want to go to shore."

He made the adjustments and their ship started to cut toward the vertical river of light. As they got closer, Flora could see it was made of thousands of threads of old-world plastic, something shiny and very well preserved. She didn't see any people around, but there were plenty of signs of them.

As Eddy rowed the dinghy toward the shore, Flora could see fishing poles and lines, piles of nets, and pails and shovels for digging shellfish.

"It all looks new," she said, laying her binoculars down on her chest. "It's not abandoned. So where is everybody?"

Eddy couldn't shrug without stopping his smooth rowing rhythm, but he brought his head down toward his shoulder in an approximation. "Maybe they're out at sea?"

Flora shook her head, looking again. "I don't see anywhere they'd moor a boat."

"Maybe they do what we do—anchor out there in the bay and come ashore some other way."

Flora couldn't shake the feeling that that wasn't the right answer, but she couldn't come up with an alternative.

On the shore, it was clear they were in a fishing village. There was a shell mound and a series of smaller middens that stank of dead fish. The firepits were recently ashed, and Eddy walked over to inspect one up close.

He put his hands cautiously near the black and gray. Warm ashes.

Bodie was yelling from the ship. Eddy's head snapped up, but he didn't understand.

Flora walked back toward the beach, her hand shielding her gray eyes.

"Boats," she said hoarsely.

She would have said a number if she could count them. They came so swiftly up the shoreline and in such a score that she couldn't keep them straight in her eyes long enough to count them. Each was sleek, long and pointed, and each had oars over the side, moving in perfect sync as though they were rowed by one person with eight arms.

There were four on each boat, Flora saw as they grew larger and larger between her and the ship. They were bare-chested and she searched frantically for any women among them.

She saw none.

They beached their boats and came ashore on light bare feet. They carried fishing spears and nets. Each of them had a tattoo, inked from their bottom lip to their chin, stretching down like a beard on an otherwise hairless face.

One ran up faster than the others, taking the advance position and training a spear on them. Flora could see his muscles working, sliding beneath his skin. He raised the hand not holding a spear as if in invitation for them to speak.

They did not. Flora saw out of the corner of her eye that Eddy had laid one hand behind him, on his gun. Hers was somewhere under yards and yards of silk. She wasn't ready.

"Librarians!" The man's voice was smooth and youthful, and he did not seem angry, though the word was shouted.

"What?" Flora stepped forward, cocking her head to the side. "I'm sorry, we don't—"

"Librarians," he yelled once more. His voice went up at the end, as though it were a question.

Flora and Eddy looked at each other. Eddy's lips flexed downward a little, an approximation of a shrug.

They turned back to the man, and this time Eddy spoke.

"Listen. We don't want any—"

A weapon Flora had never seen appeared in the air, whipping toward them at a blurring speed. A tangle of leather cords struck Eddy about the neck faster than he could raise his hands. Weights at the ends of the lines snapped back as the lines caught, thudding against the back and side of his head. Flora saw him go down, bonelessly flopping onto the sand.

She was still staring at the heap he had become when she was knocked out herself.

Flora came to slowly, trying to figure out how her hammock had fallen in the night and left her sitting up against the mast.

She opened her eyes and saw that the boat was on fire. No, that wasn't right. Her vision was doubled, and it was only one fire, contained in a circle of stones.

Then she remembered being off the ship, the fishermen and their spears.

She turned her head to the side too fast and everything swam again. She blinked hard, trying to get her brains in order.

Eddy was there, tied to a pole just as she was. He was still knocked out.

Flora looked up, trying to assess how bad things were. Above her, a bundle of fish hanging on her pole shivered and rained down drops of salt water.

Twenty men, maybe more. Almost all armed.

She rotated her rib cage, trying to sense the weight of her gun against her body. It was there.

Maybe they don't know that I'm armed?

She looked over and saw the butt of Eddy's gun where it always sat. With his hands tied behind him, it wasn't even really out of reach. He could pull it, but aiming it would be a challenge.

Still, it could start enough chaos. Maybe they don't have guns here. Maybe they don't know what they are.

The men were not paying attention to her. Night had fallen, and they had all turned their backs on Eddy and Flora to watch the sea. Flora scanned the horizon, looking for Bodie, for the *Ursula*. She saw nothing.

Fog lay heavy against the flat sea. The tide was out. Flora thought about making a sound but did not.

Then the glow from a ship lit up the fog but did not break through it. Flora saw it like a tiny moon advancing on the shore. She shook her head again.

What the hell is that?

Beside her, Eddy was beginning to stir.

"Eddy," she hissed through her teeth. "Eddy! Eddy, can you hear me?"

Eddy rolled his head on a limp neck, looking at her out of one eye. "What the fuck?"

Flora shrugged. She saw Eddy immediately move his hand to check for his gun. He had his finger on the trigger at once, the muzzle laid against the sand.

"Wait," Flora said. "Just wait."

Eddy's jaw set, but he did wait.

Through the fog there came two dinghies. In the front of each sat a person holding a flaming torch. Flora looked back at the moon-ship, veiled behind the wall of fog.

It's torches. They've got a boat covered in torches.

As they came ashore, Flora knew they were women. It wasn't their clothes; many of them wore leather wrap-dresses over breeches. It wasn't their hair; two or three of them were shaved like Eddy preferred to be. But it was in every line of them; the way they braced their weight in their hips before flexing muscular arms to haul their boats up the beach. It was in the way they stood and looked at one another.

I ought to feel safer, Flora, thought, squirming. *So why don't I?*

She thought of Alma and the women of Shy. She thought about herself, keeping watch over Eddy in Estiel.

It doesn't mean that they'll be better. Just that they might understand.

As the women came closer to the fires on the beach, Flora saw that they too wore tattoos that lay across their chins, as if ink had dripped from their bottom lips and dried there.

One of them stopped and spoke to the spear-bearers.

"You've got two?"

The man bowed his head. "I do, Mother. As I signaled."

"Are they well? Are they young?"

He nodded again, gesturing toward the place where Eddy and Flora were staked to the sand.

The woman who had spoken stepped forward. She was broad in the shoulders and hips, the wrap of her dress accentuating the hourglass shape of her body. Her hair was long and loose, black shot all over with gray and woven with the feathers of seabirds. A string of sea-glass beads hung just below her ear. Flora saw it catching in the firelight.

She searched the woman's eyes and saw no malice. She sat up straighter and prepared to speak, but the woman turned to Eddy first.

"Are you a keeper?"

Eddy cocked his head to the side. Flora saw him dragging the gun, straining against his bonds. "A what?"

"A keeper," the woman said in a low, calm voice that just carried over the sound of the sea. "Are you a keeper of women?"

She inclined her head toward Flora. "Is this woman your property?"

"Oh," Eddy said at once. "You mean am I a slaver? No, I'm not a fucking slaver."

"Is that true?" The woman turned to Flora, searching her face. "Are you free?"

Flora shrugged. "Right now, I'm tied to a pole. Usually I'm free. Eddy doesn't own me. We don't do that."

The woman nodded, then bent down to free Flora. Standing up again, she said, "I am Dell, and I am the Mother Librarian. Forgive the fishermen for binding you. It's my orders. We are always searching for women."

Flora stood up and rotated her shoulders a few times. "I've had worse. Why bother tying us? Couldn't they have just asked us to stay and meet you?"

Dell fixed her with a quizzical eye. "Why would you stay when we might be slavers? Only slavers have boats."

Flora looked down at Eddy, still tied.

"Mother Dell," Eddy said. "How about it?"

Dell looked him over again, her black eyes critical. She looked back to Flora.

"He's really okay," she said.

Dell shrugged and freed Eddy, who stood and put his gun neatly away.

"I'm sorry to treat you this way. We have a real problem with slavers up and down the coast. Most of them are coming from the Bay, we think. We've had to become more aggressive in our precautions."

Flora turned to look as if these precautions would be clear to see, but was immediately distracted. Women had come off the ship in numbers she hadn't expected. There were forty or more spread out over the beach. They were eating roasted fishes and fresh oysters. They were standing grouped and talking with one another, all of them dressed somewhat like Dell.

But a dozen or more sat in the sand, each cradling a full-grown man in their laps. They were breastfeeding. Flora took in the same scene over and over again: a man curled up, blissful with his eyes closed, a hand resting on the breast to which he was not currently connected at the mouth. Cheeks working and working.

Dell followed Flora's eye line. "Would you like one? I'm sure one of the librarians would be happy to have you."

"No," Flora said quickly. "Thank you. Why do you do that?"

Dell shrugged. "A man needs milk. So where are you travelers from?"

Eddy stepped forward, tearing his eyes away from the strange sight. "We're from far, far inland. Near the river called the Misery. We've come all the way around from Florda to find the Midwife's Bay."

Dell looked up at the starlit sky. "Misery. Missouri, do you mean? And Florida?"

Flora and Eddy exchanged a glance. "Place names are different," Eddy said uncertainly. "But that sounds the same."

"And this Midwife's Bay you mentioned. Is that the San Francisco Bay?"

They looked at one another again. Flora, who had been rereading the Midwife recently, thought that was correct. "I think so, yes. Based on her book."

Dell's eyes lit up and she reached out a hand to Flora. "What book? Show me."

Flora smiled nervously. "I don't have it on me. It's on our ship . . . which was right out there. I don't know where it is now."

Dell nodded. "We spotted her as she was moving away from the shoreline. She's not far. But you must tell me more about this book."

So they sat by the fire and tried not to notice the men lining up for milk in the cool of the evening. Eddy told Dell about the Midwife, about Nowhere, and about them. Flora broke in here and there, but mostly she listened to Eddy speak.

He never talks this long to any of us, she thought. *Not even Alice. I don't think I've ever heard him say this many words at once.*

Dell's smile never faded, and only seemed to become more knowing as the story went on. When Eddy had run out of words, she spoke again.

"We are all librarians," she told him. "Do you know what that means?"

Meg Elison

Flora spoke up. "I've raided libraries in a couple of cities. I've seen pictures of old-world librarians. They were women who kept books, so that people could share their knowledge. They taught children to read."

Dell nodded. "We keep books of the old world, but our mission is to collect the books of the new world. There is often only one copy of each. We copy and collect and preserve. We keep them safe from fire and invaders and slavers. We are the library of the new world."

She said all this with a simple grandeur. Flora thought she saw a glint in Eddy's eye.

"We would like to collect the story of your Midwife. To copy it, before you move on."

"I don't know," Flora began. "It's over twenty volumes, and we may not have the time to—"

"I can give you one woman per volume," Dell said, looking over her people on the beach. "That's not a problem."

Eddy looked at Flora. "I don't see why not," he said.

"We have to get back to the *Ursula*. I want to check on my kid, anyway."

"You have a living child?" Dell's eyes were sharp.

"I have a living child," Flora agreed. "But not of my body."

Dell nodded. She arranged for two women to row them in one of the small boats back to where she had come from. Once they passed through the fog and Flora saw its full size, she gasped out loud.

CHAPTER 37

The Book of Flora
Shore to ship to ship . . . who knows where we are now
Winter, cold fog at sea
104N

We see the boat like a city rising out of the sea. It's lit with torches, but only at the prow. The rest of it runs dark, and that helps hide its size. It's enormous.

The hull is gray metal, and the sides rise up so tall that we can hear our voices echo off of it and come bouncing back at us.

"What the hell runs that thing?" Eddy asks, his head cranked back all the way to look up at the edge of it, blacker than the night. It blots out the stars.

"This thing is called the Alexandria," Dell says, looking mildly offended. "And we have a reserve. It's stored offshore and no one knows about it."

"A reserve of what?"

"Diesel," she says. Above us, someone throws down a rope ladder. The drop is so long that it seems to hang in the air before unrolling toward us.

"Deez," I say, low, to Eddy.

"Yeah," he says. "But how much must something this size burn through?"

"Can you climb?" Dell looks back over her shoulder.

I nod, thinking about the endless ascent out of Ommun. If I can do that, surely I can do this. But the rope ladder will not hold still and I'm knocked against the metal side of the ship more than once, bashing my shoulder or my hip. Eddy holds the bottom of the ladder and that makes it a little easier, but I'm not looking forward to coming down the same way.

Eddy follows me up and Dell comes last. Our pilots stay on our rowboat, which helps me relax and accept the idea that I'm not trapped here. Once I'm on the deck, I can't help but look for the Ursula. There are no other lights on the sea. Black night in every direction but the beach, which is a haze of orange through the fog.

There's a lookout in the crow's nest, and women come and go across the space of the deck. No one pays much attention to us. The ship is as broad as a town square and twice as wide. Its surface is black as an old road and mostly smooth. It's so large that I can barely feel the movement of the water. Not at all like the Ursula, which is always rocking and tossing beneath my feet. This is like an island. It's unnerving.

Dell beckons to us. "This way. Let me show you."

She walks us to a doorway that opens on a set of stairs leading down. The ship has electric lights below, unlike the torches on deck.

She sees me looking. "The system is old, but we've kept it in very good shape. We have stations where we can get replacement copper wire and other supplies. They won't last forever, but they may not have to. This way."

She makes a right turn and takes us deeper down into the ship. It's labyrinthine and metal; it reminds me immediately of Ommun. But the people are very different.

Coming and going throughout the ship, I see only women. I think about Shy and the place Kelda was from, Womanhattan. I think about the places I saw with Archie, how many of them kept men and women separate. I think about how many places I never felt that I could belong, because I would not be sorted correctly when the time came to put me on one side of the wall or the other.

I look over at Eddy and wish I knew if he was thinking the same thing. He is lost to me, has been lost to me, since we found each other in that cave. Estiel only made it worse. I won't ever really know his mind, and I grieve for what might have been. For that wall.

But maybe I'm not as far off as I think, because Eddy opens his mouth and says what I'm thinking. "The ship is all women."

Dell nods, not turning around. "That's right. Boys live on the beach, they learn to fish and weave and fight. Girls stay on the ship and learn to do library work. We come to shore twice a week."

"What if a child is neither?"

"Don't be silly," Dell said. "Everybody is one or the other."

"Are men allowed on the ship?" Eddy is catching up to Dell.

"No, never," Dell says equably.

"But you let me on," Eddy says at once.

Dell laughs a little. "I know what you are. We have women like you on board." She looks over her shoulder at me, giving me the once-over I know so well. "Like you, too."

Eddy's jaw sets, but if he is going to say something else, he misses the moment. "Here," Dell says.

She turns a wheel that moves two enormous lockbolts, and opens the metal door.

The air inside is fragrant with the smell of books and old papers. For just a moment I am reminded of Estiel, and my heart pounds, but then I realize it is only the scent of a cat. A small one.

"You keep cats on board?"

Dell turns to face me. "They control the rats. No avoiding them, I'm afraid, and they'll destroy our work. And the cats are happy to eat the guts out of a fish."

She gestures to the shelves lining the walls. There are some old-world books, as she said there would be. But most of it is diaries, journals, note-books, and collections of papers.

I can't help it—I want to touch everything. I reach out and very gently handle a notebook bound with a spiral made of thin metal.

"How long has this library existed?"

Dell sighs. "Since the plague."

"The Dying," Eddy counters.

Dell nods. "There are many names for it. There's a whole section of diaries from that time. We are particularly interested in those, of course. The ones that told us how this world came to be."

She pushes her heavy dark hair off her shoulder. "Beyond that, we have extensive collections of writings from people all over this continent, from the last century. We have the complete story of our attempts at civilization, in all the forms it has taken. Every one with the same goals, every one taking a different route to get there."

"I've seen some of that," Eddy says. "I have stories to tell. There's no way you've got it all."

Dell looks him over. "Maybe you'd stay with us awhile, and help us with this work."

I don't think Eddy would have considered it at all if Alice hadn't got-ten pregnant. But one by one, we had all left him. I had not been who he wanted me to be, and I had Connie. Alice had never been satisfied with one, and had always taken other lovers. And Bodie had done for her what Eddy never could. Kelda had chosen to return to Ommun, for all her end-less devotion to Eddy. Ina had died. Eddy looked so alone, staring around at those books.

And then he burst into tears.

"*This is what I was supposed to do,*" *he says between sobs.* "*My mother. Always wanted me to leave a book behind. To be like the Unnamed. I am like her. I was. But I picked to be like her in just the one way. I could have done more.*"

Dell looks shocked, and doesn't quite know what to do with this weeping stranger.

I go to Eddy and take his hands. "*There's still time,*" *I tell him.* "*You aren't done. You're here with the Midwife's book. You still have your story to tell. And you don't have to be anybody but who you are.*"

But he's shaking his head. Never letting me in.

"*You don't understand,*" *he says.*

I drop his hands. I think I do, but there's no winning that fight. Here I am, with my own journal in constant work, and knowing that he never writes anything down. Here I am, trying to always record what new places and new people are like. Here I am, tucking Connie's drawings into my pages, making the record complete. The work of this ship makes sense to me, but he's the one having the breakdown.

"*Are you taking on women?*" *I ask Dell, turning from Eddy.*

Dell nods. "*And their stories. Forever, as long as the boat can float. This is the work that women do. We keep the fire of civilization burning, by collecting and protecting stories. It's what we've always done.*"

I think of the library in Demons, the pictures of the old-world women who did the same job then. Everyone seems to have an idea of what women do, what we are. But Dell's makes more sense to me than most.

Shouting from above, as a message is passed from mouth to mouth. Dell lifts up her head.

"*Sailboat off the port,*" *comes the report.*

Dell looks at us.

"*That's our boat,*" *I tell her.*

We go back up to the deck and see that it is Bodie, steering the tiny Ursula toward us, with Alice waving on the bow.

I wave back, hoping Connie can see me.

"Why would they approach this huge ship?" Eddy asks, scanning the water behind them.

But the library crew has sprung to life all around us, because they already know the answer to that question.

A slave ship is pulling into the harbor just behind them.

CHAPTER 38

THE *ALEXANDRIA*

The ship was too big to turn around quickly, but the crew began to prime the engines and bring the ship about. Eddy and Flora sought cover but found none. They were exposed on the flat deck of the ship, and nobody was paying any attention to them.

"Gunner," yelled Dell. "Don't fire until we're between the smaller vessel and the slave ship."

"Aye," a redheaded woman yelled back. The ship lurched forward, churning against the shallow water and thrumming all over as the ancient engines stirred to life. When it began to move, it was surprisingly fast.

Across the bay, Bodie immediately took the hint. He brought the *Ursula* into the shadow of the mighty *Alexandria*, slipping behind her as a chick seeks the warmth beneath a mother hen's wing. Flora leaned over the railing, hoping for a glimpse of Connie, but the child must have gone below.

The slave ship was fully visible now, and it was a monster. Three masts of aged black wood, with men swarming over her decks like ants.

"Gunner," Dell yelled again from a perch halfway up to the crow's nest. "Fire at will!"

"Wait," Eddy yelled, his brow furrowing. "What about the—"

The guns fired immediately, a booming, earsplitting thud that rocked the whole ship. And then a second and a third. Across the water, the slave ship splintered pitifully, struck twice by whatever ammunition something so large could offer. Fire engulfed the fragments as they began to sink.

Eddy watched in horror, his mouth hung agape. Flora looked around the deck of the ship, staring in disbelief at the women on board celebrating such a malicious, forgone victory.

"What the hell?" She could barely hear herself speak. She reached out to the woman nearest her and dragged her close. "What the hell? What about the slaves on board?"

The woman pushed her off. "We'll rescue anyone who's in the water who isn't male. Come on. Don't be ridiculous. We did them a favor."

Flora staggered off and reached for Eddy. She looked at his face and saw something there that terrified her. He had moved past his earlier consternation. He was wearing an expression of wild satisfaction. He was glad.

And this was what you always wanted. An unambiguous, untainted victory. A commitment to an absolute, no matter what it costs. They kill slavers the way you always wanted to: immediately, without negotiation or hesitation. Those guns on your body will never match what the guns on this ship can do.

Below, Flora saw that they had indeed dispatched rescue boats to search for survivors. She didn't think they'd come back with many.

She looked for Dell but didn't find her. She grabbed Eddy by the arm. "Come on," she said. "We've got to get back to Bodie and Alice and Connie. Come on."

She found Eddy was hard to move, but in the end he went with her.

◆ ◆ ◆

Aboard the *Ursula*, Connie was all eyes. "What happened? Who's on that big ship? How did they get those big guns?"

Flora reached out and cupped Connie's cheek. "It's a library ship," she said. "They keep books and stories, and they kill slavers. That's all it is."

"A library ship?"

Flora nodded. "It's new to me, too."

Alice stared over the bow at the wreckage of the slave ship, one hand on her belly. "They could have just as easily fired on us. They don't know we're not a slave ship."

"We were there to tell them," Eddy said. "You were never in any danger."

Alice gave a short little laugh. "As if that's ever been true."

"So, are we ready to push up the coast?" Bodie asked. "We're not far from Midwife Bay now."

Eddy shook his head. "They say there's nothing up there. Nothing at all, no reason to push on."

Bodie shrugged. "Then what now?"

Eddy was staring at the huge gray ship, ignoring the small boats that picked up survivors. "I don't know yet." His voice was low, but his eyes were up.

You do know, Flora thought. Because she knew, too.

CHAPTER 39

The Book of Flora
Midwife's Bay
Coldest part of the year, but it's not as cold here
104N

Bodie's map says it's San Francisco Bay, but we're calling it Midwife's Bay, because that's what it is. Because the story is what matters. Eddy's map could have been updated, and I think he would have liked the change. But Eddy is gone.

I can barely stand it. I keep thinking he's just belowdecks or out on the shore. He's like a hole where a tooth used to be, and I keep putting my tongue in it. I can't get used to it. I can't accept that I ever will.

Alice believes that we'll meet again. She says that if we found Errol, then Eddy can find us again. That it's possible. Eddy knows which way we're headed, but nothing more. He doesn't know where we'll end up. I don't know where that ship will go. We have nothing tying us to one another. I guess we never did.

We lingered in the bay a few days. We watched the fishermen come and go. Connie sat and watched the men take milk. I could tell that they wanted to try it but were afraid to ask.

"It's alright if you want that," I told them. "The women are offering."

"Why do they do that?" Their eyes were shiny, and I tried to remember what it was like to be that young, to still want to be comforted like a child but also ready to fuck like an adult.

"It's a gift," I said. "A way to connect. It's how Mothers feed their babies, you know."

"I know," they said quickly. "I know about babies. I'm not stupid."

I didn't answer. I waited.

"But there are no babies," they said, their voice eager. "They just give milk, even though there's no one who needs it."

I shrugged. "Women often nurse someone else's child, if the Mother is sick. Or keeping nursing for years, if the child still needs it. I don't know how they start or stop. It just happens."

"Maybe they can just make it happen," Connie said. "Maybe it happens because they want it to, and they know that they can."

"Maybe," I said, because I didn't know how to argue it. I keep returning to the place where I am certain that they don't really know or believe the truth of how people have children. It kept coming up in the days before Eddy left. The other night was the last straw. I'm still reeling.

We were all on the deck. Alice was weaving a patch for one of Bodie's bad nets. He's taught us all how to do it. I've been weaving since I was Connie's age, so it was nothing to me. The open, even weaving of nets is no task at all compared to the tight, hot-fingered weaving of wool. Connie struggles with it. They have never really developed a trade, in all the chaos of their life. Eddy refused to do it at all. Alice is neat-handed, smart, and patient. She's as good as I am, now that she's been at it awhile.

Connie was watching her do it. They'd been staring at her off and on since she told us she was pregnant. I didn't think much of it, since pregnant women are always a source of wonder and fascination for the people around them. Connie is no different from that. But still, something about the intensity of their gaze worried me. Does everyone on this ship want to fuck Alice? I figured I was about to find out.

"How did it happen?" Connie just blurted it out, giving Alice a little jump of fright.

"What?" she said, turning her neck away from her work to look at them. "The net?"

They shook their head. "No, the baby. You said you're having Bodie's baby. So how did it happen?"

Alice smiled a little awkwardly. "I told you when you asked, child. We did the thing that makes them. I got pregnant, as women often do."

They looked around the deck, spotting Eddy in the prow, staring at the lights of the library ship, and me with the Midwife's book. "Yes, but you've done that with Eddy and Flora, too. So how do you know it's Bodie's?"

Bodie smiled and put a hand on the back of his neck. He was as embarrassed as a child, that leathery old seaman! "Yes, child. But I have man seeds in my body. I can give them to her. These others can't, you see?"

Connie's brow dropped at once. "What? Don't we all have the seeds of children inside us?"

I walked over to them and put a hand on their shoulder. "It has to be a man and a woman," I told them gently. "That's the only combination that makes a pregnancy."

"Then why don't you have Eddy's baby?"

Eddy and I looked at one another, and then away.

"Eddy and I weren't born with the right bodies to do that," I told them. "Well, actually, we were. But things have happened since then. I was cut as a small child, and Eddy—"

"Cut how?" Connie asked at once.

I cringed. "Connie, this is awfully personal. Why do you need to know?"

"I don't understand," Connie said. "I don't understand why sometimes people have babies and sometimes they don't. Sometimes babies die and *sometimes they're born wrong. Sometimes they're like me. Can I have a baby? Can I get someone pregnant?"*

"Nobody knows what their future will look like," Eddy said. He did not turn around and look at us. "Nobody knows the answer to that."

"That's right," said Bodie. "It's luck. Or it's magic. You cast your lot and what comes up is what you deal with."

Connie shook their head. "How can I accept that? When it's so important. When it's everything."

"I know what you're feeling," I said, trying to draw them near. "I know it's hard to settle into your body and feel welcome in it, take control of it."

"You don't know what it's like," Connie said, breathing harder. "I was a girl. I had everything. I could have had a Hive, could have had endless children. Then one day I became something else and nobody could love me."

"That's not true," I told them. "You can still have a Hive. You can get children other ways; look at how I got you. Eddy rescued a dozen girls from slavers, and any of them could have become his child."

Eddy did not add anything.

"Not like Alice has it." Their voice was shaking. "And you could, too. If you wanted to. Being cut doesn't change that."

"Connie," I said, my voice low. "I don't have a womb any more than you do. I don't think you understand how this works."

"I can talk you through the process," Alice offered, standing up. "It's a little mysterious, but not that complicated, in the end. Lend me a piece of your charcoal and I'll sketch it out."

Connie shook their head. They looked at Eddy, Alice, and me in succession, over and over. They laid their hands against their chest and belly, mimicking Eddy when he breathes, Alice when she feels for her child. They were silent a moment.

"What is a woman?"

"I'm going to become a librarian," Eddy said, out of nowhere.

"What?" I was asking them both.

"I'm so sick of this," Eddy said. "Of all of it. We're never going to find what we're looking for, because it doesn't exist. I don't want to fight. Not even the little fights that happen when you try to build with other people. I don't ever want to live around men again. I don't ever want to have to define myself to anyone, ever again. I'm going."

Alice stood up. Her voice trembled. "Eddy, you can't leave us. We've known each other our whole lives. I wanted to raised my child with you."

Eddy looked over at Bodie. "No you didn't."

Alice gave that little smile and one-shoulder shrug that seemed to work on everyone. She had washed her hair with rainwater, and her ringlets were perfect again. In the light of the rising moon, she was blue-white and as beautiful as any woman I've ever seen. "I had to get it somewhere," she said in a low voice. "And I wasn't going to get it from you. It could still be ours. Since when does any man have a claim on a child?"

I saw Connie watching avidly, trying to figure it all out.

"Eddy is free to go where he wants," I said, my heart breaking inside me the way a wave breaks on the rocks. "Isn't that the point?"

Eddy smiled at me for the first time in I don't know how long. Since the cave, maybe? It seemed like forever.

"Maybe that's why your book is blank," I said.

He looked at me with such nakedness that I could barely stand it. "What do you mean?"

"Because you're not meant to leave a story behind. Or a child. Maybe you're meant to watch the stories of others."

He walked down the length of the deck and took both my hands in his. "Thank you. I won't forget."

Alice cried on him endlessly as he tried to say his goodbyes. She clung to him as though she were drowning. He extricated himself and gathered his pack. He was resolute, never wavering. I believe I saw relief on his face and not much else.

He bid Connie and Bodie goodbye somewhat less warmly. Connie seemed stunned and distant. *That child has had enough goodbyes to last them forever (haven't we all?).*

Eddy came back to me again. "I have all the guns I'll ever need, from Ommun. My bag is still almost too heavy with bullets." He hooked his thumb at the gray ship over his shoulder and grinned. "And you've seen what they've got. I don't think I'll need most of this."

He pulled two of the pistols from Ommun out of his pack, added a long box of bullets, and handed them to Alice. "Take care of yourself," he said.

Alice sobbed and wouldn't take the parcel. Bodie did it for her.

"Mighty fine gift. She'll thank you one day."

Eddy nodded. He pulled one of his knives out of a deep place in his binder and gave it to Connie. "This is a good one. Take care of it, and it'll take care of you."

Connie looked at the piece of shining steel in openmouthed wonder. "Thank you," they breathed. Eddy put a hand on their shoulder, and they regarded each other a minute. That was all of it.

He came to me and held out the revolver that his mother had given him. The one that had been passed down through Nowhere all those years, that had come to him from the Midwife.

"You're following her now. You have her books. You carry this. You go on. I'm done. This should be yours."

I couldn't take it. I knew what it meant to him, and I opened my mouth to argue.

"You have to keep it wiped down," he said, pressing it into my hand. "You have to take care of it. If you touch your hand to it at night, it'll keep you safe. This is the gun that killed the Lion. This is my heart. It always has been. But it's time I grew a new one."

I took his warm metal heart from his hands and held it to my chest the way one holds a child. I wish I had known what to say.

He called to one of the small boats as it passed, taking the librarians away when all their milk was gone. They brought him on without any questions. I took my last look at him against the purpling sky, outlined in black next to a woman whose still-exposed breasts seemed to glow in the dark. Then he was gone.

I used to think that the losses in my life would slow down or maybe cease, that I wouldn't always be mourning and saying goodbye. But the older I get, the more constant that state becomes.

There is nothing in San Francisco. The stories were true. Much of the old city is under water, and storms have wrecked boats all over the bay, washing them in from the sea and getting them caught there. No fires at night, no signs of life. Alice and I sat on the railing of the ship, watching whales glide through the water among the wrecks. We saw one calving, thrashing her offspring free with a bright plume of blood in the water.

"How do they do that?" Connie asked, their hands moving over their sketchpad.

I didn't have an answer. Nobody does.

The boat seems emptier than it should be with only one person missing. Alice is wrapped tight around Bodie; they look like a couple of snakes entwined. Connie's sketchbook is full of nothing but drawings of Alice. Alice from the back, from the side, from above. Connie must have climbed into the crow's nest to get that angle: Alice's nose jutting like a blade out over the roundness of her belly. A few other drawings, from memory or from the sea. A litter of kittens. Bodie's hand sunk into a gravid fish, her night-bright shining eggs spilling out over his hands.

I remember the way he put his fingers in his mouth, sucking their raw saltiness and rolling his eyes up in his head. "Unborn," he had said. "Magnificent."

The Midwife is no comfort now. She makes me think of Eddy and almost nothing else. I think of my silence when he burned Ina's body, and when he was strapped to the Lion's bed. What should I have done? What could I have said? Is there some other life where we held it all together? Should we have just stayed in Nowhere and tried to rebuild?

Is there even a right answer? Is there any way in this life to feel less pain?

I feel old. I suppose that makes sense. I'm older now than I've ever been. But I feel old in the way that means there is nothing ahead. And that is what hurts the most. There is nothing on the horizon now, as we sail ever northward. Connie gets taller and Alice gets rounder, and I get nothing but older, day after day.

CHAPTER 40

The Bambritch Book
High summer, long hot days
144N

I thought I was old then. I didn't know what old looked like yet, how it would settle on me like invisible weights, bowing my back and making my hips ache. I didn't know that age would bring the cold into my bones like splinters made of glass, or that it would make my bowels untrustworthy and unpredictable.

The young have no idea the kind of pain and degradation that await. It's just as well. It would be hard to go on at all if you knew what the end of the line looked like. My prize for fighting, for not dying all those times, is a broken heart and very dry skin.

There is no entry in my book for when Connie left. I knew there would be none, but it still shocked me to come to the place where that book just stops. I closed it and didn't open it again for many years. When I was ready, I simply began in a new book. I wanted something that had never held a mention of Eddy, or of Connie. I wanted to start over, and so I did.

When we reached Bambritch, Eddy had been gone half a year. The sea was a cold and bitter gray, and it was sleeting into our faces half the time. Connie was sleeping with me out of sheer desperation for warmth. Alice was as big as a house.

Settle was a fairly large city even then, all those years ago. I can't believe how many are there now. The last few times I've gone over to do any training, it's been totally overwhelming. Thousands, packed all over that narrow strip of land across the sea.

But when we arrived back then, the city was full of plague. We came to the docks and tried to moor, but there were signs up all over, plus masked people warding us off.

It was absolute chaos beyond. Some of the people in masks were clearly ill themselves. Some of the signs said "Yellow Fever," others said "Scarlet Fever" or simply "POX" in three huge, ominous letters.

Alice took one look at that and disappeared belowdecks. There was no way we could expose her to that, even if we had wanted to try. But we had been at sea for so long. Supplies of anything but fish and salt were dangerously low, so we had to press on.

Someone at the docks told us to try the islands. There were so many, Bodie simply pointed and headed for one. It turned out to be Bambritch.

There was almost no structure here when we arrived. Just a handful of folks living and fishing and farming together. Connie was so excited to see people who weren't actively waving us off, they slipped on the way down the ladder and ended up soaked. It was Hortensia who took us in that night, who fed us and put us in front of her fire. She had an old-world stethoscope and she handed it over to Alice, who found her child's fluttering heartbeat within seconds.

Connie and I took a house, the same house I live in now. Alice and Bodie took another. Connie was at their house constantly, waiting on

Alice hand and foot, bringing her little treasures they had bartered for with their drawings.

Alice indulged Connie. At the time, I thought it was sweet of her, but now I know it was too much. Too much. I had no idea how far it would go.

They were sleeping over there, hovering over Alice every day as her time drew nearer. They were sketching her day and night, avoiding me or anyone else. They hated to be away from Alice for any reason.

In one of our rare moments alone, Alice looked at me with the raw, hunted expression of an animal. Her skin looked thin and bruised, and the darkness under her eyes made them like wells in her face.

"They keep asking me the same questions," she said, looking around the room to make sure Connie wasn't there. "I've explained everything a thousand times. I got a medical textbook from the library, showed them the parts and the fetal development timeline and everything. They just keep telling me that that can't be how it happens. There's nothing I can do to convince them. It's starting to scare me a little."

I tried not to frown too hard. Connie was stubborn, that was clear. But why argue with the reality of conception? What would be the point?

"What are they driving at?" I asked her. "Is it jealousy or just ignorance?"

"Neither," Alice said, swallowing hard and looking around again. "They think I fragged myself."

"Oh, come on," I said, scoffing and settling back in my chair. "That's the most ridiculous thing I ever heard." I picked up my cup of pine-needle tea and found it cold but still agreeable. "They can't really think that."

Alice shrugged. "I don't know what they can think," she said. "We don't really know where they came from, Flora. They might have been damaged somehow as a child, so that this will never make sense. Maybe they need to believe in something impossible because of what they are."

I bristled a little at the "what they are" comment. People in Bambritch had been fairly accepting of Connie, but there were a few who could not get used to calling them "they." There were still others who laughed at or embroidered on Connie's personal history, because they have never heard of a guevedoces here. I've never heard of one anywhere else, but that shouldn't matter. It's Connie's body and they were there when it happened. The truth of it belonged to them.

Connie came of the age to start being interested in someone sexually, but they never seemed to look at anyone that way except Alice. If Alice had wanted to bring them into her Hive back then, I'd have opposed it. Connie was too young to be with anyone in that way. But I couldn't have stopped it.

"That doesn't matter," I told her. "Everybody has a body, every body has a story. Plenty of children have trouble believing anything we tell them about babies, because the stories are so inconsistent and mixed with rumor. And the books we have don't predict how many will die in childbirth, or seem to understand how rare and dangerous it is. They come from another world."

Alice nodded. "That's it exactly. They tell me that those old-world books can't predict this. That we've become something else than what we were. They say the future is frags. I don't know what to say to that."

She and I had spoken many, many times on the necessity of teaching some science to the kids. We wanted the children of Bambritch to be able to read and write, but they needed to know how the world worked, as well. Alice had stressed to me time and time again that it was impossible to teach her trade to a youngster who had no basic understanding of life science, the body, the world of plants, or even the difference between applying heat and applying cold.

Not understanding these basic processes was what let people fall into abject superstition, believing that they needed to make sacrifices or offer some kind of ritualized devotion in order to be fed or be safe. There are hundreds of people in Settle who wear the bones of plague dead in order to ward off the sickness themselves. Without any science, they match like to like and assume that these charms and nonsense will work. It's that kind of ignorance that allows plague to spread, because they won't listen to people like Alice who talk about germ theory, sterilization, or even properly washing their hands.

When Connie came back, I told them they had to come home with me that night.

"Why?" they whined.

I looked them over. They had the barest patch of hair on their upper lip. They were sleeping more and more, and seemed to constantly be in a mood. The change was heavy on them; I could smell them every time they were near.

"Because I miss you," I said, not wanting to tell them that Alice was exhausted and nearly due, and she wanted them out of her hair.

"Fine," they growled. "Bye, Alice!"

She waved to them over her shoulder, already headed out.

We walked home. The way was short, but I wasn't sure how to begin, so we arrived there before I had figured out what to say.

We sat at our kitchen table. The house reminded me of my little place in Jeff City. The kitchen was cheery, on the back of the house and flooded with sunlight. The night was quiet; it wasn't warm enough yet for frogs or bugs. There was nothing but humming silence between the two of us.

I cooked us eggs in crushed tomatoes and herbs, and I still had bread. This was their favorite, always. We sat down and I watched them begin to shovel it in. I managed a few bites, but my stomach was flipping and churning. I was fairly certain this was going to be a fight, but I didn't know how bad it would get.

"So, you know Alice is telling you the truth, right?"

"What do you mean?" They slurped up a whole egg and burst the yolk in their mouth. I had seen them do it a hundred times, but tonight it seemed somehow predatory, like watching a snake raid a bird's nest.

"When she tells you how she got pregnant, that's the actual story. That is how absolutely everyone who has ever gotten pregnant ended up that way."

"That's not true," they said, raking a piece of bread through the red trench of tomatoes and bringing it to their mouth. "In the books, it says there used to be lots of ways. A doctor could help. Or people could take semen from someone and do it all alone."

I tried not to roll my eyes. "Alright, yes. You're right. In the old world, there were more ways to do it."

Another slurp. "And now, there might be new ways."

"Connie, there is no such thing as fragging."

They looked up at me, and I saw such a stranger in their eyes that I nearly gasped. I did not know them as well as I thought I did. I had taken so much for granted when they came to be with me that I think I constructed the child I wished I'd had, rather than the one I really got. I miscalculated badly. I will never be free of that.

"You have no idea what you're talking about," Connie said, their eyes narrowing in contempt.

"I do, actually. I've been around a lot longer than you," I said, trying to keep their attention.

They ran right over me. "I know you're running a little library and making your little stump speeches about teaching kids science, using soap, and dissecting worms. While you were doing all that, I was really learning. Look."

They got up and stalked away from the table. They came back with a book they had stuffed full of loose notes and sketches. It was a biology text, with all of their work packed into two sections. They opened it in front of me.

"Human evolution," they said. "We change when the environment pressures us to change. Life since the Dying has been nothing but pressure, and pressure in this one specific thing. So why wouldn't this change?"

I had no answer for that, but I dug deep. "Change like that takes a long time."

"No it doesn't." They flipped the pages to a story about moths in a smoked-out town turning from white to black and back again.

"People aren't moths," I said. "We live longer. We breed slower."

"Doesn't matter," they said, flipping forward again. "What matters is this."

They spread their hand over the book, showing me a two-page spread in that crumbling volume. The page was titled "Asexual Reproduction, Parthenogenesis, and Uniparental Offspring."

I looked it over. "Connie, these are lizards. Worms. Fish. People are something else entirely."

"Are we?" They smirked. "Don't we eat and shit and fuck just like them? Don't we die just like them? Is it really that impossible?"

Staring directly into Connie's eyes, I made the leap. "Is this about you, my living child? Are you thinking that the change that made you is at work as a force in others, giving them the power to frag like this? Is that what you're hoping? Because the thing that made you was nothing bad. You don't have to prove it can do this to redeem it, or to make it good."

Their face fell. "I'm not trying to explain myself," they sputtered. "Or you. Or Eddy. Or Hortensia, even. I'm trying to see what's next for us. I'm trying to see a world without slavers, where women don't have to be kept so that men can be sure that they'll breed."

"That isn't why they do it," I said, deadly quiet. "I know that because I was a slave, and that was never going to be possible for me."

"You don't know what's possible," Connie spat back. "It doesn't make any sense to keep slaves without believing that some lasting good will come of it."

I sighed. "Connie, people just do things that don't make sense. Not everything lines up neatly and evens out at the end. Sometimes we are just like fish or worms or lizards, doing things without thinking, just going on instinct." I tapped my finger on the page, below *Parthenogenesis*. "Sometimes we're not."

They reached down and snapped the book shut. "You're never going to understand this."

"Funny, I was thinking the same thing about you."

They left the room and I could hear them packing a bag. I walked to the foot of the stairs.

"Where are you going?"

"Out," they said. "You can't stop me because you don't own me. I'm old enough to be on my own."

I swallowed, my throat suddenly a knotted rope. "Where will you go?"

"My own place," they said behind muffling walls. "I can't stand to be around you anymore. You're so ignorant. You're so closed-minded."

"Connie," I said, trying to keep my heart out of my mouth. "Sleep on it. In the morning, you'll make a better decision."

"Morning will find me somewhere else," they said, their voice haughty.

Nothing soothes a breaking heart like anger, so I found mine. "Alice doesn't want you over there," I told them. "She says you're exhausting and scary."

They appeared at the top of the steps, bag in hand. "She did not say that," they breathed.

Oh, I had struck the heart of them. I wish I hadn't, but in the moment I was glad I did.

"She did. She doesn't want you, Connie. She's a grown woman, and she's got Bodie. Even if she does want a Hive, she won't have you in it. You're never going to be with her like that."

"Why not?" Connie asked, their nostrils suddenly flaring. "They weren't that picky about being with you. And what even are you? What could you offer her?"

I felt like they had punched me in the gut, but I didn't flinch.

"I'm an adult," I said. "I'm Flora. And I'm your mother."

"You're not my mother, you're nobody's mother. You could never do what she's doing. You're dead inside. Cut. A useless cut thing."

That was the end, and I could take no more. I got out of their way and they went through the door.

I went looking for them two days later, expecting to find them at Alice's, where they always ran when they were angry or upset. I was trying to keep the custom from Nowhere of allowing a person in childbed the privacy they would need to grieve if all did not go well, but I could not wait any longer. Word reached me on the street that the Mother and child had both lived, and I walked over in a haze of joy to find Alice in bed with a newborn, very tired but alright.

"Why didn't you call for me?" I asked her, taking the tiny pink babe out of her arms.

"I thought Connie would tell you," she said sleepily.

"Connie? Are they here?"

She yawned, nodding. "They were. They came here while I was in labor. They wanted to watch the birth, but I said no. Bodie had to scare them away from our window. That kid. I figured they would go home and tell you about it."

I didn't say anything. I touched the perfect silky folds under Alice's baby's chin. "What are you going to name her?"

"Poppy," Alice said dreamily, already falling asleep. "I've been growing her my whole life."

I waited one more day before letting go of whatever it was—pride, anger, I don't know—before openly asking around the island to find out where Connie was. I spoke to everyone I knew they were friends with and moved outward from there. Everyone told me the same thing: they hadn't seen Connie. Connie was obsessed with Alice and the pregnancy, Connie couldn't talk about anything else.

Everyone was soon in that same condition. They came from all over the island, bringing Alice and Poppy and Bodie food and old-world goods and presents and home-brewed wine and liquor. They toasted the child and touched Alice for luck. Poppy was welcomed over and over; people whispered her name like it was a cure for hopelessness. She wasn't the first child born on Bambritch, but it had been a while. She was a beacon of hope.

Finally, someone told me that Connie had left on a crab boat the day that Poppy was born. We gained one and lost one. Alice got her living child and I lost mine. I kept thinking they would come back. They didn't.

Dozens of seasons passed. Alice had more children. I had lovers who came and went. I never had another living child. I was never sure I could do any better than I had done with my lost Connie.

It's not yet dawn, but I know it will be today. This army will arrive today. They may make our shore, or they may fire on us from across the water.

I'm sure now. It's been in all my dreams and banging on the back door of my heart since I first heard the stories. Since one or two refugees told me that the army said they were looking for a person named Flora. I've known the world wasn't wide and there aren't that many people in it. I've seen Eddy find Errol and still I tried to deny that there's something that drags people back together in this world. I haven't wanted to face it, but now I know it as well as I've ever known anything: Connie will be with the army. This obsession with frags, this continual drive toward our little island, can mean nothing else. They're coming home to me, and they're trying to make a point. They always let things build up until they were ready to explode. They never were much for subtlety; I don't think I should be surprised at all that they want to tell me their feelings with tanks.

I'm ready. My living child, I'm ready. My death, I'm ready. But not for the end of us. I am not ready for that. Today, my book goes into the trunk and the trunk goes into the ground. Today, I take a drink of that old-world liquor and try to steel my nerves for what's ahead. Today, I put all my life and work behind me and face the unknown thing.

Today, I am Flora and this book is my life. Tomorrow, only one of those things will be true.

CHAPTER 41

BAMBRITCH ISLAND

The mosquito whine of the airplane motor droned closer and closer in the pink light of dawn.

Zill and her helpers had done their part; they had gotten every boat between Settle and Bambritch moved, hidden, or scuttled. The harbor was clear and the sea between was like glass.

Zill climbed up the spotting tower and handed her spyglass over to Flora without a word. Flora's gaze swept up and down the railing, looking the army over. There were thousands of bodies arranged on the opposite side, taking up their entire view of Settle's coast. Behind them, Flora counted four tanks, all with huge mounted guns. Wagons and trucks numbering in the dozens. And the airplane.

Flora looked this over carefully, seeing that the engines were running but that it was chained to the back of a large vehicle so that it could be towed. The chains were not new and not easy to remove. There was no way they intended to fly it. It was very likely they just didn't know how.

Hortensia joined them, followed by Carol and Eva.

"Look," Flora said. She pointed out the airplane. Each of them took a turn.

"They can't fly it," Hortensia said at once, somewhat triumphantly.

"You were right about that," Flora said. "Weren't you going to go with some of the people refugeeing to Vashon?"

Hortensia fixed her with a sickening eye. "Absolutely not. My place is here."

They waited. Carol put a hand on Eva's shoulder, and Eva put her hand on top of that.

They had moved everyone to the far shore of the island and advised as many as could to head elsewhere, to the other islands in the sound. There was no reason to lose everyone on Bambritch, and those who had refugeed that way agreed wholeheartedly. None of them wished to stand for the same assault again.

Without warning, one of the tanks shot off a round with a boom like a tree falling in the woods. Everyone jumped, then cringed, bracing for impact. The projectile struck water, not coming close to the island.

"A warning shot," said Eva.

"A test," Zill corrected. "To see if they could hit us from there. They can't."

The people of Bambritch became restless after the warning shot. They taunted the people on the other side, knowing that their taunts could not be heard. They milled and talked and watched while nothing at all happened. The army did not seem to go anywhere, or change its demeanor in the slightest.

"Give me the spyglass," Flora said, holding her hand out to Carol. He passed it over.

Flora saw something moving through the crowd, held over the heads of several men. She knew it was a boat before it hit the water.

"They're sending over a boat," she said. "A small one."

When it was on the water and on its way, Flora handed the glass over.

"We have to go meet them," Eva said.

"I should go alone," Flora said at once.

"What?" Hortensia's voice was sharp and cracked on the word. "Why?"

"Because it's my living child," Flora said. "Connie. They're the one who's brought this army to us. They've come back to me."

"You can't know that," Hortensia said at once, ever the skeptic.

Flora shrugged. "Nothing else makes any sense," she said. "Everything the refugees have said makes it clear. They're coming here for a reason. Some of the refugees tell me that they use my name. They have the same obsession Connie had."

"Connie was obsessed with frags?" Zill asked doubtfully.

Flora nodded. "I never knew what to do about it. I didn't know it would get like this." She turned to Carol. "Can you please send for Alice? I think she might be able to help with this."

Carol nodded and began to climb down at once.

Flora looked at the other three women. "I don't know if I'll come back from this. I don't know what to advise you to do when I'm gone. I know you'll do all you can to keep our people safe. Know that I've always loved you."

They pulled one another close and leaned their foreheads together. They spoke rapidly, in the clipped ideas that people who have shared important work use so well. It wasn't much of a plan, but it was better than nothing. In the end, they had all their bases covered.

Down on the beach, the women who had volunteered to entertain an army were ready. They had painted and rouged, and several had reddened their hair like Flora did. She smiled to see them.

"I don't know if you'll be needed, but I'm so honored that you'd try," she called out to them. They offered her grim smiles and waves, shivering in the early light.

Only the sound of seabirds overhead, the gentle lapping of the waves. The little boat was coming.

Alice arrived just before the boat made landfall. Flora looked her over. She thought the years had been kindest to Alice of everyone she knew. Alice's fair hair barely showed gray. The births of several children had softened her body, making it more generous and lovable than it had ever been. Her eyes crinkled at the edges, but they were no less lovely for that.

Flora reached out and Alice gave her hand to her old friend.

"It's Connie," Flora said.

"It's what?"

"I'm almost certain."

Alice searched Flora's eyes, her face working as she caught up slowly. Flora simply turned and led her by the hand toward the water, trying to anticipate where the little boat would land. It was close enough now that Flora could hear the whine of its deez motor and see that there were two people riding inside, rather than one.

A guard, maybe. An assistant? A partner?

The boat landed and two figures emerged, one young and one clearly struggling and obviously older.

Flora and Alice held hands and did not move.

As the other two came closer, it became clear that the taller of the two was Connie. They were broader now, in their full height and filled out like a man. They wore a red scarf over the lower half of their face, and Flora could tell at once that it was made of silk.

She strained to see Connie's eyes, to take it all in. It had been half a lifetime since she had seen her living child.

Alice squeezed her hand agonizingly hard and made a sound in her throat. Flora looked over at her and saw that her eyes were huge in her face, locked on the person walking just a few feet behind Connie.

And then Flora cried out involuntarily, feeling the air course through her body without her will.

Because the other person who had been on the boat was Eddy.

CHAPTER 42

BAMBRITCH ISLAND

Eddy raised his bound hands to them, but Alice was already running. She hit him so hard that they nearly tumbled into the rocky sand. Flora walked up slowly behind her, not watching their reunion. She had eyes only for Connie.

And Connie, of course, could only watch the two of them embrace, shutting Connie out once again. They changed course to walk toward Alice.

Good, Flora thought. *That's working as planned.*

She quickened her pace toward Connie while their attention was elsewhere. She got within ten paces and stopped. Connie's head was turned at a deep angle, showing the muscles and cords in their neck. Despite everything, something in Flora was relieved to realize that they were well and healthy, and had obviously not been hungry all this time.

They've been feeding themselves on all they could steal from the towns they've taken, the people they've killed. Get it together.

Flora took a deep breath and watched Eddy and Alice break apart. Eddy saw her, finally, came to her next.

Eddy came into her arms and Flora pulled him in, taking just a moment to see how his hair had gone gray, his face weathered by the years.

And the sea? Has he been at sea this whole time? How did Connie find the Alexandria? *How did any of this happen?*

Eddy was familiar and strange all at once, and Flora took a deep breath of his scent, holding him tight.

Whatever else they came to do, Connie brought me the two things I've lost that I've missed the most. Whatever happens now, my heart is whole.

"Tell her," Connie said, their voice deeper than Flora had ever heard it.

Eddy pulled back and put his tied hands on one side of Flora's face. "Fragging is real. I've seen it."

Alice looked at Eddy, and then at Connie.

"So? So why not go and find them, if that's true? Why kill people up and down the continent, asking for them? What are you trying to prove?"

Connie's mouth twisted to one side in something that was not quite a smile. "It's not enough to find the frags. We have to make way for them. That means that mistakes like Flora and me and Eddy here cannot exist anymore. We can make this world new and right and clean. We just have to make some space first."

Alice's cheeks were red spots of anger. "There's plenty of space, you murderer. Have you seen the empty cities out there? Nobody is trying to stop any kind of progress, if that's what it is. People are just trying to live. We don't need any more men like the Lion trying to remake the world in the way they think it should be."

Connie unwrapped their red silk, and Flora could see how closely, how carefully they had shaved their beard.

"You should untie Eddy," Alice said reproachfully. "You're just another one of them. Another little lion man."

"I don't believe there ever was a Lion," they said. "I think that's a story you all cooked up to make yourselves into heroes."

Eddy's jaw set. "You think what you want."

Flora held Eddy's hands, not daring to untie them herself. "How did they find you? Where's the *Alexandria*?"

"I don't know," Eddy said, with real pain in his voice. "They caught me in a raid and the ship left without me. I know where they'll be at midsummer, and I plan to meet them there."

"You'll be dust in the wind by midsummer," Connie said.

The Midwife's pistol is lying against my back right this minute, Flora thought. *If Connie is armed, they aren't showing it.*

As if they could hear her thoughts, Connie smiled. "Don't get any ideas, old horsewoman. If I'm not back by sunset, my army will lay waste to your island."

"With what?" Alice asked tartly. "Are they all coming over in tiny boats, one by one? We're ready for you, you know. Sending us refugees just meant you were sending us a wave of warnings."

Connie looked Alice up and down, hunger evident in their eyes. "You have no idea what we can do. What we're capable of. There are weapons we haven't used yet, things I've been saving just for this island. Just for this moment. Just for you," he said, turning his gaze back to Flora.

"Then what do you want here?" Flora asked tiredly. "I am not interested in the big show. If you came to kill me, then let's get it over with. What could you possibly want, other than some petty revenge?"

Connie's eyes rolled back to Alice. "I don't care about you, Flora. I never did. I'm here for her."

Alice froze, her face becoming a sheet of ice. "What?"

Connie took a step toward her, and Eddy stepped back. Flora had never known him to cede territory like that in a fight, and was shocked.

315

What must Connie have done to him to make him fear them this way?

"You can do it," Connie said, their voice suddenly much gentler. "I know you can. I've been studying about it for years, looking for the signs of fragging. You can do it, you just have to learn how. I'm going to take you to them, so you can learn how to do it. You'll see."

Alice gave a little laugh. "Connie, it's too late for me. I'm past the end of my blood; I've had all the children I'm going to have. With men, by the way. I had each and every one of them with a man. Because that's how it happens. Every time."

Eddy sighed behind them. "They're fucking crazy," he said. "But they really are telling the truth. There are some islands, up by Laska—"

"Shut up," Connie said over their shoulder. "I don't need you to explain this when I've always been right. When I knew from my own root and my own change that this was possible." They fixed their eyes on Alice. "I'll take you to the island. You'll see. Everything is different there."

Alice and Flora shared a look. Flora thought of her gun. Alice turned back to Connie.

"Will you tell me about this? Will you give me the choice to say yes or no?"

Connie looked her over again, the hunger of a lifetime in their eyes.

"I don't know that I will give you that choice," they said finally. "But let's talk."

Quick as a fish, they pulled a pistol from their back. Flora moved at once to draw hers, but saw that they aimed straight up. They shot an orange-red flare and reholstered at once.

"What was that?" Alice asked.

"They just bought us some time," Eddy said.

Alice settled her nerves, laying a hand against her chest. "Come with me," she said.

Absurdly, as if from some other world, Connie offered her their elbow. It was clad in an old-world leather jacket that shone with the look of someone else's labor. Alice, long used to this kind of gesture, accepted and threaded her hand through the crook of their arm.

Eddy and Flora followed a few paces back. When Alice clearly had them engaged in conversation, Flora slowed up a little more.

"Eddy, are you okay?"

"I'm too fucking old for this kind of thing," he said at once. "I was long past all this. Life in the library is so peaceful, Flora."

Flora squeezed his arm. "I keep a library, too. I know what you mean." Quieter still. "Do you remember how Estiel fell apart when the Lion was gone? How we kept thinking someone would rise to take his place, but no one did?"

"Yep," Eddy said firmly.

"Is it the same? Have you seen the army? Do they have enough leadership to go on?"

Eddy looked at Flora, not speaking. At length, he found his voice. "Can you? Can you kill Connie yourself?"

Flora looked at Connie's back, seeing only the child she had bought off an auction block in some other life. "If it means this ends. If I have to. I can."

She watched Alice dawdle, pointing things out to Connie. Getting them to remember, to share stories with her. Wasting time. She tried to guess how long it had been, but she didn't know.

How long do they need? How long until Connie realizes what we're up to?

They closed the distance before they came to Alice's house. Alice sat Connie down on her feather-filled sofa, her pride and joy. She took their jacket from them.

They noticed at once that the house was filled with drawings. "Does one of your living children draw?" they asked.

"Calyx," Alice said as she stoked up the fire and filled a teapot with water. "Not as good as you once were, though."

Connie flushed a little in their neck. "I was just wasting time," they said. "I didn't know what I was meant to do."

Flora sat on a chair opposite the sofa and gestured to Eddy to do the same. Connie had eyes only for Alice, watching her moving about her cozy little home.

Alice was accustomed to eyes upon her and moved gracefully, sensuously, disguising her years with a languid ease in her joints. She knew what she was doing.

Maybe Connie hasn't had any experience with women at all, Flora thought, watching them fall headlong into her trap. *Or maybe it's just that it's her.*

Flora's hands had begun trembling as soon as she had said it out loud to Eddy. That she could do it, if she had to. That she'd be the one to kill the tyrant this time, and save them once again. She gripped her silks and tried hard to still them.

"And what you were meant to do is murder people in some crusade," Eddy said to them. "You sure followed your destiny toward glory. You have so very much that you've built to be proud of."

Connie turned toward Eddy and smiled. "You know I only brought you here so that I could kill you in front of her, right?"

Alice dropped something. Flora seized up, not sure if she should draw the gun or not.

Do it. DO IT. THIS IS THE MOMENT. Don't hesitate now.

But she could not. She had said that she could, and meant it, but she found that she could not move a muscle.

Eddy did not look away. He did not beg for his life and he didn't even look dismayed. "I am fucking done with all of this," he said clearly. "Done with the misery people make for each other. If you're gonna do it, shut the fuck up and do it. I always knew you were a fucking coward."

Connie didn't move. They looked at Eddy, but spoke to Flora.

"I brought him back to you because I wanted to show you that you mean nothing to me. I could bring you one last moment of grief before ending your life."

Flora swallowed. "You brought me grief with your own face, Connie. You didn't need to go to any extra trouble."

"You never loved me," Connie said, faltering a little. "None of you did. Because I was a mistake. Because I was something you couldn't understand."

"No," Alice said clearly. "That's why you couldn't love yourself. Is that what all this is about? Are you just taking your own pain and spreading it around, rather than finding a way to love and be loved? You really have become a man."

Connie did move then, lashing out with an arm and slapping Alice to the floor, where she sat for a moment, blinking, her hand to her ear.

"Oh, Alice," they said. "I'm sorry. I'm sorry. I just . . . I can't control it sometimes."

"That's obvious," Alice said, not cowed one bit. "It's fine. I've had worse. Listen, let me serve us some tea before you kill my oldest friends, alright? Let's have one more minute together, then be done with this."

Connie looked down a moment, composing themselves. They pulled their gun and laid it on the table. They pointed their finger at Eddy.

"One more minute to say goodbye. Then all the mistakes in this room will be corrected."

"Does that include you?" Flora asked.

Connie's nostrils flared and their eyes went wide.

They're nothing but skinless pain. They're too volatile. This isn't going to work.

"You said you need to fix this. To make room, so that the frags can take over. That would include you, I'm pretty sure. You could just tell Alice where to go, or tell your army to take her there. The three of us could end right here. Rather poetic, right?"

Couldn't do it myself, but I could talk them into doing it. Look at them, they're halfway there now. A stable mind does not do things like this. Maybe I just topple them and end it here, now.

Connie tapped the gun on the tabletop. Alice walked back into the room with the tea tray.

Elegantly, wordlessly, with magisterial slowness, Alice made them each a cup of golden tea, one of her own blends. She passed out arrowroot cookies from a neat stack. She smiled above the rim of her teacup at Connie.

"I can do better than that," she said. She put a hand into Connie's lap and they took it at once.

"Why don't we have Flora and Eddy get out of here, and leave us alone? I still have a Hive, you know. It used to be that you were too young, but that's all over now. Why don't you stay here with me and I help you find what you're really looking for?"

Connie's eyes grew bright but did not tear up. The four of them sat, locked in the world's oldest tension, life and death playing themselves out pretending to be love and sex. The sunlight slanted across the table.

A knock at the door.

Too soon. Too soon. They won't believe it.

But the message was almost too late.

"It'll just be a minute, my love." Alice rose and brushed Connie's cheek with her hand.

Hortensia and Zill stood there when Alice opened it. "It's done," Hortensia said in her brisk, no-nonsense voice.

"The attack force in Settle took the army from behind, after we landed the boats. The people of the city gave us plenty of backup, and they're well armed over there. We've gained control of the tanks, but they pushed the plane into the sea. Some casualties, but most of them surrendered. They were all ready to stop this awful thing."

Flora stood. "You told them Connie was already dead?"

Zill nodded. "You were right. It was like a snake without a head."

Connie was on their feet, crashing toward the door, knocking over the tea tray as they went.

"That's not possible," Connie told them. "They've got two mortars aimed toward the old lighthouse, and I told them to fire if there was any kind of attack. I'd have heard it."

The moment hung in perfect silence, as golden as a cup of tea. Flora watched her only living child's face, saw cocksure security draining away and becoming the empty, openmouthed mask of betrayal. Despite what it meant for her island and herself, Flora felt her heart break in that ache-filled crystalline moment. She knew it had to happen. She didn't know it had to hurt like this.

Zill turned and ran at once, already yelling orders. Connie looked after her, rage and regret dawning on their face. They turned back to Alice, tears finally falling from their eyes.

"My love," Alice crooned. "My love. No need to get upset."

They turned toward her, their whole heart on their face. They didn't look at Flora at all.

In the relief and release of it all, Flora was finally able to pull her gun. The real fight was elsewhere. All she had to do was this small thing and surely she could do it. This was the plan, and now she had to pull the trigger. Before Connie sent up another flare, before any more time was lost. Before she lost her nerve. Her hand trembled as it held the weight of the revolver.

Eddy sighed. "The Unnamed. You still have her gun. Kind of fitting. Like a circle."

Alice smiled and raised a hand to Flora. "Don't bother. The real Midwife's weapon did the job."

Connie's body folded inward, diminishing. They fell toward Alice, their face still full of unshed longing, despite their agony. Alice cradled Connie like a child, easing them both to the floor, watching their muscles spasm and their face pull itself out of shape with twitches and grimaces. Connie's hands opened and closed and Alice slipped her fingers into one of them, riding out the contractions and waiting for the moment of emergence. Her long curls hung down and brushed Connie's forehead, so Alice pushed them back over her shoulder. Wordlessly, she crooned to Connie, trying to soothe them to peace.

Flora watched Alice midwife Connie out of their body. Flora could not move or speak. They all waited for the end in silence. The gun weighed more in her hand than her living child ever had.

Connie's eyes rolled up in their head as the poison finally reached their heart. Alice pushed the body gently off her lap, stood up, and looked down over them, utterly without remorse.

The wind blew in through the still-open door and pulled it shut. The latch clicked home as the only sound in the silent room.

EPILOGUE

Eddy waited at the appointed place for the *Alexandria* to arrive on midsummer that year. There was a small cottage big enough for the three of them to spend a few days watching the light grow longer.

Alice and Flora did not want to stay on board the library ship; they both had lives to get back to on Bambritch. But they thought a short trip couldn't hurt.

The librarians were glad to see them. Dell was long gone, replaced with a flinty-eyed commander named Di. Di greeted Eddy like an old friend, and Eddy introduced her to Flora and Alice.

They brought gifts from Bambritch in the only variety the librarians liked: books. They had collected from households that had diaries to spare, and paid scribes to copy some of the more precious ones to give to the *Alexandria*. Copies of the Book of Flora and the Bambritch Book were among them. Alice kept no narrative, but had made a copy of her personal herbal to add to their collection. The librarians received them warmly.

Eddy told Di what they wanted to see, and the leader was amenable. They sailed north, chugging with the ship's mighty engines into a frozen sea.

The island was exactly where Eddy said it would be. Di told them that there was a librarian on the island who had been left behind to study these women over a year ago. With some difficulty, they found her.

She was a woman in middle age, wrapped in furs and windburned across her high cheekbones. She offered her hand and said her name was Quinn.

"So is it true?" Flora asked without preamble. She knew that Quinn would understand.

"I don't know why it's happening," Quinn said. "But yes. They're fragmenting. It's been happening here for generations, or so they tell me. The offspring can only frag; they can't get pregnant in the usual way. Some of the frags can do both, but not the ones who are born of it. They're just different."

"Male and female?" Alice was looking at the faces of the people who came aboard the ship, looking at the strangers who had once again arrived on their shore.

Quinn shook her head. "Neither. Something else. Something new."

They held the strangeness in silence. The world was cold and just-born, and snow drifted down soundlessly.

Before they pulled out and made their way back toward home, Eddy, Alice, and Flora had one last night on that faraway shore. Di came to their shared cabin and woke them, insisting they come up top. Shivering, wrapping themselves tightly, they came.

High above, sparks and spears of color were streaking through the sky in a shimmering ribbon. The effect was startling, making Flora feel like she was flying, or blowing away on the wind. The lights were purple-red-green, not like a rainbow but like a rainbow's darker, stranger cousin. They could not look away.

They stood on the deck for as long as the lights continued. They did not argue over whether or not the lights were real, or what they meant. They simply were.

ABOUT THE AUTHOR

Photo © 2016 by Devin Cooper

Meg Elison is a high school dropout and a graduate of UC Berkeley. She is the author of *The Book of the Unnamed Midwife*, winner of the 2014 Philip K. Dick Award, and *The Book of Etta*. *The Book of Flora* is the third novel in the Road to Nowhere trilogy. The author lives in the San Francisco Bay Area and writes like she's running out of time. For more information, visit www.megelison.com.